PRAISE FOR DAVID ZINDELL

The Lightstone

"Should appeal to fans of grail legends and epic quests."
—*Library Journal*

Neverness

"Zindell's heady prose opens a gateway to a world of rich imagination."
—*Library Journal*

"One of the finest talents to appear since Kim Stanley Robinson and William Gibson—perhaps the finest."
—Gene Wolfe

The Broken God

"Zindell's combination of adventure, metaphysics, and intellectual debate works marvelously, leaving you ready for more."
—*Locus*

"Zindell draws on sources as diverse as Eastern mysticism, Eskimo culture, and linguistics for a novel of unusual depth and scope. An impressive achievement."
—*Booklist*

The Wild

"Zindell creates a universe loaded with spectacle."
—*Publishers Weekly*

"Zindell embraces a wealth of tantalizing ideas in a breathtaking saga that should match the grandeur of Herbert's *Dune* or Asimov's *Foundation*."
—*Booklist*

❌ THE LIGHTSTONE ❌

✕ THE LIGHTSTONE ✕

David Zindell

A TOM DOHERTY ASSOCIATES BOOK
NEW YORK

THE LIGHTSTONE

Copyright © 2001, 2006 by David Zindell

The Lightstone was originally published, in a substantially different form, by Voyager, an imprint of HarperCollins UK, in 2001. The Tor edition has been specially revised by the author.

Map by Richard Geiger

A Tor Book
Published by Tom Doherty Associates, LLC
175 Fifth Avenue
New York, NY 10010

www.tor.com

Tor® is a registered trademark of Tom Doherty Associates, LLC.

ISBN-13: 978-0-765-34993-4
ISBN-10: 0-765-34993-0

First Tor Edition: June 2006
First Tor Mass Market Edition: May 2007

Printed in the United States of America

0 9 8 7 6 5 4 3 2 1

TO MY DAUGHTERS, JUSTINE AND JILLIAN,
*who journeyed with me on many long and magical walks
through Ea and helped generate this story with their pointed
questions, blazing enthusiasm, dreams, and delight*

ACKNOWLEDGMENTS

I would like to thank my editor, Claire Eddy, for her many insights and suggestions that made this a better book in many, many ways.

❈ THE LIGHTSTONE ❈

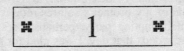

1

ON CLEAR WINTER nights, I have stood on mountains just to be closer to the stars. Some say that these shimmering lights are the souls of warriors who have died in battle; some say that at the beginning of time, Arwe himself cast an infinite number of diamonds into the sky to shine forever and defeat the darkness of night. But I believe the stars are other suns like our own. They speak along the blood in fiery whisperings of ancient dreams and promises unfulfilled. From there long ago our people came to earth bearing the cup called the Lightstone; to there we would someday return as angels holding light in our hands.

My grandfather believed this, too. It was he who taught me the stories of the Great Bear, the Dragon, and the other constellations. It was he who named me after the bright Morning Star, Valashu. He always said that we were born to shine. A Valari warrior, he once told me, should polish first his soul and then his sword. For only then can he see his fate and accept it. Or fight against it, if he is one of the few men marked out to make their own fate. Such a man is a glory and gift to the earth. Such a man was my grandfather. But the Ishkans killed him all the same.

Elkasar Elahad would have found it a strange fate indeed that on the same day King Kiritan's messengers came from Alonia to announce a great quest for the Lightstone, a whole company of knights and nobles from Ishka rode in to my father's castle to negotiate for peace or call for war. In the warmth of one of the loveliest springs that anyone could remember, with the snows melting from the mountains and wildflowers everywhere abloom, the forests surrounding Silvassu teemed with boar and deer and other animals that might be killed for food. My father's steward, upon counting the castle's guests that day, grumbled that the kitchens would require much food if any feast were to be made. And so my brothers and I, along with other knights, were called to go out and hunt for it. After all, even the murderers of a king must eat.

Just after noon I rode down from the hills upon which our ancient city is built with my eldest brother, Lord Asaru. My friend Maram and one of my brother's squires rode with us as well. We were a small hunting party, perhaps the smallest of the many to fill the woods that day. I was glad for such company, for I cared nothing for the sport of hounds yelping and men on snorting horses running down a fear-maddened pig. As for Asaru, he was like our father, King Shamesh: stern, serious, and focused on his objective with an astonishing clarity of purpose. His soul had not only been polished but sharpened until it cut like the finest Godhran steel. He had said that we would take a deer, and for that we needed small numbers and stealth. Maram, who would have preferred the pageantry of hunting with the other knights, followed him anyway. In truth, he followed me. As he liked to say, he would never desert his best friend. As he didn't like to say, he was a coward who had once seen what the razorlike tusks of a boar could do to a man's groin. It was much safer to hunt a deer.

It was a warm day, and the air smelled of freshly turned earth and lila blossoms. Every quarter of a mile or so, a stout farmhouse stood out among fields demarcated by lines of low stone walls. There was new barley in the ground and the golden sun in the sky. As we passed farther into the Valley of the Swans, the farmland gave out onto miles of unbroken forest. At the edge of a field, where the ancient oaks rose up like a wall of green, we drew up and dismounted. Asaru handed the reins of his horse to his young squire, Joshu Kadar. Joshu didn't like being left to tend the horses, and he watched impatiently as Asaru drew out his great yew bow and strung it. For a moment I was tempted to give him my bow and let him hunt the deer while I waited in the sun. I hated hunting almost as much as I did war.

And then Asaru, tall and imperious in his flowing black cloak, handed me my bow and pointed at the forest. He said, "I didn't think you would agree to go out today."

"How could I not, since you promised our father we would bring back a deer?"

"A deer," Asaru said. "Only one deer."

The questioning in his large eyes seemed to ask me why I couldn't be like any other warrior and prince. Why, I asked myself, *couldn't* I be? Why couldn't I simply let loose a steel-tipped arrow and slaughter a beautiful and innocent animal?

"There must be," I said, "hundreds of stags here."

Asaru peered off through the trees and said, "There must be. But there is good game closer to the castle. Why *these* woods, Val?"

"Why not?" I countered. Asaru, knowing how I felt about such bloodsport, had given me my choice of where to hunt that day. Although he had remained silent during our ride down from the castle, he must have known where I was leading him. "You know why," I said more gently, looking at him.

And he looked at me, fearless as all Valari would hope to be. His eyes were those of the Valari kings: deep and mysterious, as black as space and as bright as stars. He had the bold face bones and long hawk's nose of our ancient line. His skin, burnt brown in the hot spring sun, was like weathered ivory, and he had a great shock of glossy black hair, long and thick and blowing wild in the wind. Although he was very much a man of blood and steel and other elements of the earth, there was something otherworldly about him, too. My father said that we looked enough alike to be twins. But of the seven sons of Shavashar Elahad, he was the firstborn and I was the last. And that made all the difference in the world.

He drew closer and stood silently regarding me. Where I insisted on wearing a leather hunting jacket and a homespun shirt and trousers of a deep forest green, he was resplendent in a cloak and a black tunic embroidered with the silver swan and the seven silver stars of the royal house of Mesh. He would never think to be seen in any other garments. He was the tallest of my brothers, taller than I by half an inch. He seemed to look down at me, and his bright black eyes fell like blazing suns on the scar cut into my forehead above my left eye. It was a unique scar, shaped like a lightning bolt. I think it reminded him of things that he would rather not know.

"Why do you have to be so wild?" he said in a quickly exhaled breath.

I stood beneath his gaze, listening to the thunder of my heart.

"Here, now!" a loud voice boomed out. "What's this? What are you talking about?"

Maram, seeing the silent communication flowing between us, came up clutching his bow and making nervous rumbling noises in his throat. Though not as tall as Asaru, he was a big man with a big belly that pushed out ahead of him as if to knock any obstacles or lesser men from his path.

"What should I know about these woods?" he asked me.

"They're full of deer," I said, smiling at him.

"And other animals," Asaru added provocatively.

"What animals?" Maram asked. He licked his thick, sensuous lips. He rubbed his thick, brown beard where it curled across his blubbery cheeks.

"The last time we entered these woods," Asaru said, "we could hardly move without stepping on a rabbit. And there were squirrels everywhere."

"Good, good," Maram said, "I like squirrels."

"So do the foxes," Asaru said. "So do the wolves."

Maram coughed to clear his throat, then swallowed a couple of times. "In my country, I've only ever seen red foxes—they're not at all like these huge gray ones of yours that might as well *be* wolves."

Maram was not of Mesh, not even of the Nine Kingdoms of the Valari. Everything about him was an affront to a Valari's sensibilities. His large brown eyes reminded one of the sugared coffee that the Delians drink and were given to tears of rage or sentimentality as the situation might demand. He wore jeweled rings on each of the fingers of his hamlike hands; he wore the bright scarlet tunic and trousers of the Delian royalty. He liked red, of course, because it was an outward manifestation of the colors of his fiery heart. And even more, he liked standing out and being seen, especially in a wood full of hungry men with bows and arrows. My brothers believed that he had been sent to the Brotherhood school in the mountains above Silvassu as a punishment for his cowardly ways. But the truth was he had been banished from court due to an indiscretion with his father's favorite concubine.

"Do not," Asaru warned him, "hunt wolves in Mesh. It's bad luck."

"Ah, well," Maram said, twanging his bowstring, "I won't hunt them if they won't hunt *me*."

"Wolves don't hunt men. It's the bears that you have to watch for."

"Bears?"

"This time of year, especially the mothers with their cubs."

"I saw one of your bears last year. I hope I never see another."

I rubbed my forehead as I caught the heat of Maram's fear. Of course, Mesh is famed for the ferociousness of its huge brown bears, which drove the much gentler black bears into gentler lands such as Delu ages ago.

"If the Brothers don't expel you and you stay with us long enough," Asaru said, "you'll see plenty of bears."

"But I thought the bears kept mostly to the mountains."

"Well, where do you think you *are*?" Asaru said, sweeping his hand out toward the snowcapped peaks that surrounded us.

In truth, we stood in the Valley of the Swans, largest and loveliest of Mesh's valleys. Here the Kurash flowed through gentle terrain into Lake Waskaw, where the swans came each spring to swim through clear waters.

But all around rose the great white crests of the Morning Mountains: Arakel, Vayu, and sacred Telshar, on whose lower slopes my grandfather's grandfathers had built the Elahad castle. Once I had climbed this luminous mountain. From the summit, looking north, I had seen the cold white mountains of Ishka. But, of course, all my life I have tried not to look in that direction.

Now Maram followed the line of Asaru's outstretched hand. He looked into the dark, waiting forest and muttered, "Ah, where am I, indeed? Lost, lost, truly lost."

At that moment, as if in answer to some silent supplication of Maram's, there came the slow clip-clop of a horse's hooves. I turned to see a white-haired man leading a draft horse across the field straight toward us. He wore a patch over his right eye and walked with a severe limp, as if his knee had been smashed with a mace or a flail. I knew that I had seen this old farmer before, but I couldn't quite remember where.

"Hello, lads," he said as he drew up to us. "It's a fine day for hunting, isn't it?"

Maram took in the farmer's work-stained woolens, which smelled of horse manure and pigs. He wrinkled up his fat nose disdainfully. But Asaru, who had a keener eye, immediately saw the ring glittering on the farmer's gnarled finger, and so did I. It was a plain silver ring set with four brilliant diamonds: the ring of a warrior and a lord at that.

"Lord Harsha," Asaru said upon recognizing him, "it's been a long time."

"Yes, it has," Lord Harsha said. He looked at Asaru's squire, then at Maram and me. "Who are your friends?"

Asaru presented Joshu and then nodded toward Maram, saying, "And this is Prince Maram Marshayk of Delu. He's a student of the Brothers."

Lord Harsha peered out at him with his single eye. "Isn't it true that the Brothers don't hunt animals?"

"Ah, that *is* true," Maram said, gripping his bow. "We hunt knowledge. I've come along only to protect my friend in case we run into any bears."

Now Lord Harsha turned his attention toward me, and he looked back and forth between me and my brother. The light of his eye bore into my forehead like the rays of the sun.

"You must be Valashu Elahad," he said.

Just then Maram's face reddened in anger on my behalf. I knew that he didn't approve of the Valari system of honors and rank. It must have galled him that an old man of no noble blood, a mere farmer, could outrank a prince.

I looked down at the ring I wore. In it was set neither the four diamonds of a lord nor the three of a master—nor even the two sparkling stones of a full knight. A single diamond stood out against the silver: the ring of a simple warrior. In truth, I was lucky to have won it. If not for some skills with the sword and bow that my father had taught me, I never would have. What kind of warrior hates war? How is it that a Valari knight—or rather, a man who only dreamed of being a knight—should prefer playing the flute and writing poetry to trials of arms with his brothers and countrymen?

Lord Harsha smiled grimly at me and said, "It's been a long time since you've come to these woods, hasn't it?"

"Yes, sir, it has," I said.

"Well, you should have paid your respects before trampling over my fields. Young people have no manners these days."

"My apologies, sir, but we were in a hurry. You see, we got a late start."

I didn't explain that our hunting expedition had been delayed for an hour while I searched the castle for Maram—only to find him in bed with one of my father's chambermaids.

"Yes, very late," Lord Harsha said, looking up at the sun. "The Ishkans have already been here before you."

"Which Ishkans?" I asked in alarm. I noticed that Asaru was now staring off into the woods intently.

"They didn't stop to present themselves either. But there were five of them—I heard them bragging they were going to take a bear."

At this news, Maram gripped his bow even more tightly. Beads of sweat formed up among the brown curls of hair across his forehead. He said, "Well, then—I suppose we should leave these woods to them."

But Asaru only smiled, as if Maram had suggested abandoning all of Mesh to the enemy. He said, "The Ishkans like to hunt bears. Well, it's a big wood, and they've had more than an hour to become lost in it."

"Please see to it that you don't become lost as well," Lord Harsha said.

"My brother," Asaru said, looking at me strangely, "is more at home in the woods than in his own castle. We won't get lost."

"Good. Then good luck hunting." Lord Harsha nodded his head at me in a curt bow. "Are you after a bear this time, too?"

"No, a deer," I said. "As we were the last time we came here."

"But you found a bear all the same."

"It might be more accurate to say the bear found us."

Now Maram's knuckles grew white around his bow, and he looked at me with wide eyes. "What do you *mean* a bear found you?"

Because I didn't want to tell him the story, I stood there looking off into the woods in silence. And so Lord Harsha answered for me.

"It was ten years ago," he said. "Lord Asaru had just received his knight's ring, and Val must have been what—eleven? Ten?"

"Ten," I told him.

"That's right," Lord Harsha said, nodding his head. "And so the lads went into the woods alone after their deer. And then the bear—"

"Was it a large bear?" Maram interrupted.

Lord Harsha's single eye narrowed as he admonished Maram to silence as he might a child. And then he continued the story: "And so the bear attacked them. It broke Lord Asaru's arm and some ribs. And mauled Valashu, as you can see."

Here he paused to point his old finger at the scar on my forehead.

"But you told me that you were born with that scar!" Maram said, turning to me.

"Yes," I said. "That's right."

Truly, I had been. My mother's labor in bringing me into the world was so hard and long that everyone had said I wanted to remain inside her in darkness. And so, finally, the midwife had had to use tongs to pull me out. The tongs had cut me, and the wound had healed raggedly, in the shape of a lightning bolt.

"The bear," Asaru explained, "only cut the scar deeper."

"He was lucky the bear didn't break his skull," Lord Harsha said to Maram. "And both of them were lucky that my son, may he abide in peace, was walking through the woods that day. He found these lads half-dead in the moss and killed the bear with his spear before it could kill them."

Andaru Harsha—I knew the name of my rescuer very well. At the Battle of Red Mountain, I had taken a wound in my thigh protecting him from the Waashians' spears. And later, at the same battle, I had frozen up and been unable to kill one of our enemy who stood shieldless and helpless before me. Because of my hesitation, many still whispered that I was a coward. But Asaru never called me that.

"Then your son saved their lives," Maram said to Lord Harsha.

"He always said it was the best thing he ever did."

Maram came up to me and grabbed my arm. "And you think to repay the courage of this man's son by going *back* into these woods?"

"Yes, that's right," I said.

"Ah," he said, looking at me with his soft brown eyes. "I see."

And he did see, which was why I loved him. Without being told, he understood that I had come back to these woods today not to seek vengeance by shooting arrows in some strange bear but only because there are other monsters that must be faced.

"Well, then," Lord Harsha said. "Enough of bear stories. Would you like a bite to eat before your hunt?"

Because of Maram's peccadilloes, we had missed lunch, and we were all of us hungry. That wouldn't have dismayed Asaru, but rejecting Lord Harsha's hospitality would have. And so

Asaru, speaking for all of us as if he were already king, bowed his head and said, "We'd be honored."

While Lord Harsha opened his horse's saddlebags, I glanced off across the field to study his house. I liked its square lines and size and the cedar-shingled roof, which was almost as steeply gabled as the chalets you see higher in the mountains. It was built of oak and stone: austere, clean, quietly beautiful— very Valari. I remembered Andaru Harsha bringing me to this house, where I had lain in delirium for half a day while his father tended my wound.

"Here, now," Lord Harsha said as he laid a cloth on the wall. "Sit with me, and let's talk about the war."

While we took our places along the wall, he set out two loaves of black barley bread, a tub of goat cheese, and some freshly pulled green onions. We cut the bread for sandwiches and ate them. I liked the tang of the onions against the saltiness of the cheese; I liked it even more when Lord Harsha drew out four silver goblets and filled them with brown beer that he poured from a small wooden cask.

"This was brewed last fall," Lord Harsha said. He handed goblets to Asaru, me, and Joshu. Then he picked up his own. "It was a good harvest, and a better brew. Shall we make a toast?"

I saw Maram licking his lips as if he'd been stricken dumb with grief, and I said, "Lord Harsha, you've forgotten Maram."

"Indeed," he said, smiling. "But you said he's with the Brothers—hasn't he taken vows?"

"Ah, well, yes, I have," Maram admitted. "I've forsworn wine, women, and war."

"Well, then?"

"I never vowed not to drink beer."

"You quibble, Prince Maram."

"Yes, I do, don't I? But only when vital matters are at stake."

"Such as the drinking of beer?"

"Such as the drinking of *Meshian* beer, which is known to be the finest in all of Ea."

This compliment proved too much for Lord Harsha, who laughed and magically produced another goblet from the saddlebags. He picked up the cask and poured forth a stream of beer.

"Let's drink to the king," he said, raising his cup. "May he abide in the One and find the wisdom to decide on peace or war."

We all clinked goblets and drank the frothy beer. Maram, of course, was the first to finish. He gulped it down like a hound does milk. Then he held out his goblet to Lord Harsha and said, "Now *I* would like to propose a toast. To the lords and knights of Mesh who have fought faithfully for their king."

"Excellent," Lord Harsha said, refilling Maram's goblet. "Let's drink to that indeed."

Again Maram drained his cup. He licked the froth from his mustache. He held the empty cup out yet again and said, "And now, ah, to the courage and prowess of the warriors—how do you say it? To flawlessness and fearlessness."

But Lord Harsha suddenly stoppered the cask with a cork and said, "No, that's enough if you're going hunting today—we can't have you young princes shooting arrows at each other, can we?"

"But Lord Harsha," Maram protested, "I was only going to suggest that the courage of your Meshian warriors is an inspiration to those of us who can only hope to—"

"You're quite the diplomat," Lord Harsha said, laughing as he cut Maram off. "Perhaps *you* should reason with the Ishkans. Perhaps you could talk them out of this war as easily as you talked me out of my beer."

"I don't understand why there has to be a war at all," Maram said.

"Well, there's bad blood between us," Lord Harsha said simply.

"But it's the *same* blood, isn't it? You're all Valari, aren't you?"

"Yes, the same blood," Lord Harsha said, slowly sipping from his goblet. Then he looked at me sadly. "But the Ishkans shed it in ways shameful to any Valari. The way they killed Valashu's grandfather."

"But he died in battle, didn't he? Ah, the Battle of the Diamond River?"

Now Lord Harsha swallowed the last of his beer as if someone had forced him to drink blood. He tapped his eye patch and said, "Yes, it was at the Diamond. Twelve years ago now. That's where the Ishkans took this eye. That's where the Ishkans sacrificed five companies just to close with King Elkamesh and kill him."

"But that's war, isn't it?" Maram asked.

"No, that's dueling. The Ishkans hated King Elkamesh because when he was a young man such as yourself, he killed Lord Dorje in a duel. And so they used the battle as a duel to take their revenge."

"Lord Dorje," I explained, looking at Maram, "was King Hadaru's oldest brother."

"I see," Maram said. "And this duel took place, ah, fifty years ago? You Valari wait a long time to take your revenge."

I looked north toward the dark clouds moving in from Ishka's mountains, and I lost myself in memories of wrongs and hurts that went back more than a hundred times fifty years.

"Please do not say 'we Valari,'" Lord Harsha told Maram. He rubbed his broken knee and said, "Sar Lensu of Waas caught me here with his mace, and *that's* war. There's no vengeance to be taken. They understand that in Waas. They would never have tried to kill King Elkamesh as the Ishkans did."

While Lord Harsha rose abruptly and shook out the cloth of its crumbs for the sparrows to eat, I clenched my teeth together. And then I said, "There was more to it than vengeance."

At this, Asaru shot me a quick look as if warning me not to divulge family secrets in front of strangers. But I spoke not only for Maram's benefit, but for Asaru's and Lord Harsha's and my own.

"My grandfather," I said, "had a dream. He would have united all the Valari against Morjin."

At the mention of this name, dreadful and ancient, Lord Harsha froze motionless, while Joshu Kadar turned to stare at me. I felt fear fluttering in Maram's belly like a blackbird's wings. In the sky, the dark, distant clouds seemed to grow even darker.

And then Asaru's voice grew as cold as steel as it always did when he was angry at me. "The Ishkans," he said, "don't want the Valari united under our banner. No one does, Val."

I looked up to see a few crows circling the field in search of carrion or other easy feasts. I said nothing.

"You have to understand," Asaru continued, "there's no need."

"No need?" I half shouted. "Morjin's armies swallow up half the continent, and you say there's no need?"

I looked west beyond the white diamond peak of Telshar as I tried to imagine the earthshaking events occurring far away.

What little news of Morjin's acquisitions that had arrived in our isolated country was very bad. From his fastness of Sakai in the White Mountains, this warlock and would-be Lord of Ea had sent armies to conquer Hesperu and lands with strange names such Uskudar and Karabuk. The enslaved peoples of Acadu, of course, had long since marched beneath the banner of the Red Dragon, while in Surrapam and Yarkona, and even in Eanna, Morjin's spies and assassins worked to undermine those realms from within. His terror had found its most recent success in Galda. The fall of this mighty kingdom, so near the Morning Mountains and Mesh, had shocked almost all the free peoples from Delu to Thalu. But not the Meshians. Nor the Ishkans, the Kaashans, nor any of the other Valari.

"Morjin will never conquer us," Asaru said proudly. "Never."

"He'll never conquer us if we stand against him," I said.

"No army has ever successfully invaded the Nine Kingdoms."

"No, not *successfully*. But why should we invite an invasion at all?"

"If anyone invades Mesh," Asaru said, "we'll cut them to pieces. The way the Kaashans cut Morjin's priests to pieces."

He was referring to the events that had occurred half a year before in Kaash, that most mountainous and rugged of all Valari kingdoms. When King Talanu discovered that two of his most trusted lords had entered Morjin's secret order of assassin-priests, he had ordered them beheaded and quartered. The pieces of their bodies he had then sent to each of the Nine Kingdoms as a warning against traitors and others who would serve Morjin.

I shuddered as I remembered the day that King Talanu's messenger had arrived with his grisly trophy. Something sharp stabbed into my chest as I thought of worse things. In Galda, thousands of men and women had been put to the sword. Some few survivors of the massacres there had found their way across the steppes to Mesh, only to be turned away at the passes. Their sufferings were grievous but not unique. The rattle of the chains of all those enslaved by Morjin would have shaken the mountains, if any had ears to hear it. On the Wendrush, it was said, the Sarni tribes were on the move again and roasting their captured enemies alive. From Karabuk had come stories of a terrible new plague and even a rumor that a city had been burned with a firestone. It seemed that all of Ea was going up in flames while here we sat by a small green field, drinking beer and talking of yet another war with the Ishkans.

"There's more to the world than Mesh," I said. I listened to the twittering of the birds in the forest. "What of Eanna and Yarkona? What of Alonia? The Elyssu? And Delu?"

At the mention of his homeland, Maram stood up and grabbed his bow. Despite his renunciation of war, he shook it bravely and said, "Ah, my friend is right. We defeated Morjin once. And we can defeat him again."

For a moment I held my breath against the beery vapors wafting out of Maram's mouth. I had not suggested defeating Morjin but uniting against him so that we wouldn't have to fight at all.

"We should send an army of Valari against him," Maram bellowed.

I tried not to smile as I noted that in demanding that "we" fight together against our enemy, Maram meant us: the Meshians and the other Valari.

I looked at him and asked, "And to where would you send this army that you've so bravely assembled in your mind?"

"Why, to Sakai, of course. We should root out Morjin before he gains too much strength and then destroy him."

At this, Asaru's face paled, as did Lord Harsha's and, I imagined, my own. Once, long ago, a Valari army had crossed the Wendrush to assault Sakai. And at the Battle of Tarshid, Morjin had used firestones and treachery to defeat us utterly. It was said that he had crucified the thousand Valari survivors for twenty miles along the road leading to Sakai; his priests had pierced our warriors' veins with knives and had drunk their blood. All the histories cited this as the beginning of the War of the Stones.

No one knew if the Morjin who now ruled in Sakai was the same man who had tortured my ancestors: Morjin, Lord of Lies, the Great Red Dragon, who had stolen the Lightstone and kept it locked away in his underground city of Argattha. Many said that the present Morjin was only a sorcerer or usurper who had taken on the most terrible name in history. But my grandfather had believed that these two Morjins were one and the same. And so did I.

Asaru stared at Maram. "So then, you want to defeat Morjin. Do you hope to recover the Lightstone as well?"

"Ah, well," Maram said, his face falling red, "the Lightstone—now that's a different matter. It's been lost for three thousand years. Surely it's been destroyed."

"Surely it has," Lord Harsha agreed. "The Lightstone, the firestones, and other gelstei—they were all destroyed in the War of the Stones."

"Of course it was destroyed," Asaru said as if that ended the matter.

I wondered if it was possible to destroy the gold gelstei, greatest of all the stones of power, from which the Lightstone was wrought. I was silent as I watched the clouds move down the valley and cover up the sun. I couldn't help noticing that despite the darkness of the monstrous gray shapes, some small amount of light fought its way through.

"You don't agree, do you?" Asaru said to me.

"No," I said. "The Lightstone exists, somewhere."

"But three thousand years, Val."

"I *know* it exists—it can't have been destroyed."

"If not destroyed, then lost forever."

"King Kiritan doesn't think so. Otherwise he wouldn't call a quest for knights to find it."

Lord Harsha let loose a deep grumbling sound as he packed the uneaten food into his horse's saddlebags. He turned to me, and his remaining eye bore into me like a spear. "Who knows why foreign kings do what they do? But what would *you* do, Valashu Elahad, if you suddenly found the Lightstone in your hands?"

I looked north and east toward Anjo, Taron, Athar, Lagash, and the other kingdoms of the Valari, and I said simply, "End war."

Lord Harsha shook his head as if he hadn't heard me correctly. He said, "End the wars?"

"No, *war*," I said. "War itself."

Now both Lord Harsha and Asaru—and Joshu Kadar as well—looked at me in amazement as if I had suggested ending the world itself.

"Ha!" Lord Harsha called out. "No one but a scryer can see the future, but let's make this prediction anyway: when next the

Ishkans and Meshians line up for battle, you'll be there at the front of our army."

I smelled moisture in the air and bloodlust in Lord Harsha's fiery old heart, but I said nothing.

And then Asaru moved close to me and caught me with his brilliant eyes. He said quietly, "You're too much like Grandfather: you've always loved this gold cup that doesn't exist."

Did the world itself exist? I wondered. Did the light I saw shining in my brother's eyes?

"If it came to it," he asked me, "would you fight for this Lightstone, or would you fight for your people?"

Behind the sadness of his noble face lingered the unspoken question: *would you fight for me?*

Just then, as the clouds built even higher overhead and the air grew heavy and still, I felt something warm and bright welling up inside him. How could I *not* fight for him? I remembered the outing seven years ago when I had broken through the thin spring ice of Lake Waskaw after insisting that we take this dangerous shortcut toward home. Hadn't he, heedless of his own life, jumped into the black, churning waters to pull me out? How could I ever simply abandon this noble being and let him perish from the earth? Could I imagine the world without tall straight oak trees or clear mountain streams? Could I imagine the world without the sun?

I looked at my brother and felt this sun inside me. There were stars there, too. It was strange, I thought, that although he was firstborn and I was last, that although he wore four diamonds in his ring and I only one, it was he who always looked away from me, as he did now.

"Asaru," I said, "listen to me."

The Valari see a man as a diamond to be slowly cut, polished, and perfected. Cut it right and you have a perfect jewel; cut it wrong, hit a flaw, and it shatters. Outwardly, Asaru was the hardest and strongest of men. But deep inside him ran a vein of innocence as pure and soft as gold. I always had to be gentle with him lest my words—or even a flicker in my eyes—find this flaw. I had to guard his heart with infinitely more care than I would my own.

"It may be," I told him, "that in fighting for the Lightstone, we'd be fighting for our people. For all people. *We* would be, Asaru."

"Perhaps," he said, looking at me again.

Someday, I thought, he would be king and therefore the loneliest of men. And so he needed one other man whom he could trust absolutely.

"At least," I said, "please consider that our grandfather might not have been a fool. All right?"

He slowly nodded his head and grasped my shoulder. "All right."

"Good," I said, smiling at him. I picked up my bow and nodded toward the woods. "Then why don't we go get your deer?"

After that, we helped Lord Harsha put away the remains of our lunch. We slipped on our quivers full of hunting arrows. I said good-bye to Altaru, my fierce, black stallion, who reluctantly allowed Joshu Kadar to tend him in my absence. I thanked Lord Harsha for his hospitality, then turned and led the way into the woods.

2

AS SOON AS we entered the stand of ancient trees, it grew cooler and darker. The forest that filled the Valley of Swans was mostly elm, maple, and oak. Their great canopies opened out a hundred feet above the forest floor, nearly blocking out the rays of the sun. The light was softened by the millions of fluttering leaves and deepened to a primeval green.

We walked deeper into the woods across the valley almost due east toward the unseen Mount Eluru. I was as sure of this direction as I was the beating of my heart. Once a sea captain from the Elyssu, on a visit to our castle, had shown me a little piece of iron called a lodestone that pointed always toward the north. In my wandering of Mesh's forests and mountains, I had always found my way as if I had millions of tiny lodestones in my blood pointing always toward home. And now I moved steadily through the great trees toward something vast and deep that called to me from the forest farther within. What was calling me, however, I didn't quite know.

I felt something else there that seemed as out of place as a snow tiger in a jungle or the setting of the sun in the east. The air, dark and heavy, almost screamed with a sense of wrongness that chilled me to the bone. I felt eyes watching me: those of the squirrels and the cawing crows and perhaps others as well. For some reason, I suddenly thought of the lines from *The Death of Elahad*—Elahad the Great, my distant ancestor, the fabled first king of the Valari who had brought the Lightstone to Ea long, long ago. I shuddered as I thought of how Elahad's brother, Aryu, had killed Elahad in a dark wood very like this one, and then, ages before Morjin had ever conceived of such a crime, claimed the Lightstone for his own:

> *The stealing of the gold,*
> *The evil knife, the cold—*
> *The cold that freezes breath,*
> *The nothingness of death.*

My breath steamed out into the coolness of the silent trees as I caught a faint, distant scent that disturbed me. The sense of wrongness pervading the woods grew stronger. Perhaps, I thought, I was only dwelling on the wrongness of Elahad's murder. I couldn't help it. Wasn't *all* killing of men by men wrong? I asked myself.

And what of killing *itself*? Men hunted animals, and that was the way the world was. I thought of this as the scar above my eye began to tingle with a burning coldness. I remembered that once, not far from here, I had tried to kill a bear; I remembered that sometimes bears went wrong in their hearts and hunted men just for the sport of it.

I gripped my bow tightly as I listened for a bear or other large animal crashing through the bushes and bracken all about us. We Valari are taught three fundamental things: to wield a sword, to tell the truth, and to abide in the One. But we are also taught to shoot our long yew bows with deadly accuracy, and some of us are trained, as my grandfather had taught me, to move across even broken terrain almost silently. I believe that if we *had* chanced upon a bear feasting upon wild newberries or honey, we might have stepped up close to him unheard and touched him before being discovered.

That is, we might have done this, if not for Maram's continual comments and complaints. Once, when I had bent low to examine the round, brown pellets left behind by a deer, he leaned up against a tree and grumbled, "How much farther do we have to go? Are you sure we're not lost? Are you sure there are any deer in these wretched woods?"

Asaru's voice hissed out in a whisper, "Shhh—if there *are* any deer about, you'll scare them away."

"All right," Maram muttered as we moved off again. He belched, and a bloom of beer vapor obliterated the perfume of the wildflowers. "But don't go so fast. And watch out for snakes. And poison ivy."

I smiled as I tugged gently on the sleeve of his red tunic to get him going again. But I didn't watch for snakes, for the only deadly ones were the water dragons, which hunted mostly along the streams. And the only poison ivy that was to be found in Mesh grew in the mountains beyond the Lower Raaswash, near Ishka.

We walked for most of an hour while the clouds built into great black thunderheads high in the sky and seemed to press down through the trees with an almost palpable pressure. Still I felt something calling me, and I moved deeper into the woods. I saw an old elm shagged with moss, a clear sign that we were approaching a place I remembered very well. And then, as Maram drew in a quick breath, I turned to see him pointing at the exposed, gnarly root of a great oak tree.

"Look," he murmured. "What's wrong with that squirrel?"

A squirrel, I saw, was lying flat on the root with its arms and legs splayed out. Its dark eye stared out at us but appeared not to see us.

I closed my eyes for a moment, and I could feel the pain where something sharp had punctured the squirrel beneath the fur of its hind leg. It was the sharp, hot pain of infection, which burned up the leg and consumed the squirrel with its fire.

"Val?"

Something dark and vast had its claws sunk into the squirrel's fluttering heart, and I could feel this terrible pulling just as surely as I could Maram's fear of death. This was my gift; this was my glory; this was my curse. What others feel, I feel as well. All my life I had suffered from this unwanted empathy. And I had told only one other person about its terrors and joys.

Asaru moved closer to Maram and pointed at the squirrel as he whispered, "Val has always been able to talk to animals."

It was not Asaru. Although he knew of my love of animals and sometimes looked at me fearfully when I opened my heart to him, he sensed only that I was strange in ways that he could never quite understand. But my grandfather had known, for he had shared my gift; indeed, it was he who gave it to me. I thought that like the color of my eyes, it must have been passed along in my family's blood—but skipping generations and touching brother and sister capriciously. I thought as well that my grandfather regarded it as truly a gift and not an affliction. But he had died before he could teach me how to bear it.

For a few moments I stared at the squirrel, touching eyes. I suddenly remembered other lines from *The Death of Elahad;* I remembered that Master Juwain, at the Brotherhood school, had never approved of this ancient song, because, as he said, it was full of dread and despair:

> *And down into the dark,*
> *No eyes, no lips, no spark.*
> *The dying of the light,*
> *The neverness of night.*

Maram asked softly, "Should we finish him?"

"No," I said, "it will be dead soon enough. Let it be."

Let it be, I told myself, and so I tried. I closed myself to the dying animal then. To keep out the waves of pain nauseating me, by habit and instinct, I surrounded my heart with walls as high and thick as those of my father's castle. After a while, even as I watched the light go out of the squirrel's eye, I felt nothing.

Almost nothing. When I closed my eyes, I remembered for the thousandth time how much I had always hated living inside of castles. As much as fortresses keeping enemies out, they are prisons of cold stone keeping people within.

"Let's go," I said abruptly.

Where does the light go when the light goes out? I wondered. Asaru, it seemed, had also tried to distance himself from this little death. He moved off slowly through the woods, and we followed him. Soon we came upon a splintered elm that had once been struck by lightning.

Once, in this very place, I had come upon the bear that Lord Harsha had spoken of. It had been a huge, brown bear, a great-grandfather of the forest. Upon beholding this great being, I had frozen up and been unable to shoot. Instead, I had laid down my bow and walked up to touch him. I had known that the bear wouldn't hurt me: he had told me this in the playfulness of his big brown eyes. But Asaru hadn't known this. Upon seeing me apparently abandoning all sense, he had panicked, shooting the bear in the chest with an arrow. The astonished bear had then fallen on him with his mighty paws, breaking his arm and smashing his ribs. And I had fallen on the bear. In truth, I had jumped on his back, pulling at his thick, musky fur and stabbing him with my knife in a desperate attempt to keep him from killing Asaru. And then the bear had turned on me as I had turned on him; he had hammered my forehead with his sharp claws. And then I had known only blackness until I awoke to see Andaru Harsha pulling his great hunting spear out of the bear's back.

Later that night, Asaru had told our father how I had saved his life. It was a story that became widely known—and widely disbelieved. To this day, everyone assumed that Asaru had embellished my role in the bear's killing to save me from the shame of laying down my weapons in the face of the enemy.

"Look, Val," Asaru whispered, pointing through the trees.

I turned to follow the line of his outstretched finger. Standing some thirty yards away, munching the leaves of a tender fern, was the deer that we had come for. He was a young buck, his new antlers fuzzy with velvet. Miraculously, he hadn't yet seen us. He kept eating quietly even as we slipped arrows from our quivers and nocked them to our bowstrings.

Asaru, kneeling ten paces to my left, drew his bow along with me, as did Maram who stood slightly behind me and to my right. I felt their excitement heating up their quickly indrawn breaths. I felt my own excitement, too. My mouth watered in anticipation of the coming night's feast. In truth, I loved the taste of meat as well as any man, even though very often I couldn't do what I had to do to get it.

"Abide in peace," I whispered.

At that moment, as I pulled back the arrow toward my ear, the buck looked up at me. And I looked at him. His deep, liquid eyes were as full of life as the squirrel's had been of death. It was not easy to kill so great an animal as a deer, much less that infinitely more complex being called man.

Valashu.

There was something about the buck's sudden awareness of the nearness of death that opened me to the nearness of my own. The light of his eyes was like flame from a firestone melting the granite walls that I hid behind, his booming heart was a battering ram beating open the gates of my heart. More strongly than ever I heard the thunder of that deep and soundless voice that had called me to the woods that day. I heard as well another voice calling my name; it was a voice from the past and future, and it roared with malevolence and murder.

Valashu Elahad.

The buck looked past me suddenly, and his eyes flickered as he tried to tell me something. The wrongness I had sensed in the woods was now very close; I felt it eating into the flesh between my shoulder blades like a mass of twisting, red worms. Instinctively, I moved to escape this terrible sensation.

And then came the moment of death. Arrows flew. They sang from our bows, and burned through the air. Maram's arrow hit the deer in the side even as I felt a sudden burning pain in my own side; my arrow missed altogether and buried itself in a tree. But Asaru's arrow drove straight behind the buck's shoulder into his heart. Although the buck gathered in all his strength for a last, desperate leap into life, I knew that he would be as good as dead before he struck the ground.

And down into the dark. . . .

The fourth arrow, I saw, had nearly killed me. As the sky finally opened and real thunderbolts lit up the forest, I looked down in astonishment to see a feathered shaft three feet long sticking out of the side of my torn jacket. Its thick leather and the book of poetry in its pocket had entangled the arrow. I was reeling from the buck's death and something worse, but I still had the good sense to wonder who had shot it.

"Val, get down!"

And so did Asaru. Even as he shouted at me to protect myself, he whirled about to scan the forest. And there, more than hundred yards farther into the forest, a dark, cloaked figure was running away from us through the trees. Asaru, ever the battle lord, tried to follow, leaping across the bracken even as he drew another arrow from his quiver and nocked it. He got off a good shot, but my would-be murderer found cover behind a tree and then started running again. Asaru pursued, quickly closing the distance between them.

"Val, behind you!" Maram called out to my right. "Get down!"

I turned just in time to see another cloaked figure step out from behind a tree some eighty yards behind me. He was drawing back a black arrow aimed at my chest.

"Val, what's wrong with you—why don't you get down?"

I tried to heed the urgency in Maram's voice, but I found that I couldn't move. The burning in my side from the first assassin's arrow spread through my body like fire. But strangely, my hands, legs, and feet—even my lips and eyes—felt cold.

Maram, seeing my helplessness, cursed as he suddenly leaped from behind the tree where he had taken shelter. He cursed again as his fat arms and legs drove him puffing and crashing through the forest. He shot an arrow at the second assassin, but it missed, and I heard it skittering off through the leaves of a young oak tree. And then the assassin loosed *his* arrow—not at Maram but at me.

Just as the arrow was released, I felt in my chest the twisting of the man's hate. It was *my* hate, I think, that gave me the strength to turn to the side and pull my shoulders backward. The arrow hissed like a wooden snake only inches from my chin. I felt it slice through the air even as I heard the assassin howl with frustration and rage. And then Maram fell upon him like a fury, and I knew I had to find the strength to move very fast or my fat friend would soon be dead.

"Val, help me!" Maram suddenly cried out. "Please, Val!"

I felt Maram's fear quivering inside my own heart; there, I felt something deeper compelling me to move. It warmed my frozen limbs and filled my hands with a terrible strength. With a speed that astonished me, I plucked out the arrow caught in my jacket and fit it to my bowstring.

But now Maram and the assassin whirled about each other as Maram slashed at the air with his dagger and the assassin tried to brain him with an evil-looking mace. I couldn't shoot lest I hit Maram, so I cast down my bow and started running through the trees toward them. Twigs broke beneath me; even through my boots, rocks bruised my feet. I kept my eyes fixed on the assassin as he drew back his mace and swung it at Maram's head.

"No!" I cried out.

It was a miracle, I believe, that Maram got his arm up just in time to deflect the full force of the blow. But the mace's heavy iron head glanced off the side of his skull, knocking him to the ground. The assassin would surely have finished him then if I hadn't charged him with my dagger drawn and flashing with every lightning bolt that lit the forest.

Valashu Elahad.

The assassin stood back from Maram's stunned and bleeding form and watched me approach as if he recognized me. He was a huge man, thicker even than Maram, though none of his bulk appeared to be fat. His hair was a dirty, tangled, coppery mass, and the skin of his face, pale and pocked with scars, glistened with grease. He was breathing hard, and his bristly lips pulled back to reveal huge lower canines that looked more like a boar's tusks than they did teeth. He regarded me hatefully with small bloodshot eyes full of intelligence and cruelty.

And then, with frightening speed, he charged at me. Moments later, we crashed into each other. I barely managed to catch his arm even as his huge hand closed around my arm and twisted savagely to get me to drop my knife. We struggled this way, hands clutching each others arms, as we thrashed about the forest floor trying to free our weapons.

Valashu.

I pulled and shifted and raged against this monster of a man trying to kill me. His vast bulk almost crushed me under. He grunted like a wild boar, and I smelled his stinking sweat. I felt his fingernails tearing my forearm open. Suddenly I crashed against a tree. My face scraped along its rough bark, shredding off the skin. In my mouth, I tasted the iron-red tang of blood. And all the while, he kept trying to smash the mace against my head.

"Valashu," I heard my father whisper, "get away or he'll kill you."

Somehow then, I managed to turn the point of my knife into his arm. A dark bloom of blood instantly soaked through his dirty woolens. It weakened him enough that I was able to break free. With the force of sudden hate, he pulled back from me at almost the same moment and shook his mace at me as he cried out, "Damn you Elahads!"

He clenched the fist of his wounded arm and grimaced at the hurt of it. It hurt me, too. The nerves in my arm felt outraged, stunned. There was no way, I knew, that I could fight another human being and not leave myself open to the violence and pain I inflicted on him.

But I wasn't wounded in my body, and so I was able take up a good stance and keep a distance between us. I tried to clear my mind and let my will to live run through me like a cleansing river. My father had taught me to fight this way. It was he, the stern king, who had insisted that I train with every possible combination of weapons, even one so unlikely as a mace against a knife. Words and whispers of encouragement began sounding inside me; bits of strategy came to me unbidden. I found myself falling into motions drilled into my limbs by hours of exhausting practice beneath my father's grim black eyes. It was vital, I remembered, that I keep outside of the killing arc of the mace, longer than my knife by nearly two feet. Its massive head was of iron cast into the shape of a coiled dragon and rusted red. One good blow from it would crush my skull and send me forever into the land of night.

"Damn you all!" the assassin shouted as he swung the mace at my head and pressed me back. Big drops of rain splatted against my forehead, nearly blinding me; I was afraid that I would stumble over a tree root or branch and fall helpless beneath the onslaught. I feinted with my knife, trying to throw my opponent off balance and create an opening. But the assassin was a powerful man, able to check his blow and aim a new one at me almost before the head of the mace swept past me. He came straight at me in full fury, spitting and swearing and swinging his terrible mace.

He might have killed me there in the pouring rain. He had the superior weapon and the skill. But I had skill, too, and something else.

I have said that my talent for feeling what others feel can be a curse. But it is also truly a gift, like a great, shimmering double-edged sword. Now, as I felt the pounding red pain of his wounded arm, I sensed precisely how he would move almost before his muscles tensed and the mace burned past me.

It wasn't really like reading his mind. He wanted to frighten me with a feint toward my knife hand, and I felt the fear of it as an icy tingling in my fingers before he even moved; his desire to smash out my eyes formed up inside him, and I felt the sickening emotion as a blinding red pain in my own eyes. He whirled about me now, faster and faster, trying to crush me with his mace. And with each of his movements, I moved too, anticipating him by a breath. It was as if we were locked together hand to hand and eye to eye, dancing a dance of death together in the quickness of iron and steel that flashed like the storm's brilliant lightning.

And then the assassin aimed a tremendous blow at my face, and the force of it carried the mace whooshing through the air. Just then his foot slipped against a sodden tree root, and I had the opening that I had been waiting for. But I couldn't take it; I froze up with fear as I had at the Battle of Red Mountain. Instantly, the assassin recovered his balance and swung the mace back toward my chest. It was a weak blow, but it caught me on the muscle there with a sickening crunch that nearly staved in my ribs. It took all my strength to jump away from him and not let myself fall to the ground screaming in pain.

"Val, help me!" Maram screamed from the glistening bracken deeper in the trees.

I found a moment to watch as he struggled to rise grunting and groaning to his feet. And then I realized that the scream had never left his lips but was only forming up like thunder inside him. As it was inside of me.

The assassin saw Maram moving, too, and gripped his mace more tightly. His lust to kill was like a black, ravenous, twisted thing. He ached to bash open my brains. I suddenly knew that if I let him do this, he would gleefully finish off Maram. And then lie in wait for Asaru's return.

"No, no," I cried out. "Never!"

The assassin came at me again. It began hailing, and little pieces of ice pinged off the mace's iron head. I slipped and skidded over an exposed, muddy expanse of the forest floor; the assassin quickly took advantage of my clumsiness, aiming a vicious blow at me that nearly took off my face. Despite the rain's bitter cold, I could feel him sweating as he growled and gasped and damned me to a death without end.

I knew that I had to find my courage and close with him, now, before I slipped again. But how could I ever kill him? He might be a swine of a man, a terrible man, evil—but he was still a man. Perhaps he had a woman somewhere who loved him; perhaps he had a child. But certainly he himself was a child of the One, and therefore a spark of the infinite glowed inside him. Who was I to put it out? Who was I to look into his tormented eyes and steal the light?

There is something called the joy of battle. Women don't like to know about this; most men would rather forget it. Combat with another man this way in the dark woods was truly dirty, ugly, awful—but there was a terrible beauty about it, too. For fighting for life brings one closer to life. I remembered, then, my father telling me that I had been born to fight. All of us were. As the assassin raged at me with his dragon-headed mace, a great surge of life welled up inside me. My hands and heart and every part of me knew that it was good to feel my blood rushing like a river in flood, that it was a miracle simply to be able to draw in one more breath.

"Asaru," I whispered.

Some deep part of me must have realized that this wild joy was really just a love of life. And love of the finest creations of life, such as my brother Asaru and even Maram. I felt this beautiful force flowing into me like sunlight; I opened myself to it, and it filled my whole being with a terrible strength.

Maram cried out as a shot of hail struck the bloody wound on his head. The assassin glanced at him as his pulse leaped in anticipation of an easy kill. Something broke inside me then. My heart swelled with a sudden fury that I feared almost more than any other thing. I found that secret place where love and hate, life and death, were as one.

This time, when the mace swept past me, I rushed the assassin. I stepped in close enough to feel the heat steaming off his massive body. I got my arm up to block the return arc of his mace even as he snorted in anger and spat into my face. I smelled his fear, with my nostrils as well as with a finer sense. And then I plunged my dagger into the soft spot above his big, hard belly; I angled it upward so that it pierced his heart.

"Maram!" I screamed out. "Asaru!"

The pain of the assassin's death was like nothing I had ever felt before. It was like lightning striking through my eyes into my spine, like a mace as big as a tree crushing in my chest. As the assassin gasped and spasmed and crumpled to the sodden earth, I fell on top of him. I gasped for breath; I screamed and raged and wept, all at once. A river of blood spurted out of the wound where I had put my knife. But an entire ocean flowed out of me.

"Val—are you hurt?" I heard Maram's voice boom like thunder as from far away. I felt him hovering over me as he placed his hand on my shoulder and shook me gently. "Come on now, get up—you killed him."

But the assassin wasn't quite dead. Even in the violence of the pouring rain, I felt his last breath burn against my face. I watched the light die from his eyes. And only then came the darkness.

"Come on, Val. Here, let me help you."

But I couldn't move. I was only dimly aware of Maram grunting and puffing as he rolled me off the assassin's body. Maram's frightened face seemed to thin and grow as insubstantial as smoke. The colors faded from the forest; the blood seeping from his wounded head wasn't red at all but a dark gray. Everything grew darker then. A terrible cold, centered in my heart, began spreading through my body. It was worse than being caught in a blizzard in one of the mountain passes, worse even than plunging through Lake Waskaw's broken ice into freezing waters. It was a cosmic cold: vast, empty, indifferent; it was the cold that brings on the neverness of night and the nothingness of death. And I was utterly open to it.

It was as I lay in this half-alive state that Asaru finally returned. He must have sprinted when he saw me—and the dead assassin—stretched out on the forest floor, for he was panting to catch his breath when he reached my side. He knelt over me, and I felt his warm, hard hand pressing gently against my throat as he tested my pulse. To Maram he said, "The other one . . . escaped. They had horses waiting. What happened here?"

Maram quickly explained how I had frozen up after the first assassin's arrow had stuck in my jacket; his voice swelled with pride as he told of how he had charged the second assassin.

"Ah, Lord Asaru," he said, "you should have seen me! A

Valari warrior couldn't have done any better. I don't think it's too much of an exaggeration to say that I saved Val's life."

"Thank you," Asaru said dryly. "It seems that Val also saved yours."

"He did indeed," Maram said as he bowed his head to me.

Asaru looked down at me and smiled grimly. He said, "Val, what's wrong—why can't you move?"

"It's cold," I whispered, looking into the blackness of his eyes. "So cold."

"Here," Asaru said to Maram, "let's get him out of the rain."

The two of them lifted me and carried me over beneath a great elm tree. Maram laid down his cloak and helped Asaru prop me up against the tree's trunk. Then Asaru ran back through the woods to retrieve the arrow that the first assassin had shot at me.

"This is bad," he said, looking at the black arrow. In the flashes of lightning, he scanned the woods to the north, east, south, and west. "There may be more of them," he told us.

"No," I whispered. To be open to death is to be open to life. The hateful presence that I had sensed in the woods that day was now gone. Already, the rain was washing the air clean. "There are no more."

Asaru peered at the arrow and said, "They almost killed me. I felt this pass through my hair."

I looked at Asaru's long black hair blowing about his shoulders, but I could only gasp silently in pain.

"Let's get your shirt off," he said. It was one of his rules, I knew, that wounds must be tended as soon as possible. "Here, Maram, help me."

In a moment they had carefully removed my jacket and shirt. It must have been cold, with the wind whipping raindrops against my suddenly exposed flesh. But all I could feel was a deeper cold that sucked me down into death.

Asaru touched the livid bruise that the assassin's mace had left on my chest. His fingers gently probed my ribs. "You're lucky—it seems that nothing is broken."

"What about *that*?" Maram asked, pointing at my side where the arrow had touched me.

"Why, it's only a scratch," Asaru said. He soaked a cloth with some of the brandy that he carried in a wineskin and swabbed it over my skin.

I looked down at my throbbing side. To call the wound left by the arrow a scratch was to exaggerate its seriousness. Truly, no more than the faintest featherstroke of a single red line marked the place where the arrow had nicked the skin. But I could still feel the chill working in my veins.

"It's cold," I whispered. "Everywhere, cold."

Now Asaru examined the arrow, which was fletched with raven feathers and tipped with a razor-sharp steel head like any common hunting arrow. But the steel, I saw, was enameled with some dark, blue substance. Asaru's eyes flashed with anger as he showed it to Maram and said, "They tried to kill me with a poison arrow."

I blinked my eyes at the cold crushing my skull. But I said nothing against my brother's assumption that the arrow had been meant for him.

"Do you think it was the Ishkans?" Maram asked.

Asaru pointed at the assassin's body and said, "That's no Ishkan."

"Perhaps they hired him."

"They must have," Asaru said.

"N, no," I murmured. Not even the Ishkans, I thought, would ever kill a man with poison. Or would they?

Asaru quickly but with great care wrapped my torn and tainted jacket and shirt around the arrow's head to protect it from the falling rain. Then he took off his cloak and put it on me.

"Is that better?" he asked me.

"Yes," I said, lying to him despite what I had been taught. "Much better."

Although he smiled down at me to encourage me, his face was grave. I didn't need my gift of empathy to feel his love and concern for me.

"This is hard to understand," he said. "You can't have taken enough poison to paralyze you this way."

No, I thought, I couldn't have. It wasn't the poison that pinned me to the earth like a thousand arrows of ice. I wanted to explain to him that somehow the poison must have dissolved my shields and left me open to the assassin. But how could I tell my simple, courageous brother what it was like to feel another die? How I could make him understand the terror of a cold as vast and black as the emptiness between the stars?

Asaru placed his warm hand on top of mine. "If it's poison, Master Juwain will know a cure. We'll take you to him as soon as the rain stops."

My grandfather had once warned me to beware of elms in thunder, but we took shelter beneath that great tree all the same. Its dense foliage protected us from the worst of the rain as we waited out the storm.

After a while the downpour weakened to a sprinkle and then stopped. The clouds began to break up, and shafts of light drove down through gaps in the forest canopy and touched the rain-sparkled ferns with a deeper radiance. There was something in this golden light that I had never seen before. It seemed to struggle to take form even as I struggled to apprehend it. I somehow knew that I had to open myself to this wondrous thing as I had to my brother's love and to the inevitability of my death.

The stealing of the gold . . .

And then there, floating in the air five feet in front of me, appeared a plain golden cup that would have fit easily into the palm of my hand. Call it a vision; call it a waking dream; call it a derangement of my aching eyes. But I saw it as clearly as I might have a bird or a butterfly.

I was only dimly aware of Asaru kneeling by my side as he touched my throbbing head. All that I could see was the marvelous cup shimmering before me. I drank in its golden light and almost immediately, a warmth like that of my mother's honey tea began pouring into me.

"Do you see it?" I asked Asaru.

"See what?"

The Lightstone, I thought. *The healing stone.*

For this, I thought, Aryu had risen up and killed his brother with a knife even as I had killed the assassin. For this simple cup, men had fought and murdered and made wars for more than ten thousand years.

"What is it, Val?" Asaru asked, gently shaking my shoulder.

But I couldn't tell him what I saw. After a while, as I leaned back against the solidity and strength of the great elm, the coldness left my body. I prayed then that someday the Lightstone would heal me completely so that the terror of my gift would leave me as well and I would suffer the pain of the world no more.

Although I was still very weak, I managed to press my hands down into the damp earth. And then to Asaru's and Maram's astonishment—and my own—I stood up.

Somehow I staggered over to where the assassin lay atop the glistening bracken. While my whole body shook and I gasped with the effort of it, I pulled my knife out of his chest and cleaned it. Then I closed the assassin's cold blue eyes. In my own eyes, I felt a sudden moist pain. My throat hurt as if I had swallowed a lump of cold iron. Somewhere deeper inside, my belly and being heaved with a sickness that wouldn't go away. There, I knew, the cold would always wait to freeze my breath and steal my soul. I vowed then that no matter the cause or need, I would never, never kill anyone again.

In the air above me—above the assassin's still form—the Lightstone poured out a golden radiance that filled the forest. It was the light of love, the light of life, the light of truth. In its shimmering presence, I couldn't lie to myself: I knew with a bitter certainty that it was my fate to kill many, many men.

And then, suddenly, the cup was gone.

"What are you staring at?" Asaru asked.

"It's nothing," I told him. "Nothing at all."

Now a fire burned through me like the poison still in my veins. I struggled to remain standing. Asaru came over to my side. His strong arm wrapped itself around my back to help me.

"Can you walk now?" he asked.

I nodded and Asaru smiled in relief. After I had steadied myself, Asaru called Maram over to check his wounded head. He poked his finger into Maram's big gut and told him, "Your head is as hard as your belly is soft. You'll be all right."

"Ah, yes, I suppose I will—as soon as you bring back the horses."

For a moment, Asaru looked up through the fluttering leaves at the sun. He looked down at the dead assassin. And then he turned to Maram and told him, "No, it's getting late, and it wouldn't do to leave either of you alone here. Despite what Val says, there may be others about. We'll walk out together."

Asaru bent down toward the assassin. And then, with a shocking strength, he hoisted the body onto his shoulder and straightened up. He pointed deeper into the woods. "You'll carry back the deer," he told Maram.

"Carry back the deer!" Maram protested. Asaru might as well have appointed him to bear the whole world on his shoulders. "It must be two miles back to the horses!"

Asaru, straining under the great mass of the assassin's body, looked down at Maram with a sternness that reminded me of my father. He said, "You want to eat, don't you?"

Despite Maram's protests, beneath all his fear and fat, he was as strong as a bull. As there was no gainsaying my brother when he had decided on an action, Maram grudgingly went to fetch the deer.

"You look sick," Asaru said as he freed a hand to touch my forehead. "But at least the coldness is gone."

No, no, I thought, *it will never be gone.*

And neither would the burning. Now every part of my body seemed on fire. I had blood on my hands, a man's blood instead of a deer's, and that burnt down deeper than my bones.

I drew in a painful breath as I steeled myself for the walk back through the forest. I could not dispel the dread that I had damned myself. But then something bright flashed inside me. When I closed my eyes, I could still see the Lightstone shining like a sun.

With Asaru in the lead, we started walking west, toward the place where we had left the horses. Maram puffed and grumbled beneath the deer flopped across his shoulders. Asaru, I thought, would at least be happy that we had taken a deer, even as he had said we would. And so we would have something to contribute to that night's feast with the Ishkans.

3

IT WAS LATE afternoon by the time we broke free from the forest and rejoined Joshu Kadar at the edge of Lord Harsha's fields. The young squire blinked his eyes in amazement at the load slung across my brother's back; he had the good sense, however, not to beleaguer us with questions just then. He kept a grim silence and went to fetch Lord Harsha as my brother bade him.

A short time later, he returned with Lord Harsha, who rode a huge gray mare. Despite the painful creaking of his joints, the old man sat straight in the saddle like the battle lord he still was. A stout wagon laden with barrels of beer for the night's feast rolled along behind him. Its driver was a rather plump, pretty woman with raven-dark hair. She was dressed in a silk gown and a flowing gray cloak gathered in above her ample breasts with a silver broach. This was to be her first appearance at my father's castle, I gathered, and so she naturally wanted to be seen wearing her finest.

When Lord Harsha presented her as Behira, his only daughter, Maram's face flushed a deep red, and he blurted out, "Oh, my lord, what a beauty! Lord Harsha—you certainly have a talent for making beautiful things."

It might have been thought that Lord Harsha would relish such a compliment. Instead, his single eye glared at Maram like a heated iron. Most likely, I thought, he wished to present Behira at my father's court to some of the greatest knights of Mesh; he would take advantage of the night's gathering to make the best match for her that he could—and that certainly wouldn't be a marriage to some cowardly outland prince who had forsworn wine, women, and war.

"My daughter," Lord Harsha coldly informed Maram, "is *not* a thing. But thank you all the same."

Maram flushed again, this time in shame, and he bent to help Asaru load the assassin's body into the wagon. Then we all mounted our horses to begin the journey back to my father's castle.

As we plodded along the road, Maram lagged back with the wagon so that he could flirt with Behira. Above the clopping of the horses' hooves, I overheard him say, "Well, Behira, it's a lovely day for such a lovely woman to attend her first feast. Ah, how old *are* you? Sixteen? Seventeen?"

And then a few moments later, Maram told her, "I'm afraid we have no such women as you in Delu. If we did, I never would have left home."

"Well, you should have let a *woman* tend your wound," I heard Behira say to him. I could almost feel her touching the makeshift bandage that my brother had tied around Maram's head. "Perhaps when we get to the castle I could look at it."

"Would you? Would you?"

"Of course. The outlander struck you with a mace, didn't he?"

"Ah, yes, a mace." Maram's voice softened with the seductiveness of recounting his feats: "I hope you're not alarmed by what happened in the woods today. It was quite a little battle, but of course we prevailed. I had the honor of being in position to help Val at the critical moment."

According to Maram, not only had he scared off the first assassin and weakened the second, but he had willingly taken a wound to his head in order to save my life. When he caught me smiling at the embellishments of his story—I didn't want to think of his braggadocio as mere lies—he shot me a quick, wounded look as if to say, "Love is difficult, my friend, and wooing a woman calls for any weapon."

I might have smiled at his wiles, but at that moment I felt again the wrongness that I had sensed earlier in the woods. It seemed not to emanate from any one direction but rather pervaded the sweet-smelling air itself. All about us were the familiar colors of my father's kingdom: the white granite farmhouses; the greenness of fields rich with oats, rye, and barley; the purple mountains of Mesh that soared into the deep blue sky. And yet all that I looked upon seemed darkened as with some indelible taint.

It touched me as well. I felt it as a poison burning in my blood and a coldness that sucked at my soul. As we rode across the beautiful country, more than once I wanted to call a halt so that I could slip down from my saddle and sleep—either that or sink down into the dark, rain-churned earth and cry out at the terror that had awakened inside me.

And this I might easily have done but for Altaru, my great black warhorse. Somehow he sensed the hurt of my wounded side and the deeper pain of the death that I had inflicted upon the assassin; he moved with a slow, rhythmic grace that seemed to flow into me and ease my distress rather than aggravate it. The surging of his long muscles and great heart lent me a badly needed strength. I had no need to guide him or even to touch his reins, for he knew well enough where we were going: home, to where the setting sun hung above the mountains like a golden cup overflowing with light.

So it was that we finally came upon my father's castle. This great heap of stone stood atop a hill that was one of several steps forming the lower slope of Telshar. The right branch of the Kurash river cut around the base of this hill, separating the castle from the buildings and streets of Silvassu itself. At least in the spring, the river was a natural moat of raging, icy, brown waters; the defensive advantages of such a site must have been obvious to my ancestors who had entered the Valley of Swans so long ago.

As I looked out at the castle's soaring white towers, I couldn't help remembering the story of the first Shavashar, who was the great-grandson of Elahad himself. It had been he who had led the Valari into the Morning Mountains at the beginning of the Lost Ages. This was in the time after the Hundred Year March when the small Valari tribe had wandered across all of Ea on a futile quest to recover the golden cup that Aryu had stolen. Shavashar had set the stones of the first Elahad castle and had begun the warrior tradition of the Valari, for it was told that the first Valari to come to Ea—like all the Star People— were warriors of the spirit only. It was Shavashar who forged my people into warriors of the sword. It was he who had foretold that the Valari would one day have to fight "whole armies and all the demons of hell" to regain the Lightstone.

And so we had. Thousands of years later, in the year 2,292 of the Age of the Sword—every child older than five knew this date—the Valari had united under Aramesh's banner and defeated Morjin at the Battle of Sarburn. Aramesh had wrested the Lightstone from Morjin's very hands and brought the priceless cup back to the security of my family's castle. For a long time it had resided there, acting as a beacon that drew pilgrims from across all of Ea. These were the great years of Mesh, during which time Silvassu had grown out into the valley to become a great city.

"Why have you stopped?" Asaru said to me as from far away.

I remained silent as I gazed off into the past. Before us farther up the road, along the gentle slope leading up to the castle, fields of barley glistened in the slanting light where once great buildings had stood. I remembered my grandfather telling me of the second great tragedy of my people: that in the time of Godavanni the Glorious, Morjin had regained the Lightstone, and its radiance had left the Morning Mountains forever. And so, over the centuries, Silvassu had diminished to little more than a backwoods city in a forgotten kingdom. The stones of its streets and houses had been torn up to build the shield wall that surrounded the castle, for the golden age of Ea had ended and the Age of the Dragon had begun.

"It's late," Asaru said, pointing at the mural towers protecting the great wall. There, green pennants fluttered in the wind. This was a signal that the castle had received guests and a feast was to be held.

I continued staring at the great edifice of stone that dominated the Valley of the Swans. The shield wall, a hundred feet high, ran along the perimeter of the entire hill, almost flush with its steep slopes. Indeed, it seemed to rise out of the hill itself, as if the earth had flung up its hardest parts toward the sky. Higher even than this mighty wall stood the main body of the castle with its many towers: the Swan tower; the Aramesh tower with its ancient, crenelated stonework; the Tower of the Stars. And all of it had been made of white granite. In the falling sun, the whole of the castle shimmered with a terrible beauty, as even I had to admit. But I knew too well the horrors that waited inside: the sheaves of arrows tied together like so many stalks of wheat; the pots of sand to be heated red-hot and poured down upon any enemy who dared to assault the walls. Truly, the castle had been built to keep whole armies out, if not demons from hell. And not, it seemed, the Ishkans. My father had invited them to break bread with us in the castle's very heart. There, in the great hall, I would find them waiting for me, and perhaps my would-be assassin as well.

"Yes," I finally said to Asaru, "it *is* late. Let us go."

I touched my ankles to Altaru's side, and the huge horse practically leapt forward, as if to battle. We started up the north road that cut through an apple orchard before curving around the edge of Silvassu's least populated district. A short while later we passed through the two great towers guarding the Yaramesh gate and entered the castle.

In the north courtyard there was a riot of activity. Various wagons laden with foodstuffs had pulled up to the storehouses where the cooks' apprentices rushed to unload them. From the wheelwright's workshop came the sound of hammered steel, while the candlers were busy dipping tapers. We had to ride carefully through the courtyard lest our horses trample the children playing with wooden swords along the flagstones. When we reached the stables, we dismounted and gave the tending of the horses over to Joshu. There, in front of the stalls smelling of freshly spread straw and even fresher dung, we said our goodbyes. Asaru and Lord Harsha would accompany Behira to the kitchens to unload the wagon before attending to other business. And Maram and I would seek out Master Juwain.

"But what about your head?" Behira said to Maram. "It needs a proper dressing."

"Ah," Maram said, in a voice that swelled with anticipation, "perhaps we could meet later in the infirmary."

At this, Lord Harsha stepped between the wagon and Maram and stood staring down at him. "No, that won't be necessary," he said to him. "Isn't your Master Juwain a healer? Well, let *him* heal you, then."

"Please give Master Juwain my regards," Asaru said to me.

And then, looking at me strangely, he added, "Tonight there will be a feast to be remembered."

Maram and I crossed the courtyard and walked through the middle ward, which was full of chickens squawking and running for their lives. After passing through the gateway to the west ward, we found the arched doorway to the Adami tower open. I went inside and fairly raced up the worn steps that wound up through the narrow staircase; Maram puffed along behind me at a slower pace. I nearly choked on the castle's ever-present smell: rusting iron and sweating stone and the sharpness of burning tallow that over the centuries had coated the walls with layers of black smoke.

Master Juwain was in the guest chamber on the highest floor. It was the grandest such room in the castle—indeed, in all of Mesh—and many would argue that it should have been reserved for the Ishkan prince or even King Kiritan's emissaries. But by tradition, whenever a master of the Brotherhood was visiting, he took up residence there.

"Come in," Master Juwain's voice croaked out after I knocked.

I opened the great iron-shod slab of oak and stepped into a large room. It was well lit, with the shutters of its eight arched windows thrown open. Its windows were some of the few in the castle to be fitted with glass panes. Because it was rather cool, Master Juwain had a few logs burning in the fireplace along the far wall. This, I thought, was an extravagance. As were the chamber's other appointments: the tiled floor, covered with Galdan carpets; the richly colored tapestries; the shelves of books set into the wall near the canopied bed. As far as I knew, there was only one other true bed in the castle, and there my father and mother slept. The whole of the chamber bespoke a comfort at odds with the Brotherhood's ideal of restraint and austerity, but the great Elemesh had proclaimed that these teachers of our people should be treated like kings, and so they were.

"Valashu Elahad—is that you?" Master Juwain called out as I entered the room. He was as short and stocky as I remembered, and one of the ugliest men I had ever seen.

"Sir," I said, bowing. "It's good to see you again."

He was standing by one of the windows and looking up from a large book that he had been reading; he returned my bow politely and then stepped over to me. "It's good to see *you*," he said. "It's been almost two years."

To look upon Master Juwain was to be reminded at first of vegetables—and not the most attractive ones at that. His head, large and lumpy like a potato, was shaved smooth, the better to display the puffy ears that stood out like cauliflowers. His nose was a big, brown squash, and of his mouth and lips, it is better not to speak. He clasped me on the shoulder with a hand as tough as old tree roots. Although he was first and foremost a scholar—perhaps the finest in all of Ea—he liked nothing better than working in his garden and keeping close to the earth. Although he might advise kings and teach their sons, I thought he would always be a farmer at heart.

"To what honor," he asked, "shall I attribute this visit, after being ignored for so long?"

His gaze took in the rain-stained cloak that Asaru had lent me as he looked at me deeply. The saving feature of his face, I thought, was his eyes: they were large and luminous, all silver-gray like the moonlit sea. There was a keen intelligence there and great kindness, too. I have said that he was an ugly man, and ugly he truly was. But he was also one of those rare men transformed by a love of truth into a being of great beauty.

"My apologies, sir," I said. "It was never my intention to ignore you."

Just then Maram came wheezing into the room. He bowed to Master Juwain and said, "Please excuse us, sir—something has happened."

While Master Juwain paced back and forth rubbing his bald head, Maram explained how we had fought for our lives in the woods that afternoon. He conveniently left out the part of the story in which he had shot the deer, but otherwise his account was reasonably accurate. By the time I had spoken as well, the room was growing dark.

"I see," Master Juwain said, and he gazed for a moment out the window at Telshar's white diamond peak. "It's growing late, and I want to get a good look at this arrow you've brought me. And your wounds as well. Would you please light the candles, Brother Maram?"

While I gripped the black arrow, still wrapped in my torn shirt, Maram went over to the fireplace where he stuck a long match into the flames to ignite it. Then he went about the room lighting the candles in their stands.

"Here, now," Master Juwain said as his hand closed on Maram's arm. He pulled Maram over to the writing table, which was covered with maps, open books, and papers. There he sat him down in the carved oak chair. "We'll look at your head first."

Master Juwain went over to the basin by one of the windows and carefully washed his hands. Then, from beneath the bed, he retrieved two large wooden boxes, which he set on the writing table. When he opened the first box, I saw many small compartments filled with unguents, bottled medicines, and twists of foul-smelling herbs. The second box contained various knives, probes, clamps, scissors, and saws—all made of gleaming Godhran steel. I tried not to look into this box as Master Juwain lifted out a roll of clean white cloth and set it on the table.

It didn't take him very long to clean Maram's wound and wrap his head with a fresh dressing. But for me, standing by the window and looking out at the night's first stars as I tried not to listen to Maram's groans and gasps, it seemed like an hour. And then it was my turn.

I took Maram's place on the chair. Master Juwain's hard gnarly fingers gently probed my bruised chest and then touched my side along the thin red line left by the arrow. "It's hot," he said. "A wound such as this shouldn't be so hot so soon."

And with that, he dabbed an unguent on my side. The greenish cream was cool but stank of mold and other substances that I couldn't identify.

"All right," Master Juwain said, "now let's see the arrow."

As Maram crowded closer and looked on, I unwrapped the arrow and handed it to Master Juwain. He seemed loath to touch it, as if it were a snake that might at any moment come alive and sink its venomous fangs into him. With great care he held it closer to the stand of candles burning by the table; he gazed at the coated head for a long time.

"What is it?" Maram blurted out. "Is it truly poison?"

"You know it is," Master Juwain told him.

"Well, which one?"

Master Juwain sighed and said, "That we shall soon see."

He instructed us to stand off toward the open window, and we did as he bade us. Then, from the second box, he produced a scalpel and a tiny spoon whose bowl was the size of a child's fingernail. With a meticulousness that I had always found daunting, he used the scalpel to scrape off a bit of the bluish substance that covered the head of the arrow. He caught these evil-looking flakes with a sheet of white paper, then funneled them into the spoon.

"Hold your breath, now," he told us.

I drew in a draft of clean mountain air and watched as Master Juwain covered his nose and mouth with a thick cloth. Then he held the spoon over one of the candles. A moment later, the blue flakes caught fire. But strangely, I saw, they burned with an angry, red flame.

Still holding the cloth over his face, Master Juwain set down the spoon and joined us by the window. I could almost feel him silently counting the seconds to every beat of my heart. By this time, my lungs were burning for air. At last Master Juwain uncovered his mouth and told us, "Go ahead and breathe—I think it should be all right now."

Maram, whose face was red as an apple, gasped at the air

streaming in the window, and so did I. Even so, I caught the faintness of a stench that was bitter beyond belief.

"Well?" Maram said to Master Juwain. "Do you know what it is?"

"Yes, I know," Master Juwain said. There was a great sadness in his voice. "It's as I feared—the poison is kirax."

"Kirax," Maram repeated as if he didn't like the taste of the word on his tongue. "I don't know about kirax."

"Well, you should," Master Juwain said. "If you weren't so busy with the chambermaids, then you would."

I thought Master Juwain was being unfair to him. Maram was studying to become a Master of Poetry, and so couldn't be expected to know of every esoteric herb or poison.

"What is kirax, sir?" I asked him.

He turned to me and grasped my shoulder. There was a reassuring strength in his hand and tenderness as well. "It's a poison used only by Morjin and the Red Priests of the Kallimun. And their assassins."

He went on to say that kirax was a derivative of the kirque plant, as was the more common drug called kiriol. Kiriol, of course, was known to open certain sensitives to others' minds—though at great cost to themselves. Kirax was much more dangerous: even a small amount opened its victim to a flood of sensations that overwhelmed and burned out the nerves. Death came quickly and agonizingly, as if one's entire body had been plunged into a vat of boiling oil.

"You must have absorbed a minuscule amount of it," Master Juwain told me. "Not enough to kill but quite sufficient to torment you."

Truly, I thought, enough to torment me even as my gift tormented me. I looked off at the candles' flickering flames, and it occurred to me that the kirax was a dark blue hidden knife cutting at my heart, exposing it to sufferings and secrets that I would rather not know.

"Do you have the antidote?" I asked him.

Master Juwain sighed as he looked at his box of medicines. "I'm afraid there is no antidote," he said. He told Maram and me that the hell of kirax was that once injected, it never left the body.

"Ah," Maram said, "that's hard, Val—that's too bad."

Yes, I thought, trying to close myself from the waves of pity and fear that poured from Maram, it was very bad indeed.

Master Juwain moved back over to the table and gingerly picked up the arrow. "This came from Argattha," he said.

At the mention of Morjin's stronghold in the White Mountains, a shudder ran through me. It was said that Argattha was carved out of the rock of a mountain, an entire city built underground where slaves were whipped to work and dreadful rites occurred far from the eyes of civilized men.

"I would guess," Master Juwain told me, "that the man you killed was sent from there. He might even be a full priest of the Kallimun."

I closed my eyes as I recalled the assassin's fiercely intelligent eyes.

"I'd like to see the body," Master Juwain said.

Maram wiped the sweat from his neck as he pointed at the arrow and said, "But we don't *know* that the assassins are Kallimun priests, do we? Isn't it possible that one of the Ishkans has gone over to Morjin?"

Master Juwain stiffened with anger as he admonished Maram: "Please do not call him by that name." Then he turned to me. "It worries me more that the Lord of Lies has made traitor one of your own countrymen."

"No," I said, filling up with a rare anger of my own. "No Meshian would ever betray us so."

"Perhaps not willfully," Master Juwain said. "But you don't know the deceit of the Lord of Lies. You don't know his power."

He told us then that all men, even warriors and kings, knew moments of darkness and despair. At such times, when doubt shrouded the soul, they became more vulnerable to evil, most especially to the Master of Minds himself. Then Morjin might come for them, in their hatred or in their darkest dreams; he would send illusions to confuse them; he would seize the their will and control them at a distance like a puppeteer pulling on strings. These soulless men were terrible and very deadly, though fortunately very rare. Master Juwain called them ghuls; he admitted to his fear that a ghul might be waiting in the great hall to take meat with us that very night.

To steady my racing heart, I stepped over to the window to

get a breath of air. I listened to the distant howling of the wolves along the wind. As a child, I had heard rumors of ghuls, as of werewolves or the dreaded Gray Men who come at night to suck out your soul. But I had never really believed them.

"But why," I asked Master Juwain, "would the Lord of Lies send an assassin—or anyone else—to kill me with poison?"

He looked at me strangely and asked, "Are you sure the first assassin was shooting at you and not Asaru?"

"Yes."

"But how *could* you be sure? Didn't Asaru say that he felt the arrow pass through his hair?"

Master Juwain's clear, gray eyes fell upon me with the weight of twin moons. How could I tell him about my gift of sensing what lay inside another's heart? How could I tell him that I had felt the assassin's intention to murder me as surely as I did the cold wind pouring through the window?

"There was the angle of the shot," I tried to explain. "There was something in the assassin's eyes."

"You could see his eyes from a hundred yards away?"

"Yes," I said. And then, "No, that is, it wasn't really like seeing. But there was something about the way he looked at me. The concentration."

Master Juwain was silent as he stared at me from beneath his bushy gray eyebrows. Then he said, "I think there's something about *you,* Valashu Elahad. There was something about your grandfather, too."

In silence I reached out to close the cold window against the night.

"I believe," Master Juwain continued, "that this *something* might have something to do with why the Lord of Lies is hunting you. If we understood it better, it might provide us with the crucial clue."

I looked at Master Juwain then, and I wanted him to help me understand how I could feel the fire of another's passions or the unbearable pressure of their longing for the peace of the One. But some things can never be understood. How could one feel the cold light of the stars on a perfect winter night? How could one feel the wind?

"The Lord of Lies *couldn't* know of me," I said at last. "He'd have no reason to hunt the seventh son of a faraway mountain king."

"No reason? Wasn't it your ancestor, Aramesh, who took the Lightstone from him at the Battle of Sarburn?"

Could this Lord of Lies, I wondered, be the very same Morjin who had lived ages ago?

"Aramesh," I said, "is the ancestor of many Valari. The Lord of Lies can't hunt us all."

"No? Can he not?" Master Juwain's eyebrows suddenly pulled down in anger. "I'm afraid he would hunt any and all who oppose him."

For a moment I stood there rubbing the scar on my forehead. Oppose Morjin? I just wanted the Valari to stop fighting among ourselves and unite under one banner so that we wouldn't *have* to oppose him. Shouldn't that, I wondered, be enough?

"But I don't oppose him," I said.

"No, you're too gentle a soul for that," Master Juwain told me. There was doubt in his voice, and irony as well. "But you needn't take up arms to be in opposition to the Red Dragon. You oppose him merely in your intelligence and love of freedom. And by seeking all that is beautiful, good, and true."

I looked down at the carpet and bit my lip against the tightness in my throat. It was the Brothers who sought those things, not I.

Master Juwain caught my eyes and said, "You have a gift, Val. What kind of gift, I'm not yet sure. But you could have been a Meditation Master or Music Master. Or possibly even a Master Healer."

"Do you really think so, sir?" I asked, looking at him.

"You know I do," he said in a voice heavy with accusation. "But in the end, you quit."

Because I couldn't bear the hurt in his eyes, I turned to stare at the fire. Of all my brothers, I had been the only one to attend the Brotherhood school past the age of sixteen. I had wanted to study music, poetry, languages, and meditation. With great reluctance my father had agreed to this—so long as I didn't neglect the art of the sword. And so for two happy years, I had wandered the cloisters and gardens of the Brotherhood's great sanctuary ten miles up the valley from Silvassu; there I had memorized poems and played my flute and sneaked off into the ash grove to practice fencing with Maram. Though it had never occurred to my father that I might actually want to take vows and join the Brotherhood, for a long time I had nursed just such an ambition.

"It wasn't my choice," I finally said.

"Was it not? Everything we do, we choose. And you chose to quit."

"But the Waashians were killing my friends!" I protested. "Raising spears against my brothers! The king called me to war, and I had to go."

"And what have all your wars ever changed?"

"Please do not call them *my* wars, sir. Nothing would make me happier than to see war ended forever."

"No?" he said, pointing at the dagger that I wore on my belt. "Is that why you bear arms wherever you go? Is that why you answered your father's call to battle?"

"But, sir," I said, smiling as I thought of the words from one of his favorite books, "isn't all life a battle?"

"Yes," he said. "A battle of the heart and soul. It wasn't meant that this killing should go on forever."

I turned away as his sadness touched my eyes with a deep, hot pain. I suddenly recalled the overpowering wrongness that I had sensed earlier in the woods; now a bit of this wrongness, in the form of kirax and perhaps something worse, would burn forever inside me.

I wanted to look at Master Juwain and tell him that there had to be a way to end the killing. Instead, I looked into myself and said, "There's always a time to fight."

Master Juwain stepped closer to me and laid his hand on mine. Then he told me, "Evil can't be vanquished with a sword, Val. Darkness can't be defeated in battle but only by shining a bright enough light."

He let go of me suddenly and walked over to his desk. There his hand closed on a large book bound in green leather. I immediately recognized it as the *Saganom Elu,* many passages of which I had memorized during my years at the Brotherhood school. He opened it to the *Trian Prophecies* and began to recite verses that I knew well:

When earth alights the Golden Band,
The darkest age will pass away.
When angel fire illumes the land,
The stars will show the brightest day.

The deathless day, the Age of Light;
Ieldra's blaze befalls the earth;
The end of war, the end of night
Awaits the last Maitreya's birth.

The Cup of Heaven in his hands,
The One's clear light in heart and eye,
He brings the healing of the land,
And opens colors in the sky.

And there, the stars, the ageless lights
For which we ache and dream and burn,
Upon the deep and dazzling heights—
Our ancient home we shall return.

Master Juwain finished and motioned us over to the window. He pointed up at the stars, and in a voice quavering with excitement, he said, "This is the time. Our astrologers have calculated that the earth entered the Golden Band twenty years ago. I believe that somewhere on Ea, the Maitreya, the Shining One, has been born."

I looked out at the Owl constellation and other clusters of stars that shimmered in the dark sky beyond Telshar's jagged peak. It was said that the earth and all the stars turned about the heavens like a great diamond-studded wheel. At the center of this cosmic wheel—at the center of all things—dwelt the Ieldra, luminous beings who shined the light of their souls on all of creation. These great golden beacons streamed out from the cosmic center like rivers of light, and the Brothers called them the Golden Bands. Every few thousand years, the earth would enter one of them and bask in its radiance. At such times the trumpets of doom would sound and mountains would ring; souls would be quickened and Maitreyas would be born as the old ages ended and the new ones began. Although it was impossible to behold this numinous light with one's eyes, the scryers and certain gifted children could apprehend it as a deep, golden glow that touched all things.

"This is the time," Master Juwain said again as he turned toward me. "The time for the ending of war. And perhaps the time that the Lightstone will be found as well. I'm sure that King Kiritan's messengers have come bearing the news of just such a prophecy."

I gazed out at the stars and there, too, I felt a rushing of a wind that carried the call of strange and beautiful voices. The Ieldra, I knew, communicate the Law of the One not just in golden rays of light but also in the deepest whisperings of the soul.

"If the Lightstone *is* found," I said, wondering aloud, "who would ever have the wisdom to use it?"

Master Juwain looked up at the stars, too. I expected him to tell me that only the Brothers had attained the purity of mind necessary to plumb the secrets of the Lightstone. Instead, he turned to me and said, "The Maitreya would have such wisdom. It is for him that the Galadin sent the Lightstone to earth."

Outside the window, high above the castle and the mountains, the stars of the Seven Sisters and other constellations gleamed brightly. Somewhere among them, I thought, the immortal Elijin gazed upon this cosmic glory and dreamed of becoming Galadin, just as the Star People aspired to advancement to the Elijik order. There, too, dwelled Arwe, Ashtoreth, and Valoreth, and others of the Galadin. These great angelic beings had so perfected themselves and so mastered the physical realm that they could never be killed. They walked on other worlds even as men did the fields and forests of Mesh; in truth, they walked freely *between* worlds, though never yet on earth. Scryers had seen visions of them, and I had sensed their great beauty in my longings and dreams. It was Valoreth himself, my grandfather once told me, who had sent Elahad to Ea bearing the Lightstone in his hands.

For a while, as the night deepened and the stars turned through the sky, we stood there talking about the powers of the mysterious golden cup. I said nothing of my seeing it appear before me in the woods earlier that day. Although its splendor now seemed only that of a dream, the warmth that had revived me like a golden elixir was too real to doubt. Could the Lightstone itself, I wondered, truly heal me of the wound that cut through my heart? Or would it take a Maitreya, wielding the Lightstone as I might a sword, to accomplish this miracle?

I believe that I might have found the courage to ask Master Juwain these questions if we hadn't been interrupted. Just as I was wondering if those of the orders of the Galadin and Elijin had once suffered from the curse of empathy even as I did, footsteps sounded in the hallway and there came a loud knocking at the door.

"Just a moment," Master Juwain called out. He stepped briskly across the room and opened the door. And there, in the dimly-lit archway, stood Joshu Kadar breathing heavily from his long climb up the stairs.

"It's time," the young squire gasped out. "Lord Asaru has asked me to tell you that it's time for the feast to begin."

"Thank you," Master Juwain told him. Then he moved back to the desk where he had left the arrow. He carefully wrapped it in my shirt again and asked, "Are you ready, Val?"

It seemed that the answers that I sought to the great riddles of life would have to wait. And so, with Joshu in the lead, I followed Maram and Master Juwain out into the cold dark hallway.

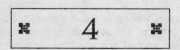

4

WE ENTERED THE great hall to the blare of trumpets announcing the feast. Along the room's north wall, hung with a black banner emblazoned with the swan and stars of the royal house of Mesh, three heralds stood blowing their brass horns. The sound that reverberated through the huge room and out into the castle was the same that I had twice heard calling the Valari to battle. Indeed, the knights of Mesh—and those of Ishka—crowded through the doorways five abreast and moved toward their various tables as if marching to war.

I found Asaru and my brothers standing by their chairs at my family's table along the north wall; there, too, my mother and grandmother waited for me to take my place, as did my father.

He stood tall and grave in a black tunic embroidered with a freshly polished silver swan and seven silver stars. As he watched me climb the steps to the dais upon which our table stood, there was reproof in his fierce gaze, but also concern and much else as well. Although Shavashar Elahad was the hardest man I knew, the well of his emotions ran as deep as the sea.

When all the guests had finally found their places, my father pulled out his chair and sat down, and everyone did the same. He took the position of honor at the center of the table, with my mother at his immediate right and my grandmother on his left. And on my grandmother's left, in order, sat Karshur, Jonathay, and Mandru, the fiercest of all my brothers. Where the other Valari knights in the room were content to wear their swords buckled to their waists, Mandru always carried his scabbarded in his three-fingered left hand, ready to draw at a moment's notice should he need to defend his honor—or his kingdom's. Asaru sat to the right of my mother, Elianora wi Solaru, who was tall and regal in her brightly embroidered gown—and said to be the most beautiful woman in the Nine Kingdoms. Her dark, perceptive eyes moved from Asaru to Yarashan and then down the line of the table from the silent and secretive Ravar to me.

She seemed to beam at me all her strength, goodness, and grace. She was the most alive being I had ever known, and the most loyal, too, and she looked at me as if to say that she would gladly lay down her life to protect me should the unknown assassin try to kill me again.

"Do you see him here?" Ravar whispered to me. The fox-faced Ravar was older than I by three years and shorter by almost a whole head. I had to bend low to hear what he was saying.

I looked out at the sea of faces in the room and tried to identify that of the assassin who had escaped us. At the table nearest the dais, on the right, sat the Brothers who were visiting the castle that night. Master Juwain was there, of course, accompanied by Master Kelem, the Music Master, and Master Tadeo and some twenty other Brothers besides Maram. I knew all of them by name, and I was sure that none of them could have drawn a bow against me.

Unfortunately, I couldn't say the same for King Kiritan's

emissaries, who had taken the next two tables. All of them—the knights and squires, the minstrels and grooms—were strangers to me. Count Dario, the king's cousin, I recognized only by description and his emblem: he wore the gold caduceus of House Narmada on his blue tunic, and his carefully trimmed hair and goatee seemed like red flames shooting from his head.

At the left of the room were the first of the Meshian tables. There Lord Harsha smiled proudly upon Behira, and Lord Tomavar and Lord Tanu sat with Lansar Raasharu and Mesh's greatest lords. If any of these old warriors were traitors, I thought, then I couldn't be sure that the sun would rise in the east the next morning.

As well I had faith in my countrymen in the second tier of tables where the master knights and their ladies waited for my father's attendants to pour the wine. And so with the many lesser knights sitting at the tables beyond, out to the farthest corners of the hall. There, almost too far away to see clearly, I studied the faces of friends such as Sunjay Navaru and other common warriors at whose sides I once had fought.

I said to Ravar, "None of them looks like the one who shot at me."

"But what of the Ishkans?" he asked, nodding at the centermost and closest of the tables below us.

As Ravar turned his sharp, black eyes upon the Ishkans, perhaps looking for weaknesses with the same concentration that he had turned on Waas's army at the Battle of Red Mountain, I did the same. And immediately my eyes fell upon an arrogant man with a great scar running down the side of his face. Although he had a great snout of a nose, his father and mother had bestowed upon him scarcely any chin. I knew him as Prince Salmelu, King Hadaru's oldest son. Five years before, at the great tournament in Taron, I had humiliated him in a game of chess, a crushing defeat that had taken only twenty-three moves. It wasn't enough that he had nearly won the gold medal in the fencing competition and had acquitted himself honorably in the long lance and archery competitions; it seemed he had to be preeminent at everything, for he took insult easily, especially from those who had bested him. It was said that he had fought fifteen men in duels—and left all fifteen dead in pools of blood. Tonight, he stared straight at me with coldness and challenge. I swallowed hard against the slimy feeling creeping into my belly. Why, I wondered, had this man always disdained me—even before our ugly chess match? At the tournament, he had called me "a clumsy young pup trying to run in the company of wolves." And then he had let himself be overheard asking if my father really could have whelped me. As I now bore the open contempt pouring out of him, I thought it was *he* who had been a dog—as a dog of a man he remained.

One of his brothers, Lord Issur, shared the table with him, along with Lord Mestivan and Lord Nadhru and other prominent Ishkans whom Ravar pointed out to me. They joined Salmelu in staring up at me.

"Do any of them look like your assassin?" Ravar asked me.

"No," I said. "It's hard to say—the man's face was hooded."

And then, even as I closed my eyes and opened myself to the hum of hundreds of voices, I felt the same taint of wrongness that I had in the woods. The red, twisting worms of someone's hate began eating their way up my spine. From what man in the hall this dreadful sensation emanated, however, I couldn't tell.

At last, the wine having been poured, my father lifted up his goblet and stood to make the opening toast. All eyes in the hall turned his way; all voices trailed off and then died into silence as he began to speak.

"Masters of the Brotherhood," he began, "princes and lords, ladies and knights, we would like to welcome you to this gathering tonight. It's a strange chance that brings King Kiritan's emissaries to Mesh at the same time that King Hadaru sends his eldest son to honor us. But let us hope that it's a good chance and a sign of good times to come."

My father, I thought, had a fine, strong voice that rang from the stones of the hall. He fairly shined with strength, both in the inner steel of his soul and in his large, long hands that could still grip a sword with all the ferocity of a lion. At fifty-four, he was just entering the fullest flower of manhood, for the Valari age more slowly than do other peoples—no one knows why. His long black hair, shot with strands of snowy white, flowed out from beneath a silver crown whose points were set with brilliant white diamonds. Five other diamonds, arrayed in the shape of a star, shimmered from his silver ring. It was the ring of a king, and someday Asaru would wear it, if no one killed him first.

"And so," my father continued, "in the hope of finding the way toward the peace that all desire, we invite you to take salt and bread with us—and perhaps a little meat and ale as well."

My father smiled as he said this, to leaven the stiffness of his formal speech. Then he motioned for the grooms to bring out what he had called "a little meat." In truth, there were many platters laden with steaming hams and roasted beef, along with elk, venison, and other game. There were fowls almost too numerous to count: nicely browned ducks, geese, pheasants, and quail—though of course no swans. It seemed that hunters such as Asaru and I had slaughtered whole herds and flocks that day. The grooms served baskets heaped with black barley bread, aged cheeses, butter, jams, apple pies, honeycomb, and pitchers of frothing black beer. There was so much food that the long wooden tables fairly groaned beneath its weight.

Although I was very hungry, my belly seemed a knot of acid and pain, and I could hardly eat. My brothers talked of war. I heard Asaru say to Ravar, "In the end, it will all come down to the mountain."

Everyone knew of which mountain he spoke: Mount Korukel, one of the guardian peaks that stood upon the border between Mesh and Ishka just beyond the feeder streams of the Upper Raaswash River. The Ishkans were pressing their old demand that the border of our two kingdoms should exactly bisect Mount Korukel, while we of the swan and stars claimed the whole mountain as Meshian soil.

"But Korukel is ours," Yarashan said as he used a napkin to neatly wipe the beer from his lips. In his outward form, he was almost as beautiful a man as Jonathay and even prouder than Asaru.

What was half a mile of rock against men's lives? I wondered. Well, if many of those rocks were diamonds, it was a great deal indeed. For the lives of men—the Valari warriors of each of the Nine Kingdoms—had been connected to the fabulous mineral wealth of the Morning Mountains for thousands of years. From their silver we made our emblems and the gleaming rings with which we pledged our lives; from its iron we made our steel. And from the diamonds we found deep underground and sometimes sparkling in the shallows of clear mountain streams, we made our marvelous suits of armor. In the Age of Swords, before the Brotherhood had broken with the Valari, it had been the Brothers who had learned to work these hardest and most beautiful of stones; they had discovered the secret of affixing them to corslets of black leather and then taught us this art. While it was not true that diamond-encrusted armor afforded the Valari invulnerability in battle—an arrow or a well-aimed spear thrust could find a chink between the carefully set diamonds—many were the swords that had broken upon it. The mere sight of a Valari army marching into battle and glittering in their ranks as if raimented with millions of stars had struck terror into our enemies for most of three long ages. They called us the Diamond Warriors, and they said that we could never be defeated by force of arms alone but only through treachery or the fire of the red gelstei.

And recently a great new vein of diamonds had been discovered running through the heart of Mount Korukel. Naturally, the Ishkans wanted to mine it for themselves.

When the last pie had finally been eaten and nearly everyone's belly groaned from much more than a little meat, it came time for the rounds of toasting. The first to stand that day was Count Dario. He was a compact man who moved with quick, deft gestures. He took up a goblet of black beer and presented it toward my father, saying, "To King Shamesh, whose hospitality is overmatched only by his wisdom."

A clamor of approval rang through the hall. Then Prince Salmelu, like the swordsman he was, took advantage of the opening that Count Dario had unwittingly presented him. Like an uncaged bear, he stood and planted his feet wide apart on the floor. He fingered the many colored battle ribbons tied to his long hair before resting his right hand on the hilt of his sword. Then with his left hand, he raised his goblet and said, "To King Shamesh. May he find the wisdom to do what we all wish for in walking the road toward peace."

As I touched my lips to my beer, he flashed me a quick, hard look as if testing me with a feint of his sword.

I knew that I should have thought of a rejoinder to his thinly veiled demand. But as he stared at me with such venomousness, my mind clouded, and I could hardly move my muscles to push up out of my chair. Instead, it was my usually stolid brother, Karshur, who stood and raised his goblet.

"To King Shamesh," he said in voice that sounded like boulders rolling down a mountain. He himself was built like an inverted mountain: as if successive slabs of granite had been piled higher and deeper from his thick legs to his massive shoulders and chest. "May he find the *strength* to do what he has to do, no matter what others may wish."

As soon as he had returned to his chair, Jonathay stood up beside him. He had all of our mother's beauty and much of her grace as well. He laughed good-naturedly, as if enjoying this duel of words. "To Queen Elianora, may she always find the patience to endure men's talk of war."

All at once, from the tables throughout the hall, the many women there raised their goblets as if by a single hand and called out, "Yes, yes, to Queen Elianora!"

As a nervous laughter spread from table to table, my mother stood and smoothed out the folds of her black gown. Then she smiled kindly. Although she directed her words out into the hall, it seemed that she was speaking right at Salmelu.

"To all our guests tonight," she said, "thank you for making such long journeys to honor our home. May the good company we bring open our hearts so that we act out of the true courage of compassion rather than fear."

So saying, she turned to Salmelu and beamed a smile at him. In her bright eyes there was only a desire for fellowship. But her natural grace seemed to infuriate Salmelu rather than soothe him. He sat deathly still in his chair gripping the hilt of his sword as his face flushed with blood. Although Salmelu had stood sword to naked sword with fifteen men in the ring of honor, he couldn't seem to bear the gentleness of my mother's gaze.

Because it would have been unseemly for him to stand again while others waited to make their toasts, he cast a quick, ferocious look at Lord Nadhru as if to order him to speak in his place. And so Lord Nadhru, a rather angry young man who might have been Salmelu's twin in his insolent nature if not appearance, sprang up from his chair.

"To Queen Elianora," he said, looking over the rim of his goblet. "We thank her for reminding us that we must always act with courage, which we promise to do. And we thank her for welcoming us into her house, even as she was once welcomed herself."

This, I thought, was the Ishkans' way of reminding her that she was as much of an outsider in the castle as they were, and therefore that she had no real right to speak for Mesh. But of course this was just pure spite on their part. For Elianora wi Solaru, sister of King Talanu of Kaash, had chosen freely to wed my father and not their greedy old king.

And so it went, toast after toast, both Ishkans and Meshians casting words back and forth as if they were velvet-covered spears. All this time my father sat as still and grave in his chair as any of our ancestors in the portraits lining the walls. Although he kept most of the fire from his eyes, I could feel a whole stew of emotions boiling up inside him: pride, anger, loyalty, outrage, love. One who didn't know him better might have thought that at any moment he might lose his patience and silence his attackers with a burst of kingly thunder. But my father practiced self-restraint as others did wielding their swords. No man, I thought, asked more of himself than he. In many ways he embodied the Valari ideal of flowingness, flawlessness, and fearlessness. As I, too, struggled to keep my silence, he suddenly looked at me as if to say, "Never let the enemy know what you're thinking."

I believe that my father might have allowed this part of the feast to continue half the night so that he might better have a chance to study the Ishkans—and his own countrymen and sons. But the toasting came to a sudden and unexpected end, from a most unexpected source.

"My lords and ladies!" a strong voice suddenly bellowed out from below our table, "*I* would like to propose a toast."

I turned just in time to see Maram push back his chair and stand away from the Brothers' table. How Maram had acquired a goblet full of beer in plain sight of his masters was a mystery. And clearly it was not his first glass either, for he used his fat, beer-stained fingers to wipe the dried froth from his mustache as he wobbled on his feet. And then he raised his goblet out toward the room, spilling even more beer on his stained tunic.

"To Lord Harsha," he said, nodding toward his table. "May we all thank him for providing this wonderful drink tonight."

That was a toast everyone could gladly drink to; all at once hundreds of goblets, both of glass and silver steel, clinked together, and a grateful laughter peeled out into the room. I looked across the hall as Lord Harsha shifted about his chair. Although he was plainly embarrassed to have been singled out for his generosity, he smiled at Maram all the same. If Maram had left well enough alone and sat back down, he might even have gained Lord Harsha's favor. But Maram, it seemed, could never leave anything alone.

"And now I would like to drink to love and beautiful women," he said. He turned to Behira. "Ah, the love *of* beautiful women—it's what makes the world turn and the stars shine, is it not?"

Master Juwain looked up at Maram, but Maram ignored his icy stare.

"It's to the most beautiful woman in the world that I would now like to dedicate this poem, whose words came into my mind like flowers opening the first moment I saw her."

He raised his goblet toward Behira. Forgetting that he was supposed to wait until *after* the toast before drinking, he took a huge gulp of beer. And all the while, Behira sat next to her father, flushing with embarrassment. But it was clear that Maram's attentions delighted her, for she smiled back at him, glowing with an almost tangible heat.

"Brother Maram," Lord Harsha suddenly called out in his gravelly old voice, "this isn't the place for your poetry."

But Maram ignored him, too, and began reciting his poem:

> *Star of my soul, how you shimmer*
> *Beyond the deep blue sky,*
> *Whirling and whirling—you and I whisperlessly*
> *Spinning sparks of joy into the night*

I stared at the rings glittering on Maram's fingers and the passion pouring from his eyes. The words of his poem outraged me. For it wasn't really his poem at all; he had stolen the verse of the great but forgotten Amun Amaduk and was passing it off as his own.

Lord Harsha pushed back his chair and called out even more strongly, "Brother Maram!"

Maram would have done well to heed the warning in Lord Harsha's voice. But by this time he was drunk on his own words (or rather, Amun's), and with childlike abandon began the second stanza of the poem:

> *From long ago we came across the universe:*
> *Lost rays of light, we fell among strange new flowers*
> *And searched in fields and forests*
> *Until we found each other and remembered.*

Suddenly, with a sound of fury in his throat, Lord Harsha drew his sword. Its polished steel glinted in the candlelight and pointed straight at Maram, who finally closed his mouth as it occurred to him that he had gone too far. And Lord Harsha, I was afraid, had gone too far to stop, too. Almost without thinking, I leaped up from my chair, crossed the dais, and jumped down to the lower level of the guests' tables. My boots hit the cold stone with a loud slap. Then I stepped in front of Maram just as Lord Harsha closed the distance between them and pointed the tip of his sword at my heart.

"Lord Harsha," I said, "will you please excuse my friend? He's obviously had too much of your fine beer."

Lord Harsha's sword lowered perhaps half an inch. I felt his hot breath steaming out of his nostrils. I was afraid that at any moment he might try to get at Maram by pushing his sword through me. Then he growled out, "Well, then he should remember his vows, shouldn't he? Particularly his vow to renounce women!"

Behind me, Maram cleared his throat as if to argue with Lord Harsha.

And then my father, the king, finally spoke. "Lord Harsha, would you please put down your sword? As a favor to me."

If Maram had been Valari then there *would* have been a death that night, for he would have had to answer Lord Harsha's challenge with steel. But Maram was only a Delian and a Brother at that. Because no one could expect a Brother to fight a duel with a Valari lord, there was yet hope.

Lord Harsha stood there staring at me as he took a deep breath and then another. I felt the heat of his blood slowly begin to cool. Then he nodded his head in a quick bow to my father and said, "Sire, as a favor to you, it would be my pleasure."

Almost as suddenly as he had drawn his sword, he slipped it

back into his sheath. When the king asked you to put down your sword—or take it up—there was no choice but to honor his request.

"Thank you," my father called out to him, "for your restraint."

"Thank you," I whispered to him, "for sparing my friend."

Then I turned to look at Maram as I laid my hand on his shoulder and pushed him back down into his chair. From the nearby table of Valari masters and their ladies, I swept up two goblets of beer and gave one to Lord Harsha.

"To brotherhood among men," I said, raising my goblet. I looked from my family's table to that of Master Juwain, and then back across the room to the table of the Ishkans. "In the end, all men are brothers."

I listened with great hope as echoes of approval rang out to the clinking of many glasses. And then Maram, my stubborn, irrepressible friend, looked up at my father and said, "Ah, King Shamesh—I suppose this isn't the best time to finish my poem?"

My father told him, "The time for making toasts is at an end. Lord Harsha, would you please take your seat so that we might move on to more important matters?"

Again Lord Harsha bowed, and he walked slowly back through the rows of tables to his chair. He sat down next to his greatly relieved daughter, whom he looked at sternly but with obvious love. And then a silence fell over the room as all eyes turned toward my father.

"We have before us tonight the emissaries of two kings," he said, nodding his head at Salmelu and then Count Dario. "And two requests will be made of us here tonight; we should listen well to both and neither let our hearts shout down the wisdom of our heads nor our heads mock what our hearts know to be true. Why don't we have Prince Salmelu speak first, for it may be that in deciding upon his request, the answer to Count Dario's will become obvious."

Without smiling, he nodded at Salmelu, who eagerly sprang to his feet.

"King Shamesh," he said in voice like a whip, "the request of King Hadaru is simple: that the border of our kingdoms be clearly established according to the agreement of our ancestors. Either that, or the king asks that we set a time and place for battle."

So, I thought, the ultimatum that we had all been awaiting had finally been set before us. I felt the hands of three hundred Meshian warriors aching to grip the hilts of their swords.

"The border of our kingdoms *is* established thusly," my father told Salmelu. "The first Shavashar gave your people all the lands from Mount Korukel to the Aru River."

This was true. Long, long ago in the Lost Ages, before the millennia of recorded history, it was said that the first Shavashar Elahad had claimed most of the lands of the Morning Mountains for his kingdom. But his seventh son, Ishkavar, wanting lands of his own to rule, had despaired of ever coming into this great possession. And so he had rebelled against his own father. Because Shavashar refused to spill the blood of his favorite son, he had given him all the lands from Korukel to the Aru, and from the Culhadosh River to the grassy plains of the Wendrush. Such was the origin of the kingdom that came to be called Ishka.

"From Mount *Korukel*," Salmelu snapped at my father. "Which you now claim for your own!"

My father stared down at him with a face as cold as stone. Then he said, "If a man gives his son all his fields from his house to a river, he has given him only his fields—not the house or the river."

"But mountains," Salmelu said, repeating the old argument, "aren't houses. There's no clearly marked boundary where one begins and ends."

"This is true," my father said. "But surely you can't think a mountain's boundary should be a line running through the center of its highest peak?"

"Given the spirit of the agreement, it's the only way *to* think."

"There are many ways of thinking," my father said, "and we're here tonight to determine what is most fair."

"You speak of fairness?" Salmelu half shouted. "You who keep the richest lands of the Morning Mountains for yourselves? You who kept the Lightstone locked in your castle for an entire age when all the Valari should have shared in its possession?"

Some of what he said was true. After the Battle of Sarburn, when the combined might of the Valari had overthrown Morjin and he had been imprisoned in a great fortress on the Isle of

Damoom, Aramesh had brought the Lightstone back to Silvassu. And it *had* resided in my family's castle for most of the Age of Law. But it had never been locked away. I turned to look at the granite pedestal against the wall behind my father's chair. There, on this dusty, old stand, now dark and empty, the Lightstone had sat in plain view for nearly three thousand years.

"All the Valari *did* share of its radiance," my father told Salmelu. "Although it was deemed unwise to move it among the kingdoms, our castle was always open to any and all who came to see it. Especially to the Ishkans."

"Yes, and we had to enter your castle as beggars hoping for a glimpse of gold."

"Is that why you invaded our lands with no formal declaration and tried to steal the Lightstone from us? If not for the valor of King Yaravar at the Raaswash, who knows how many would have been killed?"

Salmelu's small mouth set tightly with anger. "You speak of warriors being killed? As *your* people killed Elsu Maruth, who was a very great king."

Although my father kept his face calm, his eyes flashed with fire. "Was he a greater king than Elkasar Elahad, whom you killed at the Diamond River twelve years ago?"

At the mention of my grandfather's name, I stared at Salmelu, and the flames of vengeance began eating at me, too.

"Warriors die," Salmelu said, shrugging off my father's grief with an air of unconcern. "And warriors kill—as King Elkamesh killed my uncle, Lord Dorje. Duels are duels, and war is war."

"War is war, as you say," my father told Salmelu. "But there are some who say that my father's death was planned and call it murder. You'll never hear us say this. War is war, and even kings are killed on the field of battle. But the hunting of a king's son in his own woods—*that* is murder."

For a long time, perhaps as many as twenty beats of my racing heart, my father sat staring at Salmelu. His eyes were like bright swords cutting away at Salmelu's outward hauteur to reveal the man within. And Salmelu stared back at him: with defiance and a jealous hatred coloring his face. While this duel of the eyes took place before hundreds of men and women stunned into silence, I noticed Asaru exchange a brief look with Ravar. Then Asaru nodded toward a groom standing off to the side of the hall near the door that led to the kitchens. The groom bowed back and disappeared through the doorway. And Asaru stood up from the table, causing Salmelu to break eyes with my father and look at him instead.

"My lords and ladies," Asaru called out to the room, "it has come to my attention that the cooks have finally prepared a proper ending to the feast. If you'll abide with me a moment, they have a surprise for you."

Now my father looked at Asaru with puzzlement furrowing his forehead. As did Lord Harsha, Count Dario, Lord Tomavar, and many others.

"But what does all this have to do with murder?" Salmelu demanded.

And Asaru replied, "Only this: that all this talk of killing and murder must have made everyone hungry again. It wouldn't do to end a feast with everyone still hungry."

Upon these curious words, the doors to the kitchen opened, and four grooms wheeled out one of the great serving carts usually reserved for the display of whole roasted boars or other large game. It seemed that one knight or another must have indeed speared a boar earlier that day in the woods, for a voluminous white cloth was draped over what appeared to be the largest of boars. Apparently it had taken all these many hours to finish cooking. The grooms wheeled the cart right out toward the front of the room, where they left it sitting just in front of the Ishkans' table.

"Is that *really* a boar?" I heard Maram ask one of the grooms. "I haven't had a taste of a good boar in two years."

How anyone could still be hungry after all the food consumed earlier, I didn't know. But if any man could, Maram was certainly that man and he eyed the bulging white cloth along with Master Tadeo and everyone else in the room.

Asaru came down from the dais and stepped over to the serving cart. He looked straight at Salmelu. And then, with dramatic flair I hadn't known he possessed, he reached down and whisked the cloth away from the cart.

"Oh, my Lord!" Maram gasped out. "Oh, Lord, Lord, Lord!"

Others gasped out with him in astonishment. For there, laid out on bloodstained boards, was the body of the assassin that I had killed in the woods.

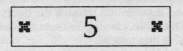

5

THE MAN'S FACE, I saw, was livid with the darkness of death. His eyes remained as I had closed them, and his dirty tunic was still moist with the blood that I had spilled.

"Who is this man?" Salmelu cried out, jumping to his feet. "Are you saying that I murdered him?"

"No," Asaru said, glancing up at me, "no one will say that."

Salmelu flicked his hand toward the cart. "But what did you mean by saying it wouldn't do to end a feast with everyone still hungry? This is no way to end a feast."

"No," Asaru agreed. "Not with all of us still hungry for the truth."

I felt sure that my father had no foreknowledge of the ugly surprise that had been presented to his guests. It had all the markings of something that Asaru and Ravar had cooked up together, so to speak. But my father immediately saw their purpose. And so did I.

Asaru now began telling of how two hooded men had tried to murder him in his father's own forest. Although he gave a full account of my killing the man upon the cart, it was obvious that he still believed the first assassin's arrow had been meant for him.

"If anyone present knows this man," he said, pointing at the dead assassin, "will he speak and tell us who he is?"

"I know him," Count Dario announced, surprising everyone. He rose and walked over to the cart to get a better look at the body. "His name is Raldu. He joined our party in Ishka, just after we had crossed the Aru River."

The other emissaries at the Alonian table, including two named Baron Telek and Lord Mingan, all looked at each other and nodded their heads in affirmation.

"But who *is* he?" Asaru asked Count Dario. "And how is it that emissaries of a great king came to share fellowship with a murderer?"

Count Dario stood pulling at his bristly red chin hairs. He evinced not the slightest sign that my brother's questions had insulted him. In a measured voice, he said, "I do not know if this man has a name other than Raldu. *He* said that he was a knight of Galda who fled that land when it fell to the Lord of Lies. He said that he had been wandering among the kingdoms in hope of finding a way to fight him. When he learned the nature of our mission, he asked to join us. Perhaps I should have questioned him more closely."

My father looked at Count Dario with a sternness softened by compassion. "It was not upon you to seek out the secrets of this Raldu's heart. But we must ask you to search your memory deeply now. Did Raldu ever speak against myself or my house? Did he ever say anything to indicate who his true lord might be?"

Count Dario moved back over to his table, where he conferred with his countrymen for a while. Then he looked up at the king and said, "No, on the journey through Ishka, he comported himself well at all times."

So, I thought, if Count Dario spoke truly, Raldu had used the emissaries as cover to enter Mesh from Ishka. And then used the hunt as an opportunity to try to murder me.

"So, then," my father said, as if echoing my thoughts, "it's clear how Raldu found his way into Mesh. But what was he doing in Ishka?"

My father turned to look at Salmelu then. Salmelu looked back at him, and his hand touched his sword as he snarled out, "If you think to accuse us of hiring assassins to accomplish what good Ishkan steel has always done quite well, then perhaps we should add *that* to the list of grievances that only battle can address."

My father's hand tightened into a fist, and for a moment it seemed that he might accuse the Ishkans of this very crime. And then Count Dario raised up his voice and said, "Mesh and Ishka: the two greatest kingdoms of the Valari. And here you are, ready to make war against each other when the Lord of Lies is on the march again. Isn't there any way I could persuade you of what a tragedy this war will be?"

My father took a deep breath and relaxed his fingers. And then he spoke not just to Count Dario but to all those present in the hall. "War," he said, "has not yet been decided. But it is growing late, and we would like to hear from anyone who would speak for or against war with Ishka."

As quickly as he could, Lord Harsha rose to his feet. He seemed in a combative mood, probably because he had lost his chance to chastise Maram. He rubbed the patch over his missing eye, then pointed at Raldu's body and said, "Whether the Ishkans hired this man, who can say? But it's plain that what the Ishkans really want is our diamonds. Well, why don't we give them a bit of Meshian steel, instead?"

With that, he patted the sheath of his sword, and the cries of many of Mesh's finest knights suddenly rang out into the hall. As he sat back down, I noticed Salmelu smiling at him.

During the whole time of the feast, my grandmother, sitting next to my father, had been quiet. She was rather small for a Valari and growing old, but once she had been Elkamesh's beloved queen. I had never known a kinder or more patient woman. Although she was shrinking in her body as the years fell upon her, a secret light seemed to be gathering in her and growing ever brighter. Everyone loved her for this deep beauty as she loved them. And so when Ayasha Elahad, the Queen Mother, arose to address the knights and ladies of Mesh, everyone fell silent to listen to her speak.

"It's been twelve years now since my king was killed in battle with the Ishkans," she called out in voice like aged wine. "And many more since my first two sons met a similar fate. Now only King Shamesh remains for me—and my grandsons by him. Must I watch them be taken away as well over a handful of diamonds?"

That was all she said. But as she returned to her chair, she looked at me as if to tell me that it would break her heart if I died before she did.

Then Master Juwain stood and gazed out at the hundreds of warriors with his clear gray eyes. "There have been thirty-three wars," he said, "over the centuries between Ishka and Mesh. What has either kingdom gained? Nothing."

That was all he said, too. He sat back down next to Master Kelem, who sagely nodded his hoary old head.

"It's to be expected that Master Juwain would feel thusly,"

Salmelu called out. "The Brothers always side with the women in avoiding matters of honor, don't they?"

It is one of the tragedies of my people that the other Valari, such as the Ishkans, do not esteem the Brotherhood as do we of Mesh. They suspect them of secret alliances and purposes beyond the teaching of meditation or music—all true. But the Brothers, Maram notwithstanding, have their own honor. I hated Salmelu for implying that they—and noble women whom I loved—might be cowards.

I rose to my feet then. I took a drink of beer to moisten my dry throat. I knew that almost no one would want to hear what I had to say. But the kirax was beating like a hammer in my blood, and I still felt the coldness of Raldu's body in my own. And so I looked at Salmelu and said, "My grandfather once told me that the first Valari were warriors of the spirit only. And that a true warrior would find a way to end war. It takes more courage to live life fully with an open heart than it does to march blindly into battle and die over a heap of dirt. This is something women understand."

Salmelu gave me barely enough time to return to my chair before firing his sneering words back at me: "Perhaps young Valashu has been spending too much time with the Brothers *and* the women. And perhaps it's well that his grandfather is no longer alive to spread the foolishness of myths and old wives' tales."

Again, as if I had drunk a cup full of kirax, a wave of hatred came flooding into me. I couldn't tell if this poisonous emotion originated from myself or from Salmelu. Certainly he had hated *me* since the moment I had bested him at chess. But did this prince of Ishka hate me deeply enough to shoot arrows at me?

"You should be careful," my father warned Salmelu, "of how you speak of a man's ancestors."

"Thank you, King Shamesh, for sharing your wisdom," Salmelu said, bowing with exaggerated punctilio. "And *you* should be careful of what decision you make tonight. The lives of many depend on this famous wisdom."

As my father caught his breath and stared out at the great wooden beams that held up the roof of the hall, I wondered why the Ishkans had really come to our castle. Did they wish to provoke a war, here, this very night? Did they truly believe that they could defeat Mesh in battle? Well, perhaps they could. The Ishkans could field some twelve thousand warriors and knights to our ten, and we couldn't necessarily count on our greater valor to win the day as we had at the Diamond River. But I thought it more likely that Salmelu and his countrymen were bluffing: trying to cow us into ceding them the mountain by displaying their eagerness to fight. They couldn't really want war, could they? Who, I wondered, would ever want a war?

My father asked everyone to sit then, and so we did. He called for the council to continue, and various lords and ladies spoke for or against war according to their hearts. Lord Tomavar, a long-faced man with a slow, heavy manner about him, surprised everyone by arguing that the Ishkans should be allowed to keep their part of the mountain. He said that Mesh already had enough diamonds to supply the armorers for the next ten years and that it wouldn't hurt to give a few of them away. Other lords and knights—and many of the women—agreed with him. But there were many more, such as the fiery Lord Solaru of Mir, who did not.

Finally, after the candles had burned low in their stands, my father held up his hand to call an end to the debate. "Thank you all for speaking so openly. But now it is upon me to decide what must be done."

As everyone waited to hear what he would say and the room fell quiet, he took a deep breath and turned toward Salmelu. "Do you have sons, Lord Salmelu?" he asked him.

"Yes, two," he said, cocking his head and waiting for the point of the question.

"Very well, then as a father you will understand why we are too distraught to call for war at this time." He paused to look first at Asaru and then at me. "Two of *my* sons were nearly murdered today. And one of the assassins still walks free, perhaps taking meat here this night."

At this, many troubled voices rumbled out into the hall as men and women cast nervous glances at their neighbors. And then Salmelu rebuked my father, saying, "That's no decision at all!"

"There's no need to hurry this war, if war there must be," my father told him. "We must determine the extent of the diamond deposits before deciding if we will cede them. And an assassin remains to be caught."

My father went on to say that the end of summer, when the harvest was in, would be soon enough for battle.

"We've come here to bring you King Hadaru's request," Salmelu said, staring at my father, "not to be put off."

"And we've given you our decision," my father told him.

"Yes, and it's a *dangerous* decision," Salmelu snapped out. "You would do well to reflect upon just how dangerous it might prove to be."

Truly, I thought, my father was taking a great chance. For thousands of years, the Valari had made war upon each other, but never toward the end of conquest. But if a king tried to avoid a formal war such as the Ishkans had proposed, then he ran a very real risk that a war of ravage, rapine, and even annihilation might break out.

"We live in a world with danger at every turn," my father told Salmelu. "Who has the wisdom always to see which of many dangers is the greatest or the least?"

"So be it, then," Salmelu snarled, looking away from him.

"So be it," my father said.

This pronouncement answered the first of the requests asked of him that night. But no one seemed to remember that a second remained to be made. And then Count Dario finally stood to address us.

"King Shamesh," he called out, "may I speak now?"

"Please do—it has grown very late."

Count Dario touched the golden caduceus shining from his tunic, then cast his voice out into the hall. "This night I have watched the noblest lords of Ishka and Mesh nearly come to blows over past grievances that no one can undo," he said. "Who has the wisdom to overcome this discord? Who has the power to heal old wounds and bring peace to the lands of Ea? *I* know of no such man now living, neither king nor Brother nor sage. But it is said that the Lightstone has this power. And that is why, with the Red Dragon uncaged once again, it must be found."

He paused to take a deep breath and look around the room as my father nodded at him to continue.

"And it *will* be found," he said. "This is the prophecy that the great scryer, Ayondela Kirriland, gave us before she was murdered. It is why King Kiritan has sent messengers into all the free lands."

Although it was not Salmelu's place to speak, he looked Count Dario up and down and demanded, "What are the words of this prophecy, then?"

"Her words are these," he said, casting Salmelu an icy look. Everyone looked at him as he told us, "The seven brothers and sisters of the earth with the seven stones will set forth into the darkness. The Lightstone will be found, the Maitreya will come forth, and a new age will begin."

A new age, I thought as I gazed at the empty stand behind our table where once the Lightstone had shined. *An age without killing or war.*

"My king," Count Dario continued, "has asked for all knights wishing to fulfill the prophecy to gather in Tria on the seventh day of Soldru. There he will give his blessings to all who vow to make this quest."

"And a very noble quest this is," my father finally said.

"King Kiritan has asked that all kings of the free lands send knights to Tria. He would make this request of you, King Shamesh."

My father nodded his head respectfully, then looked across the hall at his seneschal, Lansar Raasharu. "Very well, but before this decision is made, we would like to hear counsel. Lord Raasharu?"

Lord Raasharu was renowned for his loyalty to my family. He had long iron-gray hair, which he brushed back from his plain face as he stood and said, "Sire, how can we trust the prophecies of foreign scryers? Are we to risk the lives of knights on the words of this Ayondela Kirriland? And this at a time when the Ishkans are demanding our diamonds?"

Now Lord Tanu, a fierce old warrior whose four diamonds flashed brilliantly in his ring, said simply, "This quest is a fool's errand."

His sentiment seemed to be that of most of the lords and knights in the hall. For perhaps another hour, my countrymen arose one by one to speak against King Kiritan's request. And nearly all this time, I sat staring at the empty granite stand behind my father's chair.

"Enough," my father finally said, raising his hand. He turned to address Count Dario. "We said earlier that hearing King Hadaru's request first might help us decide King Kiritan's request. And so it has. It seems that we of Mesh are all agreed on this, at least."

He paused a moment and turned to point at the empty stand. "Other kings have sent knights to seek the Lightstone—and few of these knights have ever returned to Mesh. The Lightstone is surely lost forever. And so even one knight would be too many to send on this hopeless quest."

Count Dario listened as many knights rapped their rings against the tables in affirmation of my father's decision. Then his face clouded with puzzlement as he half shouted, "But once your people fought the Lord of Lies himself for the Lightstone! I don't understand you Valari!"

"It may be that we don't understand ourselves," my father said gravely. "But we know a fool's errand when we hear of one."

In the quiet that fell upon the hall, I could almost hear the beating of my heart. The candles in their stands near the wall had now burned very low; this changed the angle of the rays of light cast against the great banner, so that the silver swan and the seven silver stars seemed to shimmer with a new radiance.

"Then you will send no knights to Tria?" Count Dario asked.

"No, no knights will be sent," my father said. "However, no one who truly wants to go will be kept from going."

Although I listened to my father speak, I did not really hear him. For on the wall behind our table, scarcely ten feet from my throbbing eyes, the largest of the banner's seven stars suddenly began gleaming brightly. It cast a stream of light straight toward the surface of the dusty stand. The silvery light touched the white granite, which seemed to glow with a soft, golden radiance. I remembered then the ancient prophecy from the *Epics* of the *Saganom Elu:* that the silver would lead to the gold.

I looked at my father as he called out to the many tables below ours: "Is there anyone here who would make this quest?"

All at once, the many whispering voices grew quiet, and almost everyone's gaze pulled down toward the floor. Their lack of interest stunned me. Couldn't they see the silver star blazing like a great beacon from the center of the banner? What was wrong with them that they were blind to the miracle occurring before their eyes?

I turned back toward the stand then, and my astonishment

made my breath stop and my heart catch in my throat. For there, on top of the stand, a golden cup was pouring its light out into the hall. It sat there as clear for all to see as the goblets on the tables before them.

The Lightstone will be found, I heard my heart whisper. *A new age will begin.*

Ravar, who must have seen me staring at the stand as if drunk with the fire of angels, suddenly began staring, too. But all he said was, "What are you looking at, Val?"

"Don't you see it?" I whispered to him.

"See *what*?"

"The Lightstone," I said. "The golden cup, there, shining like a star."

"You're drunk," he whispered back to me. "Or you're dreaming."

Now Count Dario called out to the knights and nobles in the room: "Is there anyone here who will pledge himself to making this quest?"

While Lord Harsha scowled and traded embarrassed looks with Lord Tomavar, most of the knights present, both Ishkan and Meshian, kept staring at the cold floorstones.

"Lord Asaru," Count Dario called out, turning toward my brother, "You are the eldest son of a long and noble line. Will you at least make the journey to Tria to hear what my king has to say?"

"No," Asaru told him. "It's enough for me to hear what *my* king has said: that this is no time for hopeless quests."

Count Dario closed his eyes for a moment as if praying for patience. Then he looked straight at Karshur as he continued his strategy of singling out the sons of Shavashar Elahad.

"Lord Karshur," he said, "will you make this journey?"

Karshur gathered in his great strength as he looked at Count Dario. In a voice that sounded like an iron door closing, he said, "No, the Lightstone is lost or destroyed, and not even the most adamant knight will ever find it."

As Count Dario turned to query Yarashan, to the same result, I looked out toward the far wall at the portraits of the Elahad kings. I stared at the most recent one. And the bright eyes of my grandfather, Elkamesh, stared back at me out of bold face bones and a mane of flowing white hair. The painter, I thought, had done well in capturing the essence of his character. The love that he had always held for me seemed still to live in dried pigments of black and white. If my grandfather were here in the flesh, I knew what he would say to me—and to King Kiritan's summons to make the quest.

Count Dario asked his question of Jonathay and Ravar, and then turned to the last of my brothers. "Sar Mandru, will you be in Tria on the seventh day of Soldru?"

"No," Mandru said, fiercely gripping the sheath of his sword in his three fingers, "my duty lies elsewhere."

Now Count Dario paused to take a breath as he looked at me. All of my brothers had refused him, and I, too, felt the pangs of my loyalty to my father pressing at my heart.

"Valashu," he asked, "what does the last of King Shamesh's sons say?"

I opened my mouth to tell him that I had my duty as did my brothers, but no words came out. And then, as if seized by a will that I hadn't known I possessed, I pushed back my chair and rose to my feet. In less than a heartbeat, it seemed, I crossed the ten feet to where the Lightstone gleamed like a golden sun on its ancient stand. I reached out to grasp it. But my fingers closed upon air, and even as I blinked my eyes in disbelief, the Lightstone vanished into the near-darkness of the hall.

"Valashu?"

Count Dario, I saw, was looking at me as if I had fallen mad. Asaru had pushed back his chair and had turned to look at me, too.

"Will you make the journey to Tria?" Count Dario said to me.

I turned to stare at the stand that had held the Lightstone. But it did not reappear.

"Valashu Elahad," Count Dario asked me formally, "will you make this quest?"

"Yes," I whispered to myself, "I must."

"What? What did you say?"

I took a deep breath and tried to fight back the fear churning in my belly. I touched the lightning-bolt scar on my forehead. And then, in a voice as loud and clear as I could manage, I called out to him and all the men and women in the hall: "Yes, I will make the quest."

Some say that the absence of sound is quiet and peace; but

there is a silence that falls upon the world like thunder. For a moment, no one moved. Asaru was staring at me as if he couldn't believe what I had said, as were Ravar and Karshur and my other brothers. Everyone in the hall was staring at me, my father the most intently of all.

"Why, Valashu?" he finally asked me. I felt the deeper question burning inside him like a heated iron: *why have you disobeyed me?*

And I told him, "Because the Lightstone must be found, sir."

I had a hard time looking at my father then. The tightness in his throat was like a choking in my own. Despite his anger, though, his love for me was no less real or deep than my grandfather's had been. And I loved him as I did the very sky and wanted badly to please him. But there is always a greater duty, a higher love.

"My last born," he suddenly called out to the nobles in the hall, "has said that he will journey to Tria, and so he must go. It seems that the House of Elahad *will* be represented in this quest, after all, if only by the youngest and most impulsive of its sons."

He paused and then turned toward Salmelu. "It would be fitting, would it not, if your house were to send a knight on this quest as well. And so we ask you, Lord Salmelu, will you journey to Tria with him?"

My father was a deep man, and he could be cunning. I thought that he wished to weaken the Ishkans—either that, or to shame Salmelu in front of the greatest knights and nobles of our two kingdoms. But if Salmelu felt any disgrace in refusing to make the quest that the least of Shamesh's sons had promised to undertake, he gave no sign of it. Quite the contrary. He sat among his countrymen, rubbing his sharp nose as if he didn't like the scent of my father's intentions. And then he looked from my father to me and said, "No, I will not make this quest. My father has already spoken of his wishes. *I* would never leave my people without his permission at a time when war threatened."

My ears burned as I looked into Salmelu's mocking eyes. It was one of the few times in my life I had seen my father outmaneuvered by an opponent.

"However," Salmelu went on, smiling at me, "let it not be said that Ishka opposes this foolish quest. As our kingdom offers the shortest road to Tria, you have my promise of safe passage through it."

"Thank you for your graciousness, Lord Salmelu," I said to him, trying to keep the irony from my voice. "But the quest is not foolish."

"No? Is it not?" He pointed toward the empty stand behind me. "Do you think *you* will ever recover what the greatest Valari knights have failed even to find?"

"We will not speak words of discouragement tonight," my father told Salmelu. "The Lightstone may indeed never be found. But we should at least honor those who attempt to find it."

So saying, he arose from his chair and walked toward me. He was a tall man, taller even than Asaru, and for all his years he stood as straight as a spruce tree.

"Although Valashu is the wildest of my sons, there is much to honor in him tonight," he said. He pointed at Raldu's body, which still lay stretched out on the cart at the center of the hall. "A few hours ago he fought and killed an enemy of Mesh— possibly he saved my eldest son's life, and Brother Maram's as well. We believe that he should be recognized for his service to Mesh."

My father, I thought, had managed to save face by honoring my rebelliousness instead of chastising it, and it seemed that Salmelu hated him for that. He sat sulking in his chair and staring at me.

"I won't have my son going to Tria as a warrior only," my father said. He reached inside the pocket of his tunic and removed a silver ring set with two large diamonds. They sparkled like the five diamonds of his own ring. "Val, come here, please."

I stood up and went over to where he waited for me by the banner at the front of the hall. I knelt before him as he bade me. I noticed my mother watching proudly but with great worry, too. Asaru's eyes were gleaming. Maram looked on with a huge smile lighting up his face; one would have thought that he congratulated himself for somehow bringing about this honor that no one could have anticipated. And then, before my family and all the men and women in the hall, my father pulled the warrior's ring from my finger and replaced it with the ring of a full knight. I sensed that he had kept this ring in his pocket for a long time, waiting for just such an occasion.

"In the name of Valoreth," he said, "we give you this ring."

My new ring felt cold and strange on my finger. But the heat of my pride was quickly warming it.

My father then drew his sword from its sheath. It was the marvelous Valari kalama: a razor-sharp, double-edged sword that was light enough and well-enough balanced for a strong man to swing with one hand from horseback, and long and heavy enough to cut mail when wielded with two hands. Such swords had struck terror into even the Sarni tribes and had once defeated the Great Red Dragon. The sword, it is said, is a Valari knight's soul, and now my father brought this shimmering blade before me. With the point held upward as if to draw down the light of the stars, he pressed the flat of the blade between my eyes. The cold steel sent a thrill of joy straight through me. It made me want to polish my own inner sword and use it only to cut through the darkness that sometimes blinded me.

"May you always see the true enemy," my father told me, repeating the ancient words of our people. "May you always have the courage to fight it."

He suddenly took the sword away from me and lifted it high over his head. "Sar Valashu Elahad," he said to me, "go forth as a knight in the name of the Shining One and never forget from where you came."

That was all there was to the ceremony of my being knighted. My father embraced me and signaled to his guests that the feast had come to an end. Immediately Asaru and my brothers gathered close to congratulate me. Although I was glad to receive the honor they had long since attained, I was dreadfully afraid of where my pledge to recover the Lightstone might take me.

"Val, congratulations!" Maram called out to me as he pressed through the circle of my family. He threw his arms around me and pounded my back with his huge hands. "Let's go back to my room and drink to your knighthood!"

"No, let's not," I told him. "It's very late."

In truth, it had been the longest day of my life. I had hunted a deer and been wounded with a poison that would always burn inside me. I had killed a man whose death had nearly killed me. And now, before my family and all my friends, I had promised to seek that which could never be found.

"Well," Maram said, "you'll at least come say good-bye to me before you set out on this impossible quest of yours, won't you?"

"Yes, of course," I told him, smiling as I clasped his arm.

"Good, good," he said. He belched up a bloom of beer and then covered his mouth as he yawned. "I've got to find Behira and tell her the rest of the poem before I pass out and forget it. Would you by chance know where she might be quartered in this huge heap of stones of yours?"

"No," I told him, committing my first lie as a knight. I pointed at Lord Harsha as he made his way with his daughter and several lords out of the hall. "Perhaps you should ask Lord Harsha."

"Ah, perhaps I *won't,* not just now," Maram said as he stared at Lord Harsha's sheathed sword. It seemed that he had seen one kalama too many that night. "Well, I'll see you in the morning."

With that, he joined the stream of people making their way toward the door. Although I was as tired as I had ever been, I lingered a few more moments as I watched the Alonians and Ishkans—and everyone else—file from the hall. Once more I opened myself to see if I could detect the man who had fired the arrow at me. I couldn't. One last time I turned toward the white granite stand to see if the Lightstone would reappear, but it remained as empty as the air.

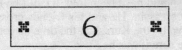

THE NEXT MORNING, the Ishkans departed our castle in a flurry of pounding hooves and muffled curses. Likewise, the Alonians continued on their journey toward Waas and Kaash, where they would tell King Talanu and my cousins at his court of the great quest. I spent much of the day going around the castle's storerooms gathering supplies for my journey: cheeses and nuts, dried venison and apples and battle biscuits so hard they would break one's teeth if they weren't first dipped in a cupful of brandy or beer. These vital beverages I poured into small oak casks, which I carefully balanced on the back of my packhorse.

When all was ready, I decked myself out as for war. By law, no knight could leave Mesh alone wearing our diamond armor; such displays were likely to incite the envy and hatred of robbers, who would murder to gain the priceless gems. So instead, I donned a mail suit made of silver steel. Over its gleaming rings I pulled a black surcoat bearing the swan and stars of Mesh. As well I bore a heavy charging lance, five lighter throwing lances, and, of course, the shining kalama that my father had given me on my thirteenth birthday. The massive war helm, with its narrow eye slits and silver wings projecting out from the sides, I would not put on until just before I was ready to leave the castle.

When I was nearly ready, Lansar Raasharu, my father's seneschal, found me saddling Altaru in the stables. He told me that I should keep a tighter watch over my own lips than I did over even the Ishkans.

"They're a hotheaded bunch," he said, "who will fashion your own words into weapons and hurl them back at you toward disastrous ends."

"Better that," I said, "than poison arrows fired in the woods."

Lord Raasharu rubbed his sad face and cocked his head, looking at me in surprise. He asked, "Hasn't Lord Asaru spoken to you?"

"No, not since before the feast."

"Well, you should have been told: it can't be Prince Salmelu who was your assassin. He and his friends crossed my path in the woods down by the Kurash at the time of your trouble."

"And you're sure it was he?"

"As sure as that you're Valashu Elahad."

"That is good news!" I said. I hadn't wanted to believe that Salmelu would have tried to murder me. "The Ishkans may be Ishkans, but they're Valari first."

"That's true," Lord Raasharu said. "But the Ishkans are still Ishkans, so you be careful once you cross the mountains, all right?"

And with that, he clapped his hand across my shoulder hard enough to make the rings of mail jingle and said good-bye.

It distressed me that I could find neither Maram nor Master

Juwain to tell them how much I would miss them. According to Master Tadeo, who still remained in the Brothers' quarters, both Master Juwain and Maram had left the castle in great haste at dawn while I had been sleeping. Apparently there had been some sort of altercation with Lord Harsha, who had ridden off in a fury with Behira and their wagon. But it seemed I had not been forgotten. Master Tadeo handed me a sealed letter that Maram had written; I tucked it behind the belt girdling my surcoat to read later.

There remained only the farewells to be made with my family. Asaru insisted on meeting me by the east gate, as did my mother, my grandmother, and my other brothers. In a courtyard full of barking dogs and children playing in the last of the day's sun, I stood by Altaru to take my leave of them. They each had presents for me and a word or two of wisdom as well.

Mandru, the fiercest of my brothers, gave me his treasured sharpening stone made of pressed diamond dust and said to me, "Keep your sword sharp, Val. Never yield to our enemies."

After he had embraced me, Ravar presented me with his favorite throwing lance, while Jonathay gladly yielded up his beloved chess set. Yarashan handed me a well-worn copy of the *Valkariad*, which was his favorite book of the *Saganom Elu*. He, too, embraced me, then stepped aside so that Karshur could give me his favorite hunting arrow.

Then Asaru approached me. "Please take this," he said. From around his neck, he pulled loose the thong binding the lucky bear claw that he always wore. He draped it over my head and told me, "Never lose heart—you have a great heart, Val."

Although he fell silent as he clapped me on the shoulder, the tears in his eyes said everything else there was to say.

My mother, too, was weeping as she came forward to give me the traveling cloak that I knew she had been weaving as a birthday present. With its thick black wool trimmed out with fine silver embroidery and a magnificent silver brooch with which to fasten it, it was a work of love that would keep me warm on even the stormiest of nights.

"Come back," was all she told me. "Whether you find this cup or not, come home when it's time to come home."

She kissed me then and fell sobbing against me. It took all her will and dignity to pry herself loose and stand back so that my grandmother could give me the white wool scarf that she had knitted for me. Ayasha Elahad, whom I had always called Nona, tied the simple garment around my neck. She stood in the darkening courtyard looking up at me in adoration. Then she pointed at the night's first stars and told me, "Your grandfather would have made this quest, you know. Never forget that he is watching you."

I hugged her tiny body against the hardness of the mail that encircled mine. Even through this steel armor with its hundreds of interlocked rings, I could feel the beating of her heart. This frail woman, I thought, was the source of love and joy in my family, and I would take this most precious of gifts with me wherever I went.

At last I stood away from her and looked at my family one by one. No one spoke; no one seemed to know any more words to say. I had wondered if my father would come to say good-bye, but it seemed that he was too angry to bear the sight of me. And then, even as I turned to take Altaru's reins and mount him, I heard footsteps sounding hard against the packed earth. I looked out to see my father emerge from the gateway to the castle's adjoining middle courtyard. He was dressed in a black and silver tunic, and he bore on his arm a shield embossed with a silver swan and seven stars against a triangular expanse of glossy black steel.

"Val," he said as he walked up to me, "it's good you haven't left yet."

"No, not yet," I said. "But it's time. It seemed you wouldn't come."

"It seemed that way to me, too. But farewells should be said."

I stared at my father's sad, deep eyes and said, "Thank you, sir. It can't be easy for you seeing me leave like this."

"No, it's not. But you always went your own way."

"Yes, sir."

"And you always accepted your punishments when you did."

"Yes," I said, nodding my head.

"But you never complained."

"No—you taught me not to."

"And you never apologized, either."

"No, that's true."

"Well," he said, looking at my war lance and glistening armor, "this time the hardships of your journey will be punishment enough."

"Very likely they will."

"And dangers," he continued. "There will be dangers aplenty on the road to Tria—and beyond."

I nodded my head and smiled bravely to show him that I knew there would be. But inside, my belly was fluttering as before a battle.

"And so," he said, "it would please me if you would take this shield on your journey."

He stepped closer, all the while keeping a watchful eye upon the snorting Altaru and his great hooves. Not wishing to arouse the ferocious stallion's protective instincts, he slowly held his shield out to me.

"But, sir," I said, looking at this fine piece of workmanship, "this is your war shield! If there's war with Ishka, you'll need it."

"Please take it all the same."

For a long moment, I gazed at the shield's swan and silver stars.

"Would you disobey in this, as well?"

"No, sir," I said at last, taking the shield and thrusting my forearm through its leather straps. It was slightly heavier than my own shield but somehow seemed to fit me better. "Thank you—it's magnificent."

He embraced me then, and kissed me, once, on my forehead. He looked at me strangely in a way that I had never seen him look at Karshur or even Asaru. Then he told me, "Always remember who you are."

I bowed to him, then hoisted myself up onto Altaru. The great beast's entire body trembled with the excitement of setting out into the world.

Just then there came the sound of a horse galloping up the road beyond the open gate. A cloaked figure astride a big panting sorrel came pounding into the courtyard. The rider wore a saber strapped to his thick black belt and bore a lance in his saddle's holster but seemed otherwise unarmed. His clothes were of bright scarlet. I smiled because it was, of course, Maram.

"Val," he called out to me as he reached forward to stroke and calm his sweating horse. "I was afraid I'd have to intercept you on the road."

I smiled again in appreciation of what must have been a hard ride down from the Brotherhood Sanctuary. My family all looked upon him approvingly for this act of seeming loyalty.

"Thank you for coming to say good-bye," I told him.

"Say good-bye? No, no—I've come to say that I'd like to accompany you on your journey. That is, at least as far as Tria, if you'll have me."

This news surprised everyone, except perhaps my father, who gazed at Maram quietly.

"Will I *have* you?" I said to him. I felt as if the weight of my unaccustomed armor had suddenly been lifted from my shoulders. "Gladly. But what's happened, Maram?"

"Didn't you read my letter?"

I patted the square of paper still folded into my belt. "No, my apologies, but there wasn't time."

"Well," he began, "I couldn't just abandon my best friend to go out questing alone, now could I?"

"Is that all?"

Maram licked his lips as he glanced from my mother to Asaru, who was eyeing him discreetly. "Well, no, it is not all," he forced out. As he went on to relate, Lord Harsha had caught him earlier that morning with Behira; he had again drawn his sword and chased him up and down the women's guest quarters. Only Lord Harsha's broken knee and Maram's greater agility, much quickened by his panic, enabled Maram to evade him. After Lord Harsha's temper had cooled somewhat, he had told Maram to leave Mesh that day or face his sword when they next met. Maram had fled from the castle and returned to the Brotherhood Sanctuary to gather up all his belongings. And then returned as quickly as he could to join me.

"Lord Harsha has threatened to cut off my, ah . . . head," he told me. "Let's be off. I'd at least like to be out of this district by midnight."

"It would be an honor to have you with me," I told him. "But what about your schooling?"

"I've only taken a leave of absence," he said. "I'm not quite ready to quit the Brotherhood altogether."

And, it seemed, the Brotherhood wasn't ready to quit him.

Even as Maram started in his saddle at the sound of more horses coming up to the castle, I looked down the road to see Master Juwain riding another sorrel and leading two pack-horses behind him. He made his way through the gateway and came to a halt near Maram. He glanced at the weapons that Maram bore. Maram must have persuaded him that the lance and sword would be used only for their protection and not war. Master Juwain shook his head at having yet again to bend the Brotherhood's rules on Maram's behalf.

Master Juwain explained that the news of the quest had created a great stir among the Brothers. For three long ages they had sought the secrets of the Lightstone. And now it seemed that, if the prophecy proved true, the cup of healing might finally be found. And so the Brothers had decided to send Master Juwain to Tria to determine the veracity of the prophecy.

"Then it isn't your intention to make this quest?" my father asked Master Juwain.

"Not at this time. I'll accompany Val only as far as Tria, if that's agreeable with him."

"Nothing could please more, sir." I smiled, unable to hide my delight. "But it's my intention to take the road through Ishka, and that may not prove entirely safe."

"Where can safety be found these days?" Master Juwain said, looking up at the great iron gate and the castle walls all around us. "Lord Salmelu has promised you safe passage, and we'll have to hope for the best."

"Very well, then," I told him.

I turned to look at my brothers one last time. I nodded my head to my grandmother and my mother, who was quietly weeping again. Then I smiled grimly at my father and said, "Farewell, sir."

"Farewell, Valashu Elahad," he said, speaking for the rest of my family. "May you always walk in the light of the One."

At last I put on the great helm, whose hard steel faceplates cut out the sight of my weeping mother. I wheeled Altaru about and nudged him forward with a gentle pressure of my heels. Then, with Master Juwain and Maram following, I rode out through the gate toward the long road that led down from the castle. And so my father finally had the satisfaction of seeing me set out as a Valari knight in all his glory.

It was a clear night with the first stars slicing open the blue-black vault of the heavens. To the west, Arakel's icy peak glowed blood red in light of the sun lost somewhere beyond the world's edge. To the east, Mount Eluru was already sunken in darkness. The cool air sifted through the slits in my helm, carrying the scents of forest and earth and almost infinite possibilities. Soon, after perhaps half a mile of such joyous travel, I took off my helm, the better to feel the starlight on my face. I listened to the measured beat of Altaru's hooves against the hardpacked dirt even as I looked out at the wonder of the world.

It seemed almost a foolish thing to begin such a long journey with night falling fast and deep all around us. But I knew that the moon would soon be up, and there would be light enough for riding along the well-made North Road that led toward Ishka. With the wind at my back and visions of golden cups blazing inside me, I thought that I might be able to ride all night. The seventh day of Soldru would come all too soon, and I wanted very badly to be in Tria with the knights of the free lands when King Kiritan called the quest. Six hundred miles, as the raven flies, lay between Silvassu and Tria to the northwest. But I—we—would not be traveling as a bird flying free in the sky. There would be mountains to cross and rivers to ford, and the road toward that which the heart most desires is seldom straight.

And so we moved north through the gently rolling country of the Valley of the Swans. After an hour or so, the moon rose over the Culhadosh range and silvered the fields and trees all about us. We rode in its soft light, which filled the valley like a marvelous shimmering liquid. The farmhouses we passed sent plumes of smoke curling up black against the luminous sky. And in the yards of each of those houses, I thought, no matter how tiring the day's work had been, warriors would be practicing at arms while their wives taught their children the meditative discipline so vital to all that was Valari. Only later would they take their evening meal, perhaps of cheese and apples and black barley bread. It came to me that I would miss these simple foods, grown out of Meshian soil, rich in tastes of the star-touched earth that recalled the deepest dreams of my people. I wondered if I were seeing my homeland for the last time even while strangely beholding it as if for the first time. It came to me as well that a Valari warrior, with sword and shield and a lifetime of discipline drilled into his soul, was much more than a dealer of death. For all the things around me—the rocks and earth, the wind and trees and starlight—were just the things of life, and ultimately a warrior existed only to protect life and the land and people that he loved.

We made camp late that night in a fallow field by a small hill off the side of the road. The farmer who owned it, an old man named Yushur Kaldad, came out to greet us with a pot of stew that his wife had made. Although he hadn't been present at the feast, he had heard of my quest. After giving us permission to make a fire, he wished me well and walked back through the moonlight toward his little stone house.

Maram began gathering rocks for a firepit and said, "A good blaze will keep away the bears."

"Don't worry," I told him, "the bears will leave us alone if we leave them alone."

Although Maram smiled bravely at my reassurance, he put more faith in fire. And so he moved off toward the hill where he found some dried twigs and branches among the deadwood beneath the trees. With great care, he arrayed the tinder and kindling into a pyramid at the center of the pit. Then from his pocket he produced a flint and steel, and coaxed the sparks from them into a cone of bright orange flames.

"You have a talent with fire," Master Juwain told him. He dropped his gnarly body onto his sleeping fur and began ladling out the stew into three large bowls. Despite his years, he moved with strength and suppleness, as if he had practiced his healing arts on himself. "Perhaps you should study to be an alchemist."

Maram's sensuous lips pulled back in a smile as he held his hands out toward the flames. His large eyes reflected the colors of the fire, and he said, "It has always fascinated me. I think I made my first fire when I was four. When I was fourteen, I burned down my father's hunting lodge, for which he has never forgiven me."

At this news, Master Juwain rubbed his lumpy face and told him, "Perhaps you *shouldn't* be an alchemist."

Maram shrugged off his comment with a good-natured smile. He clicked his fire-making stones together and watched the sparks jump out of them.

"What is the magic in flint and steel?" he asked, speaking

mostly to himself. "And what is the secret of the flames bound up in wood? How is it that logs will burn but not stone?"

Of course, I had no answers for him. I sat on my furs watching Master Juwain pulling at his jowls in deep thought. To Maram, I said, "Perhaps if we find the Lightstone, you'll solve your mysteries."

"Well, there's one mystery I'd like solved more than any other," he confided. "And that is this: how is it that when man and woman come together, they're like flint and steel throwing out sparks into the night?"

I smiled and looked straight at him. "Isn't that one of the lines of the poem you recited to Behira?"

"Ah, Behira, Behira," he said as he struck off another round of sparks. "Perhaps I should never have gone to her room. But I had to know."

"Did you . . . ?" I started to ask him if he had stolen Behira's virtue, as Lord Harsha feared, but then decided that it was none of my business.

"No, no, I swear I didn't," Maram said, understanding me perfectly well. "I only wanted to tell her the rest of my poem and—"

"*Your* poem, Maram?" We both knew that he had stolen it from the *Book of Songs,* and so perhaps did Master Juwain.

"Well," Maram said, flushing, "I never said outright that *I* had written it, only that the words came to me the first moment I saw her."

"You parse words like a courtier," I said to him.

"Well, I was courting Behira, wasn't I?"

"Were you? But what of your vow?"

"What of it? I'm only a man, aren't I? Yes, just a man, and that's why I went to her room. You see, I had to know if she was the one."

"What one, Maram?"

"The woman with whom I could make the ineffable flame— the fire that never goes out." He turned to stare at the blazing wood that he had ignited. "You spoke of finding your golden cup. Well, if ever I held the Lightstone in my hands, I'd use it to discover the place where love blazes eternally like the stars. *That's* the secret of the universe."

For a while, no one spoke as we sat there eating our midnight meal beneath the stars. Yushur had brought us an excellent stew full of succulent lamb, new potatoes, carrots, onions, and herbs; we consumed it down to the last drop of gravy, which we mopped up with the fresh bread that Master Juwain had brought down from the sanctuary. To celebrate our first night together on the road, I cracked open a cask of beer. True to his vows, Master Juwain took only the smallest sip of it, but of course Maram had much more. After his first serving, as his rumbling voice built castles in the air, I had to ration the precious black liquid into his cup. But as the time approached for sleeping, it became apparent that I hadn't measured out the beer carefully enough.

"Ah, yes, love," he said. He belched, then sighed and rubbed his eyes. "The elusive dream. As elusive as the Lightstone itself."

In a voice full of self-pity, he declared that the Lightstone had certainly been destroyed and that neither he nor anyone else was ever likely to find his heart's deepest desire.

Master Juwain had so far endured Maram's drinkfest in silence. But now he glared at him and said, "*My* heart tells me that the prophecy will prove true. Starlight is elusive, but we do not doubt that it exists."

"Ah, well, the prophecy," Maram muttered. "But who *are* these seven brothers and sisters? And what are these seven stones?"

"*That,* at least, should be obvious," Master Juwain said. "The stones must be the greater gelstei."

He went on to say that although there were hundreds of types of gelstei, only seven types were considered the great stones: the white, blue, green, purple, and black stones; the red fire-stones; and the noble silver. Of the gold gelstei there was only one, known as *the* Gelstei, and that was the Lightstone.

"So many have sought the master stone," he said.

"Sought it and died," I said. "No wonder my mother wept for me."

"Do not speak so," Master Juwain chastened me.

"But this whole business," I said, "seems such a narrow chance."

"Perhaps it is, Val. But even a scryer can't see all chances. Not even Ashtoreth herself can."

For a while we fell silent as the wind pushed through the valley and the fire crackled within its circle of stones. I thought of

Morjin and his master, Angra Mainyu, one of the fallen Galadin who had once made war with Ashtoreth and the other angels and had been imprisoned on a world named Damoom; I thought of this, and I shuddered. Then, to raise my spirits, Maram began singing the epic of Kalkamesh from the *Valkariad* of the *Saganom Elu* while Master Juwain kept time by drumming on one of the logs waiting to be burned. I brought out my flute and took up the song's boldly defiant melody. I played to the wind and earth and to the valor of the legendary being who had walked into the hell of Argattha to wrest the Lightstone from the Lord of Lies himself. It was a fine thing we did together, making music beneath the stars. My thoughts of death—the stillness of Raldu's body and the coldness of my own—seemed to vanish like the flames of the fire into the night.

We slept soundly after that on the soft soil of Yushur Kaldad's field. No bears came to disturb us. It was a splendid night, and I lay on top of my furs wrapped only in my new cloak for warmth. When the sun rose over Mount Eluru the next morning to the crowing of Yushur's cocks, I felt ready to ride to the end of the world.

And ride we did. After breaking camp, we set out through the richest farmland of the valley. It was a fine spring day with blue skies and abundant sunshine. The road along this part of our journey was as straight and well-paved as any in the Morning Mountains. My father had always said that good roads make good kingdoms, and he had always gone to pains to maintain his. Both Master Juwain and Maram could ride well, and Maram was tougher than he looked. And so we made excellent progress through the wind-rippled fields.

Around noon, after we paused for a quick meal, the country began to change. Toward the northern end of the Valley of the Swans, the terrain grew hillier and soil more rocky. There were fewer farms and larger stands of trees between them. Here the road wound gently around and through these low hills; it began to rise at an easy grade toward the greater hills and mountains to the north. But still the traveling was easy. By the time the sun had crossed the sky and began dipping down toward the Central Range, we found ourselves at the edge of the forest that blankets the northernmost districts of Mesh.

Our camp that night was much cooler, and we were very glad

for the fire that Maram made. After dinner, we edged close to the flames and listened to the wolves howling high in the hills around us. Then we gathered our cloaks around us and fell soundly asleep.

The next morning dawned cloudy and cool. The sun was no more than a pale yellow disk behind sheets of white in the sky. Since I wanted to be well through the pass into Ishka by nightfall, I encouraged the groggy Maram to get ready as quickly as he could. A few miles of hard travel brought us to Ki, a small city of shops, smithies, and neat little chalets with steep roofs to keep out the heavy mountain snows that fell all through winter. At the town's center, the Kel Road from the east intersected the larger North Road. The Kel Road was one of the marvels of Mesh. It wound through the mountains around the entire perimeter of our kingdom connecting the kel keeps that guarded the passes. There were twenty-two of these high mountain fortresses spaced some twenty miles apart. I had spent a long lonely winter at one of them, watching for an invasion of the Mansurii tribe that never came.

For seven miles between Ki and the kel keep situated near Raaskel and Korukel, the Kel Road ran contiguous with the North Road. Here, as the horses' hooves strove for purchase against the worn paving stones, the road rose very steeply. Thick walls of oak trees, mixed with the elms and birch, pressed the road from either side, forming an archway of green leaves and branches high above it. But after only a few miles, the forest began changing, giving way to stands of aspen and spruce growing at the higher elevations. The mountains rose before us like steps leading to the unseen stars.

In many places, the road cut the sides of the fir-covered foothills like a long curved scar against the swelling green. I knew that we were drawing close to the pass, although the lower peaks blocked the sight of it. Maram had doubts about the land that we were approaching. After I had recounted my conversation with Lansar Raasharu, he wondered aloud who the second assassin might be, if he wasn't one of the Ishkans. Might this unknown man, he asked, stalk us along the road? And if he did, what were we doing venturing into Ishka, where he might more easily finish what he had begun in the woods? With every step we took closer to this unfriendly kingdom, these questions seemed to hang lower in the air like the cold mist sifting down from the sky.

Around noon, just as we crested a low rise marked with a red standing stone, we had our first clear view of the pass. We rested the horses and gazed out at the masses of Korukel and Raaskel that rose up like great guardian towers only a few miles to the north. The North Road curved closer to Raaskel, the smaller of the two mountains. But with its sheer granite faces and snowfields, I thought, it was forbidding enough. Korukel, whose twin peaks and great humped shoulders gave it the appearance of a two-headed ogre, seemed ready to pelt us with spears of ice or roll huge boulders down upon us. If not for the diamonds buried within its bowels, it was hardly a mountain worth fighting for.

"Look!" Maram said, pointing up the road. "The Telemesh Gate. I've never seen anything like it."

Few people had. There, across the barren valley just beyond the massive fortress of the kel keep, cutting the ground between the two mountains, was the work of my ancestors and one of the wonders of Ea: it seemed that a great piece of mountain a fifth of a mile wide had simply been sliced out of the earth as if by the hand of the Galadin themselves. In truth, as Maram seemed to know, King Telemesh had made this rectangular cut between the two mountains with a firestone that he had brought back from the War of the Stones. According to legend, he had stood upon this very hill with his red gelstei and had directed a stream of fire against the earth for most of six days. And when he had finished and the acres of ice, dirt, and rock had simply boiled off into the sky, a great corridor between Mesh and Ishka had been opened.

"It's too bad the firestones have all perished," Maram said wistfully. "Else all the kingdoms of Ea might be so connected."

"It's said that Morjin is searching for the secret of reforging the firestones," I told him.

At this, Master Juwain looked at me sharply and shook his head. Many times he had warned Maram—and me—never to speak the Red Dragon's true name. And with the utterance of these two simple syllables, the wind off the icy peaks suddenly seemed to rise; either that, or I could feel it cutting me more closely. Again, as I had in the woods with Raldu and later in the castle, I shivered with an eerie sense that something was watching me. It was as if the stones themselves all about us had eyes. It consoled me not at all that my countrymen here in the north called Raaskel and Korukel the Watchers.

For half a mile we walked our horses down to the keep at the center of the valley. There we stopped to pay our respects to Lord Avijan, the garrison's commander. He told me that Salmelu and the Ishkans had gone up into the pass that morning: "They were riding hard for Ishka. As you had better do, if you don't want to be caught in the pass at nightfall."

After he had wished me well on my quest, we took his advice. We continued along the North Road where it snaked up the steeply rising slopes of the valley. About two miles from the keep, as we approached the Telemesh Gate, it grew suddenly colder. The air was thick with a moisture that wasn't quite rain or mist or snow. But there was still snow aplenty blanketing the ground. Here, in this bleak mountain tundra where trees wouldn't grow, the mosses and low shrubs in many places were still covered in drifts.

"It's cold," Maram complained as his gelding drove his hooves against the road's wet stone. "I don't like the look of this place."

I peered through the gray air at the Telemesh Gate now only a hundred yards farther up the road. It was a dark cut through a wall of rock, an ice-glazed opening into the unknown.

"Come on," I said as I urged Altaru forward. But he nickered nervously and didn't move. As Master Juwain came up to join us, the big horse just stood there with his nostrils opening and closing against the freezing wind.

"What is it, Val?" Master Juwain asked me.

I shrugged my shoulders as I scanned the boulders and snowfields all about us. The tundra seemed as barren as it was cold. Not even a marmot or a ptarmigan moved to break the bleakness of the pass.

"Do you think it could be a bear?" Maram asked, looking about, too.

"No, it's too early for bears to be up this high," I told him.

In another month, the snow would be gone, and the slopes

around us would teem with wildflowers and berries. But now there seemed little that was alive save for the orange and green patches of lichen that covered the cold stones.

Again, I nudged Altaru forward, and this time he whinnied and shook his head angrily at the opening to the Telemesh Gate. He began pawing at the road with his iron-shod hoof, and the harsh sound of it rang out into the mist-choked air.

"Altaru, Altaru," I whispered to him, "what's the matter?"

There was something, I thought, that he didn't like about this cut between the mountains. There was something I didn't like myself. I felt a deep wrongness entering my bones as from the ground beneath us. It was as if Telemesh, the great king, the grandfather of my grandfathers, in burning off the tissues of the mountain with his firestone, had wounded the land in a way that could never be healed. And now, out of this open wound of fused dirt and blackened rock, it seemed that the earth itself was still screaming in agony. What man or beast, I wondered, would ever be drawn to such a place? Well, perhaps the vultures who batten on the blood of the suffering and dying would feel at home here. And the great Beast who was called the Red Dragon— surely he would find a twisted pleasure in the world's pain.

It came then out of the dark mouth of the fire-scarred gate. It was, even as Maram feared, a bear. And not merely a Meshian brown bear but one of the rare and horribly tempered white bears of Ishka. I guessed that he must have wandered through the gate into Mesh. And now he seemed to guard it, standing up on his stumpy hind legs to a height of ten feet as he sniffed the air and looked straight at me.

"Oh, Lord!" Maram called out. "Lord, Lord!"

Now Altaru, seeing the bear at last, began snorting and stomping at the road. The wind carried down from the mountain, and we could both smell its rank scent, which fairly reeked with an illness that I couldn't identify. I couldn't help staring at his small, questing eyes as my hand moved almost involuntarily to the hilt of my sword. And all the while, he kept sniffing at me with his black nose; I had the strange sense that even though he couldn't catch my scent, he could smell the kirax in my blood.

And then suddenly, without warning, he fell down onto all fours and charged us.

"He's coming!" Maram cried out. "Run for your life!"

True to his instincts, he wheeled his horse about and began galloping down the road. I reached toward my packhorse for my bow and arrows, but just then, Altaru reared with a surge of bunching muscles, throwing back his head and flashing his hooves in challenge at the bear. I was badly unbalanced and went flying out of my saddle. Tanar, my screaming packhorse, almost trampled me in his panic. If I hadn't rolled behind Altaru, he would have brained me with his wildly flailing hooves.

"Val!" Master Juwain called to me. "Get up and draw your sword!"

It is astonishing how quickly a bear can cover a hundred yards, particularly when running downhill. I didn't have time to draw my sword. Even as Master Juwain tried to get control of his own bucking horse, the bear bounded down the snowy slope toward us. Tanar screamed again in terror, all the while trying to get out of the way. And then the bear closed with him, and I thought for a moment that he might tear open his throat or break his back with a blow from one of his mighty paws. But it seemed that the stout horse was not intended to be the bear's prey. The bear only rammed him with his shoulder, knocking him aside in his fury to get at me.

"Run, Val!" I heard Maram calling me as from far away.

The bear would certainly have fallen upon me then if not for Altaru's courage. As I struggled to stand and regain my breath, the horse reared again and struck a glancing blow off the bear's head. His sharp hoof cut open the bear's eye, which filled with blood. The stunned bear roared in outrage and swiped at Altaru with his long black claws. He grunted and brayed and shook his sloping white head at me. I smelled his musty white fur and felt the growls rumbling up from deep in his throat. His good eye fixed on mine like a hook; he opened his jaws to rip me open with his long white teeth.

"Val, I'm coming!" Maram cried out to the thunder of hooves against stone. "I'm coming!"

The bear finally closed with me, locking his jaws onto my shoulder with a crushing force. He snarled and shook his head furiously and tried to pulp me with his deadly paws. And then Maram reached us. Unbelievably, he had managed to wheel his horse about and urge it forward in a desperate charge at the bear. He had his lance drawn and couched beneath his arm like a knight. But although trained in arms, he was no knight; the point of the lance caught the bear in the shoulder instead of the throat, and the shock of steel and metal pushing into hard flesh unseated Maram and propelled him from his horse. He hit the ground with an ugly slap and whooshing of breath. But for the moment, at least, he had succeeded in driving the bear off of me.

"Val," Maram croaked out from the blood-spattered road, "help me!"

The bear snarled at Maram and moved to rend him with his claws in his determination to get at me. And in that moment, I finally slid my sword free. The long kalama flashed in the uneven light. I swung it with all my might at the bear's exposed neck. The kalama's razor edge, hardened in the forges of Godhra, bit through fur, muscle, and bone. I gasped to feel the bear's bright lifeblood spraying out into the air as his great head went rolling down the road into a drift of snow. I fell to the road in the agony of the bear's death, and I hardly noticed the bear's body falling like an avalanche on top of Maram.

"Get this thing off me!" I heard Maram call out weakly from beneath the mound of fur.

But as always when I had killed an animal, it took me many moments to return to myself. I slowly stood up and rubbed my throbbing shoulder. If not for my armor and the padding beneath it, the bear would surely have torn off my arm. Master Juwain, having collected and hobbled the frightened horses, came over then and helped me pull Maram free from the bear. He stood there, checked us for wounds in the driving sleet as Maram looked at me and said, "I thought the bears would leave us alone if we left *them* alone."

Strange, I thought, that a bear should fall upon three men and six horses with such ferocious and single-minded purpose. I had never heard of a bear, not even a ravenous one, attacking so boldly.

Master Juwain stepped over to the side of the road and examined the bear's massive head. He looked at his glassy dark eye and pulled open his jaws to gaze at his teeth. "It's possible that he was maddened with rabies," he said. "But he doesn't have the look."

"What made him attack us, then?" Maram demanded.

Master Juwain's face fell gray as if he had eaten bad meat.

He said, "If the bear were a man, I would say his actions were those of a ghul."

I stared at the bear, and it suddenly came to me that the illness I had sensed in him had been not of the body but the mind.

"A ghul!" Maram cried out. "Are you saying that Mor . . . ah, that the Lord of Lies had seized his will? I've never heard of an animal ghul."

No one had. With the wind working at the sweat beneath my armor, a deep shiver ran through me. I wondered if Morjin—or anyone except the Dark One himself, Angra Mainyu—could have gained that much power.

As if in answer to my question, Master Juwain sighed and said, "It seems that his skill, if we can call it that, is growing."

While Maram looked about nervously, I began cleaning the blood off me. After retying Tanar to Altaru, I mounted my black stallion and turned him up the road.

"You're not thinking of going *on*?" Maram asked me.

I pointed at the opening of the gate. "Tria lies that way."

Maram looked down at the kel keep and the road that led back to the Valley of the Swans. He must have remembered that Lord Harsha was waiting for him there; it occurred to me that he had finally witnessed firsthand the kind of work that a kalama could accomplish, for he rubbed his curly beard worriedly and muttered, "Ah, we *can't* go back, can we?"

He mounted his trembling sorrel, as did Master Juwain his. I smiled at Maram and bowed my head to him. "Thank you for saving my life," I told him.

"I *did* save your life, didn't I?" he said. He smiled back at me as if I had personally knighted him in front of a thousand nobles. "Well, allow me to save it again. Who really wants to go to Tria, anyway? Perhaps it's time I returned to Delu. We could all go there. You'd be welcomed at my father's court and—"

"No," I told him. "Thank you for such a gracious offer, but my journey lies in another direction. Will you come with me?"

Maram sat on his horse and looked back and forth between the headless bear and me. He blinked his eyes against the stinging sleet. He licked his lips, then finally said, "Will I come with you? Haven't I said I would? Aren't you my best friend? Of *course* I'm coming with you!"

And with that he clasped my arm, and I clasped his. As if Altaru and I were of one will, we started moving up the road together. Maram and Master Juwain followed close behind me. I regretted leaving the bear unburied in a shallow pond of blood, but there was nothing else to do. Tomorrow, perhaps, one of Lord Avijan's patrols would find him and dispose of him. And so we rode our horses into the dark mouth of the Telemesh Gate and steeled ourselves to go down into Ishka.

■　　　7　　　■

OUR PASSAGE THROUGH the gate proved uneventful and quiet save for Maram's constant exclamations of delight. For, as he discovered, the walls of rock on both sides of us sparkled with diamonds. The fire of Telemesh's red gelstei, in melting this corridor through the mountain, had exposed many veins of the glittering white crystals. In honor of his great feat, the proud Telemesh had ordered that they never be cut, and they never had been. I thought that the beauty of the diamonds somewhat made up for this long wound in the earth. But many visitors to Mesh—the Ishkans foremost among them—complained of such ostentatious displays of my kingdom's wealth. King Hadaru had often accused my father of mocking him thusly. But my father turned a stony face to his plaints; he would say only that he intended to respect Telemesh's law even as he would the Law of the One.

"But can't we take just *one* stone?" Maram asked when we were almost through the gate. "We could sell it for a fortune in Tria."

Maram, I thought, didn't know what he was saying. Was anyone more despicable than a knight who became a diamond seller? Yes—those who sold the bodies of men and women into slavery.

"Come," he said. "Who would ever know?"

"*We* would know, Maram," I told him. I looked down at the corridor's stone floor, which glittered with more than one diamond beneath patches of windblown grit and the occasional droppings of horses. "Besides, it's said that any man who steals a stone will himself turn into stone—it's a very old prophecy."

For many miles after that—after we debouched from the pass and began our descent into Ishka—Maram gazed at the rock formations by the side of the road as if they had once been thieves making their escape with illicit treasure in their hands. But as dusk approached, his desire for diamonds began to fade with the light. His talk turned to fires crackling in hearths and hot stew waiting to be ladled out for our evening meal. The sleet, which turned into a driving rain on the heavily wooded lower slopes of the mountain, convinced him that he didn't want to camp out that night.

When we reached the Ishkans' fortress that guarded their side of the pass, the fortress's commander directed us to the house of a woodcutter who lived only a mile farther down the road. We continued plodding on through the icy rain until we found the house: a square chalet no different from ones that dot the mountains of Mesh. And the house's occupants—Ludar Narath and his family—reminded me of mountain families of my home. Ludar's wife, Masha, served us fried trout and a soup made of barley and mushrooms. His eldest daughter drew up a hot bath in the huge cedarwood tub where we soaked our battered bodies. All the Naraths seemed determined that Ishkan hospitality should not suffer when compared to that of Mesh.

With morning came the passing of the storm and the rising of the sun against a blue sky. After a good breakfast, we thanked Ludar and his family for the grace of their house and continued our journey. We rode through a misty country of high ridges and steep ravines. Although I had never passed this way before, the mountains beyond Raaskel and Korukel seemed strangely familiar to me. By early afternoon we had made our way through the highest part of them; stretching before us to the north was a succession of green-shrouded hills that would eventually give way to the Tushur river valley. With every mile we put behind us, the hills grew lower and less steep. The road, while not as well-paved as any in Mesh, wound mostly downhill, and the horses found the going rather easy. By the time we drew up in a little clearing by a stream to make camp that night, we were all in good spirits.

The next day we awoke early to the birds singing their morning songs. We traveled hard through the rolling hill country, which gradually opened out into the broad valley of the Tushur. There, the road curved east through the emerald farmland toward the golden glow of the sun—and toward Loviisa, where King Hadaru held his court. We debated making a cut across this curve and rejoining the road much to the north of the Ishkans' main city. It seemed wise to avoid the bellicose Salmelu and his friends. As Maram pointed out: "What if Salmelu *hired* the assassin who shot at us in the woods?"

"No, he couldn't have. No Valari would ever dishonor himself so."

"But what if the Red Dragon has gotten to him, too? What if he's been made a ghul?"

I looked off at the gleaming ribbon of the Tushur where it flowed through the valley below us. I wondered for the hundredth time why Morjin might be hunting me. I said, "Salmelu is no ghul. If he hates me, it's of his own will and not the Red Dragon's."

After stopping for a quick meal, we decided that making a straight cut through the farms and forests of Ishka would only delay us and pose its own dangers: there would be the raging waters of the Tushur to cross and perhaps bears in the woods. In the end, it was the prospect of encountering another bear that persuaded Maram that we should ride on to Loviisa, and so we did.

We planned to spend the night in one of Loviisa's inns; the following morning we would set out as early and with as little fanfare as possible. But other plans had been made for us. It seemed that our passage through Ishka had not gone unnoticed. As night approached and we rode past the farms near the outskirts of the city, a squadron of knights came thundering up the road to greet us. Their leader was Lord Nadhru, whom I recognized by the long scar on his jaw and his dark, dangerous look. He bowed his head toward me and said, "Sar Valashu, we meet again. King Hadaru has sent me to request your presence in his hall tonight."

At this news, I traded quick looks with both Maram and Master Juwain. There was no need to say anything; when a king "requested" one's presence, there was nothing else to do except oblige him.

And so we followed Lord Nadhru and his knights through Loviisa, whose winding streets and coal-fired smithies reminded me of Godhra. He led us past a succession of square stone houses up a steep hill at the north of the city. And there, on a heavily wooded palisade overlooking the icy Tushur, we found King Hadaru's palace all lit up, as if in anticipation of guests. As Ludar Narath had told me, the king disdained living in his family's ancient castle in the hills nearby. And so instead he had built a palace fronted with flower gardens and fountains. The palace itself was an array of pagodas, exquisitely carved on its several levels out of curving sweeps of various kinds of wood. Indeed, it was famed throughout the Morning Mountains as the Wooden Palace. Ludar himself had cut dozens of rare shatterwood trees to provide the paneling of the main hall. Inside this beautiful building, if the stories proved true, we would find beams of good Anjo cherrywood and ebony columns that had come all the way from the southern forests of Galda. It was said that King Hadaru had paid for his magnificent palace with diamonds from the overworked Ishkan mines, but I did not want to believe such a slander.

We entrusted our horses to the grooms who met us at the palace's front door. Then Lord Nadhru led us down a long corridor to the hall where King Hadaru held his court. The four warriors guarding the entrance asked us to remove our boots before proceeding within. They allowed me to keep my sword sheathed by my side. One might better ask a Valari knight to surrender his soul before his sword.

The Ishkan nobles, Salmelu and Lord Issur foremost among them, stood waiting to welcome us near King Hadaru's throne. This was a single piece of white oak carved into the shape of a huge bear squatting on its hind legs. King Hadaru seemed almost lost against this massive sculpture, and he was no small man. He sat very straight in the bear's lap with the great white head projecting up and out above him. He himself seemed somewhat bearlike, with a large head covered by a mane of snowy white hair that showed ten red ribbons. He had a large, predatory nose like Salmelu's and eyes all gleaming and black like polished shatterwood. As we walked through the hall, its massive oak beams arching high above us, his dark eyes never left us.

After Lord Nadhru presented us, he took his place near Salmelu and Lord Issur, who stood near their father's throne. Other prominent knights attended the king as well: Lord Mestivan and Lord Solhtar, a proud-seeming man with a heavy black beard that was rare among the Valari. I noticed Maram staring with a barely contained heat at a beautiful young woman. This proved to be Irisha, Hadaru's queen. Her hair was raven-black and her skin almost as fair as the oak of King Hadaru's throne. She was the daughter of Duke Barwan of Adar in Anjo, and it was said that King Hadaru had coerced him into giving her as his bride after his old queen had died. She stood in a bright green gown close to the king's throne, closer even than Salmelu. It was somewhat barbaric, I thought, that even a queen should be made to stand in the king's presence, but that was the way of things in Ishka.

"Sar Valashu," the king said in a voice thickened with age. "I would like to welcome you and your friends to my home."

King Hadaru favored me with a smile as brittle as the glass of the hall's many windows, and I gazed out at the splendid place. The vast roof, supported by great ebony columns, opened out in sweeping curves high above us. The panels of the walls were of the blackest shatterwood and red cherry, carved with battle scenes of Ishka's greatest victories. In their polished surfaces was reflected the light of the thousands of candles burning in their stands. The glossy oak floor was unadorned by any carpet. Its grainy whiteness was broken only by a circle some twenty feet across in front of the throne; no one stood upon this disk of red rosewood. I guessed that it symbolized the sun or perhaps one of the stars from which the Valari had come. I couldn't see a speck of dust upon it, nor on any other surface in the hall, which smelled of lemon oil and other exotic polishes.

The king peered at me from beneath his bushy eyebrows and said, "I've heard that you've pledged yourself to making this foolish quest."

"That is true," I said, as everyone near the throne gazed at me.

"Well, the Lightstone will never be found. Your ancestor gave it to a stranger in Tria when he would have done better to bring it to Loviisa."

His thin lips pulled together in distaste as if he had eaten a lemon. I felt the resentment burning inside him. It occurred to me then that love frustrated turns to hate; hope defeated becomes the bitterness of despair.

"But what if the Lightstone *were* found?" I asked him.

"By you?"

"Yes—why not?"

"Then we have no doubt that you would bring it back to your drafty old castle and lock it away from the world."

"No, the Lightstone's radiance was meant to be shared by everyone," I told him. "How else could we ever bring peace to the world?"

"Peace?" he snarled out. "How can there ever be peace when there are those who would claim what is not theirs?"

At this, Salmelu traded sharp looks with Lord Nadhru, and I heard Lord Solhtar murmuring something about Korukel's diamonds. Lord Mestivan, standing next to him in a bright blue tunic, nodded his head as he touched the red and white battle ribbons tied to his long black hair.

"Perhaps someday," I said, "all will know what is rightfully theirs."

At this, King Hadaru let out a harsh laugh like the growl of a bear. "You, Valashu Elahad, are a dreamer—like your grandfather."

"All men have dreams," I said. "What is yours, King Hadaru?"

This question caught the king off guard, and his whole body tensed as if in anticipation of a blow. Something bright and vital inside him seemed to struggle to breathe. He suffered, I thought, from a stinginess of spirit in place of austerity, a brittle hardness instead of true strength. He strove for a zealous cleanliness when he should have longed for purity. And yet despite these turnings of the Valari virtues, I also sensed in him a secret desire that both he and the world could be different. He might fight against Mesh with all the cool ferocity for which he was famed, but his greatest battle would always be with himself.

"I dream of diamonds," he said as his sad, dark eyes found mine. "I dream of the warriors of Ishka shining like ten thousand perfect diamonds as they stand ready to fight for the riches they were born for."

Now it was my turn to be caught off guard. My grandfather had always said that we were born to stand in the light of the One and feel its radiance growing ever brighter within our hearts.

King Hadaru glanced at Lord Nadhru and asked, "And of what do *you* dream, Lord Nadhru?"

Lord Nadhru stroked the hilt of his sword, and without hesitation, said, "Justice, sire."

Then King Hadaru looked at Salmelu. "Of what do you dream, my son?"

Salmelu seemed to have been waiting for this moment. "*I* dream of war. Isn't that what a Valari is born for? To stand with his brothers on the battlefield and feel his heart as hard as a diamond, to see his enemies fall before him—is there anything better than this?"

"Peace is better," I said as I gazed at the two diamonds of my knight's ring. "We were born to be warriors of the—"

"*I* myself saw your father give you that ring!" Salmelu snarled. His malice toward me rose inside him like an angry snake. "But I can hardly believe what I see now: a Valari warrior who does everything that he can to avoid war."

I breathed deeply to cool the heat rising through my belly. Then I said, "If it's war you want, why not unite against the Red Dragon and fight *him*?"

"Because *I* do not fear him as you seem to. No Ishkan does."

This, I thought, was not quite true. King Hadaru paled at the utterance of this evil name. It occurred to me then that he might not, after all, desire a war with Mesh that would weaken his kingdom at a dangerous time. Why wage war when he could gain his heart's desire merely by making threats?

"It's no shame to be afraid," King Hadaru said. "True courage is marching into battle in the face of fear."

At this Salmelu traded quick looks with both Lord Nadhru and Lord Mestivan. I sensed that they were the leaders of the Ishkan faction that campaigned for war.

"Yes," Salmelu said. "Marching into *battle,* not merely banging on our shields and blowing our trumpets."

"Whether or not there is a battle with Mesh," the king reminded him, "is still not decided. As I recall, the emissaries I sent to Silvassu failed to obtain a commitment for battle."

At this, Salmelu's face flushed as if he had been burned by the sun. He stared at his father and said, "If we failed, it was only because we weren't empowered to declare war immediately in the face of King Shamesh's evasions and postponements. If I were king—"

"Yes?" King Hadaru said in a voice like steel. "What *would* you do if you were king?"

"I would march on Mesh immediately, snow or no snow in the passes. It's obvious that the Meshians have no real will toward war."

"Then perhaps it is well that you're not king," his father told him. "And perhaps it's well that I haven't yet named an heir."

At this, Irisha smiled at King Hadaru as she protectively cupped her hands to cover her belly. Salmelu glared at her with a hatefulness that I had thought he reserved only for me. He must have feared that Irisha would bear his father a new son, who would simultaneously push him aside and justify King Hadaru's claims on the domains of Anjo.

King Hadaru turned to me and said, "Please forgive my son. He is hotheaded and does not always consider the effects of his acts."

Despite my dislike of Salmelu, I felt a rare moment of pity for him. Where my father ruled his sons with love and respect, Salmelu's father ruled with fear and shame.

"No offense is taken," I told the king. "It's clear that Lord Salmelu acts out of what he believes to be Ishka's best interest."

"You speak well, Sar Valashu," the king told me. "If you weren't committed to making this impossible quest of yours, your father would do well to make you an emissary to one of the courts of the Nine Kingdoms." He sat back against the white wood of his throne, regarding me deeply. "You have your father's eyes, you know. But you favor your mother. Elianora wi Solaru—now *there* is a beautiful woman."

King Hadaru, I thought, was trying to win me with flattery, toward what end I couldn't see. But his attentions only embarrassed me. And they enraged Salmelu. He must have recalled that his father had once wooed my mother in vain and had only married *his* mother as a second choice.

"Yes," Salmelu choked out. "I agree that Sar Valashu should be made an emissary. Since it's clear that he's no warrior."

Maram, standing next to me, made a rumbling sound in his

throat, as if he might challenge Salmelu's insult. But the sight of Salmelu's sheathed kalama helped him keep his silence. As for me, I looked down at the two diamonds sparkling in my ring and wondered if Salmelu was right, after all.

Then Salmelu continued, "*I* would say that Sar Valashu does favor his father, at least in his avoidance of battle."

Why, I wondered, was Salmelu now insulting both my father and me in front of the entire Ishkan court? Was he trying to call me out? No, I thought, he couldn't challenge me to a duel, since that would violate his pledge of a safe passage through Ishka.

"My father," I said, breathing deeply, "has fought many battles. No one has ever questioned his courage."

"Do you think it's *his* courage I question?"

"What do you mean?"

Salmelu's eyes stabbed into mine like daggers as he said, "It seems a noble thing, this pledge of yours to make your quest. But aren't you really just fleeing from war and the possibility of death in battle?"

I listened as several of the lords near Salmelu drew in quick breaths; I felt my own breath burning inside me as if I had inhaled fire. Was Salmelu trying to provoke me into calling *him* out? Well, I wouldn't be provoked. To fight him would be to die, most likely, and that would only aid him in inciting a war that might kill my friends and brothers. I was a diamond, I told myself, a perfect diamond, which no words could touch.

And then despite my intentions, I found myself suddenly gripping the hilt of my sword as I said to him, "Are you calling me a coward?" If he called me a coward, to my face, than that *would* be a challenge to a duel that I would have to answer.

As my heart beat inside my chest so quickly and hard that I thought it might burst, I felt Master Juwain's hand grip my arm firmly as if to give me strength. And then Maram finally found his voice; he tried to make a joke of Salmelu's deadly insult, saying, "Val, a coward? Ha, ha—is the sky yellow? Val is the bravest man I know."

But his attempt to quiet our rising tempers had no effect on Salmelu. He stared at me coldly and said, "Did you think I was calling you a coward? Then please excuse me—I was only raising the question."

"Salmelu," his father said to him sternly.

But Salmelu ignored him, too. "All men," he said, "should question their own courage. Especially kings. Especially kings who allow their sons to run away when battle is threatened."

"Salmelu!" King Hadaru half shouted at him.

Now I gripped my sword so hard that my fingers hurt. To Salmelu, I said, "Are you calling my father a coward, then?"

"Does a lion beget a lamb?"

These words were like drops of kirax in my eyes, burning me, blinding me. Salmelu's mocking face almost disappeared into the angry red sea closing in around me.

"Does an eagle," he asked, "hatch a rabbit from its eggs?"

The wily Salmelu was twisting his accusations into questions, evading the responsibility for how I might respond. Why? Did he think I would simply impale myself on his sword?

"It's good," he said, "that your grandfather died before he saw what became of his line. Now there was a brave man. It takes true courage to sacrifice those we love. Who else would have let a hundred of his warriors die trying to protect him rather than simply defending his honor in a duel?"

As I choked on my wrath and stopped breathing, the whole world seemed to come crushing down upon my chest. I allowed the terrible lie to break me open, so that I might know the truth of who Salmelu really was. And in that moment of bitterness and blood, his hate became my hate, and mine fed the fires of his, and almost without knowing what I was doing, I whipped my sword from its sheath and pointed it at him.

"Val," Maram cried out in a horrified voice, "put away your sword!"

But there was to be no putting away of swords that night; some things can never be undone. As Salmelu and his fellow Ishkans quickly drew their swords, I stared in silent resignation at this fence of gleaming steel. I had drawn on Salmelu. Despite his taunts, I had done this of my own free will. And according to ancient law that all Valari held sacred, by this act it had been I who had thus formally challenged him to a duel.

"Hold! Hold yourselves now, I say!" King Hadaru's outraged voice cut through the murmurs of anticipation rippling through the hall. Then he arose from his throne and took a step forward. To Salmelu, he said, "I did not want this. I would not have you make this duel tonight—you needn't accept Sar Valashu's challenge."

Salmelu's sword wavered not an inch as he pointed it toward me. He said, "Nevertheless, I do accept it."

The king stared at him for a long moment, then sighed deeply. "So be it, then. A challenge has been made and accepted. You will face Sar Valashu in the ring of honor when you are both ready."

At this, Salmelu and the other lords slid their swords back into their sheaths, and I did the same. So, I thought, the time of my death had finally come. There was nothing more to say; there was nothing more to do—almost nothing.

Because Valari knights do not fight duels wearing armor, the king excused me for a few minutes so that I might remove my mail. With Maram and Master Juwain following close behind me, I repaired to an anteroom off the side of the hall. It was a small room, whose rosewood paneling had the look and smell of dried blood. I stood staring at yet another battle scene carved into wood as the heavy door banged shut and shook the entire room.

"Are you mad!" Maram shouted at me as he shook his huge fist in the air. "That man is the best swordsman in Ishka, and you drew on him!"

"It . . . couldn't be helped," I said.

"Couldn't be helped?" he shouted. He seemed almost ready to smack his fist into me. "Well, why don't you help it now? Why not just apologize to him and leave here as quickly as we can?"

At that moment, with my legs so weak that I could hardly stand, I wanted nothing more than to run away. But I couldn't do that. A challenge had been made and accepted. There are some laws too sacred to break.

"Leave him alone now," Master Juwain said as he came over to me. He helped me remove my surcoat and began working at the catches to my armor. "If you would, Brother Maram, please go out to the horses and bring Val a fresh tunic."

Maram muttered that he would be back in a few moments, and again the door opened and closed. With trembling hands, I began pulling off my armor. With my mail and underpadding removed, it was cold in that little room. Indeed, the entire palace was cold: out of fear of fire, the king allowed no flame hotter than that of a candle in any of its wooden rooms.

"Are you afraid?" Master Juwain asked as he laid his hand on my trembling shoulder.

"Yes," I said, staring at the dreadful red wall.

"Brother Maram is an excitable man," he said. "But he's right, you know. You could simply walk away from all this."

"No, that's not possible," I told him. "The shame would be too great. My brothers would make war to expunge it. My father would."

"I see," Master Juwain said. He rubbed his neck, and then fell quiet.

"Master Juwain," I said, looking at him, "in ancient times, the Brothers would help a knight prepare for a duel. Will you help me now?"

Master Juwain looked at me sadly. "That was long ago, Val, before we forswore violence. If I helped you now and you killed Salmelu, I would bear part of the blame for his death."

"If you don't help me and he kills me, will you not bear part of the blame for mine?"

For as long as it took for my heart to beat twenty times, Master Juwain stared at me in silence. And then he bowed his head in acceptance and said, "All right."

He instructed me to gaze at the stand of candles blazing in the corner of the room. I was to single out the flame of the highest candle and concentrate on its flickering yellow tip. Where did a candle's flame come from when it was lit? He asked me. Where did it go when it went out? He steadied my breathing then as he guided me into the ancient death meditation. Its purpose was to take me into a state of zanshin, a deep and timeless calm in the face of extreme danger. Its essence was in bringing me to the realization that I was much more than my body and that therefore I wouldn't fear its wounding or death.

"Breathe with me now," Master Juwain told me. "Concentrate on your awareness of the flame. Concentrate on your awareness, in itself."

Was I afraid? He told me to ask myself. Who was asking the question? If it was *I* who asked, what was the "I" who was aware of the one who asked? Wasn't there always a deeper I, a truer self—luminous, flawless, indestructible—that shined more brightly than any diamond and blazed as eternally as any star? What was this one radiant awareness that shined through all things?

For once in my life, my gift was truly a gift. As I opened myself to Master Juwain's low but powerful voice, his breathing became one with my breathing and his calm became my own. After a while, my hands stopped sweating and I found that I could stand without shaking. Although my heart still beat as quickly as a child's, the crushing pain I had felt earlier in my chest was gone.

And then suddenly, like thunder breaking through the sky, Maram came back into the room with my tunic, and it was time to go.

"Are you ready?" Master Juwain said as I pulled on the simple garment and buckled my sword around my waist.

"Yes," I said, smiling at him. "Thank you, sir."

We returned to the main hall. King Hadaru and his court had gathered in a circle around the disc of rosewood at the center of the room. In Mesh, when a duel was to be fought, the knights and warriors formed the ring of honor at any convenient spot. But then, we did not fight duels nearly so often as did the blood-thirsty Ishkans.

As I made my way toward the red circle, the floor was so cold beneath my bare feet that it seemed I was walking on ice. Salmelu was waiting for me inside the ring of his countrymen. He had his sword drawn, and Lord Issur stood by his side. Although it took me only a few moments to join him there, with Maram acting as my second, it seemed like almost forever. Then we began the rituals that precede a duel. Salmelu handed his sword to Maram, who rubbed its long blade with a cloth soaked in brandy, and I gave Lord Issur mine. After this cleansing was finished and our swords returned, we closed our eyes for a few moments of meditation to clear our minds.

"Very good," King Hadaru called out. "Are the witnesses ready?"

I opened my eyes to see the ring of Ishkans nod their heads and affirm that they were indeed ready. Maram and Master Juwain now stood among them toward the east of the ring, and they smiled at me grimly.

"Are the combatants ready?"

Salmelu, standing before me with his sword held in two hands by the side of his head, smiled and called out, "I'm ready, sire. Sar Valashu was lucky at chess—let's see how long his luck holds here."

The king waited for me to speak, then said, "And you, Sar Valashu?"

"Yes," I told him. "Let's get this over."

"A challenge has been made and accepted," King Hadaru said in a heavy voice. "You must now fight to defend your honor. In sight of all our ancestors who have stood on this earth before us, you may begin."

For a few moments no one moved. So quiet was the ring of knights and nobles around us that it seemed no one even breathed. Some duels lasted no longer than this. A quick rush, a lightning stroke of steel flashing through the air, and as often as not, one of the combatants' heads would be sent rolling across the floor.

But Salmelu and I faced each other across a few feet of a blood-red circle of wood, taking our time. Asaru had once observed that a true duel between Valari knights resembled nothing so much as a catfight without the hideous screeching and yowling. As if our two bodies were connected by a terrible tension, we began circling each other with an excruciating slowness. After a few moments, we paused to stand utterly still. And then we were moving again, measuring distances, looking for any weakness or hesitation in the other's eyes. I felt sweat running down my sides and my heart beating like a hammer up through my head; I breathed deeply, trying to keep my muscles relaxed yet ready to explode into motion at the slightest impulse. I circled slowly around Salmelu with my sword held lightly in my hands, waiting, waiting, waiting. . . .

And then there was no time. As if a signal had been given, we suddenly sprang at each other in a flurry of flashing swords. Steel rang against steel, and then we locked for a moment, pushing and straining with all our might against each other, trying to free our blades for a deadly cut. We grunted and gasped, and Salmelu's hot breath broke in quick bursts against my face. And then we leapt back from each other and whirled about before suddenly closing again. Steel met steel, once, twice, thrice, and then I aimed a blow downward that might have split him in two. But it missed, and his sword burned the air scarcely an inch above my head. And then I heard Salmelu cry out as if in pain; I cried out myself to feel a sudden sharp agony cut through my leg almost down to the bone.

"Look!" Lord Mestivan called out in his high, nervous voice. "He's cut! Salmelu has been cut!"

As Salmelu and I stood away from each other for a moment to look for another opening, I noticed a long red gash splitting the blue silk of his trousers along his thigh. It seemed that my blow hadn't missed him after all. The gash ran with fresh blood, but it didn't spurt, so most likely he wasn't fatally wounded. It was a wonder, I thought, that I had wounded him at all. Asaru had always said that I was very good with the sword if I didn't let myself become distracted but I had never believed him.

Gasps of astonishment broke from knights and lords in the ring around me. I heard Lord Nadhru call out, "He's drawn first blood! The Elahad has!"

Standing across the circle from him, Maram let out a sudden bellowing cheer. He might have hoped that Salmelu and I would put away our swords then, but the duel wouldn't end until one of us yielded.

Salmelu was determined that it would not be he. The steel I had put in his leg had sent a thrill of fear through him, and his whole body trembled with a panic to destroy me. I felt this dreadful emotion working at me like ice rubbed along my limbs, paralyzing my will to fight. I remembered my vow never to kill again, and I felt the strength bleed away from me. And in my moment of hesitation, Salmelu struck.

He sprang off his good leg straight at me, whirling his sword at my head, all the while snarling and spitting out his malice like a cat. Once again, his hate became my hate, and the madness of it was like a fire burning my eyes. As he cut at me, I barely managed to get my sword up to parry his. Again and again he swung his sword against mine, and the sound rang out into the hall like the beating of a blacksmith's hammer. Somehow I managed to lock swords with him and forestall his furious onslaught. He broke free, however, and lunged straight at my heart. It was only by the miracle of my gift that I felt the blade pushing into my breast—and I pulled frantically aside a moment before the point actually broke through. But the blow took me in my side beneath my arm. His sword drove clean through the knotted muscle there and out my back. I cried out for all to hear as he wrenched his sword free; I jumped backward and held my sword in my good hand as I waited for him to come for me again.

"Second blood to Ishka!" someone called out. "The third blood will tell!"

I stood gasping for breath as I watched Salmelu watching me. He took his time circling nearer to me; he moved as if in great pain, careful of his wounded leg. My left arm hung useless by my side; in my right hand, I gripped my long, heavy kalama, the bright blade that my father had given me. I was almost certain that Salmelu would soon find a way to cut through my feeble defenses. I felt myself almost ready to give up. But the combat, I reminded myself, wouldn't end until one of us yielded—yielded in death.

Again, Salmelu came at me. His little jaw worked up and down as if he were already chewing open my entrails. He now seemed supremely confident of cutting me open there—or in some other vital place. He had the strength and quickness of wielding his sword with two practiced arms, while my best advantage was in being able to dance about and leap out of his way. But the circle was small, and it seemed inevitable that he would soon catch me up near the edge of it. The seeming certainty of my approaching death unnerved me. Despite the fury of the battle, I began shivering. So badly did my body tremble that I could hardly hold my sword.

It was my gift, I believe, that saved me. I had just time enough to sense where Salmelu intended to thrust his flashing sword and avoid it by a feather's edge, by a breath. And my gift opened me to much else. I felt the deep calm of Master Juwain meditating at the edge of the circle, and my hate for Salmelu began dying away. I remembered my mother's love for me and her plea that I should someday return to Mesh; I remembered my father's last words to me: that I must always remember who I was. And who was I, really? I suddenly knew that I was not only Valashu Elahad who held a heavy sword in a tired hand, but the one who walked always beside me and would remain standing when I died: watching, waiting, whispering, shining. To this one who watched, the world and all things within it moved with an exquisite slowness: a scything sword no less than an Ishkan lord named Salmelu. I saw his kalama's steel flash at me then in a long sweeping arc. There came an immense stillness and clarity. In that timeless moment, I leaned back to avoid the point, which ripped a ragged tear across my tunic. And then, quick as a lightning bolt, I slashed my sword in a counterstroke. As I had intended, it cut through the muscles of both of Salmelu's arms and across his chest. Blood leapt into the air, and his sword went flying out of his hands. It clanged against the floor even as Salmelu screamed out that I had killed him.

But I hadn't. The wound wasn't fatal, although it was terrible enough, and he would never hold a sword so easily again.

"Damn you, Elahad!" he snarled at me. He gazed down in disbelief at his bloody sword and the gashes it had torn in the wood of the floor. And then he looked at me in hatred as he waited for me to take his life away.

"Finish him!" King Hadaru commanded in a voice stricken with grief. "What are you waiting for?"

As the blood flowed in streams from Salmelu's useless arms, his hateful eyes drilled into me. I felt his malice eating at my eyes like red, twisting worms. I wanted nothing more than to kill him so that I could keep this dreadful thing from devouring me or anyone else.

"Send him back to the stars!" Maram cried out.

The Brotherhood teaches that death is but a door that opens upon another world. The Valari believe that it is only a short journey not to be feared. I knew differently. Death was the end of everything and the beginning of the great nothingness. It was the dying of the light and a terrible cold. I looked at Salmelu almost ready to collapse in terror into the pool of his own blood, and I was even more afraid to kill him than I was to be killed.

"No," I said to King Hadaru, "I can't."

"All duels are to the death," he reminded me. "If you stay your sword, you do my son a grave dishonor and bring no honor to yourself."

I gripped my sword hard in my trembling hand. I watched as Salmelu's strength finally gave way and he collapsed to the floor. From the blood-soaked boards there, he stared up at me fearfully, all the while waiting, waiting, waiting. . . .

"No, there will be no killing," I finally said. "No more killing."

I walked over to Maram, who handed me a cloth to clean the blood from my sword. Then, with a loud ringing sound, I slid it back into its sheath.

"So be it," King Hadaru said to me.

At that moment, the swords of Lord Issur and Lord Nadhru—and two dozen others—whipped out and pointed at me. By denying Salmelu his honorable death, I had shamed him even more seriously than he had me. And now his brother and friends meant to avenge my deadly insult.

"I challenge you!" Lord Issur shouted at me.

"I challenge you, too!" Lord Nadhru snarled out. "If Lord Issur falls, then you will fight me!"

And so it went, various knights and lords around the ring of honor calling out their challenges to me.

"Hold!" King Hadaru commanded. He pointed his long finger at the blood still flowing from my side. "Have you forgotten he's wounded?"

Valari codes forbade the issue of challenges to wounded warriors. And so Lord Nadhru and the others very angrily put away their swords.

"You have dishonored my house," King Hadaru said, gazing at me. "And so you are no longer welcome in it."

He turned to look at Lord Nadhru, Lord Issur, and other knights, and finally at his gravely wounded son. Then, in a trembling voice, he said, "Valashu Elahad, you are no longer welcome in my kingdom. No one is to give you fire, bread, or salt. My son has promised you safe passage through Ishka, and that you shall have. But what happens after you cross our borders to another land is only justice and your fate."

The sudden gleam in Lord Nadhru's eyes gave me to understand that he and his friends would pursue me into other kingdoms to exact vengeance—perhaps they would pursue me to the ends of the earth.

"So be it," I said to King Hadaru.

There was nothing else do to. When a king ordered you to leave his kingdom, it was foolish to remain.

And so I turned to lead the way back into the anteroom

where I had left my armor. The Ishkan lords and ladies only reluctantly broke the ring of honor to allow me pass from the circle. It was something of a miracle that no one drew his sword.
But as we made our way through the long cold hall, I felt
dozens of pairs of eyes stabbing into me like so many kalamas.
The pain of it was almost worse than that of the wound Salmelu
had opened in my side.

8

MASTER JUWAIN DRESSED my wound in that cold little room
off the main hall. He told me that I was lucky that Salmelu's
sword had cut the muscle lengthwise, along the grain. Such
wounds usually healed of their own with no more treatment
than being sewn shut. It hurt when Master Juwain punctured
my flesh with a sharp little needle and piece of thread. Working
on my armor and surcoat hurt even more. And then it was time
to go.

Outside the palace we found the grooms waiting for us with
our horses. Lord Nadhru and Lord Issur—and a squadron of
Ishkan knights mounted on their stamping horses—were waiting for us there, too.

With a sharp gasp, I used my good arm to pull myself onto
Altaru's back. The beast's glossy coat was like black jade in the
moonlight; he angrily shook his head at the Ishkan knights and
their horses. We made our way down the tree-lined road leading
away from King Hadaru's palace. The sound of the horses'
hooves striking the paving stones seemed very loud against the
stillness of the quiet grounds. It was now full night and falling
cold. In the sky there were many stars. They rained their silver
light upon the tinkling fountains and the rows of flowers that
perfumed the air. Even though I vowed not to do so, I turned in
my saddle to see the bright starlight glinting off the points of
the Ishkans' lances and armor. The knights followed us at a

good distance; as we turned onto the road leading to the bridge that crossed the Tushur, I was afraid that they intended to follow us all the way to Anjo.

"Perhaps you should return to Mesh," I said to Maram. I turned to Master Juwain riding his sorrel to my right. "And you, too, sir. It's not you that the Ishkans want."

Master Juwain looked at me with concern and said, "But who will tend you if you fall to fever? And we can't just leave you alone to the Ishkans' lances, can we, Brother Maram?"

Maram, casting a glance back at Lord Nadhru and the other knights, sighed and then smiled at me and said, "No, I suppose we can't."

Loviisa, although not a large city, was spread out on both sides of the Tushur. We crossed the river, with its gurgling, black waters, and so did Lord Nadhru and his knights. After a mile, the buildings thinned out and gave way to the rolling farmland of the surrounding countryside. The moon shone upon fields of barley and wheat, whose new leaves glistened in the soft light. More than once, Maram cast a longing glance toward one of the little houses in the fields off the side of the road. We all listened to the lowing of cows and smelled the maddening aroma of roasting meat that wafted on the wind. We were very hungry, but all we had to eat was a few wheels of cheese and some battle biscuits pulled from the packhorses' bags. Maram complained that the iron-hard biscuits hurt his teeth; he bemoaned my duel with Salmelu, and then chided me, saying, "Why couldn't you at least wait until *after* King Hadaru had feted us before drawing on him?"

Eating the biscuits hurt my teeth, too. Everything about that nighttime flight from Ishka hurt. As always, Altaru sensed my condition and moved so as to ease the discomfiture of my wound. Even so, I could feel my outraged body throbbing with every beat of my heart. Around midnight, some clouds came up, and it rained. It grew suddenly colder. Maram pulled his cloak tightly around himself and then shook his fist at the sky as he growled out, "I'm cold; I'm tired; I'm wet—and I'm still hungry. The merciless Ishkans can't expect us to ride all night, can they?"

It seemed they could. Soon after that, Master Juwain insisted that we stop to make camp for the night. But even as we were tethering our horses to the fence edging a field, Lord Nadhru came thundering up the road on a huge warhorse. He stared straight at me and said, "You've been denied any hospitality while in Ishka. Mount your horses, and don't try to stop again."

"Are you mad?" Maram snapped at him. "We've ridden since dawn, and our horses are exhausted, we are too, and—"

"Mount your horses," Lord Nadhru commanded again, "or we'll bind you with ropes and drag you from Ishka!"

Just then Lord Issur came riding up. He sat high on his horse while he regarded us through the rain. He was a spirited, graceful man, perhaps even kind in his own way, and I thought I might have liked him if we had met under different circumstances.

"Please mount your horses," he told us. "We've no liking to do as Lord Nadhru has said."

Master Juwain stepped forward and looked up at the two towering knights on their horses. "My friend is badly wounded and needs rest. If you have any compassion, you'll let us be."

"Compassion?" Lord Issur cried out. "If Sar Valashu had any compassion, he would have slain my brother rather than condemning him to live in shame."

"At least your brother is still alive," Master Juwain said. "And so there's always hope that he'll find a way to undo his shame, is there not?"

"Perhaps," Lord Issur said. "But I still must ask you to mount your horses, or I'll have to let Lord Nadhru fetch his ropes."

There was no arguing with him. Kind he might be, deep in his heart, but there was steel in him, too, and he seemed determined to execute King Hadaru's wishes no matter how bravely Master Juwain stood before him.

After he and Lord Nadhru had ridden back to the other knights, we prepared to set out again. Then Maram suddenly drew his sword and shook it at the dark road in their direction.

"How they speak to you!" he called out to me. "Didn't they see what you did to Salmelu? *I've* never seen such sword work in my life! Tie us with ropes, they say! Why, if they even lay a hand on you, I'll—"

"Maram, please," I broke in. "Save your fight for our passage into Anjo. Now let's ride while we still can."

The Sarni warriors, it is said, eat and sleep in the saddle and let a little blood from a vein in their horses' necks for drink. Riding hard, they can cover a hundred miles in a day. We rode hard ourselves that night, although we did not cover nearly so many as a hundred miles. As the rain pelted my cloak and the farmland gave way to rougher country, I struggled to remain awake. The pain in my side helped me. As for Maram, more than once he nodded off with a loud snoring, only to be jolted rudely awake when he felt himself slipping off his horse. Master Juwain, however, seemed to need little sleep. He admitted that his daily meditations had nearly overcome his need for such sweet oblivion. Beneath his vow of nonviolence and his kindly ways, he was a very tough man, as many of the Brothers are.

Sometime before morning, the rain stopped and the clouds pulled back from the night's last stars. Daybreak found us in a broad, green valley more than half the way to Anjo. To the east, a low range of mountains cut the golden-red disk of the rising sun. Its streaming rays fell upon us, not so warmly that it dried our garments, but not so weakly that we didn't all feel a little cheered. To the west, framed by the great snow-capped peaks of the Shoshan range, the sunlight glinted off an expanse of blue water: Lake Osh, I guessed. And to the south, a couple of hundred yards behind us, many brightly colored surcoats flapped in the early wind as King Hadaru's knights urged their horses forward.

We rode, too, as hard and steadily as we dared. The morning deepened around us as the sun grew ever brighter. It heated up my armor, and I was grateful for the surcoat that covered most of its searing steel rings. The warmth of the day made me drowsy, and I scarcely noticed the rocky slabs of the mountains to the east or the higher peaks that lay ahead of us. By noon, we had passed well beyond Yarwan, a pretty little town that reminded me of Lashku in Mesh. I guessed that the border to Anjo—and the Aru-Adar bridge—lay only ten or twelve miles farther up the road. And so I eased Altaru to a halt and turned to talk with Maram and Master Juwain.

"It would be best if you go on from here without me," I told them. I pointed up the road, which led north like a ribbon of gleaming stone. "The Ishkans won't follow you across the bridge."

"But where are you going?" Maram asked me.

Now I pointed west to the hilly country that lay between Lake Osh and the mountains to the north. "If what my father's minstrel once told me is true, there's a way through the mountains farther to the west. We'll part company for a few days and meet in Sauvo."

In Sauvo, I explained, King Danashu would give us shelter, and there the Ishkans would not go.

Master Juwain nudged his horse over to me and touched his cool hand to my forehead. "You're very hot, Val—you have a fever, and that might kill you before the Ishkans do. We won't leave you alone."

"No, we won't," Maram told me. Then, as he realized what he had committed himself to, doubt began to eat at his face, and he summoned up the bravado to bluster his way through it. "We'll follow even through the gates of hell, my friend."

"How did you know," I said with a smile, "where we were going?"

And with that, I turned Altaru toward the west and left the road. We began riding easily through the soft, green hills. The Ishkans, obviously alarmed at our new tack, tightened their ranks and followed us more closely. The soil beneath our horses' trampling hooves was too poor for crops, and so there were few farms about. Few trees grew, either, having been cut long ago for firewood or the Ishkans' wasteful building projects. I had hoped for more cover than this from Lord Issur's and Lord Nadhru's unrelenting vigilance. In truth, I had hoped for a thick forest into which we might dash and make our escape.

And so I followed the sun, and Maram and Master Juwain followed me. It was the longest day of my life. My side felt as if Salmelu's sword was still stuck there, and every bone in my body, particularly those of my trembling legs, hurt. After some hours, the country around us seemed to dissolve into a sea of blazing green. I dozed in my saddle and I dreamed feverish dreams. More than once, I almost toppled off Altaru's back; but each time he moved with a knowing grace to check my fall. I marveled at the trust he had in me, leading him on toward a destination that none of us had ever seen. My trust in him—his sure-footedness and his plain good sense—grew with every mile we put behind us; it seemed even more solid than the earth over which we rode.

Nightfall made our journey no easier. Indeed, if not for the full moon that rose over the hills about us, we wouldn't have been able to journey at all. I tried to set my gaze on a white-capped peak that swelled against the black sky straight ahead; there the lesser mountains to the north met the Shoshan range like a great hinge of rock. But my eyes were dry as stones, and I could hardly keep them open. I was so tired that I couldn't even eat the pieces of biscuit that Master Juwain kept trying to urge into my mouth like a mother bird. It was all I could do to gulp down a few swallows of water. Soon, I knew, I would slip from Altaru's back, no matter the great horse's agility and love for me. I would find oblivion in the sweet heather that blanketed the hills. And then Lord Nadhru would have to come for me with his ropes.

It was the Lightstone, I believe, that kept me going. I held the image of the golden cup close to my heart. From its deep hollows welled a cool, clear liquid that seemed to flow into me and give my body a new strength. It woke me up, at least enough so that my eyes didn't close in darkness.

It awakened me, too, to the sorry state of my friends, for they were nearly as tired as I was. And they were even more fearful of the unknown lands ahead. Their plight struck to my heart, and I vowed to do all that I could for them so long as any strength remained to me.

I rode with them over the silver hills. And then, around midnight, just as we topped a hill crowned with many sharp rocks, I caught a moist, disturbing scent that jolted me wide awake. I stopped Altaru as I gazed at a depression that seemed out of place in the generally rising terrain. Patches of mist hung over it, like cotton balls floating in a great bowl. On the east side of it, the range of mountains along which we had been riding came to a sudden end. On the west side, farther ahead of the dark scoop in the earth, was the mountainous wall of the great Shoshan range. Here, at last, was the hinge in the mountains that I had been seeking. And as I had hoped, the hinge was broken at its very joint, and the way into Anjo lay open before us.

"What is it?" Master Juwain said as he stared across the moonlit land.

Now a whiff of decay fell over me, and the air seemed suddenly colder. And then I said, "It's a bog—and not a small one, either."

I went on to tell him that this was an evil wound upon the land. For once, in the Age of Law, a mountain had stood upon this spot. The Ishkans of old had named it Diamond Mountain in honor of the richest deposits of these gems ever to be found in the Morning Mountains. In their lust for wealth, they had used firestones to burn away layers of useless rock and uncover the veins of diamonds. Such wasteful mining, over centuries, had burned away the entire mountain. It had left a poorly drained depression that filled with silt and sand so that now, a whole age later, only a foul-smelling bog remained.

Maram, staring in horror at the miles-wide patch of ground, took my arm and said, "You can't mean to ride down into that, can you? Not at night?"

If my father had taught me anything about war, it was that a king should never rely on mountains, rivers, forests—or even bogs—for protection. Such seemingly impenetrable natural barriers are often quite penetrable, sometimes much more readily than one might suspect. Often, hard work and a little daring sufficed for forcing one's way through them.

"Come on," I said to Maram, "it won't be so bad."

"Oh no?" he said. "Why do I suspect that it will be worse than bad?"

As we were debating the perils of bogs—Maram held that the quicksands in them could trap both man and horse and suck them down into a dreadful death—the Ishkans came riding up. Lord Issur and Lord Nadhru led eighteen grim-faced knights who seemed nearly as tired as we were. They sat shifting about uneasily in their saddles as the line of their horses stretched across the top of the hill.

"Sar Valashu!" Lord Issur called out as he pointed into the bog. "There is no way out of Ishka in this direction. Now you must return as you have come, and set out through one of the passes to the north."

"No," I said, "we'll go this way."

"Through the Black Bog?" he asked as his knights laughed uneasily.

Maram wiped the sweat from his bulging forehead. "The Black Bog, is it called? Excellent—now *there* is a name to inspire courage."

"It will take more than courage for you to cross it."

"How so?" Maram asked.

"Because it is haunted. There's something in there that devours men. No one who has ever gone into it has ever come out again."

Now Master Juwain looked at me as I felt his belly suddenly tighten. But his steely will kept his fear from overcoming him; I smiled at him to honor his courage, and he smiled back.

To Lord Issur, I said, "Nevertheless, we will go into it."

"Go back," Lord Issur urged me. There was a tightness in his own voice which I suspected he didn't like. "It is death to go into this bog."

"It is death for me to go into any of the passes if you follow so closely behind me."

"There are worse things than death," he said.

I stared down into the misty depression but said nothing.

"At least," Lord Issur said, nodding at Master Juwain and Maram, "it will be your own death only. And you may die fighting with a sword in your hand."

Just then, Altaru let out a whinny of impatience, and I patted his trembling neck to steady him. "No, there's been enough fighting," I said.

"Master Juwain?" Lord Issur called out. "Prince Maram Marshayk—what will you do?"

In a voice as cool as the wind, Master Juwain affirmed that he would follow me into the bog. Maram looked at me for a long moment as our hearts beat together. After taking a deep breath, he said that he would go with me, too. And then he muttered to the sky, "The Black Bog indeed—why don't you just kill us here and save us the misery?"

For a moment it seemed that the Ishkans might do exactly that. The eighteen knights each gripped their lances more tightly as they looked at Lord Nadhru and Lord Issur and waited for their command. I waited, too. Many miles before, I had foreseen that the Ishkans might kill me on this very spot—and kill as well Master Juwain and Maram as witnesses to such a crime. But I had counted on them honoring Salmelu's promise that I wasn't to be harmed while on Ishkan soil. In the end, one is either Valari or not.

"We won't follow you there," Lord Issur said. "It would be death."

At this, many of his knights sighed gratefully. But Lord Nadhru edged his horse closer to us and let his hand rest upon the hilt of his sword. To Lord Issur, he said, "But what of the king's command that Sar Valashu and his friends leave Ishka?"

Again, Lord Issur pointed down into the bog. "*That* is no longer part of Ishka. It belongs to no kingdom on earth."

He turned to me and said, "Farewell, Valashu Elahad. You're a brave man, but a foolish one. We'll tell your countrymen, as we will our own, that you died in this accursed place."

There was nothing to do then but go down into the bog. I said farewell to Lord Issur, then urged Altaru down the hill. Maram hesitated as he stared at the misty, uncertain ground before us, and he muttered to himself: "They laughed when I wouldn't go swimming in the ocean with the other boys; well, they wouldn't laugh *now*."

Then he and Master Juwain, with the packhorses tied behind their sorrels, followed behind me. And so, for a few hundred yards, did the Ishkans. They watched us through the wavering moonlight to make sure that we did as we had said we would.

The slope of the hill gradually gave way to more even ground as we rode down into the depression. And the heather beneath our horses' hooves gave way to other vegetation: sedges and grasses and various kinds of moss. There was no clear line demarcating the bog from the land around it. But there came a point where the air grew suddenly colder and smelled even more pungently of decay. There Altaru suddenly planted his hooves in the moist ground and let out a great whinny. He shook his head at the mist-covered terrain before us and would not go any farther.

"Come on, boy," I said as I patted his neck. "We have to do this."

Master Juwain and Maram came up to us, and their horses pawed the ground uneasily, too.

"Come on," I said again. "It won't be so bad."

I tried to clear my feverish head as Master Juwain had taught me. Some part of the calm I achieved must have passed into Altaru, for he turned his head to look back at me with his great, trusting eyes. And then he began moving slowly forward, into the bog.

The other horses followed him, and their hooves made moist

squishing sounds in the cold ground. It was strange, I thought, that although the ground over which we rode oozed with water, it seemed solid enough to look at. In few places were there actually patches of standing water. These almost black meres we avoided easily enough as we kept pressing forward. Our path through the bog, while not perfectly straight, was direct enough that I was sure we would soon be out of it.

I tried to keep us oriented toward the north so that we wouldn't lose direction in the trackless waste. After a while, I looked back to fix our position by the hill where we had left the Ishkans. Although it was hard to see very far, even in the bright moonlight, I thought I could make out their forms far off as they watched us from the top of the hill. And then a mist came up, covering us as it obliterated all sight of them. When it pulled back a few minutes later, the hill seemed barren of knights, or indeed, of any living thing. I couldn't even perceive the jagged rocks along the hill's crest. The hill itself seemed flatter and wider; it was as if the heavy air over the bog were like a spectacle maker's lens that distorted the world all around us.

"Val," Maram said behind me, "I feel sick—it's like I'm falling."

I, too, felt a strange, sinking sensation in the pit of my stomach. It was something like the time Asaru and I had jumped off the cliffs above Lake Silash into the dark, freezing waters. It seemed that the bog was pulling at us, pulling us down into the inconstant earth, even though at no point did its seeping water rise much above the horses' fetlocks.

"It will be all right," I said as the mist slid along the ground and wrapped its gray-black tendrils around us. "If we keep moving, it will be all right."

And then, even as the mist opened slightly and I looked up at the sky, I knew that it would *not* be all right. For something about this accursed bog was distorting the sight of the very stars. The brightest of them—Solaru, Aras, and Varshara—seemed strangely dulled and slightly out of place. I blinked my eyes and shook my head in disbelief. And the feeling of falling down into an endless dark hole grew only stronger.

"Maram," I said. "Master Juwain—there's something wrong here!"

I turned to tell them that we should stay close together. But when I peered through the swirling mist, I couldn't see them. And that was very strange because I had thought they were no more than ten yards behind me.

"Maram!" I called out. "Master Juwain—where are you?"

I stopped Altaru and listened as carefully as I could. But the bog was quiet and deathly still. Not even a cricket chirped.

"Maram! Master Juwain!"

The shock of being suddenly alone was like a hammer striking me beneath my ribs. For many moments, I had trouble breathing the dank, stifling air. Had both Maram and Master Juwain, I wondered, plunged into a quicksand that had instantly sucked them down without a sound? Had they simply vanished from the earth?

I felt the sweat beading along my skin beneath my armor and clothing. My whole body felt icy cold even as I shivered uncontrollably. I covered my forehead and rubbed my fevered eyes. Was I mad? I wondered. Was I ill to my death and forever lost in this choking mist?

"Altaru," I whispered as I stroked the coarse, long hair of his mane, "where are they? Can you smell them?"

Altaru nickered nervously, then turned his head right and left. He pawed the sodden ground and waited for me to tell him what to do.

"Maram! Master Juwain!" I shouted. "Why can't you hear me?"

There came a booming sound then as if the whole earth was shaking. It took me a while to realize that it was only the beating of my heart and not some gigantic drum. And then Maram called to me—but not from behind me, as I had expected. A moment later, the mist parted again, and I could see him and Master Juwain riding their horses barely twenty yards ahead of me.

"Why did you leave me?" I called out as I rode up to them.

"Leave *you*?" Maram said. He leaned over on his horse and grasped my good arm with his as if to reassure himself that I was really there. "It was you who left us."

"Don't play games, Maram. How did you get ahead of me?"

"How did you get behind us?"

Because I had no strength to argue, I just sat astride Altaru looking at him in relief. I had never thought that the sight of his thick brown beard and weepy eyes could please me so greatly.

Then Master Juwain came over to us and said, "There *is*

something wrong with this place. I've never heard of anything like it. Why don't we tie the horses together and stay closer to each other now?"

Both Maram and I agreed that this was an excellent idea. With some rope that we found in one of the horses' packs, we tied the sorrels close behind Altaru and the packhorses behind them.

"Let's go," I said, not wanting to spend another minute there. "It can't be much more than a few miles to drier ground."

Again, with me in the lead, we moved off toward what I thought was due north. In places, the mist was so thick that we couldn't see more than ten feet in any direction. The ground beneath us now was mostly of large, spongy mosses that made sucking sounds as the horses trampled over them. The air was cold and wet and smelled of dark scents that were strange to me. There were no animals to be seen or to be heard either. Even so, as we made our way across the drowned sedges and grasses and muck, I felt something following us. Although I thought that it couldn't be an animal—and certainly nothing like a wolf or a bear—I had an uneasy sensation that it could smell me from miles away even through the thickest of mists. And then I closed my eyes for a moment, and I was certain of nothing at all. For in my mind, I could see gray shapes on horseback riding hard in our pursuit. I was afraid that Lord Issur had changed his mind after all and was coming to murder us.

I pressed Altaru more urgently then; the other horses, tied to my saddle with short lengths of rope, quickened their paces. We rode in near silence for what seemed a long time. I couldn't guess how many miles we covered, for both time and distance in this terrible bog seemed to be different from that of the mountains and valleys in which I had spent my whole life. With every bit of sodden ground that we passed over, the sense that something or someone was following us grew stronger. I couldn't understand why we hadn't found the bog's northern edge and the safety of Anjo. And then, even as the mist thinned, Maram let out a cry of terror because he had found something else.

"Look!" he said as he pointed at the ground ahead.

Now the moonlight seemed to wax stronger for a moment as it fell upon a form half-sunken into the mosses and muck. It was a man, I saw, or rather the remains of one. His bones, gleaming a dull white, were spread out along the ground. His eyeless skull seemed to stare straight at us, and his finger joints were wrapped around the hilt of a great, rusted sword. Almost the whole of his skeleton was encased in a suit of slowly rotting diamond-studded armor. Its hundreds of stones, although smeared with mud, still had some fire to them. They caught my eye with their sparkle even as Maram and Master Juwain drew up beside me.

"How long," Maram asked, "do you think this knight has been here?"

"That's hard to say," I told him.

"Do you think he got lost? Do you think he ran out of food and starved?"

There was a note of panic in his voice, and Master Juwain took hold of his arm and gently shook him. He said, "There are some things it's better not to ask and better not to know. Now let's leave this place before we unnerve each other completely."

Maram quickly agreed to that, and we rode hard for an hour or so. At those rare moments when I could see the sky, I tried to steer by the stars. But they kept shifting about in strange new patterns that didn't make sense to me. Master Juwain suggested trying to fix our position by the bright disk of the moon, and this I tried to do. But then, some miles from the spot where we had left the knight, I looked up to see half the moon missing as if some great beast had taken a bite out of it. I shook my head in disbelief, and sat there on top of Altaru blinking my eyes.

"Perhaps it's only an eclipse," Master Juwain said to encourage me.

I looked at him and smiled as I shook my head. And then, as Maram let out a shriek of terror, I looked up at the sky again, and the moon was completely gone.

"Let us ride," I said. "Let's find a way out of here before we all lose our minds."

Yet again we set out in a direction that might have been north, south, east, or west—or some entirely new direction that would take us nowhere forever. We rode hard for what seemed many hours. There was nothing to do but listen to the splashing that the horses made and breathe the chill air. Once, the stars returned to their familiar positions within their ancient constellations, and more than once, the full moon again burned a silvery circle through the black sky. We might have taken comfort from this bright disk, but then, as we were gazing up at it, a dark shape like that of a dragon or an impossibly huge bat flew straight across it. And then a moment later the moon vanished, and the mist closed around us like a wet, gray shroud.

"Val," Maram said to me in a low voice, "I'm afraid."

"We all are," I told him. "But we have to keep going."

And then, seeing that my words had done little to cheer him, I nudged Altaru closer to him and gripped his hand in mine. I said, "It's all right—I won't let anything happen to you."

As we rode on in silence over the sucking mosses, I was very afraid that the pain and fever of my wounded side would soon set me to screaming. But even worse than this throbbing agony was the sensation of something squirming in my head, clawing my eyes from inside. I could still feel something or someone following us through the mist. And something else—it felt like a vast, black, bloated spider—was watching us and waiting for us even as it somehow called us toward the darkest of places at the bog's very center. The more I tried to evade this dreadful thing, the closer I seemed to be drawn to it—and Maram and Master Juwain with me. It was only a matter of time, I thought, until it seized me and tore me open to suck out my mind.

Before fear maddened me completely, I tried to use my mind to reason our way out of the bog. Hadn't we been traveling through it for at least twelve hours? Shouldn't we then have covered at least forty miles and not merely the four or five miles of the bog's true width? Were we moving in circles? Was the black mere to our right new to us or one that we had left behind many miles ago? And if we kept the mountains of the Shoshan range always to our left—during those rare moments when the mist lifted and we could see them—shouldn't we have long since found our way into Anjo?

"Val, I'm so tired," Maram said. He waved his hand about as if to dispel the mist nearly blinding us. "Where *are* we? Will this night never end?"

I had no answers for him. My command of direction, on which I had always prided myself, seemed to have abandoned me utterly. I could neither see nor sense my way out this forsaken place. Perhaps there *was* no way out, even as Lord Issur had said. Soon, we would all slip off our horses and have to rest. We might awaken, once, twice, or even twenty more times to continue our journey into the endless night. But in the end, our food would run out and we would weaken beyond repair; we would fall into the sleep from which there is no awakening, even as the poor knight had. And then we would die in this desolate bog. Perhaps someday another knight would find *our* bones and behold the fate that awaited him.

At last, I slumped forward in my saddle and threw my good arm around Altaru's neck to keep from myself plunging to the ground. And then I whispered in his ear, "We're lost, my friend, we're very lost. My apologies for bringing you here. Now go where you will, and bring yourself out, if you can."

I closed my eyes then, and tried to hold on to his thickly muscled neck as the long column of it vibrated with a sudden nicker. He seemed to understand me, for he nickered again and surged forward with a new strength. Master Juwain's and Maram's sorrels, tied to him along with the pack horses, followed closely behind him. As I felt the rocking of Altaru's great body, my mind emptied and I drifted toward sleep. I was only dimly aware of him pausing before various meres and sniffing the air as he circled right or left and wound his way across the squishing mosses. My only thought was to keep hold of him and not let myself fall into the bog.

How long we traveled this way, I couldn't say. The heavy mist devoured both moon and stars. The darkness of the night seemed ever to deepen into a blackness as thick as ink. Although I knew that the fever must be working at me, my entire body felt as cold as death, and I couldn't stop shivering.

On and on we rode for many miles. I fell into a sleep in which I was strangely aware that I was sleeping. I dreamed that Altaru somehow found true north, and I felt the ground beginning to rise beneath us. And then this horse that I loved beyond all others let loose a tremendous whinny that shook me fully awake. The mist fell away from me. I opened my eyes to see both moon and stars and the jagged mountains of the Shoshan rising up to the west. Behind us—we all turned to look—the hazy bog steamed silver-gray in the soft light. But ahead of us, a mile away on top of a steep hill, a castle stood limned against the glowing sky. Maram called out that we were saved, even as I let out a cry of joy. And then I finally let myself slip from Altaru's back, and I lay down against the hard, rocky, sweet, beautiful earth.

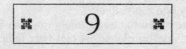

WE WERE AWAKENED from our sleep by the sound of trampling horses. Five knights with green falcons emblazoned on their shields and surcoats—the emblem of the Rezu clan, who ruled Anjo's westernmost duchy—rode up to us through the morning's bright light and demanded that we accompany them. The short ride up to the castle nearly killed me. It was a small castle with only four towers and a single keep that also held the living quarters and great hall. The walls, though not particularly high, were of a blue granite and seemed in good repair. We entered it across a moat on which floated many ducks and geese. I noted that the great chains that worked the drawbridge were free of rust and freshly greased. In the single courtyard, where some sheep milled about baahing nervously, a sharp-faced man with sharp quick eyes stood waiting to greet us. He wore a fresh black tunic and a kalama whose sheath was scarred with gouges. He greeted us warily and then presented himself as Duke Rezu of Rajak.

"And who are you," he asked me, "who encamps in my domain without my leave? From where have you come?"

"My name," I said hoarsely, "is Valashu Elahad." Then I turned to present Master Juwain and Maram. "We've come from Mesh."

Duke Rezu stared at my torn and bloodstained surcoat. "From Mesh, indeed—that I can see. But how did you come from there to here?"

In answer, I could only point in the direction of the bog.

"Through the bog? No, that's not possible—no one has ever come *out* of the Black Bog."

Now his fist tightened around his sword, and he looked at us as if we had better give him a true accounting of our journeys.

"Nevertheless, we did," I told him. "We crossed it last night and—"

A sudden shiver of pain tore through my side, and I had to hold on to Altaru's neck to keep from falling. Then Master Juwain said to Duke Rezu, "My friend has been wounded. Is there any way you can help us?"

The duke regarded me for an uncomfortably long time. Then he said, "Sar Valashu Elahad—I met your father at the tournament in Nar. You have his eyes. And I hope you have his honesty as well: I can't believe that the son of Shavashar Elahad would tell anything other than the truth. Even so, it's hard to believe that you crossed the bog. It seems that you have stories for us. However, we won't ask you to recount them just now. You are wounded and need rest. That you shall have. And fire, salt, and bread as well."

And with that he bowed to me, stepped forward, and took my hand in his to offer his hospitality. He summoned a groom to care for our horses. Then he instructed a young squire to take us into the castle's living quarters.

I spent most of the next three days lying abed in our well-lighted rooms high in the keep. Maram washed away the muck of the bog and tended to my needs with a care that I hadn't known he possessed. Master Juwain made me a strong, bitter tea that tasted of turpentine and mold; he said it would fight my fever. After eating a little of the bread and chicken soup that Duke Rezu sent up for dinner, I slept through the night and long into the next morning. I awoke to find that my fever had broken, and I ate a much larger meal of bacon, fried eggs, and porridge. And so it went for the next two days, the rhythm of my life settling in to successive rounds of eating and sleeping.

On the evening of the third day, the duke summoned us to dinner. It seemed that the castle had guests whom he wished us to meet. And so I put on my tunic, then we all went down to take our meal together.

The duke's hall was not nearly so large as my father's. With its low smoke-stained beams and wooden floor lined with woven carpets, it seemed a rather cozy room for feasting. In it were crammed six smallish tables for Duke Rezu's warriors and knights, and a longer one that served his family and guests. That evening, only this longer table, made of planks of rough-cut hickory, was set with dishes.

The duke stood waiting for us by his chair at the head of the table, while his wife took her place at the opposite end. Along the north side of the table gathered various members of the Rezu clan: his youngest son, Naviru, and a nephew named Arashar; Chaitra, the duke's recently widowed (and beautiful) niece, and his mother, Helenya, a small, dour woman whose features were as sharp as flints. Next to her stood an old minstrel named Yashku. Master Juwain, Maram, and I took our places at the table's south side along with the duke's two other guests. The first of these he presented as Thaman of Surrapam, a barbaric man whose mottled, pinkish skin, red hair, and icy blue eyes tempted one to stare. Instead of offending him with the insolence of my gaze, I turned to regard the duke's other guest.

He was a man with the strange and singular name of Kane. His loose gray-green woolens were without emblem and almost concealed the suit of mail beneath. I wondered from what land he had come. Although not as tall as many Valari, he had the brilliant black eyes and bold face bones of my people. His accent sounded strange, as if he had been born in some kingdom far from the Morning Mountains, and he wore his snowy white hair cropped close to his head. I couldn't tell how old he was: the hair suggested an age of sixty, while his sun-beaten features were those of a forty-year-old man. He moved, however, like a much younger warrior. In the highlands of Kaash, I had once seen one of the few snow tigers left in the world; Kane reminded me of that great beast in the power and grace of his muscular body and most of all, in the fire I sensed blazing inside him. His dark eyes were hot, angry, wild, and pained, as if he were used to looking upon death, and I immediately mistrusted him.

"So, Valashu Elahad," he said, drawing out the syllables of my name after the duke had introduced us and we had all sat down. I felt his gaze cutting into the scar on my forehead. "Of the Meshian Elahads—now there's a name that even *I* have heard."

"Heard . . . where?" I asked, trying to ferret out his homeland.

But he only stared at me with his fathomless eyes as he scowled and the muscles above his tense jaws stood out like blocks of wood.

"So," he continued. "The duke tells me you came through the bog."

"Yes, we did," I said, looking at Master Juwain and Maram.

Here the duke's wife—she was a harsh-looking woman named Durva—fingered her graying hair and said, "We've always counted on the bog as being impassable. It's bad enough having to guard our border with Adar, to say nothing of the Kurmak raids. But if we have to worry about the Ishkans coming at us from the south, then we might as well just go into the bog ourselves and let the demons devour us."

I shook my head as I smiled at her. Then I said, "There aren't any demons in the bog."

"No?" she asked. "What *is* there in the bog?"

"Something worse," I said.

While the duke called for our goblets to be filled so that we could begin our rounds of toasting, I told of our passage through the bog. I had to explain, of course, why we had chosen to flee into it, and that led to an account of my duel with Salmelu and my reasons for leaving home. When I had finished my story, everyone sat looking at me quietly.

"Remarkable," Duke Rezu said, staring at me down the ridge of his sharp nose. "A sun that never rises, and a moon that vanishes like smoke! Who could believe such wonders?"

At this, Kane took a long pull of his beer, then said, "A man who has never seen a boat won't want to believe that mariners could cross the sea in one. There are many bad places in the world. And there are many things in Ea left from the War of Stones that we don't understand. This Black Bog is only one of them, eh?"

After that Duke Rezu finally called for our meal to begin. His grooms brought out of the kitchen many platters of food: fried trout and rabbit stew, goose pie and nut bread and a big salad of spring greens—and much else. I found myself very hungry. I piled trout and potatoes on my plate, and I watched as Maram, too, began to eat with a good appetite. After some moments of clanking dishes and beer being sloshed into our quickly emptied goblets, Maram nudged his elbow into my side. He nodded toward Kane, then whispered, "I thought that *you* were the only one who could eat more than I."

Not wanting to be too obvious, I glanced down the line of the table to see Kane working at his meal with a startling intensity. At the duke's encouragement, he had taken a whole leg of lamb for himself. Using a dagger that he shook out of the sleeve of his tunic, he sliced off long strips of the rare meat with the skill of a butcher. His motions were so graceful and efficient that his hands and jaws—his whole body—seemed to flow almost languidly. He ate quite neatly, almost fastidiously. But as I watched his long white teeth tear into the meat, I realized that he was devouring it with great speed. And with great relish, too: there was blood on his lips and fire in his eyes. In the time it took me to finish my first fillet of fish, he downed many gobbets of meat, all the while giving sound to murmurs of contentment from deep in his throat.

Duke Rezu urged upon him other dishes and poured his beer with his own hand. From comments that he made and the silent trust of their eyes, I understood that Kane had done services for him in the past—what kinds of services I almost didn't want to know.

"So, you wounded Lord Salmelu and left him alive," Kane said to me as he looked up from his bloody work with his dagger. He smiled at me without humor. "You should never leave enemies behind you, eh?"

I smiled, too, with no humor, and said, "The world is full of enemies—we can't kill them all."

At this, Durva shook her head and said, "I wish you *had* killed Salmelu. And I wish your countrymen would kill the Ishkans, as many as possible. That would keep them from looking north, wouldn't it?"

"Perhaps," I said. "But there must be better ways to discourage the wandering of their eyes."

Duke Rezu sighed at this and then pointed at the hall's empty tables. "Even as we take this meal behind the safety of these walls, my eldest son, Ramashar, and my knights are riding the border of Adar. And we can only hope that the Kurmak clans won't mount an invasion this summer. Sad to say, we have enemies all around us. And so long as we do, the Ishkans will never be discouraged."

"Enemies we have no lack of," Durva agreed. Then she glared at her husband. "Yet you chose this time to let our son go off on a hopeless quest."

Duke Rezu took a gulp of beer as he regarded his outspoken wife. And then, to me and his other guests, he explained, "Count Dario and the Alonians passed through Anjo before coming to Mesh. Tanar, my secondborn, has answered the call to quest even as Sar Valashu and his friends have. He left for Tria ten days ago."

This news encouraged me, and I felt a warmth inside as if I had drunk a glass of brandy. At least I wouldn't be the only Valari knight in Tria.

The duke looked at Thaman, who had hardly spoken ten words all night. Then he asked, "And how is it in Surrapam? Have King Kiritan's emissaries reached your land, too?"

Thaman, dressed in stained woolens that had seen better days, ran his fingers through his thick red beard and said, "Yes, they have. But this is not the time for us to be making such quests."

"How so?" Duke Rezu asked him.

Thaman lifted back his head and drained the beer from his goblet. He grimaced, as if he found the taste of the thick black brew very bitter. Then he said, "The emissaries came too late. On the eighth of Viradar, at the Red Dragon's bidding, the armies of Hesperu marched against us. They've conquered our entire kingdom up to the line of the Maron River."

At these words, everyone at the table grew still and looked at Thaman. These were the worst tidings to come to the Morning Mountains since the story of Galda's fall.

"I don't know how long we'll be able to hold," Thaman continued. "The Hesperuks fight like demons. The Red Dragon's men have done things I cannot speak of. My wife, my children. . . ."

Thaman's voice died into the silence of the room. Although he kept his face as cold as stone and stared off dry-eyed, I felt tears burning to break out from my own eyes at the great sorrow he held inside.

Duke Rezu refilled Thaman's goblet; bitterness or no, he drank the black beer almost in one gulp. Then, to Duke Rezu, he said, "You Valari speak of having enemies all around you. But for the peoples of Ea, there is only one true enemy, and his name is Morjin."

At the sound of this name, I felt the arrow again bite into my side and the kirax burning in my blood. I turned to see Kane staring at Thaman with great intensity.

"The Red Dragon's armies," Thaman said, "will soon control the entire south of Ea except for the Crescent Mountains and the Red Desert.

At the mention of the Red Dragon, I felt Kane begin to burn with the heat of a hatred. I couldn't comprehend.

"My king," Thaman said, looking at Duke Rezu and then me, "King Kaiman, has sent me to your land because it's said that the Valari are the greatest warriors in Ea. He hopes that you'll attack Sakai from the east before the Red Dragon swallows up what is left of Surrapam and all the west."

I felt the sudden pressure of Maram's fat hand squeezing my leg beneath the table. Then he winked at me. This was the very plan that he had proposed in Lord Harsha's field just before Raldu had almost murdered me.

Duke Rezu clenched his fist as he said to Thaman, "Once we Valari fought our way across the Wendrush to attack the Red Dragon. He burned our warriors with firestones and crucified the survivors."

At this, Thaman drew his sword and rapped his wedding ring against it. The steel blade rang out like bell as he said, "Someday, and sooner than you think, the Red Dragon will do worse than that to all your people."

Duke Rezu shook his head sadly. "This is not the time for the Valari to fight the Red Dragon together."

"What would it take, then, to unite you?"

"I'm afraid," the Duke said, "that nothing less than an invasion of the tribes of the northern Sarni would unite Anjo. And to unite all the Valari kingdoms? Who can say? Only Aramesh was ever able to accomplish that, and we'll never see his like again."

Despite myself, a thrill of pride swelled inside me. Aramesh was the great-grandfather of my grandfathers, and his blood still ran through my veins.

At that moment, I felt something like a dagger cutting into my forehead. I turned to see Kane staring at me, and the sharpness of his gaze seemed to tear me open.

"It doesn't always take the united armies of the Valari to oppose Morjin," he growled out. He nodded at Yashku and asked him, "Do you know the Song of Kalkamesh and Telemesh?"

"Yes, I do," Yashku said.

"So—sing it for us, then."

Yashku looked at the duke to gain his assent. Duke Rezu slowly nodded his head and told him, "We could use a song to hearten us tonight. But let's fill our goblets before you begin—if I remember, it's a very long song."

We began passing the big, brown jugs full of beer as I stared at the candles throwing up their bright flames. The duke's grooms came out of the kitchen to remove the dishes, and the rattle of silverware and plates seemed very loud against the sudden quiet. Then Yashku, a wizened man with worn teeth, began pulling at his long white hair as he prepared to recite the many verses of this epic poem.

The first part of it, which he sang out in a strong, mellow voice, told of the great crusade to liberate the Lightstone from Morjin at the end of the Age of Law. Yashku sang of the alliance between Mesh, Ishka, Anjo, and Kaash, and how these four kingdoms had sent armies across the Gray Prairies to join the Alonian army in assaulting Morjin's fortress of Argattha. He recounted the heroics and evil deeds of the Battle of Tarshid. There, against the Law of the One, King Dumakan of Alonia had used a red gelstei against Morjin's armies. But Morjin used the Lightstone to turn the firestones against the alliance. Some of the firestones had exploded, destroying much of the Alonian army. Morjin had then turned his own firestones on the Valari armies, almost completely annihilating them. The survivors he had crucified along the road leading to Argattha. Then he and his priests had drunk the blood of their pierced hands in a great victory rite, which heralded the coming of the Age of the Dragon. Yashku's words cut like swords into my heart:

> A thousand men were bound in chains
> Along the road where terror reigns,
> And one by one were laid on wood
> Where once Valari knights had stood.
>
> In breaking of their flesh and bones,
> Priests took up hammers hard as stones,
> And iron spikes they drove through flesh,
> And thus they killed the men of Mesh.

Their life poured out and reddened mud;
The Dragon's priests—they caught the blood
In clutching hands and golden bowls,
Then made a toast and drank their souls.

Here Yashku paused to take a sip of beer. Then he began singing about the courage of two men some eighty years after this terrible event. The first of these was Sartan Odinan, Morjin's infamous priest who had burnt the city of Suma to the ground with a firestone. But, in soul-searing remorse for his great crime, he had finally found his humanity and turned against Morjin. And so he made an alliance with a mysterious man named Kalkamesh—who was said to be the very same Kalkamesh who had fought beside Aramesh at the Battle of Sarburn thousands of years before. Vowing to regain the Lightstone by stealth where great armies had failed to take it by force, they had entered Argattha in secret. After miles of dark passageways and many perilous encounters, they had finally found the Lightstone locked away in one of Morjin's deepest dungeons at the very center of the city. Kalkamesh had managed to open the dungeon's iron door, but just as he was about to take the Lightstone in his hands, they were discovered.

What happened then in Argattha three millennia before, as told by Yashku, brought a gleam to everyone's eyes. While Kalkamesh had turned to fight Morjin's guards with a rare and terrible fury, Sartan had made his escape with the Lightstone. He had fled Argattha with the golden cup into the snowy wastes of Sakai where he and it had vanished from history.

"Very good," Kane growled out as Yashku again paused to wet his throat. "And now for Kalkamesh and Telemesh."

The many verses of the poem, to this point, had been only a sort of preamble to the poet's true subject. This was the incredible valor of Kalkamesh and Telemesh. As we settled back in our chairs and sipped our beer, Yashku told of how Morjin had captured and tortured Kalkamesh. Believing that Kalkamesh must have known where Sartan intended to take the Lightstone, he had ordered Kalkamesh crucified to the mountain out of which was carved the city of Argattha. He had questioned him day and night, but Kalkamesh had only spat into his face. There, bolted naked to the side of the mountain, he endured every morning the rising of the blistering sun. And every morning as the sun's first rays touched Kalkamesh's writhing body, Morjin had arrived personally to cut open his belly with a stone knife and tear out his liver. He then used a green gelstei to aid this immortal man's already astonishing regenerative powers, and each night Kalkamesh's liver had grown back. It had been the beginning of the Long Torture that would last ten years.

But Morjin was never able to break Kalkamesh. The story of his suffering and courage spread into every land of Ea. High in the Morning Mountains, the young Telashu Elahad, who would one day ascend the Swan Throne to become King Telamesh, heard of Kalkamesh's torment and vowed to end his misery. He had set out on his quest and crossed the Wendrush all alone. And then, on a night of lightning and storm, he had climbed Mount Skartaru in the dark to free Kalkamesh from his terrible fate. Yashku's words now rang out like silver bells deep in my soul:

> *The lightning flashed, struck stone, burned white—*
> *The prince looked up into the light;*
> *Upon Skartaru nailed to stone*
> *He saw the warrior all alone.*
>
> *Through rain and hail he climbed the wall*
> *Still wet with bile, blood, and gall.*
> *Where dread and dark devour light,*
> *He climbed alone into the night.*
>
> *And there beneath the blackened sky,*
> *He met the warrior eye to eye,*
> *The ancient warrior, hard as stone—*
> *He raised his sword and cut through bone.*
>
> *The lightning flashed, struck stone, burned red,*
> *And still the warrior wasn't dead.*
> *Where eagles perch and princes walk,*
> *He left his hands upon the rock.*
>
> *And down and down they climbed as one*
> *To beat the rising of the sun.*
> *Through rain and ice and wind that wailed,*
> *With strength and nerve that never failed.*

They came into a healing place
Beneath Skartaru's bitter face.
And there, the One, the sacred spark,
Where love and light undo the dark.

The lightning flashed, struck stone, burned clear;
The prince beheld through rain and tear
The hands that held the golden bowl,
The warrior's hands again were whole.

"Very good," Kane growled out after Yashku had finished reciting the poem. "You sing well, minstrel. Very well indeed."

Kane sat sipping his dark beer, which he had asked Duke Rezu's grooms to serve him hot like coffee. He was a hard man to read and an even harder one to look at. There was a heart-piercing poignance beneath the brilliance of his black eyes, and he might have been considered too beautiful but for the harsh, vertical lines of a perpetual scowl that scarred his face. A scryer, it is said, with the aid of a crystal sphere can look into the future. There was something about him ageless and anguished as if he could look far into the past and recall all its hurts as his own. I wondered if he, like Thaman, had lost his family to the depredations of the Red Dragon. How else to explain the volcanic love and hate that threatened to erupt from him at every mention of Morjin's name?

"So," he said, "Kalkamesh and Telemesh—Sartan, too—defied Morjin. And shook the world, eh? I think it's shaking still."

After we thanked Yashku for singing us the poem, Maram turned to Master Juwain and asked, "What befell Kalkamesh after Argattha?"

"It's said that he perished in the War of the Stones."

Thaman turned to regard Kane. "And what of Sartan Odinan? He might have spirited away the Lightstone, but to where? The song doesn't say."

Master Juwain cleared his throat, then put in, "But there are other songs that tell of that."

We all turned to regard him with surprise. It was the first time on our journey from Silvassu that he had spoken of the Lightstone's fate.

"There is the Song of Madhar," he went. "And the Lay of

Alanu, recorded in the Book of Beasts. This tells that Sartan hid the Lightstone in a castle high in the Crescent Mountains and studied its secrets. It's said that he, too, gained immortality and used it to create an order of secret masters who have journeyed across Ea for thousands of years opposing the Lord of Lies. And there are other legends, almost too many to mention."

"Books, legends!" Thaman spat out. "It's not words we need now but men with strong arms and sharp swords."

Master Juwain's bushy eyebrows suddenly narrowed as he pointed his finger at my side. He said, "Strong arms and swords we have in abundance here in the Morning Mountains. But without the knowledge of how to use them, they're worse than useless."

"Use them against Morjin, then."

"The Lord of Lies," Master Juwain said, "will never be defeated by the force of arms alone."

"Then you think to defeat him by finding this golden cup that your legends tell of?"

"Does knowledge defeat ignorance? Does truth defeat a lie?"

"But what if the Lightstone has been destroyed?"

"The Lightstone," Master Juwain said, "was wrought of gold gelstei by the Star People themselves. It cannot be destroyed."

Thaman gave up arguing with Master Juwain and returned to his beer. He took a long drink of it and then asked, "What do you think, Sar Kane?"

"Just Kane, please," Kane said. "I'm no knight."

"Well," Thaman asked him, "will the Lightstone ever be found?"

Kane's eyes flashed just then, and I was reminded of lightning bolts lighting up the sky on a hot summer night. "The Lightstone *must* be found," he said, "Or else the Red Dragon will never be defeated."

"But defeated *how?*" Thaman asked, pressing him. "Through knowledge or through the sword?"

"Knowledge is dangerous," Kane said with a grim smile. "Swords are, too. Who has the wisdom to use either, eh?"

"There's still wisdom in the world," Master Juwain said.

"There's still knowledge aplenty for those who open their minds to it."

"*Dangerous,* I say," Kane repeated, looking at Master Juwain. "Long ago, Morjin opened *his* mind to the knowledge bestowed by the Lightstone, and he gained immortality, so it's said. Who on Ea has benefited from this precious knowledge?"

As Duke Rezu's grooms arrived to bring out fresh pitchers of beer, Master Juwain sipped from the cup of tea that he had ordered. He studied Kane, obviously considering how to respond to his arguments.

"The Lord of Lies is the Lord of Lies," he finally said. "If he's truly the same tyrant who crucified Kalkamesh so long ago, then he makes a mockery of the immortality that is the province of the Elijin and Galadin."

At this mention of the names of the angelic orders, Kane's eyes grew as empty as black space. I felt myself falling into them; it was like falling into a bottomless black pit.

"So," Kane finally said, staring at Master Juwain, "it's knowledge of the angels that you ultimately seek, isn't it?"

"Is that not what the One created us to seek?"

"How would *I* know about that, dammit?" Kane growled out.

His vehemence startled all of us, our host especially. Duke Rezu was used to battles, but not in his own hall. After lifting up his goblet and making a toast to the courage of Telemesh and Kalkamesh, he nodded at Kane. "I think we're all agreed, at least, that we must oppose Morjin, however we can."

"*That* I will agree to," Kane said. "I'll oppose Morjin even if it means seeking the Lightstone myself, and if I find it, letting the Brotherhood take from it what knowledge they can."

It was a noble thing for him to say, and his words warmed Master Juwain's heart. But not mine. I found that I could no more trust Kane than I could a tiger who purred softly one moment and then stared at me with hungry eyes the next.

"As it happens," he told Master Juwain, "I've business in Tria myself. If you'll let me, I'll accompany you there."

Master Juwain sat sipping his tea as he slowly nodded his head. I sensed that he relished the opportunity to reopen his arguments with Kane. He said, "I would be honored. But the decision is not mine to make alone. What do you think, Brother Maram?"

Maram, who was busy making eyes with Chaitra, tore his gaze away from her and looked at Master Juwain. He was more than a little drunk, and he said, "Eh? What do *I* think? I think that even four is too few to face the dangers ahead that I don't even want to think about. The more the merrier!"

So saying, he turned back to Duke Rezu's widowed niece and flashed her a winning smile.

Master Juwain smiled too, in exasperation at the task of taming Maram. Then he said to me, "What about you, Val?"

I turned toward Kane, who was staring at me with his unflinching gaze. It hurt to look at him too long, and so instead I glanced at the dagger that he still held in his large hands. And then I asked, "What is your business in Tria?"

"My business is *my* business," he growled at me. "And *your* business, it would seem, is in reaching Tria without being killed. I'd think that you'd welcome the opportunity to increase your chances."

Truly, I would, but did that mean welcoming this stranger to our company? I glanced at the sword sheathed at his side; it looked like a kalama. I thought that we might all welcome its sharp edges in fighting the unknown dangers that Maram was so afraid of. But a sword, as my grandfather used to say, can always cut two ways.

"We've come this far by ourselves," I said to Kane. "Perhaps it would be best if we continued on as we have."

"So," Kane said, "if Morjin's men hunt you down in the forests of Alonia, you think to make it easy for them, eh?"

How, I wondered, had Kane sensed that Morjin might be pursuing me? Had Maram, in his drunken murmurings, blurted out clues that Kane had pieced together? Had the story of Raldu nearly murdering me somehow reached this little duchy of Rajak ahead of us?

"There is no reason," I said, "for the Lord of Lies to be hunting us."

"You think not, eh? You're a prince of Mesh—King Shamesh's seventh son. Do you think Morjin needs any more reason than that to kill you?"

Kane spoke Morjin's name with so much hate that if words were steel, Morjin would now be dead. Watching Kane's neck tendons popping as he ground his teeth together, I couldn't doubt that he was Morjin's bitter enemy. But the enemy of my enemy, as my father liked to say, was not necessarily my friend.

"My apologies," I said to him, "but perhaps you can find other company."

"Other company, you say? The outlaws who've taken over the wild lands beyond Anjo? The bears that infest the deeper woods?"

At the mention of Maram's least favorite beast, my love-stricken friend broke off his flirtation with Chaitra and said, "Ah, Val, perhaps we *should* considering taking this Kane with us. To, ah, protect him from the bears."

Kane turned toward me to see what I would say. I felt his deep, driving determination, like an enormous boulder used to crushing the will out of others.

"No," I said, struggling to breathe. "The bears will leave him alone if he leaves them alone. Surely he has enough woodcraft to avoid them."

Both Master Juwain and Maram knew me well enough not to try to dissuade me. Master Juwain smiled at Kane and said, "I'm sorry, but perhaps we can meet in Tria and continue our discussion there."

Kane ignored Master Juwain and continued to stare at me. He snarled out, "Then you insist on making this journey alone, eh?"

"Yes," I told him, trying to hold his gaze.

"So be it, then," he said with all the finality of a king pronouncing a sentence of death.

After that, Duke Rezu tried to return our conversation to the legends of the Lightstone. But the mood was broken. As it had grown very late, Yashku excused himself and went off to bed, followed in short order by old Helenya, who complained of her aching joints and sleeplessness. Maram, of course, would have stayed there all night flirting with Chaitra if she hadn't suddenly winked at him and announced her need to go finish some undone knitting. As for me, the wound in my side pained me almost as much as the anguish of Kane's wounded soul puzzled me. Who was this man, I wondered, whose eyes looked as if they were forged in some hellish furnace out of black iron fallen down from the stars? From where had he come? To where did he really intend to go? As we all pushed back our chairs and stood up from the table, I thought that I would never know the answers to these questions.

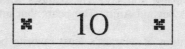

✱ 10 ✱

As THE MORNING sun brightened the bluish peaks of the Aakash range to the east of the castle, we gathered in the courtyard to make our goodbyes to Duke Rezu. It was cool and clear, a good day for travel. The duke warned us to avoid the barony of Vishal and other parts of the broken kingdom of Anjo. After that we clasped hands, and I thanked him again for his hospitality.

We rode down from the castle to the sound of the wind blowing across the heath. It was a high, fair country that the duke called home, with mountains lining our way both on the east and west. There were only a few trees scattered across the green hills of Rajak's central valley, and our riding was easy, as the duke had promised. Most of the land near his castle was given over to pasture for the many flocks of sheep basking in the early sun; their thick winter wool was as white and puffy as the clouds floating along the blue sky. But there were farms, too. Patches of emerald green, marked off by lines of stone walls or hedgerows, covered the earth before us like a vast quilt knit of barley and oats and other crops that the duke's people grew. Here and there, a few fields lay fallow, casting up colors of umber and gold.

Despite the pain in my side, it was good to be in the saddle again. It was good to smell grass and earth and the thick horse scent of Altaru's surging body. With neither the Ishkans nor any enemy we knew pursuing us, we set a slow pace toward the lands that awaited us farther to the north.

Beautiful country or no, Maram could barely keep his eyes open to behold it. All that morning, he slumped in his saddle, yawning and sighing. Finally Master Juwain took him to task for once again breaking his vows.

"I heard you get up last night," Master Juwain told him. "Did you have trouble sleeping?"

"Yes, yes, I did," Maram said as he rode beside me. "I wanted to take a walk around the walls and look at the stars."

"I see," Master Juwain said, riding beside him. "*Shooting* stars, they were, no doubt. The light of the heavenly bodies."

"Ah, it's a wonderful world, isn't it?"

"Wonderful, yes," Master Juwain admitted to him. "But you should be careful of these midnight walks of yours. One night you might find yourself plunging off the parapets."

Maram smiled at this, and so did I. Then he said, "I've never been afraid of heights. To fall in love with a woman is the sweetest of deaths."

"As you've fallen for Chaitra?"

"*Have* I fallen for Chaitra?" Maram asked as he pulled at his thick brown beard.

"But she's a widow," Master Juwain said. "And a newly made one at that. Didn't the duke say that her husband had been killed last month in a skirmish with Adar?"

"Yes, sir, he did say that."

"Don't you think it's cruel, then, to take walks in the starlight with a bereaved woman and then leave her alone the next day?"

"Cruel? Cruel, you say?" Maram was wide awake now, and he seemed genuinely aggrieved. "The wind off Arakel in Viradar is cruel. Cats are cruel to mice, and bears live only to make me suffer. But a man's love for a woman, if it be true, can never be cruel."

"No," Master Juwain agreed, "*love* can't be."

Maram rode on a few paces, all the while muttering that he was always misunderstood. And then he said, "Please, sir, listen to me a moment. I would never think to dispute with you the declensions of the pronouns in Ardik or the declinations of the constellations in Soldru. Or almost anything else. But about women—ah, women. Widows, especially. There's only one way to truly console a widow. The Brotherhood teaches us to honor our vows but also that compassion is more sacred yet. Well, to make a woman sing where previously she has been weeping is the soul of compassion. When I close my eyes and smell the perfume that clings to my lips, I can hear Chaitra singing still."

Maram's worldly ways obviously vexed Master Juwain. I thought that he might upbraid him in front of me or perhaps lay upon him some punishment. But instead he gave up on instilling in Maram the Brotherhood's virtues—at least for the moment. He sighed as he turned to me and said, "You young people these days do as you will, don't you?"

"Are you speaking of Kane?" I asked him.

"I'm afraid I am," he said. "Why did you refuse his company?"

I looked out at a nearby hill where a young shepherd stood guarding his sheep against marauding wolves; I thought a long time before giving him a truthful answer to his question.

"There's something about Kane," I said. "His face, his eyes—the way he moves the knife in his hands. He . . . burns. Raldu's accomplice put a bit of kirax in my blood, and *that* still burns like fire. But in Kane, there's more than a little bit of hell. He hates so utterly. It's as if he loves hating more then he could ever love a friend. How could anyone trust a man like that?"

Master Juwain rode next to me, thinking about what I had said. Then he sighed and rubbed the back of his head, which gleamed like a large brown nut in the bright sunlight. He said, "You know that Kane has Duke Rezu's trust."

"Yes, the duke has need of men with quick swords," I said. For a moment I listened to the thump of our horses' hooves against the stony soil. "It's strange, isn't it, that this Kane showed up at the Duke's castle at the same time we escaped from the bog?"

"Perhaps it's just a coincidence," Master Juwain said.

"You taught me not to believe in coincidences, sir."

"What do you believe about Kane, then?"

"He hates the Lord of Lies, that much seems certain," I said. "But *why* does he hate him so much?"

"It's only natural to hate that which is pure hate itself."

"Perhaps," I said. "But what if it's more than that?"

"What, then?"

"There's something about Kane," I said again. "What if it was he who shot at me in the forest? And then somehow followed me into Anjo?"

"You think that it was *Kane* who tried to assassinate you?" Master Juwain asked. He seemed astonished. "I thought we had established that it was the Lord of Lies who wished you dead. As you've observed, Kane hates him. Why should he then serve him?"

"That is what's puzzling me, sir. Perhaps the Lord of Lies has made a ghul of him. Or perhaps he has captured Kane's family and threatens them with death or worse."

"Now *that* is a dark thought," Master Juwain said. "I'm afraid there's something dark about you, Valashu Elahad, to be thinking such thoughts on such a beautiful morning."

I was afraid of the same thing, and I lifted up my face to let the bright sun drive away the coldness gnawing at my insides.

"Well," Master Juwain continued, "it's said that ghuls sometimes retain enough of their souls to hate their master. As for your other hypothesis, who knows? The Lord of Lies is capable of doing as you said—and much worse."

Master Juwain stopped to let his horse eat some grass. He began pulling at the flesh beneath his chin. Then he said, "But I don't think either hypothesis accounts for what I've seen of our mysterious Kane."

"What do you think then, sir?"

He sat there on his horse on the middle of a gently rising hill, all the while regarding me with his large gray eyes. And then he asked, "What do you know of the different Brotherhoods, Val?"

"Only what you taught me, sir."

And that, I thought, was not very much. I knew that early in the Age of Law, in a time of rebirth known as the Great Awakening, the Brotherhood had come out from behind the Morning Mountains to open schools across all of Ea. The different schools took on different names according to the colors of the gelstei that were to become the soul of that brilliant civilization; each school specialized in pursuing knowledge that related to its particular stone, and eventually became its own Brotherhood. Thus the Blue Brotherhood concerned itself with communications of all sorts, especially languages and dreams, while the Red Brotherhood sought understanding of the secret fire that blazed inside rocks and earth and all things. And so on. For two thousand years, the Brotherhoods had led civilization's rise into a golden age. And then, with the release of Morjin from his prison on the Isle of Damoom and his stealing of the Lightstone, had come the fall.

During the Age of the Dragon, the various Brotherhoods had

dwindled or were destroyed by Morjin's assassin-priests. Now, only the original Brotherhood remained to spread the light of truth throughout Ea.

"All the Brotherhoods were destroyed," I said to Master Juwain. "All except one."

"Hmmm, were they indeed?" Master Juwain said. "What do you know of the Black Brotherhood?"

"Only that they were once strongest in Sakai. And that when the Kallimun priests established their fortress in Argattha, they hunted down the Brothers and razed every one of their schools to the ground. The Black Brotherhood was completely destroyed early in the Age of the Dragon."

Maram, taking an interest in our conversation, nudged his horse forward to hear better what we were saying.

Master Juwain turned about in his saddle, left and right, scanning the empty hills around us. And then, in a much lowered voice, he said, "No, the Black Brotherhood was never destroyed. The Kallimun only drove them out of Sakai into Alonia."

He went on to tell us that the Black Brotherhood, seeking to understand the fire-negating properties of the black gelstei and the source of all darkness, had always been different from the other Brotherhoods. Early in the Age of Law, when the Brotherhoods had renounced war, the Black Brothers had rebelled against the new rule of nonviolence. Believing that there would always be darkness in the world, they began taking up knives and other weapons to fight against it. And they fought quite fiercely, for thousands of years. As the other Brotherhoods— the Blue and the Red, the Gold and the Green—closed their schools all through the Age of the Dragon, the Black Brotherhood opened schools in secret in almost every land.

When Master Juwain had finished, Maram sat very erect on his horse and said, "I've never heard anyone speak of that."

"We *don't* speak of it," Master Juwain said. "Not to novices. And not usually to any Brother before he has attained his mastership."

At this, Maram, who was no more likely to attain a mastership than I was to become a king, slowly nodded his head, as if proud to be taken into Master Juwain's confidence. And then he said, "I didn't know there were any black gelstei left in the world for *anyone* to study."

"There may not be," Master Juwain said. "But the Black Brothers gave up the pursuit of such knowledge long ago. Now they live to hunt the Kallimun priests who once hunted them. And ultimately, to slay the Red Dragon."

Here he turned toward me and said, "And that brings us back to Kane. I suspect that he might be of the Black Brotherhood. From what I've read about the Black Brothers, he has their look. Certainly he has their hate."

I stared off at the soft green hills and the purplish Aakash mountains just beyond them. The sun poured down its warmth upon the earth, and a sweet wind rippled the acres of grass. On such a lovely day, it seemed strange to speak of dark things such as the Black Brotherhood. Almost as strange as Kane himself.

"And so you asked Kane to ride with us," I said to Master Juwain. "Why, sir? Because you thought he might scare away any of the Red Dragon's men who might be hunting us? Or because you want to know more about the Black Brotherhood?"

Master Juwain laughed softly as he looked at me with his deep eyes. Then he said, "You know me well, Val. I *do* seek knowledge, sometimes even in dark places. It is my curse."

I looked up at the sun then as I thought about my own curse; I thought about the way that Kane's grief had nearly sucked me down into the dark whirlpool of his soul. Would I, I wondered, ever find that which would heal me of my terrible gift of experiencing the sufferings of others?

"If Kane *is* of the Black Brotherhood," I finally said to Master Juwain, "why would he press to accompany us?"

But Master Juwain, who knew so much about so many things, only looked at me in silence and slowly shook his head.

For the rest of the morning, as we journeyed north along the Aakash range, we talked about the Brotherhoods' role in the study and fabrication of the seven greater gelstei stones. The fine day opened into the long hours of the afternoon even as the valley through which we rode opened toward the plains of Anjo. The hills about us gradually lessened in elevation and began to flatten out. Late in the day, with the sun arching down toward the jagged Shoshan mountains to the west, we crossed into the domain of Daksh, ruled by Duke Gorador. As Duke Rezu had advised us, we found his ally's castle some five miles farther up the valley.

Duke Gorador proved to be a heavy man with a long face like a horse and long lower lip, at which he pulled with his steely fingers as we told him our story. He seemed glad to hear that I had made enemies of Lord Salmelu and the Ishkans; apparently he regarded the enemy of his enemy as his friend, for he immediately offered us his hospitality, and ordered that we be feted and well cared for that night.

We slept well to the music of the wolves howling in the hills. Early the next morning, we rode into the soft, swelling heath around the duke's castle. The sky was as blue as cobalt glass; the soft wind smelled of dandelions and other wildflowers that grew on the grassy slopes. In the east, the sun burned with a golden fire even as I burned with hope.

It was a fine day for traveling, I thought, perhaps our finest yet. As the noon hour approached, the mountains to our east grew lower and lower like great granite steps leading down into the plains of Anjo. Their forested slopes gradually gave way to grassier terrain. At the border of Daksh, we urged our horses up the last of these hills so that we might look out and take our bearings. To the west, the Shoshan range still rose like a vast wall of rock and ice, but I knew that their jagged peaks concealed a great gap some seventy-five miles to the northwest. Forty miles due north, the raging Santosh river flowed down from these mountains into the distant blue haze of the Alonian Sea. The Santosh formed the border between Alonia and Anjo's wild lands that both Duke Rezu and Duke Gorador had warned us against. From our vantage above them, they didn't seem so wild. Long stretches of swaying grass and shrubs were cut by stands of trees in an irregular patchwork of vegetation. The ground undulated with soft swells of earth, as of the contours of a snake, but nowhere did it appear hilly or difficult to cross.

Maram, who had no feel for this pretty country, sat on top of his horse composing aloud a poem to his most recent beloved, I heard him say, "Val, which line do you think Chaitra would like better? 'Her eyes are pools of sacred fire?' Or 'Her eyes are windows to the stars?' Val, are you listening to me? What's wrong?"

I was barely listening to him. A sudden coldness struck into me as of something serpentine wrapping itself around my spine. It seemed to contract rhythmically, grinding my backbones together even as it ate its way into my skull. Despite the dreadful chill I felt spreading through my limbs, I began to sweat. My belly tightened with a growing sickness.

Master Juwain nudged his horse over to me and laid his hand on my head to see if my fever had returned. He asked, "Are you ill, Val?"

"No, it's not that." I saw great concern on both my friends' faces. And I was loath to alarm either of them, especially Maram. But they had to know, so as gently as I could, I told them, "Someone is following me."

At this news, Maram fairly leaped in his saddle and began scanning the world in every direction. And so, more calmly, did Master Juwain. But the only moving things they detected were a few hawks in the sky and a rabbit startled out of the grass by Maram's wheeling his horse back and forth across the top of the hill.

"Are you sure we're being followed?" Master Juwain asked me.

"Yes," I said.

"Do you think it's Kane?" Maram asked. He turned south to peer more closely through the valley leading back to Duke Rezu's castle. "Could it be the Ishkans? No, no—they wouldn't dare ride this far into Anjo. Would they?"

But I had no answers for him, nor for myself. All I could do was to smile bravely so that the flames of Maram's disquiet didn't spread into a raging panic.

Master Juwain, who had an intimation of my gift, nodded his head as if he trusted what I had told him. He asked, "What should we do, Val?"

I pointed down at the wild lands before us. "If it *is* Kane who is after us, then he knows that Duke Rezu advised us to avoid this direction. If it's someone else, then likely they'll try to intercept us somewhere along the Nar Road where it crosses through Yarvanu."

"Of course they would," Maram muttered. "That's the only way over the Santosh into Alonia."

"Perhaps not the only way," I said.

"What do you mean?" Maram asked in alarm.

Again I pointed down into the wild country that began at the base of our hill. "We could journey straight for the Santosh. And then into Alonia. If we keep northwest toward the Shoshan range and then strike out north again, we should intercept the Nar road in the gap, far from any of our pursuers."

Maram looked at me as if I had suggested crossing the Alonian Sea on a log. Then he called out, "But what of the robbers and outlaws we were warned against? And how will we cross the Santosh if there's no bridge? And if by some miracle we *do* cross it without drowning, how will we find our way through Alonia? I've heard there's nothing there but trackless forest."

Some men are born to fear the familiar dangers that they see before their eyes; some take their greatest terror in the unknown. Maram was cursed with a sensibility that found threat everywhere in the world, from a boulder poised on the side of a hill to his most wild imaginings. I knew that nothing I could say would assuage the dread rising inside him like a flood. Dangers lay before us in every direction. All we could do was to choose one way or another to go.

Even so, I grasped his hand in mine to reassure him. It was one of the times in my life that I wished my gift worked in reverse, so that some of my great hope for the future might pass into him. I fancied that some of it did.

We held council on top of the barren hill. We all agreed that when facing an opponent, it was best to do the unexpected. And so in the end we decided on the course that I had suggested.

After packing up our food, we rode down into the wild lands, communicating a new haste to our horses. We moved at a bone-jolting trot over fields overgrown with shrubs and weeds; but upon entering the various woods that lay upon the our line of travel, we had to pick our way more slowly. The country through which we rode had once been rich farmland, some of the richest in the Morning Mountains. But now all that remained of civilization were the ruins of low stone walls or an occasional house, rotting or fallen in upon itself. We saw no other sign of human beings all that long afternoon. When evening came, we made camp in a copse of stout oaks. We risked no fire that night. We ate a cold meal of cheese and bread and then agreed to take our sleep in turns so that one of us might always remain awake to listen for our pursuers. I took the first watch, followed by Maram. When it came time for me to rest, I fell asleep to the sound of wolves howling far out on the plain before us.

I was awakened just before dawn by a dreadful sensation that one of these wolves was licking my throat. I sprang up from the dark, damp earth with my sword in my hand; I believe I lunged at the gray shapes of beasts lurking in the shadows of the trees. And then, as I came truly awake and my eyes cleared, I saw nothing more threatening than a few rotting logs among the towering oaks.

"Are you all right?" Master Juwain whispered. "Was it a dream?"

"Yes, a dream," I told him. "But perhaps it's time we were off."

We roused Maram then and quickly broke camp. Upon emerging from the woods, we rode straight toward the north star over a dark and silent land. But soon the sun reddened the sky in the east and drove away the darkness. With every yard of dew-dampened ground that we covered, it seemed that the world grew a little brighter. I took courage from this golden light. By the time full day came, I could no longer feel the serpent writhing along my spine.

After hours of hard riding, urged on by clouds of biting black flies, we found a track through the broad swath of woods along the Santosh. We heard the river's great surge of water through the trees before we could see it: the oaks and willows grew like a curtain right down to the bank. Then the track straightened and rose toward the causeway, which led to an old bridge spanning the river. At the foot of the rickety structure, we paused to look down into the river's raging brown waters.

"Excellent!" Maram cried out, looking at the bridge, "we're saved!"

Crossing the bridge proved to be an exercise in faith. We all dismounted and led our horses across the bridge one by one, the better to distribute our weight across its rotten planks. Even so, Altaru's hoof broke through one of them with a sickening crunch, and it was all I could do to extricate it without my startled horse breaking his leg. Master Juwain and Maram, with their lighter sorrels and the packhorses, encountered no problems.

As darkness was now coming on, we camped there on the low ground near the river. We ate a joyless dinner in the damp, all the while listening for the sound of hooves pounding against the drumlike boards of the bridge. It was a cold, uncomfortable night. Sleep brought only torment. The season's first mosquitoes whined in my ear, bit, drew blood. After a time, I gave up slapping them and in exhaustion slipped down into the land of dreams. But there the whining grew only louder and swelled to a dreadful whimpering as of a prelude to a scream. Toward dawn I finally came screaming out of my sleep. Or so I thought. When my mind cleared, I realized that it was not I but Maram who was screaming: it turned out that a harmless garter snake had slithered across his sleeping fur and sent him hopping up from it on all fours like a badly frightened frog.

We were very glad to begin the day's journey. And very glad at last to have planted our feet on Alonian soil, if only the most southern and eastern part of it. It was a land that human beings had deserted many years ago. If any habitation had ever existed on this side of the river, the forest had long since swallowed it up. The oaks and the moss-covered elms through which we passed were more densely clustered than those of Mesh. The undergrowth of bracken and ferns was a thick, green blanket almost smothering the forest floor. It would have been difficult to force our way through it if the forest had proved as trackless as Maram had feared. But the old road leading from the bridge turned into a track leading northwest through the trees. It seemed that no one except a few wandering animals had used it for a thousand years.

All that day we kept to the track and to others we found deeper in the woods. As I had intended, we traveled on a fairly straight line toward the gap in the Shoshan range through which the Nar Road passed. We saw no sign of man, and I began to hope that our cut across the wild lands of Anjo had confounded whoever was hunting us. We slept that night at a higher elevation, where we saw neither mosquitoes nor snakes.

Our next day's journey took us across several rills and streams flowing down from the mountains toward the Santosh. Toward evening we encountered a bear feasting on newberries; we left him alone, and he left us alone. On our third day from the bridge, we entered the gap in the Morning Mountains, where the land became hilly again. Here the trees lifted up their branches toward the sun and breathed their great, green breaths that sweetened the air.

"Where *are* we?" Maram grumbled two days later as we made our way west beneath the great crowns of the trees high above us. Through their leaves the sun shined as if through thousands of green windows. "Are you sure we're not lost?"

"Yes," I told him for the hundredth time. "As sure as the sun itself."

"I hope you're right. You were sure we wouldn't get lost in the bog, either."

As Altaru trod over earth nearly overgrown with ferns, I looked off at some lilies growing by the side of the track. "We're only a few miles beyond the gap. We should find the Nar Road a few miles north of here."

"We *should* find it," Maram agreed. "But what if we don't?"

"And what if the sun doesn't rise tomorrow?" I countered. "You can't worry about everything, you know."

"Can I not? Can I not? My friend, I was born to worry."

Soon our track cut across a rocky shelf on the side of the hill. It was one of the few places we had found where trees didn't obstruct our view and we could look out at the land we were crossing. It was a rough, beautiful country we saw, with green-shrouded hills to the north and west. A soft mist, like long gray fingers, had settled down into the folds between them.

"I don't see the road," Maram said as he stood staring out to the north. "If it's only a few miles from here, shouldn't we see it?"

"Look," I said, pointing at a strangely formed hill near us. After rising at a gentle grade a few hundred feet, it seemed to drop off abruptly as if cut with cliffs on its north face. At its top, it was barren of trees and all other vegetation except a few stunted grasses. "If we climb it, we should be able to see the road from there."

I led us down into a mist-filled vale that gave out onto the barren hill to our north. After riding along a little stream for perhaps half a mile, the skin at the back of my neck began to tingle and burn. I had a sickening sense of being hunted, by whom or what I did not know.

And then, as suddenly as thunder breaking through a storm, the blare of battle horns split the air. *Ta-roo, ta-roo, ta-roo*—the same two notes kept braying as if someone was blowing a trumpet high on the hill before us. I tightened my grip around Altaru's reins and began urging him toward the hill; it was as if the horn—or something else—were calling me to battle.

"Wait, Val!" Maram called after me. "What are you doing?"

"Going to see what's happening," I said simply.

"I hate to know what's happening," he said. He pointed behind us in the opposite direction. "Shouldn't we flee while we still have the chance?"

I listened for a moment to the din shaking the woods, and then to a deeper sound inside me. I said, "But what if brigands live in these hills? What if they have trapped some traveller here?"

"What if they trap *us* there? Come, please, while there's still time!"

"No," I told him, "I have to see."

So saying, I pressed Altaru forward. Maram followed me reluctantly, and Master Juwain followed him trailing the packhorses. We rode along the dale and then through the woods leading up the side of the hill. As if someone had scoured the hill with fire, the trees suddenly ended in a line that curved around the hill's base. There we halted in their shelter to look out and see who was blowing the horn.

"Oh, no!" Maram croaked out.

A hundred yards from us, ten men were advancing up the hill. They were squat and pale-skinned, nearly naked, with only the rudest covering of animal skins for clothing. They bore long oval shields, most of which had arrows sticking out of them. In their hands they clutched an irregular assortment of weapons: axes and maces and a few short, broad-bladed swords. Their leader—a thickset and hairy man with daubs of red paint marking his face—paused once to blow a large blood-spattered horn that looked as if it had been torn from the head of some animal. And then, pointing his sword up the hill, he began advancing again toward his quarry.

This was a single warrior who stood staring down at the men from the top of the hill. I immediately noted the long blond hair that spilled from beneath the warrior's conical and pointed helmet; I couldn't help staring at the warrior's double-curved bow and the studded leather armor, for these were the accouterments of the Sarni, which tribe I couldn't tell. A ring of dead men lay in the stunted grass farther down the hill, fifty yards from the warrior. Arrows stuck out of them, too. In all Ea, there were no archers like the Sarni and no bows that pulled so powerfully as theirs. But this warrior, I thought, would never pull a bow again, because his quiver was empty and he had no more arrows to shoot. All he could do was to stand near his downed horse and wait for the hill-men to advance through the ring of their fallen countrymen and begin the butchery they so obviously intended.

"All right," Maram murmured at me from behind his tree, "you've seen what you came to see. Now let's get out of here!"

As quickly as I could, I nudged Altaru over to my packhorse where I untied the great helmet slung over his side. I untied as well the shield that my father had given me and thrust my arm through it. My side still hurt so badly that I could barely hold it. But I scarcely noticed this pain because I had worse wounds to bear.

"What are you doing?" Maram snapped at me. "This isn't our business. That's a Sarni warrior, isn't it? A *Sarni,* Val!"

Master Juwain agreed with him that the course of action on which I was setting out perhaps wasn't the wisest. But since the Brotherhood teaches showing compassion to the unfortunates of the world, neither did he suggest that we should flee. He just stood there in the trees weighing different stratagems and wondering how the three of us—and one Sarni warrior—could possibly prevail against ten fierce and vengeful hill-men.

I slipped the winged helmet over my head. I took up my lance and couched it beneath my good arm. How could I explain why I did this? I could hardly explain it to myself. After many miles of being hunted, I couldn't bear the sight of this warrior being hunted and bravely preparing to die. For Master Juwain, compassion was a noble principle to be honored wherever possible; for me it was a hot, white pain piercing my heart. For some reason I didn't understand, I found myself opening to this doomed warrior. A proud Sarni he might be, but something inside him was calling for help, even as a child might call, and hoping that it might miraculously come.

"That man," I told Maram, "could have been Sar Tanar. He could be my brother—he could be you."

And with that, I touched my heels to Altaru's sides and rode out of the trees. I pressed my horse to a gallop; it was a measure of his immense strength that he quickly achieved this gait, driving his hooves into the ground that sloped upward before us. I felt the great muscles of his rump bunching and pushing us into the air. He wheezed and snorted, and I felt his lust for battle. The hill-men had now drawn closer to the warrior, who stood waiting for them with nothing more than a saber and a little leather shield. His ten executioners, with their painted faces and bodies, advanced as a single mass, clumped foolishly close together. Their leader blew his bloody horn again and again to give them courage; they struck their weapons against their wooden shields as they screamed out obscenities and threatened fiendish tortures. This din must have drowned out the sound of Altaru pounding toward them, for they didn't see me until the last moment. But the warrior, looking downhill, did. It must have mystified him why a Valari knight would ride to help him. But he left all such wonderings for a later moment. He let out a high-pitched whoop and charged the hill-men even as I lowered my lance and prepared to crash into them.

Just then, however, one of the hill-men turned toward me and let out a cry of dismay. This alerted the others, who froze wide-eyed in astonishment. I might easily have pushed the lance's point through the first man's neck. Altaru's snorting anger, and my own, drove me to do so; the nearness of death touched me with a terrible exhilaration. But then I remembered my vow never to kill anyone again. And so I raised the lance, and as we swept past the man, I used its steel-shod butt to strike him along the side of his head. He fell stunned to the side of the hill. One of his friends tried to unhorse me with a blow of his mace, but I caught it with my father's shield. Then the infuriated Altaru struck out with his hoof and broke through the hill-man's shield and shoulder with a sickening crunch. He screamed in agony, even as I bit my lip in effort not to scream, too.

Through the heat of the battle, I was somehow aware of the Sarni warrior closing with the hill-men's leader and opening his throat with a lightning slash of his saber. I immediately began coughing at the bubbling of blood I felt in my own throat. Then one of the hill-men swung his axe at my back, and only my Godhran-forged armor kept it from chopping through my spine. I whirled about in my saddle and struck him in the face with my shield. He stumbled to one knee, and I hesitated for an endless moment as I trembled to spear him with my lance.

And in that moment, the Sarni warrior cut through to him and ruthlessly finished him as well. A mail bevor fastened to the warrior's helm hid most of his face, but I could see his blue eyes flashing like diamonds even as his saber flashed out and struck off the man's head. The Sarni's prowess of arms and rare fury—and, I supposed, my own wild charge—had badly dispirited the hill-men. When an arrow came whining suddenly out of the trees below us and buried itself in the ground near one of the hill-men to my right, he pointed downhill at Maram standing by a tree with my hunting bow and cried out, "They'll kill us all—run for your lives!"

In the panic that followed, the Sarni warrior managed to kill one more of the hill-men before his comrades turned their backs to us and fled down the hill toward the east, where a slight rise in the ground provided some cover against Maram's line of fire. I believe that the warrior might have pursued them to slay a few more if I hadn't slumped off my horse just then.

"No, please—no more killing," I said as I held my hand palm outward and shook my head. I stood by Altaru and grasped the pommel of his saddle to keep from falling.

"Who are you, Valari?" the warrior called to me.

I looked down the hill where the seven surviving men had disappeared into the woods. I looked at Maram and Master Juwain now making their way up the hill toward us. Except for the heavy breath steaming out of Altaru's huge nostrils and my own labored breathing, the world had grown suddenly quiet.

"My name is Valashu Elahad," I gasped out. I felt weak and disconnected from my body, as if my head had been cut off like the hill-man's and sent spinning into space. I pulled off my helm then, the better to feel the wind against me. "And who are you?"

The warrior hesitated a moment as I pressed my hand to my side. I felt the blood soaking through my armor. The battle had reopened the wound there, as well as the deeper wound that would never be healed.

"My name is Atara," the warrior said, removing his helm as well. "Atara Manslayer of the Kurmak. Thank you for saving my life."

I gasped again, but not in pain. I stared at the long golden hair flowing down from Atara's head and the soft lines of Atara's golden face. It was now quite clear that Atara was a woman—the most beautiful woman I had ever seen. And though our enemies were either dead or dispersed, something inside her still called to me.

"Atara," I said as if her name were an invocation to the angels who walked the stars, "you're welcome."

I suddenly knew that there was much more than a bond of blood between us. I looked into her eyes then, and it was like falling—not into the nothingness where she had sent the hill-men, but into the sacred fire of two brilliant blue stars.

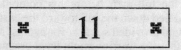

FOR WHAT SEEMED forever, Atara held this magical connection of our eyes. Then, with what seemed a great effort of will, she looked away and smiled in embarrassment as if she had seen too much of me—or I of her.

She said, "Please excuse me, there's work to be done."

She walked back and forth across the hill, scanning the tree line for any sign that the hill-men might attack again. Then she quickly went about the bloodstained slope cutting her arrows out the bodies of the fallen men. As she went from man to man, she counted out loud, beginning with the number five. At first, I thought her accounting had something to do with the number of arrows she recovered. But when she reached the body of the hill-men's leader, whom no arrow had struck, she said, "Fourteen." And the headless body of the man she had beheaded was fifteen, whatever that might mean.

And then, as Maram and Master Juwain drew closer, I reflected upon Atara's strange second name: Manslayer. I remembered Ravar once telling of a group of woman warriors of the Sarni called the Manslayer Society. It was said that a few rare women from each tribe practiced at arms and gave up marriage in order to join the fearsome Manslayers. Membership in their society was almost always for life, for the only way that a Manslayer could be released from her vows was to slay a hundred of her enemies. Atara, in having slain four before she reached this dreadful hill, had already accounted for more men than many Valari knights. And in sending on twelve more, with arrow and sword, she had accomplished a great if terrible feat.

I stood watching her in awe as she cleaned the blood from her arrows and dropped them down into the quiver slung over her back. I thought that she couldn't be much older than I. She was a tall women and big-boned, like most of her people. And she had their barbaric look. Her leather armor—all black and hardened and studded with steel—covered only her torso. A more supple pair of leather trousers provided protection for her legs. Her long, lithe arms were naked and burnt brown by the sun. Golden armlets encircled the upper parts of them. A golden torque, inlaid with lapis, encircled her neck. Her hair was like beaten gold, and the ends of it were wrapped with strings of tiny lapis beads. But it was her eyes that kept capturing my gaze; I had never hoped to see eyes like hers in all the world. Like sapphires they were, like blue diamonds or the brightest of lapis. They sparkled with a rare spirit, and I thought they were more precious than any gem.

Just then, Maram and Master Juwain rode up to us, and Maram said, "It really *is* a woman!"

"A woman, yes." I was instantly jealous of the interest he showed her. I said to him, "May I present Atara Manslayer of the Kurmak tribe?"

I gave Master Juwain's and Maram's names, and Atara greeted them politely. Then she pointed to the top of the hill where her horse lay moaning, and she said, "Excuse me, but I have one more thing to attend to."

She walked straight up to her horse, a young steppe pony whose belly had been cut open. Much of his insides had spilled out of him and lay steaming on the grass. She sat down beside him; gently, she lifted his head onto her lap. She began stroking the side of it as she sang out a sad little song and looked into his dark eye. She stroked his long neck and then—even as I turned Altaru facing downhill—she drew her saber across his throat almost more quickly than I could believe.

For a while Atara sat there on the reddening grass as she stared up at the sky. Her struggle between pride of decorum and grief touched me keenly. And then, at last, she buried her face in her horse's fur and began weeping softly. I blinked as I fought to keep from weeping as well.

After a while, she stood up and came over to us. Her hands and trousers were as bloody as a butcher's. She pointed at the bodies of the hill-men and said, "They accosted me in the woods as I was climbing the hill. They demanded that I pay a toll for crossing their country. *Their* country, hmmph. I told them all this land belonged to King Kiritan, not them."

"What else could you do?" Maram said. "Who has gold for tolls?"

Here Atara moved back to her horse, where she freed a purse from his saddlebag. As she weighed it in her hand, it jangled with coins, and she said, "It's not gold I lack—only a willingness to enrich robbers."

"But they might have killed you!" Maram said.

"Better death than the dishonor of doing business with such men."

Maram stared at her as if this principle were utterly alien to him.

"But why were you even in the hill-men's country?" I asked her. I thought it more than strange that we should meet in the middle of this wilderness. "And why were you climbing this hill?"

Atara pointed to the hill's ragged, rocky crest above us and said, "I thought I might be able to see the Nar Road from here."

We looked at each other in immediate understanding. I admitted that I needed to be in Tria on the seventh day of Soldru to answer King Kiritan's call to find the Lightstone. As did Atara. She told us of her journey then. She said that when word of the great quest had reached the Kurmak tribe, she had bade her people farewell and had ridden north along the western side of the Shoshan Mountains. Only by keeping close to these great peaks had she been able to bypass the Long Wall, which ran for four hundred miles across the prairies from the Shoshan to the Blue Mountains. Once, of course, in the time of Tulumar Elek, the united Sarni tribes had found a way to breach the immense fortifications of the wall: working at night, they had spread across its stone a mysterious substance called relb. Relb, a forerunner of the red gelstei, looked much like paint or fresh blood; at the touch of the sun's rays it burst into flame, melting stone to lava—thus was the Long Wall broken long ago. But long ago it had been repaired, and so Atara had been forced to seek a way around it.

"I found a goat path through the rocks," she told us. "And then other tracks through the forest. But I had hoped to cut the road by now."

"You didn't see it from the top of the hill?" Maram asked her.

"No, I didn't have time to look. But why don't we look now?"

Together, we walked the twenty yards to the hill's top. There the ground dropped off suddenly, as if a giant axe had chopped off the entire north part of the hill. We stood looking out. Forty or fifty miles away, the northern spur of the Shoshan Mountains was buried in the clouds. A cottony mist lay over the hill country leading up to the range. We couldn't see much more of it than humps of green sticking out above the silvery swirls. But just below us, a blue-gray band of rock cut through the trees. It was wider than any road I had ever seen, and I knew that it must be the ancient Nar Road, which had been built from Tria to Nar before even the Age of Swords.

The question now arose as to what we should do. Maram, of course, favored the familiarity of good paving stones beneath his feet, while I might have preferred to keep to the woods. But Master Juwain observed that if the hill-men were bent upon revenge, they could fall upon us anywhere in these hills that they chose. Therefore, he said, we might as well make our way down to the road. Atara agreed with him, although she thought the hill-men were unlikely to attack us after losing so many men— especially since the arms of a Valari knight had now been added to the power of her great bow.

"And what about *my* bow?" Maram protested. He held up my hunting bow as if it belonged to him. "It was *my* arrow, was it not, that finally frightened the men away?"

Atara looked down the hill to where Maram's arrow still stuck out of the grass. She said, "Oh, you're right—what a magnificent shot! You probably managed to kill a mole or at least a few earthworms."

I tried not to smile as Maram's face flushed beet red. And it was good that I didn't, for Atara had her doubts about me as well.

"I've heard that the Valari are great warriors," she told me.

Yes, I thought, Telemesh and my grandfather were. My father is.

Atara pointed down at the body of the man I had spared. "It must be hard to be a great warrior who is afraid to kill his enemies."

Her eyes, beautiful as diamonds, could be as cold and hard as these stones, too. They cut right through me and seemed to strip me naked. "Yes," I told her, "it is hard."

"Why did you ride to help me, then?"

My gift, which sometimes let me see others' motivations so easily, often left me quite blind to my own. What could I say to her? That I had felt compassion for her plight? That even now I was afraid I might feel something more? Better then to say nothing, and so I stared off at the mist swirling over the hills.

"Well, you *did* help me, after all," Atara finally said. "You saved my life. And for that, I owe you a debt of blood."

"No," I said, looking at her, "you owe me nothing."

"Yes, I do. And I should ride with you until this debt is repaid."

I blinked my eyes at the strangeness of this suggestion. A Sarni warrior ride with a Valari knight? Did wolves run with lions? How many times over the ages had the Sarni invaded the Morning Mountains—always to be beaten back? How many Valari had the Sarni sent on, and the Sarni slain of the Valari? Not even a warrior of the Manslayer Society, I thought, could count such numbers.

"No," I said again, "there is no debt."

"Yes, of course there is. And I must repay it. Do you think I would ride with you otherwise?"

Upon looking at the way she impatiently moved her hands as if to sweep away my obduracy, I sensed that she might well prefer to make her own way out of this wilderness—or even to fight me for the sheer joy of fighting.

"If the hill-men return," she said, "you'll need my bow and arrows."

I touched my hand to my kalama and said, "We Valari have always done well enough with our swords—even against the Sarni."

We might have stood there arguing all day if Master Juwain hadn't observed that the sun wouldn't stop to listen and neither would the earth stand still to see who had prevailed. We should move on, and soon. Then he pointed out that Atara had no horse, and he asked me if I truly intended to leave her alone in the woods.

"Are you sure you want to ride with us?" I asked her. Then I told her about Kane and the unknown men whom we suspected of hunting us since Anjo, and who might be hunting us still.

If I had thought to discourage her, however, I was disappointed. In answer to my question, she just stood there cleaning the blood from her sword and smiling as if I had proposed a game of chess on which she might gladly bet not only her bag of gold but her very life.

I looked at the bodies of the hill-men she had slain. Truly, she was the enemy of my enemies, but her people were also the enemy of mine. Was my enemy, then, so easily to become my friend?

"I pledge my life to the protection of yours," she said simply. "But I can't keep the hill-men away—or anyone else—if I don't ride with you."

I could almost feel her will to keep her word. I saw in her a bright light and a basic goodness that touched me to the core. Even as I feared the fire building in me: if I let it, it might burn through me and consume me utterly. But if I ran away from this ineffable flame as I always had, then how would I be able to protect *her* should evil men come for her again?

"Please," I said, "ride with us. We'll be glad for your company."

I clasped hands with her then, and I felt the blood on her palm warm and wet against my own.

We spent most of the next hour readying ourselves for our journey. While Master Juwain redressed my wound, Maram shared out some of my hunting arrows with Atara. With her pony dead, we decided to convert my packhorse, Tanar, to a mount. The big gelding was quite strong, but it had been a long time since he had borne a human being on his back. When Atara buckled her saddle around him, he shook his head and stamped his hoof. Atara, however, had a way with horses. After convincing Tanar to accept the iron bit in his mouth, she rode him about the hill for a while and announced that he would have to do until she could buy a better horse in Suma or Tria.

We found our way down the hill then, into the valley we had seen from its top. A short distance through the trees brought us to a sudden break into bright sunlight where the Nar Road cut across the land. I marveled at the road's width: it was like a river of stone flowing through the forest. Grass grew in the many small cracks in it, and here and there, a tree grew out of a break in its surface. But it still seemed quite serviceable. Whole armies, I thought, could pass down this road. Whole armies had.

For the rest of the day we traveled northeast along it. We rode four abreast with the two remaining packhorses trailing behind us. If the hill-men were watching us from behind the walls of trees along the road, they didn't dare to show themselves. Even so, Atara and Maram kept their bows strung and close at hand as we all listened for breaking twigs or rustling leaves.

I watched Atara riding easily on top of her new mount; she was as supple and strong as her great Sarni bow. I was moved to wonder if other Sarni were making the journey to Tria, and so I asked her about this.

"None from the Kurmak," she told me. "As for other tribes, who can say? But there may be those who seek the gold that is not the true gold."

"What do you mean?" I asked her.

"I mean that Morjin has offered a thousand-weight of gold to anyone who would bring the Lightstone to him. And he is trying to win the tribes with promises of even greater treasure."

"Are the tribes listening to the Red Dragon then?"

"Some of them are. The Zayak and Marituk have practically pledged their swords to him. And half the clans of the Urtuk, it is said, favor an alliance with Sakai."

At this news, I ground my teeth together. The Urtuk commanded the steppe just to the west of the mountains of Mesh. "And what about the Kurmak?" I asked her. "Will your people ride with the Red Dragon?"

"Never!" Atara said. "Sajagax himself would slay any warrior of the clans who even suggested following Morjin."

She went on to tell us that this fierce old chief of the Kurmak was her grandfather, and that he would use the Lightstone to defeat Morjin. As would Atara. "The Gelstei," she said simply, "*must* be found."

As we made our way through the lovely afternoon, I thought about what Atara had said. I thought about her as well. I liked her forceful and sportive temperament, and I liked her passion for justice even more. She had a wisdom I had never seen in a woman her age. And kindness, too. That evening, when it came time to make camp, she told me that since I was wounded, I should rest and allow her to do much of the work. She insisted on unsaddling Altaru and brushing him down. When I insisted that my unruly horse might kill her if she drew too close to him, she simply walked up to his side and told him that they must be friends. Something in the dulcet tones of her voice must have worked a magic on Altaru, for he nickered softly and allowed her to breathe into his great nostrils. She stroked his neck for a long time then, and I could feel the beginning of love stirring in his great chest.

I was forced to admit that it was good that Atara had joined us; we all appreciated her enthusiasm and easy laughter. But she managed to vex us as well. Over the days of our journey, Master Juwain, Maram, and I had grown used to each other and had established a certain rhythm in making camp. Atara changed all that. She was as meticulous in performing chores as she was precise in shooting her arrows. Water must be taken from a stream at its exact center so as to avoid collecting any unwanted sediment; the stones for the fire had to be set around the pit in an exact circle and the firewood neatly trimmed so as to fit the pit perfectly. For Atara, I thought, there was a right way and a wrong way of doing everything, and she attended each little action as if the fate of the world hung in the balance.

The next day dawned bright and clear with the music of a million birds filling the forest. We traveled through some of the most beautiful country I had ever seen. The hills were on fire with a deep and pure green, and they glowed like huge emeralds; the sun was a golden crown melting over them. Wildflowers grew everywhere along the side of the road. With spring renewing the land, every tree was in leaf, and every leaf seemed to reflect the light of every other so that the whole forest shimmered with a perfect radiance.

Everything about the world that day touched me with astonishment at its perfection. It pleased me to see the squirrels scurrying after new shoots, and the sweetness of the buttercups and daisies filled my lungs with every breath. But I took my greatest delight from Atara, for she seemed the greatest of the world's creations. At those rare moments when she relaxed and let down her guard, her wild joy of life came bubbling up out of her like a fountain. Sometimes she rode on ahead with Maram, and I listened as they talked spiritedly or as Atara laughed at one of Maram's rude jokes. My ears couldn't seem to get enough of the sound; my eyes drank in the sight of her long, browned arms and her flowing yellow hair and were unquenchably thirsty for more. I marveled at even her hands, for they were graceful and finely made, with long, tapering fingers—not at all the hands of a warrior. The image of her whole being seemed to burn itself into me: straight, proud, laughing, wise, and allied with all the forces of life, a woman as a woman was born to be.

On the next day of our journey, we left the hills behind us, and the forest grew flatter. Around noon, I found myself riding beside Maram while Atara and Master Juwain went on ahead some thirty yards. I couldn't keep myself from admiring Atara's poise in the saddle, the way that the play of her hip and leg muscles seemed to guide Tanar effortlessly along. And Maram couldn't keep himself from noticing my absorption—and commenting on it.

"You're in love, my friend," he said to me. "At last, in love."

His words caught me completely by surprise. The truth often does. It is astonishing how we can deny such things even when it is in our eyes and hearts. "You think I'm in *love*?" I said stupidly. "With Atara?"

"No, with your packhorse, whom you've been watching all morning." He shook his head at my doltishness. "Of *course* with Atara!"

"But I thought it was you who loved her."

"*I?* But what made you think that?"

"Well, she is a woman, isn't she?"

"Ah, a woman she is. And I'm a man. So what? A stallion smells a mare in heat, and it's inevitable that the inevitable will happen. But *love,* Val?"

"Well, she is a beautiful woman."

"Beautiful, yes. So is a star. Can you touch one? Can you wrap your arms around such a cold fire and clasp it to your heart?"

"I don't know," I said. "If you can't, why should you think I can?"

"Because you're different from me," he said simply. "You were born to worship such impossible lights."

He went on to say that the very feature I loved most about Atara unnerved him completely. "The truth is, my friend, I can't bear looking at her damn eyes. Too blue, too bright—a woman's eyes should flow into mine like coffee, not dazzle me like diamonds."

I looked down at the two diamonds of my knight's ring but couldn't find anything to say.

"She loves you, you know," he suddenly told me.

"Did she say that?"

"Well, no, not exactly. In fact, she denied it. But that's like denying the sun."

Again I looked at the stones of my ring shining in the bright morning light. "No, no," I murmured, "it is not possible."

"It *is* possible, dammit! She told me she was drawn to that wild thing in your heart you always try to hide. When you walk into a clearing, don't you see the way her eyes light up as if *you* were the sun?"

"No, it is not possible," I said again.

"Listen, my friend, and listen well!" Here Maram grasped my arm as if his fingers might convince me of what his words could not. "You should tell her that you love her. Then ask her to marry you, before it's too late."

"*You* say that?" I couldn't believe what I had heard. "How many women have *you* asked to marry you, then?"

"Listen," he said again. "I may spend the rest of my life looking for the woman who was meant for me. But you, by rare good chance and the grace of the One—you've found the woman who was meant for you."

We made camp that night off the side of the road in a little clearing where a great oak had fallen. A stream ran through the forest only fifty yards from our site; it was a place of good air and the clean scents of ferns and mosses. Maram and Master Juwain drifted off to sleep early while I insisted on staying awake to make the night's first watch. In truth, with all that Maram had said to me, I could hardly sleep. I was sitting on a flat rock by the fire and looking out at the stars when Atara came over and sat beside me.

"You should sleep, too," I told her. "The nights are growing shorter."

Atara smiled as she shook her head at me. In her hands she held a couple of stones and a length of wood, which she intended to shape into a new arrow. "I promised myself I'd finish this," she said.

We spoke for a while of the Sarni's deadly war arrows, which could pierce armor, and their great bows made of layers of horn and sinew laminated to a wooden frame. Atara talked of life on the Wendrush and its harsh, unforgiving ways. She told me about the harsh, unforgiving Sajagax, the great war chief of the Kurmak. But of her father, she said little. I gathered only that he disapproved of her decision to enter the Manslayer Society.

"For a man to see his daughter take up arms," I said, "must come as a great shock."

"Hmmph," she said. "A warrior who has seen many die in battle should not complain about such shocks."

"Are you speaking of me or your father?"

"I'm speaking of men. They claim they are brave and then almost faint at the sight of a woman with a bow in her hands or bleeding a little blood."

"That is true," I said, smiling. "For me to see my mother or grandmother wounded would be almost unbearable."

Atara's tone softened as she looked at me and said, "You love them very much, don't you?"

"Yes, very much."

I stopped talking then, and listened to the stream flowing through forest and the wind rustling the leaves of the trees. Atara was quiet for a few moments while she regarded me in the fire's soft light. And then she told me, "I've never known a man like you."

I watched as she drew the length of wood between the two grooved pieces of sandstone that she held in her hand, shaping the new arrow. Then I said, "Who has ever seen a woman like you? In the Morning Mountains, the women shoot different kinds of arrows into men's hearts."

She laughed at this in her spirited way, then her face fell grave as she said, "Men only reap what they sow."

"No, there must be another way," I told her. I drew my sword and watched the play of starlight on its long blade. "This is not the way the world was meant to be."

"Perhaps not," she said, staring at this length of steel. "But it's the way the world *will* be until we make it differently."

"And how will we ever do that?"

She fell quiet for a long time as she sat looking at me. And then she said, "Sometimes, late at night or when I look into the waters of a still pool, I can see it. *Almost* see it. There is a woman there. She has incredible courage but incredible grace, too. There hasn't been a true woman on Ea since the Age of the Mother. Maybe not even then. But this woman of the waters and wind—she has a terrible beauty like that of Ashtoreth herself. This is the beauty that every woman was born for. But that woman I will never be until men become what they were meant to be. And nothing will ever change men's hearts except the Lightstone itself."

"Nothing?" I asked, dropping my gaze toward her arrow.

Here she laughed nicely for a moment and then admitted, "Someday, I would like to see all men united. All men and all women."

"That is a lovely thought," I told her. "And you are a lovely woman."

"Please don't say that."

"Why not?"

"Please don't say that the *way* that you say that."

"My apologies," I said, looking down as she slid the arrow between her sanding stones.

I fell silent as I listened to the sweet song of a nightingale crescendoing out from somewhere in the tall trees around us. Then Atara said to me simply, "You are Valari, and I am Sarni."

"Yes, a Sarni of the *Manslayers,*" I said as I looked at her.

She continued shaping her arrow, then told me, "That is our world. And what can any child do who is born into it the way it is now?"

I glanced down at her arrow in new understanding. "So then, if you kill enough bad men, the world will be a better place for children?"

"Yes—that is why I joined the society and made my vow."

"Would you never consider breaking it, then?"

"As Maram breaks his?"

"A hundred men," I said, staring off at the shadows between the trees. Not even Asaru or Karshur, I thought, had slain so many.

"A vow is a vow," she said sadly.

What kind of woman, I wondered, would vow to slay so many men? And what kind of man would vow never to slay again even though that might prove his fate?

"Have you slain Valari, then?" I asked her.

"Have *you*?" she countered. She looked at me as if taking my measure.

I put away my sword and took out my flute. I said, "When I was a boy, I would have hoped to spend my time playing *this*. I've no love of killing."

She must have hated the way that I looked at her then, for her back stiffened, and she said, "And you think *I* do?"

I shrugged my shoulders at this. "You are a Sarni, and a Manslayer at that. My father once told me that the Sarni make their children gut their captives alive to encourage a taste for blood."

"And *my* father," she said, "once told me that the Valari are marauders and savages who slay their own brothers for the sport. Should we believe the tales that old men have told us, or the truth of our eyes and hearts?"

What *was* the truth of this beautiful woman? I wondered. As she sat up straight and pointed her arrow at me, I saw her as a perfect warrior who would slay anyone who stood against her pursuit of her impossible ideals. At that moment, as the fire illumined the unyielding features of her face, she seemed less beautiful than terrible. A coldness came into her. In seeing the way that I looked at her, her anger grew as icy as a river flowing down from frozen mountains.

"You were right—I should sleep now," she told me. She rose up with a suddenly released tension like that of bow snapping straight. "Goodnight, Valari."

And without another word, she circled the fire to return to her blanket.

For a long time her doubt of me hung in the air like black

smoke. In truth, I doubted myself—and more, if I really did love her as Maram had said. I doubted if I *could* love her. Although I might indeed long to clasp her to me, first I would have to open my heart.

■ **12** ■

TOWARD THE DARKEST hours of morning, as I lay anguishing over what had occurred with Atara, my nightmares began again. It seemed that my fever had returned, and with it, a lancinating pain that drove straight through my head. I was vaguely aware that I was writhing and sweating on top of my sleeping furs for what seemed entire ages. And then suddenly I found myself somehow awakening many miles away in a large room with rich furnishings. I stood by a magnificently canopied bed, marveling at the gilded chests and wardrobes along the walls. There I saw three long mirrors, framed in ornate gold as well. An intricately woven carpet showing the shapes of animals and men covered the floor. I couldn't find any window or door. I stood sweating in fear because I couldn't imagine how I had come to be there.

And then the mirror opposite me began rippling like still water into which someone had thrown a stone. A man suddenly stepped out of it. He was slightly above average height, slim and well-muscled, with skin as fair as snow. His short hair shined like spun gold, and the fine features of his face radiated an almost unearthly beauty. I gasped to behold his eyes, for they were all golden, too. His golden tunic was embroidered with a emblem that held my eyes fast: it was the coiled shape of a large and ferocious red dragon.

"You're standing on my head," he told me in a strong, deep voice. "Please get your dirty boots off of it."

I looked down to see that I was indeed standing on the eyes of a red dragon woven into the wool at the center of the carpet.

I instantly found myself moving backward. No king I had ever known—neither King Hadaru nor even my father—spoke with such command as did this beautiful man.

"Do you know who I am?" he asked me.

"Yes," I said. I was sweating fiercely now; I wanted to close my eyes and scream, but I couldn't look away from him. "You're the Red Dragon."

"I have a name," he said. "You know what it is—please say it."

"No, I won't."

"Say it now!"

"Morjin," I said, despite my resolve. "Your name is Morjin."

"*Lord* Morjin, you should call me. And you are Valashu Elahad. You killed one of my knights, didn't you?"

"No, that's not true—are assassins knights?"

"You put your knife into him. You killed this man, and so you owe him a life. And since he was *my* man, you owe me your life."

"No, that's a lie," I said. "You're the Lord of Lies."

Morjin smiled, revealing small white teeth as lustrous as pearls. He asked me, "Have you never lied, then?"

"No—my mother taught me not to lie. My father, too."

"*That* is the first lie you've told me, Valashu. But not the last."

"Yes, it is!" I said. I pressed my hand to my throbbing head. "I mean, no, it isn't—I wasn't lying when I said it's wrong to lie."

"Is it really?" he asked me. He took another step closer and said, "It pleases me that you lie to me. Why not be truthful about what all men do? Please listen to this truth, young *Elahad*: he who best knows the truth is most able to tell a falsehood. Therefore the man best at lying is the most true."

"That's a lie!" I half shouted. But my head hurt so much I could hardly tell what was true and what was not.

He stood there smiling at me nicely, as if he were my best friend. And then the music began pouring off his silver tongue again: "We already know the truth about each other, deep in our hearts, don't we, Valashu?"

"No—you know nothing about me!"

"Do I not?" Morjin pointed his long finger at my chest and said, "Don't you doubt the wisdom of making this quest? Don't you doubt yourself?"

I knew that I shouldn't listen to him, so I stood there pressing my hands over my temples and ears. It felt like some beast was trying to break its way into my head.

"You suffer so terribly, don't you? Because of your gift; because you can't bear to bear others' pain. Don't you long for the suffering to end?"

Morjin's fine hands moved dramatically as if to emphasize the poignancy of his words; it seemed that such bright fires burned inside him that he couldn't stop moving. Then he took another step closer to me.

"No!" I told him. I shook my head, which throbbed with a deep agony at every beat of my heart.

"Please don't deny me."

Now he took the final step toward me and smiled again. I was suddenly aware that he smelled of roses. I tried to move back but found that I didn't want to. I told myself that I mustn't be afraid of him, that he had no power to harm me. Then he reached out his hand and touched his forefinger to the scar on my forehead; the tip of it was warm, and I could almost feel it glowing with a deep radiance. He traced this finger slowly along the zigzags of the scar. It was like a serpent sinuously impressing itself into me. He smiled warmly as he then cupped the whole of his hand around my head. Despite the delicacy of his fingers, I sensed that there was iron there and that he had the strength to crush my skull like an eggshell. But instead he only touched my temples with exquisite sensitivity and breathed deeply as if drawing my pain into him. And suddenly my headache was gone.

"There," he said, stepping away from me. "You're deciding if your Valari manners permit you to thank me, aren't you? Is it so hard to say the words?"

"To the Lord of Lies? To the Crucifier?"

"Men have called me that—they don't understand."

"They understand what they see," I said.

"And what do *you* see, young Valashu?"

Again he smiled, and the room lit up as with the rising of the sun. For a moment, I couldn't help seeing him as an angel of light, as what I imagined the Elijin to be.

"They understand what you *do*," I said. "You've enslaved half of Ea and tortured everyone who has opposed you."

"Enslaved? When your father accepts homage from a knight, is that enslavement? When he punishes a man for treason, is that torture?"

"My father," I said, "is a king."

"And I am a king of kings," he said. "My realm is Sakai—and all the lands east, west, north, and south. A long time ago, the land that you and your friends are traveling through belonged to me, and it will once again."

"No, you're a usurper. Perhaps not even the same Morjin of ages past."

"I am," he told me, "more than seven thousand years old. And I didn't come by my immortality by accident."

"No—you gained immortality by stealing the Lightstone."

"But how can a man steal what is his?"

"What do you mean? The Lightstone belongs to all of Ea."

"It belongs to him who made it." He formed his hands into a cup and smiled at me. "*I* forged the Lightstone myself late in the Age of Swords."

I searched his face for the truth. His golden eyes seemed so bright and compelling that I didn't know what to think.

"The Lightstone belongs to me. And you must help me regain it."

"No, I won't."

"You *will*," he told me. "Scrying isn't the greatest of my talents, but I'll tell you this: someday you'll deliver it into my hands."

"No, never."

"You owe me your life," he told me. "A man who doesn't repay his debts is a thief, is he not?"

"No—there is no debt."

"And *still* you deny me!" he thundered. Suddenly, he smacked his fist into his open hand. His face grew red and hard to look at. "Just as you still shelter one who is worse than a thief."

"What do you mean?"

"Who is that standing behind you?" he said, pointing his finger at me.

"What do you mean—there's no one behind me!"

But it seemed that there was. I turned to see a boy standing in the shadow that I cast upon the carpet. He was about six years old, with bold face bones, a shock of wild black hair, and a scar shaped like a lightning bolt cut into his forehead.

"There," Morjin said, stabbing at him with his long finger. "Why are you trying to protect him?"

Morjin tried to step around me to get at the boy. When I raised my arm to stop him, he touched my side with something sharp. I looked down to see that his finger had grown a long black claw tipped with a bluish substance that looked like kirax. My whole body began burning, and I suddenly couldn't move.

"Come here, Valashu," Morjin said. Quick as a snapping turtle, he grabbed up the boy and stood shaking him near the wall. But the boy spat in his face and managed to bite off his clawlike finger. Morjin looked at the gaping wound in his hand and said to me, "You'll have to help me now."

"No, never!" I said again through my clenched teeth.

"Give me the arrow!" Morjin told me.

With one hand pinning the struggling boy against the wall, he reached out his other hand to me. I saw to my amazement that I was holding in my hand an arrow fletched with raven feathers and tipped with a razor-sharp steel. It was the arrow that the unknown assassin had shot at me in the forest.

"Thank you," Morjin said, taking it from me. He suddenly plunged it into the boy's side, and we both screamed at the burning pain of it. In moments, the kirax froze the boy's limbs so that he couldn't move.

"Do you have the hammer?" Morjin said to me. "Do you have the nails?"

He turned from the boy and took from me the three iron spikes that I held in my left hand and the heavy iron maul in my right. I saw then that I had been mistaken, that there really was a door in the room: it was a thick slab of oak set into the wall just next to the boy. Morjin used the hammer to nail the child's hands and legs to it. I couldn't hear the ringing of iron against iron, so loud were the boy's screams.

"There," he said when he had finished crucifying the child. Morjin smiled sadly at me and continued, "And now you must give me what is mine."

"No!" I cried out. "Don't do this!"

"A king," he said to me, "must sometimes punish, even as your father punished you. And a warrior must sometimes slay in pursuit of a noble end, even as you have slain."

"But the boy! He's done nothing—he's innocent!"

"Innocent? He's committed a crime worse than treason or murder."

"What is this crime?" I gasped.

"He coveted the Lightstone for himself," he said simply. "He could not bear the gift that the One bestowed upon him, and so when he heard his grandfather speak of the golden cup that heals all wounds, he dreamed of keeping it for himself."

"No—that is not true!"

Morjin moved closer to the boy. The great beast opened his mouth and let the blood streaming from the boy's pierced hand run into it.

"No, don't," I said.

"You must help me," he said to me.

"No."

"You must do me homage, Valashu Elahad, son of kings. You must surrender to me what is mine."

The whole of my body below my neck couldn't move, but I could still shake my head.

"You must open your heart to me, Valashu."

His eyes now began to burn like two golden suns. Long black claws like those of a dragon grew from his hands in place of fingers.

"Don't hurt him!" I cried out. "You can't hurt him!"

"*Can't* I?"

"No, you can't—this is only a dream."

"Do you think so?" he asked. "Then see if you can wake up."

So saying, he turned to the terrified boy and made cooing sounds of pity as he tore him apart. When he was finished, he held the boy's still-beating heart in his claws so that I could see it.

You killed him! I wanted to scream. But the only sound that came from my ravaged throat was a burning sob.

"It is said that if you die in your dreams, you die in life." He looked at the throbbing heart and said, "But no, Val, I *haven't* killed him, not yet."

And with that, he placed the heart back into the boy's chest and sealed the wound with a kiss from his golden lips. The boy opened his eyes then and stared at Morjin hatefully.

"Do you see?" he said to me with a heavy sigh. "I can't *demand* that you open your heart to me. Such gifts must be truly given."

I bit my lip then and tasted blood. The dark, salty liquid moistened my burning throat, and I cried out, "That will never happen!"

"No?" he asked me angrily. "Then you will truly die."

Now his head grew out from his body, huge and elongated and red and covered with scales. His eyes were golden-red and glowed like coals. His forked tongue flicked out once as if tasting the fear in the air. Then he opened his jaws to let out a gout of fire that seared the boy from his head to his bloody feet. The boy screamed as his flesh began to char; Morjin screamed out his hatred in his fiery roar. And I screamed too as I pleaded with him to stop.

But he didn't stop. He let the fire pour out of his fearsome mouth as if venting ages of bitterness and hate. I felt my own skin beginning to blister; I knew that Morjin would soon renew it with the touch of his lips so that he could burn me again and again until I finally surrendered to him or died. I sensed that if I fought against the terrible burning, it would go on forever. And so I surrendered to it. I let its heat burn deep into my blood; I felt it burning the kirax *in* my blood. And suddenly I found myself able to move again. I swung my fist like a mace at the side of Morjin's head; it was like striking iron. But it stunned him long enough so that I could rush through the flames streaming from his mouth to the blackened, bloody door. The boy was now black and twisted and screaming for me to help him. I somehow wrenched him free from the door with a great tearing of flesh and bones. And then, holding him close to me where I could feel the wild beating of his heart and his screams as my own, I opened the door.

I opened my eyes then to see Atara bending over me and pressing a cool, wet cloth against my head, which she held cradled in her lap. I was lying back against my sweat-soaked sleeping furs near the fire. I took me a moment before I realized that I was screaming still. I closed my mouth then and bit my bloody lip against the burning in my body. Master Juwain, brewing up some tea, held my hand in his, testing my pulse.

Maram, who sat beside me, looked at me gravely and said, "We couldn't wake you. But *you* were screaming loud enough to wake the dead."

Atara's fingers—calloused from years of pulling a bowstring—were incredibly gentle as she brushed back my sodden hair. Whatever anger I had aroused in her earlier seemed to be forgotten. I squeezed her hand to thank her for her watching over me, and then I sat up. I found that I was still clutching my other hand against my heart, but the wounded boy I thought to find there was gone.

"Are you all right now?" Maram asked me.

I blinked my eyes against the burning there. I looked out at the trees, which were immense gray shapes in the faint light filtering through the forest. The crickets were chirping in the bushes, and a few birds were singing the day's first songs. It was that terrible time between death and morning when the whole world struggled to fight its way out of night.

I stood up, wincing against the flames that still scorched my skin. I took a step away from the fire.

"It is still night," Atara said. "Where are you going?"

"Down to the stream, to bathe," I said. I wanted to wash away the charred skin from my hands and let the stream's rushing waters cool my burning body.

"You should not go alone," she told me. "Here, let me get my bow—"

"No!" I said. "It will be all right—I'll take my sword."

So saying, I bent to grab up my kalama, which I always kept sheathed next to my bed when I was sleeping. And then I walked off by myself toward the stream.

It was eerie moving through the gray-lit woods. I imagined I saw dark gray shapes watching me through the trees. But when I looked more closely I saw that they were only bushes or shrubs: arrowwood and witch hazel and others whose names I couldn't remember. I plodded along the forest floor and crunched over twigs and old leaves. I smelled animal droppings and ferns and the sweaty remnants of my own fear.

Suddenly I broke free from the trees and came upon the stream. It gurgled along its rocky course like a silver ribbon beneath the stars. I looked up at the glowing sky, grateful that could I see its blazing points of light. In the east, the Swan constellation was just rising over the dark rim of the forest. Near it shined Valashu, the Morning Star—so bright that it was almost like a moon. Even as I bent to lave the stream's cool water over my head, I kept my eyes fixed upon the familiar star that gave me so much hope.

And then I felt a cold hand touch my shoulder. For a moment I was angry because I thought that Maram or Atara had followed me. But when I turned to tell them that I really did want to be alone, I saw that the man standing beside me was Morjin.

"Did you really think you could escape me?" he asked.

I stared at his golden hair and his great golden eyes, now touched with silver in the starlight. The claws were gone from his hands, and he was wearing a wool traveling cloak over his dragon-emblazoned tunic.

"How did you come here?" I gasped.

"Don't you know? I have been following you since Mesh."

I gripped the hilt of my sword as I stared at him. Was this still a dream? I wondered. Was it an illusion that Morjin had cast like a painter covering a canvas with brightly colored pigments? He *was* the Lord of Illusions, wasn't he? But no, I thought, this was no illusion. Both he and the fiery words that hissed from his mouth seemed much too real.

"I must congratulate you on finding your way out of my room," he said. "It surprises me that you did, though it pleases me even more."

"It pleases you? Why?"

"Because it proves to me that you are capable of waking up."

He gave me to understand that much of what had passed in my dream had been only a test and a spur to awaken my being. This seemed the greatest of the lies that he had told me, but I listened to it all the same.

"I am sorry, Valashu, but sometimes compassion must be cruel."

"*You* speak of compassion?"

"I do speak of it, because I know it better than any man."

He told me that my gift for feeling others' sufferings and joys had a name, and that was *valarda*. This meant both the heart of the stars and the passion of the stars. He pointed up at the Morning Star and the bright Solaru and Altaru of the Swan constellation. All the Star People, he said, who still lived among these lights had this gift. As did Elahad and others of the Valari who had come to Ea long ago. But the gift had mostly been lost during the savagery of many thousands of years.

"There is a terrible beauty to this *valarda*, is there not?" he said. "It makes one suffer so deeply! But there is a way to make the suffering end."

"How?" I asked.

He cupped his hands in front of his heart then, and they glowed with a soft golden radiance like that of a polished bowl. He said, "Do you burn, Valashu? Does the kirax from my arrow still torment you? Would you like to be cured of this poison and your deeper suffering as well?"

"How?" I asked again. Despite the coolness spraying up from the stream, my whole body raged with fever.

"I can relieve you of your gift," he told me. "Or rather, the pain of it."

Here he pointed at the kalama that I still held sheathed in my hand. "You see, the *valarda* is like a double-edged sword. But so far, you've known it to cut only one way."

He told me that a true Valari, which was his name for the Star People, could not only experience others' emotions but make them feel his own.

"Do you hate, Valashu? Do you sometimes clench your teeth against the fury inside you? I *know* that you do. But you can forge your fury into a weapon that will strike down your enemies. Shall I show you how to sharpen the steel of *this* sword?"

"No!" I cried out. "That is wrong! It would be twisting the bright blade that the One himself forged. Staining it as with blackened blood. The *valarda* may be double-edged, as you say. But I must believe that it is sacred. And I would never pervert it by turning it inside out to harm anyone. No more than I would use my kalama to kill anyone."

"But you *will* kill again, and with that sword," he said, pointing at my kalama. "And with the *valarda*, as well. You see, Valashu, inflicting your own pain on others is the only way not to feel *their* pain—and your own."

I closed my eyes as I looked inside for this terrible sword that Morjin had spoken of. I feared that I might find it. And this was the worst torment I had ever known.

"What you say, all that you say, is wrong," I gasped out. "It is evil."

"Is it wrong to slay your enemies, then? Isn't it *they* who are evil for opposing your noblest dream?"

"You don't know my dream."

"Don't I? Isn't it your dearest hope to end war? Listen to me, Valashu, listen as you've never listened before: there is nothing I desire more than an end to these wars."

I listened to the rushing of the stream and the words from his golden lips. I was afraid that he might be telling me the truth. He went on to say that many of the kings and nobles of Ea loved war because it gave them the power of life and death over others. But they, he said, were of the darkness while dreamers such as he and I were of the light.

"It is death itself that is the great enemy," he said. "And that is why we must regain the Lightstone. Only then can we bring men the gift of true life."

"It is written in the *Laws*," I said, "that only the Elijin and the Galadin shall have such life."

Morjin's eyes seemed to blaze out hatred into the gray light of the dawn. He told me, "All the Galadin were once Elijin, even as the Elijin were once men. But they have grown jealous of our kind. Now they would keep men such as you from making the same journey that they once did."

"But I don't seek immortality," I told him.

"That," he said softly, "is a lie."

"All men die," I said.

"Not *all* men," he told me, smoothing the folds from his cloak.

"It's no failing to fear death," I said "True courage is—"

"Lie to me if you will, Valashu, but do not lie to yourself." He grasped my arm, and his delicate fingers pressed into me with a frightening strength. And then he spoke the words to a poem I knew too well:

> *And down into the dark,*
> *No eyes, no lips, no spark.*
> *The dying of the light,*
> *The neverness of night.*

"There is way to keep the light burning," he told me as he gently squeezed my shoulder. "Let me show you the way."

His whole being was like a portal to other worlds from which men had journeyed long ago—and on which men who were more than men still lived. I felt his longing to return there. It was as real as the wind or the stream or the earth beneath my feet. I felt his immense loneliness in the bittersweet aching of my own. Something unbearably bright in him called to me as if from the wild, cold stars. I knew that I had the power to save him from a dread almost as dark as death, even as I had saved Atara from the hill-men. And this knowledge burned me even more terribly than had his dragon fire or the kirax in my veins.

"Let me show you," he said, forming his hands into a cup again. A fierce golden light poured out of them, almost blinding me.

"Servants I have many," he told me. "But friends I have none."

I felt him breathing deeply as I drew in a quick, ragged breath.

"I will make you King of Mesh and all the Nine Kingdoms," he told me. "Kings I have as vassals, too, but a king of kings who comes to me with an open heart and a righteous sword— that would be a wondrous thing."

I gazed at the light pouring from his hands, and I couldn't breathe.

"Help me find the Lightstone, Valashu, and you will live forever. And we will rule Ea together, and there will be no more war."

Yes, yes, I wanted to say. *Yes, I will help you.*

There is a voice that whispers deep inside the soul. Each of us has such a voice. Sometimes it is as clear as the ringing of a silver bell; sometimes it is faint and far off, like the fiery exhalations of the stars. But it always knows. And it always speaks the truth, even when we don't want to hear it.

"No," I said at last.

"No?"

"No, you lie," I told him. "You're the Lord of Lies."

"I'm the Lord of Ea, and you will help me!"

I gripped the hilt of the sword that my father had given me as I slowly shook my head.

"Damn you, Elahad! You damn yourself to death, then!"

"So be it," I told him.

"So be it," he told me. And then he said, "I will tell you the true secret of the *valarda:* the only way you will ever expiate your fear of death is to make others die. As I will make *you* die, Elahad!"

The hate with which he said this was like lava pouring from a rent in the earth. I realized then that fear of death leads to hatred of life. Even as my fear of Morjin led me to hate him. I hated him with black bile and clenched teeth and red blood suddenly filling my eyes; I hated him as fire hates wood and darkness does light. Most of all, I hated him for lying to me and playing on my fears and making me sick to my soul with a deep and terrible hate.

It took only a moment for his dragon's head to grow out from his body and for his claws to emerge. But before his jaws could open, I whipped my kalama from its sheath. I plunged the point of it through the dragon embroidered on his tunic, deep into his heart. It was like I had ripped out my own heart. The incredible pain of it caused me to scream like a wounded child even as my sword shattered into a thousand pieces; each piece lay burning with an orange-red light on the ground or hissed into the stream and sent up plumes of boiling water. I watched in horror as Morjin screamed, too, and his face fell away from the form of a dragon and became my own. Clots of twisting red worms began to eat out his eyes, *my* eyes, and his whole body burst into flames. In moments his face blackened into a rictus of agony. And then the flames consumed him utterly, and he vanished into the nothingness from which he had come.

For what seemed a long time, I stood there by the stream, waiting for him to return. But all that remained of him was a terrible emptiness clutching at my heart. My fever left me; in the darkness of the dawn, I was suddenly very cold. Inside me beat the words to another stanza of Morjin's poem that I could never forget:

> *The stealing of the gold,*
> *The evil knife, the cold.*
> *The cold that freezes breath,*
> *The nothingness of death.*

13

A FEW MOMENTS later, Atara and Master Juwain came running into the clearing by the stream, Maram puffing close behind them. Atara held her strung bow in her hand, and Maram brandished his sword; Master Juwain had a copy of the *Saganom Elu* that he had been reading, but nothing more. The thought of him reciting passages or throwing his book at a man such as Morjin made me want to laugh wildly.

"What is it?" he asked me. "Who were you shouting at, Val?"

"At Morjin," I said. "Or perhaps it was just an illusion."

I looked at the steel gleaming along the length of my sword, and I wondered how it had been remade.

"Morjin was *here?*" Atara asked. "How? Where did he go?"

I pointed toward the glow of the sun rising in the east. Then I pointed at the woods, north, west, and south. Finally I flung my hand up toward the sky.

"Take Val back to camp," Atara said to Master Juwain. She nodded at Maram, too, as if issuing a command. Then she started off toward the woods.

"Where are you going?" I asked her.

"To see," she said simply.

"No, you mustn't!" I told her. I took a step toward her to stop her, but my body felt as if it had been drained of blood. I stumbled and was only saved from falling by Maram, who wrapped his thick arm around me.

"Take him back to camp!" Atara said again. And then she moved off into the trees and was gone.

Maram and Master Juwain threw my arms across their shoulders and dragged me back to camp as if I were a drunkard. They sat me down by the fire, and Maram covered me with his cloak. But the icy nothingness with which Morjin had touched my soul still remained.

"What did the Lord of Illusions do to you?" he asked me.

I tried to tell Master Juwain and Maram something of my dream—and what had happened by the stream afterward. But words failed me. It was impossible to describe a terror that had no bottom or end.

After a while, my head began to clear and I came fully awake. Dawn began to brighten into morning as the sun's light touched the trees around us. I listened to the *shureet shuroo* of a scarlet tanager piping out his song from the branch of an oak; I gazed at the starlike white sepals of some goldthread growing in the shade of a birch tree. The world seemed marvelously and miraculously real, and my senses drank in every sight, sound, and smell.

Just as I was steeling myself to strap on my sword and go look for Atara, she returned. She stepped out from behind the cover of the trees as silently as a doe. In the waxing light, her face was ashen. She came over and sat beside me by the fire.

"Well?" Maram asked her. "What did you see?"

"Men," Atara said. With a trembling hand, she reached for a mug of tea that Master Juwain handed her. "Gray men."

"What do you mean, *gray men*?" Maram said.

"There were eleven of them," Atara said. "Or perhaps more. They were dressed all in gray; their horses were gray, too. Their faces were hideous: their flesh seemed as gray as slate."

She paused to take a sip of tea as beads of sweat formed up on Maram's brow.

"It was hard to *see*," Atara said. "Perhaps their faces were only colored by grayness of the dawn. But I don't think so. There was something about them that didn't seem human."

Master Juwain knelt beside her and touched her shoulder. He told her, "Please go on."

"One of them looked at me," she said. "He had no eyes—no eyes like those of any man I've ever seen. They were all gray, as if covered with cataracts. But he wasn't blind. The *way* that he looked at me. It was as if I was naked, like he could see everything about me."

She took another sip of tea, then grasped my hand to keep her hand from shaking.

"I shouldn't have looked into his eyes," she said. "It was like looking into nothing. So empty, so cold—I felt the cold freezing my body. I felt his intention to do things to me. I . . . have no words for it. It was worse than the hill-men. Death I can face. Perhaps even torture. But this man—it was like he wanted to kill me forever and suck out my soul."

We were all silent as we looked at her. And then Maram asked, "What did you *do?*"

"I tried to draw on him," she said. "But it was as if my arms were frozen. It took all my will to pull my bow and sight on him. But it was too late—he rode off to join the others."

"Oh, excellent!" Maram said, wiping his face. "Men *are* after us—gray men who devour souls."

As the sun rose higher, we sat by the fire debating who these men might be. Maram worried that the man who had faced down Atara might be Morjin himself—how else to explain the terrible dream and illusion I had suffered? Master Juwain held that they might be only in Morjin's employ; as he told us: "The Lord of Lies has many dreadful servants."

"But why should *Morjin* be hunting Val?" Atara wanted to know.

Master Juwain turned to me, wondering how much he should tell her. I looked at him and nodded my head. And so he went on to recount how an assassin's arrow tipped with kirax had wounded me in the woods outside of Silvassu. He explained how the priests of the Kallimun sometimes used kirax to slay horribly at Morjin's bidding.

"Oh, but you make evil enemies, don't you?" Atara said to me.

"It would seem so," I said. Then I smiled at the three of them. "But also the best of friends."

Atara returned my smile, then asked, "But why should Morjin wish you dead?"

That was one of the questions I most wanted answered. Because I had nothing to say, I shrugged my shoulders and stared off into the woods.

Maram, after wiping the sweat from his brow, stared, too, and then said, "What are we going to do, Val?"

I thought for a moment. "So long as we keep to the road, we'll be easy prey. Perhaps we should take to the forest again."

I said that the Nar Road curved north toward Suma, where the forest ended and the more civilized reaches of Alonia began. "If we cut straight for Suma, there will be hills to hide us and streams in which to lose our tracks."

"You mean, rivers to drown us," Maram said. "Hills to hide *them.*"

I guessed that Suma lay some eighty miles to the northwest.

After we broke camp, we set out through the trees toward it. As the day warmed toward noon, the ground rose away from the stream. The trees grew less thickly, though they seemed taller, with the oaks predominating over the poplars and chestnuts. I could find no track through them. Still, the traveling wasn't difficult, for the undergrowth was mostly of lady fern and maidenhair, and the horses had no trouble finding footing. We rode in near silence beneath the great leafed archways of the trees. I took the lead, followed by Master Juwain and the two packhorses. Maram and Atara brought up the rear. All of us—except Master Juwain—rode with bows strung and swords close at hand.

We saw many squirrels and a few deer munching on leaves but no sign at all of the Stonefaces, as Maram named the gray men. I never doubted that they were somehow tracking us through the woods. With the sun high above the world, my fever came raging back, and my blood felt heavy as molten iron. It seemed as though someone was aiming arrows of hate at me, for I could almost feel a succession of razor-sharp points driving into my skull.

Master Juwain rode up beside me and touched my forehead. Then he told me, "Your wound is healing nicely, so I'm sure it's not infection that's firing your fever."

"Perhaps it's the kirax," I said.

He watched me rubbing my head and looked at me with great concern. "I'm sorry I have no cure for what ails you."

"Perhaps there is no cure," I told him. Then I said, "The Red Dragon is so evil—how can anyone be this evil?"

"Only out of blindness," Master Juwain said, "so that he can't see the difference between evil or good. Or only out of the delusion that he is doing good when actually bringing about the opposite."

The Red Dragon, he said, was certainly not evil by his own lights. No one was. But I wasn't as sure of this. Something in Morjin's voice seemed to delight in darkness, and this haunted me.

"He spoke to me," I told Master Juwain. "And I listened to him. Now his words won't leave my head."

How, I asked myself, could I know what was the truth and what was a lie if I didn't listen?

To the rough walking gait of his horse, Master Juwain began thumbing rhythmically through the pages of the *Saganom Elu*. When he had found the passage he wanted, he cleared his throat and read to me from the *Healings*.

"I would advise you to meditate, if you can," he told me. "Do you remember the Second Light Meditation? It used to be your favorite."

I nodded my head painfully. I remembered it well enough: I was to close my eyes and dwell on the dread brought on by the fall of night. And then, after gazing upon the blackness of the sky there as long as I could, I was to envision the Morning Star suddenly blazing as brightly as the sun. This fiery light I would then hold inside me as I would the promise that day would always follow night.

"It's hard," I told him after a some long moments of trying to practice the meditation. "The Lord of Illusions has made light seem like darkness and darkness light."

"The worst lie," Master Juwain said, "is that which misuses truth to make falseness. You must never listen to him, not even in your dreams."

"Are my dreams mine to make, then? Or are they his?"

"Your dreams are always *your* dreams," he told me. "But you must fight to keep them for yourself even more fiercely than you would to keep an enemy's sword from piercing your heart."

"How, then?"

"By learning to be awake and aware in your dreams."

"Is that possible?"

"Of course it is. There are exercises in the dreamwork that you would have been taught if you hadn't left our school."

"Can you teach me them now?"

"I can try, Val. But the art of dreaming at will takes years to learn."

As we rode deeper into the woods, he explained some of the fundamentals of this ancient art. Every night while falling asleep, I was to resolve to remain aware of my dreams. And more, I was to create for myself an ally, a sort of dream self who would remain awake and watch over me while I slept.

"Do you remember the zanshin meditation I taught you before your duel with Lord Salmelu?"

"Yes—it is impossible to forget."

"You may make use of that, then," he said. "You must concentrate on the question, Who am I? When you think you know, ask yourself: who is doing the knowing? This 'who,' this one who knows—this is your ally. It is he who remains always beside you, and is awake even as you sleep."

That evening we made camp on a hill beneath the tall oaks. There was little enough cover to hide us—nothing more than some thickets of laurel—but at least we would have a more or less clear line of sight should the gray men try to charge at us up the hill. I fell asleep to Master Juwain's meditation. It did me little good, however, for I had terrible dreams throughout the night. My cries kept the others awake. They were true allies, of flesh and blood, and they kept watch over me where Master Juwain's more ethereal ally did not.

All the next day and the one following, in the moist woods full of amanita and destroying angels and other poisonous mushrooms, I felt a mailed fist pounding at my head and trying to wear me down. When we made camp by a stream that gurgled like an opened throat, Atara and Maram joined me in nightmare. Only Master Juwain seemed shielded against the terrible images that Morjin sent to rob us of sanity and sleep. But even he awoke the next morning with a fever and a fierce headache. Maram wondered if we had managed to drink some tainted water, perhaps from a stream poisoned by a dead animal who had eaten some of the overly abundant mushrooms. But Master Juwain doubted this possibility. He stood rubbing his bald head by his horse as he told Maram, "This is no taint of rotten flesh or the poisoning of plants. No, Brother Maram, I'm afraid these Stonefaces are getting bolder."

For the next two days, we fled as quickly as we could through the dense woods. Mosquitoes bit us, and blackberry brambles scratched the horses' flanks bloody. During one of our hard gallops, it pained me to see the froth building up along Altaru's jaw. However, he made little complaint; he just charged on through the moss-hung trees hour after hour, and day after day, driving at the earth with his great hooves. Maram's and Master Juwain's horses had a harder time of it. And Atara's horse was no mount at all.

I did not know how long we could go on this way. We had been on the road for most of a month. The journey had worn the flesh off our bodies, and even Maram was beginning to look gaunt. We were dirty, our clothes torn by thorns and stained with mud. The hard riding had reopened the wound in my side; beneath my armor, I felt the dampness of blood. I was afraid that soon I would faint and fall off my horse.

More than once, I drifted off to sleep, only to come jolting awake as we splashed across one stream or another. It was hard to keep Altaru to our course to the northwest. At each of my lapses in consciousness, I found him turning toward the south. I sensed in him a fierce desire to move in that direction; it was as if he could smell a mare deeper in the woods, and every muscle in his body trembled to find her. It was only by his instincts, I remembered, that we had escaped from the Black Bog. Perhaps his instincts might now help us escape the Stonefaces. And so, without telling the others what was happening, I let Altaru go where he wished.

Thus we traveled quite a few miles due south. I sensed a gradual change in the air, and I thought that the trees here grew taller. Their green crowns towered over the forest floor perhaps as high as 120 feet. From somewhere in their spreading branches and fluttering leaves, I heard the voice of an unfamiliar bird: his cry was something like the *raaark* of a raven but was deeper and harsher and seemed to warn us away. Other things warned us away as well. I had a disquieting sense that I was crossing an invisible border into a forbidden realm. Whenever I tried to peer through the woods to see what might be drawing Altaru, however, it seemed that a will greater than my own caused me to become distracted and look away. It was as if the earth itself here was guarded by some sentinel I could not see. But strangely, I was never quite conscious of a being or entity watching the woods. At precisely those moments when I tried to bring these sensations into full awareness, I found myself touching my wounded side or gazing at the blood on my hand—or wondering if I had really fallen in love with Atara. It was as if my mind had slipped off the surface of a gleaming mirror to behold only myself.

I knew that the others, too, sensed something strange about

the woods. I felt Atara's reluctance to go any farther and Maram's doubt pounding in him like a heartbeat that seemed to say: *Go back, go back, go back.* Even Master Juwain's great curiosity about the woods seemed blunted by his fear of them.

And then, after perhaps a couple of miles, the soft breeze grew suddenly cooler and cleaner. The sweet scent of the numinous seemed to hang in the air. I found that I could breathe more easily, and I gasped to behold the heights of the trees, for here the giant oaks grew very high above us, at least two hundred feet. The forest floor was mostly free of debris, being covered by a carpet of golden leaves. But there were flowers, too: violets and goldthread and others that I had never seen before. One of these had many red pointed petals that erupted from its center like flames. I called it a fireflower; but its fragrance filled me as if I had drunk from a sparkling stream. I felt my fever cooling and then leaving me altogether. My head pain vanished as well. All my senses seemed to grow keener and deeper. I could almost see the folds in the silvery bark of an oak three hundred yards away and hear the sap streaming through its mighty trunk.

How far we rode into these great trees I could not tell. In the abiding peace of the oaks, both distance and direction seemed to take on a new depth of dimension. Something about the earth itself here seemed to dissolve each moment into the next so that the whole forest opened onto a secret realm as timeless as the stars. I might have been walking these same woods a million years in the past—or a million years hence.

"What *is* this place?" Maram wondered as he stopped his horse to look up at the leaves fluttering high above us.

I climbed down from Altaru to give him a rest and stretch my legs. I reached down to touch a starflower growing out of a little plant. Its five white petals shined as if from a light within.

"My headache is gone," Maram said. "My fever, as well."

Atara and Master Juwain admitted that they, too, had been miraculously restored. With Maram, they climbed off their horses and joined me on the forest floor. Then Master Juwain said, "There are places on the earth of great power. Healing places—this must be one of them."

"Why haven't I heard of these places?" Maram asked.

"Yes, indeed, why *haven't* you, Brother Maram? Do you not remember the *Book of Ages* where it tells of the vilds?" Master Juwain then recited:

> *"There is a place tween earth and time,*
> *In some forgotten misty clime*
> *Of woods and brooks and vernal glades,*
> *Whose healing magic never fades.*
>
> *"An island in the greenest sea,*
> *Abode of deeper greenery*
> *Where giant trees and emeralds grow,*
> *Where leaves and grass and flowers glow.*
>
> *"And there no bitter bloom of spite*
> *To blight the forest's living light,*
> *No sword, no spear, no axe, no knife*
> *To tear the sweetest sprigs of life.*
>
> *"The deeper life for which we yearn,*
> *Immortal flame that doesn't burn,*
> *The sacred sparks, ablaze, unseen—*
> *The children of the Galadin.*
>
> *"Beneath the trees they gloze and gleam,*
> *And whirl and play and dance and dream*
> *Of wider woods beyond the sea*
> *Where they shall dwell eternally."*

After he had finished, Maram rubbed his beard and said, "I thought that was just a myth from the Lost Ages."

"I hope not," Master Juwain said.

"Well, wherever we are," Maram said, smiling at him, "it seems that at least we've finally lost the Stonefaces. Val, what do you think?"

I closed my eyes for a moment trying to feel for the snake wrapping its coils around my spine. My whole being seemed suddenly free from any wrongness. Even the burning of the ki-rax was cooled by the breeze blowing through the woods.

"We might have lost them," I agreed. All around us grew fireflowers and starflowers and violets. In the trees, a flock of blue birds like none I had ever seen was trilling out the sweetest of songs. I had only ever dreamed of a place that felt so alive as this.

"Well, then," Maram said, "why don't we celebrate? Why don't we break out some of your father's fine brandy that we've been toting all the way from Mesh?"

We all agreed that this was a good idea; even Master Juwain consented to breaking his vows this one time. After Maram had cracked the cask and filled our cups with some brandy, Master Juwain touched his tongue to the dark liquor and grimaced; one might have thought he was touching fire. Then Maram raised his cup and called out, "To our escape from the Stonefaces. Surely these woods won't abide any evil."

Just as he was about to fasten his thick lips around the rim of his cup, a lilting voice called back to him from somewhere in the trees: "Surely they won't, Hairface."

A man suddenly stepped from behind a tree thirty yards away. He was short and slight, with curly brown hair, pale skin, and leaf-green eyes. Except for a skirt woven of some silvery substance, he was naked. In his little hands he held a little bow and a flint-tipped arrow.

The unexpected sight of him so startled Maram that he spilled his brandy over his beard and chest. Then he managed to splutter, "Who are you? We didn't know anyone lived here. We mean you no harm, little man."

Quick as a wink, the man drew his arrow straight at Maram and piped out, "Sad to say, we mean *you* harm, big man. So sad, too bad."

And with that, even as Maram, Atara, and I reached for our weapons, the little man let loose a high-pitched whistle that sounded like the trilling of blue birds. Immediately, others of his kind appeared from behind trees in a great circle around us two hundred yards across. There were hundreds of them, and they each held a little bow fitted with an arrow.

"Val, what shall we do?" Maram cried out.

As I drew my sword, the man said, "Put down your weapons!"

At another of his whistles, the circle of little people began to close around us as both men and women approached us through the trees. There was nothing to do except put down our weapons as he had said.

"Come, come," he told me from in front of a tree where he had stopped ten yards away. The others had now closed their circle some twenty yards around us. "Now stand away from your beasts, please—we don't want to pierce them."

"Val!" Maram called to me. "They mean to murder us—I really think they do!"

So did I think this. It seemed a bitter fate that after facing seeming worse dangers together, we should have to die like cornered prey in this strange and beautiful woods.

"Come, come," the man said again, "stand away. It's sad to die, and bad to die like this—but it will be worse the longer we put it off."

There was nothing to do, I thought, but die as he had said. For each of us, a time comes to say farewell to the earth and return to the stars. Now, at the sight of two hundred arrows pointing at our hearts, each of us faced the approach of death in his or her own way. Master Juwain began chanting the words to the First Light Meditation. Maram covered his eyes with his forearm, as if blocking out the sight of the fierce little people might make them go away. He cried out that he was a prince of Delu, and he promised them gold and diamonds if they would put down their bows. Atara calmly reached back into her quiver for an arrow. She obviously intended to slay at least one more man and end her life in a joyous fight. I did not. It was bad enough that I should feel the great nothingness pulling me down into the dark; why, I wondered, should I inflict this terrible cold on men and women who sought only to protect their forest kingdom? And so, at last, I stood away from Altaru. I stood as tall and straight as I could. I lifted my hand from the hilt of my sword to brush back my hair, which my sweat had plastered to the side of my face. Then I looked at the man with the leaf-green eyes and waited.

For a moment—the longest of my life—the little man stood regarding me strangely. Then his drawn bow wavered; he relaxed the pull on his bowstring and pointed straight at my forehead. To the other men and women behind and all around him he said, "Look, look—it is the mark!"

A murmur of astonishment rippled around the circle of little people. I noticed then that on each of their bows was burned a jagged mark like that of a lightning bolt.

"How did you come by the mark?" the man asked me.

"It was there from my birth," I told him truthfully.

"Then you are blessed," he said. "And I am glad, so glad, for there will no killing today."

Maram let out a cry of thanksgiving while Atara still held her arrow nocked on her bowstring. The man asked her if she would consent to putting it away; otherwise, he said, his people would have to shoot *their* arrows into her arms and legs.

"Please, Atara," I said to her.

Although hating to disarm herself, Atara put her arrow back into her quiver and stowed her bow in the holster strapped to her horse.

"Too bad that we must bind you now," the man said. "But you understand the need for it, don't you? You big people are so quick with your weapons."

So saying, he whistled again, and several women came forward with cords to bind our hands behind our backs. It seemed that our journey to Tria would have to wait—how long, I didn't know. But there seemed no help for it.

When they were finished, the man said, "My name is Danali. We will take you to a place where you can rest."

After presenting myself and each of the others in turn, I asked him, "What *is* this place? And what is the name of your people?"

"This is the Forest," he said simply. "And we are the Lokilani."

And with that, he turned to lead us deeper into the woods.

■ 14 ■

WE WALKED IN line, trailing our horses, the Lokilani swarming around us. With the abandon of children, they touched our garments and let out cries of surprise at Atara's leather trousers and most of all, at the steel links of my armor. I gathered that none of them had seen such substances before. They were all dressed as was Danali, in skirts of what appeared to be silk. Many wore emerald or ruby pendants dangling from their delicate necks; a few of the women also sported earrings but were otherwise unadorned. None of them wore shoes upon their leathery feet.

Danali led us beneath the great oaks and elms, which seemed to grow still greater with every mile we moved into them. In places, however, we passed through groves of much lesser trees that were scarcely any taller than those of Mesh. They appeared all to be fruit trees: apple and cherry, pear and plum. Many were in full flower with little white petals covering them like mounds of snow; many were laden with red apples or dark red cherries. That they should bear fruit in Ashte seemed a miracle, and not the only one of those lovely woods. It amazed me to see deer in great numbers walking through the apple groves as if they had nothing to fear from the Lokilani with their bows and arrows.

When Maram suggested that Danali should shoot a couple of them to make a feast for dinner, he looked at him in horror and said, "*Shoot* arrows into an animal? Would I shoot my own mother, Hairface? Am I wolf, am I weasel, am I a bear that I should hunt animals for food?"

The Lokilani, we found, wouldn't even eat the eggs taken from birds' nests or honey from the combs of the bees. Neither did they cultivate barley or wheat or any such vegetables as carrots, peas, or beans. The only gardens they kept grew other glories from the earth: crystals such as clear quartz, amethyst, and starstone, as well as garnets, topaz, tourmaline, and more precious gems. I marveled at the many-colored stones erupting from the forest floor like so many new shoots. They seemed always to be planted—if that was the right word—in colorful concentric circles around trees whose like I had seen only in my dreams. Though not very tall, they spread out like oaks, and their bark was silver like that of maples. But it was their leaves in all their splendor that made me gasp and wonder; they shimmered like millions of golden shields and were etched with a webwork of deep green veins. Danali called them astors. I thought that the astors—and the bright gemstones growing around them—must be the greatest miracles of the Forest, but I was wrong.

By a circuitous route that seemed to follow no logic or path,

Danali led us through the trees to the Lokilani's village. This was no simple assemblage of buildings. Indeed, there were no real buildings here; neither were there streets, for the only dwellings the Lokilani had were spread out over many acres, each house being built beneath its own tree.

Danali escorted us toward one of these strange-looking houses. Its frame was of many long poles set into the ground in a circle and leaning up against each other so as to form a high cone. The poles were woven with long strips of white bark like that of birch. Inside we found a circular expanse of earth covered with golden astor leaves. A small firepit had been dug into the ground at the house's center, but there was no furniture other than beds of fresh green leaves. Danali explained that this was a house of healing; here we would remain until our bodies and spirits were whole again.

After setting a guard around our house, Danali saw to our every need. He had food and drink brought to us; he had our clothes taken away to be mended and cleaned. That evening he led us under escort to a hot springs that bubbled up out of the ground near a grove of plum trees. Several of the Lokilani women climbed into the water with us and used handfuls of fragrant-smelling leaves to scrub us clean. One of them, a pretty woman named Iolana, captured Maram's eye. She had long brown hair and the green eyes of all her people, but she was almost as small as a child, standing no higher than the top of Maram's belly. The difference in their sizes, however, did not discourage him. When I remarked the incongruity of a moose taking up with a roe deer, he told me, "Love will find a way, my friend. It always does. I'll be as gentle with her as a leaf settling onto a pond. Don't you find that there's something about these little people that inspires gentleness?"

I had to admit that their bows and arrows notwithstanding, the Lokilani were the least warlike people I had ever met. And perhaps the kindest, too. That evening, Danali sent a beautiful woman named Pualani into our house. She had flowing, chestnut hair and eyes as green as the emerald she wore around her neck. With great gentleness, she pressed her warm fingers into my skin all around the wound that Salmelu had cut into me. Then she had me drink a sweetish tea that she made and told me to lie back against my bed of leaves.

Almost immediately, I fell asleep. But strangely, all night long I was aware that I was sleeping, and also aware of Pualani pressing pungent-smelling leaves against my side. I thought I felt as well the coolness of her emerald touching me. My whole body seemed to burn with a cool, green light. When I awoke the next morning, I was amazed to discover that my wound had completely healed. Not even a scar remained to mark my flesh and remind me of my sword fight.

"It's a miracle!" Maram exclaimed when he saw what Pualani had done. In the soft light filtering through the curving white walls of our house, he ran his rough hand over my side. "This wood is full of magic and miracles!"

Later that day, Danali came to our house to escort us to a feast held in our honor. We all put on our best clothes: Maram found a fresh red tunic in the saddlebags of his packhorse while Master Juwain had only his newly cleaned green woolens. Atara, however, unpacked a yellow doeskin shirt embroidered with fine beadwork; it made a stark contrast with her dark leather trousers, but I liked it better than her studded armor. As for myself, I wore a simple black tunic emblazoned with the silver swan and seven stars of Mesh.

The whole Lokilani village had assembled nearby in a stand of great astor trees. There must have been nearly five hundred of them: men, women, and children sitting on the leaf-covered ground and gathered around many long mats woven of long, green leaves. I saw at once that these mats served as tables, for they were heaped with bowls of food. Danali invited us to sit at a table beneath the boughs of a spreading astor, along with his wife and five children. And then, just as we were taking our places, Pualani walked into the glade. Her hair was crowned with a garland of blue flowers, and she wore a silvery robe that covered her from neck to ankle. Although we had supposed her to be quite young, she was accompanied by her grown daughter, who turned out to be none other than Iolana. With them walked her husband, a slender but well-muscled man whom Danali introduced as Elan. He surprised us all by telling us that Pualani was the Lokilani's queen.

Pualani took the place of honor at the head of the table with Elan to her left. Master Juwain, Maram, Atara, and I sat to one side of the table facing Danali and his family. Iolana knelt directly beside Maram, and they both seemed quite happy with this arrangement. She gazed at him much more openly than would any maid of Mesh.

Without fanfare, toasting, or speeches, the meal began as Pualani reached out to pass a bowl of fruit to Elan. There was much food to heap on our plates, which were nothing more than single but very large leaves. As Danali had told us, all of our meal had come from trees or bushes in the Forest. Fruits predominated, and I had never seen so many served in one place: blackberries and raspberries, gooseberries, apples, and plums. There were cherries, too, as well as a greenish, apple-like thing that they called starfruit. And others. It was all ripe, and every piece I put into my mouth burst with fresh juices and sweetness. The Lokilani made good use of their woods' many seeds and nuts, which included not only familiar ones such as walnuts and hickories but also some very large brown nuts they called treemeats. Danali said that they were more sustaining than the flesh of animals; they tasted rich and earthy and seemed full of the Forest's strength. The Lokilani cooked them into a thick stew, even as they baked a bread of bearseed and spread it with various nut butters and jams. As well, we were passed bowls of green shoots that I had thought only a squirrel could eat, and at least four kinds of edible flowers. For drink, we had cups of cool water and elderberry wine. Although it seemed this last was too sweet to drink in quantity, Maram proved me wrong. He let the Lokilani refill his cup again and again, even more times than he refilled his own plate.

"What a meal," he said as reached for a pitcher of maple syrup to drizzle over his bread. "I've never eaten like this before."

None of us had. The food was not only more delicious than any I had ever tasted, it was more alive. It seemed that the essence of the Forest was passing directly into our bodies as if breathed into our blood.

At the end of our feast, Pualani sat quietly regarding us. Her deeply set eyes caught up the color of the emerald necklace she wore, and I thought that she was not only beautiful but wise. And then, in a calm, clear voice thick with the Lokilani's lilting accent, she said to us, "We have much to discuss, and so why don't we begin at the beginning? We would all like to know how you found your way into our wood, and why."

Since I—or rather, Altaru—had led our way here, Master Juwain, Maram, and Atara all looked at me to answer her.

"The 'why' of it is easy enough to tell," I said. "We were fleeing our enemies, and our path took us here."

"Well, Sar Valashu, that *is* a beginning," Pualani said. "But only the very beginning of the beginning, yes? You've told us the circumstances of your flight into the Forest but not *why* you've come to us. But perhaps you don't yet know, too bad."

Maram, after taking yet another pull of his wine, looked at her and slurred out, "Not everything has a purpose, my lady."

"But of course, all things do," she said. "We just have to look for it."

"You might as well look for the reason that birds sing or men drink wine."

She smiled at him and said, "Birds sing because they're glad to be alive, and men drink wine because they're not."

Pualani turned toward me and said, "Why don't we put aside the purpose of your coming here and try to understand just how you entered our woods."

"Well, we walked into them," I told her.

"Yes, of course—but *how* did you do this? No one just walks into the Forest."

She explained that just as some peoples built walls of stone to protect their kingdoms, the Lokilani had constructed a different kind of barrier around their woods. She told us very little of how they did this. She hinted at the power of the great trees to keep strangers away and at a secret that the Lokilani seemed to share with each other but not with us.

"Here the power of the earth is very great," she said. "It repels most people. Even many of the bears, wolves, and higher beasts. A man walking in our direction would find that he doesn't want to walk this way. His path would take him a great circle around the Forest or away from it."

"Perhaps it would," I said, remembering the sensations I had felt the day before. "But if he came close enough, he would see the great trees."

"Men come close to many things they never see," Pualani

said as she smiled mysteriously. "Looking toward the Forest from the outside, most men would see *only* trees."

"But what if they were looking *for* the Forest?"

"Men look for many things they never find," she said. "And who knows even to look? Even a Lokilani, upon leaving our woods, can forget what real trees are like and have a hard time finding his way back in."

"Our coming must have been a wild chance, then."

"No one comes here by chance, Sar Valashu. Few come at all."

I pointed off toward a tree a hundred yards away where a young woman stood with a strung bow and arrow. I said, "Your people don't hunt animals—what do they hunt, then?"

Pualani's face clouded for a moment as she exchanged dark looks with Elan and Danali. Then she said, "For many times many years, the Earthkiller has sent his men to try to find our Forest. A few have come close, and these we've had to send back to the stars."

"Who is this Earthkiller, then?"

"The Earthkiller is the Earthkiller," she said simply. "This is known from the ancient of days: he cuts trees to burn in his forges. He cuts wounds in the earth to steal its fire. By forge and fire he seeks the making of that which can never be made."

Her words sounded familiar to me, as they must have to Master Juwain. I nodded at him as he pulled out his *Saganom Elu;* with great excitement, he read from the *Book of Fire:*

> *He hates the flowers, soft and white,*
> *The grass, the forest's gentle breath,*
> *For all that lives and leaps with light*
> *Recalls the bitterness of death.*
>
> *With axe and pick and poison flame*
> *He wreaks his spite upon the land;*
> *His armies burn and hack and maim*
> *The ferns and flowers, soil and sand.*
>
> *And down through rocky vein and bore*
> *With evil eye and sorcery*
> *He plumbs the earth for golden ore*
> *In search of immortality.*

Thus wounding earth to steal her fire
And feeding trees to forge and flame,
He turns upon himself his ire
And burns his soul with bitter blame.

For golden cups that blaze too bright
Make hateful, mortal men afraid,
And that which makes the stellar light,
In love, cannot itself be made.

When he had finished, Pualani sighed deeply and said, "It would seem that your people know of the Earthkiller, too."

"We call him the Red Dragon," Master Juwain said.

"You have named him well, then," Pualani said. Then she pointed at his book and asked, "But what is this animal skin encasing the white leaves crawling with bugs?"

We were all astonished that Pualani had never seen a book. Just as it astonished her and all the Lokilani when Master Juwain explained how the sounds of language could be represented by letters and read out loud.

"You bring marvels into our woods," she said. "Great mysteries, too."

She took a sip of wine and slowly swallowed it. Then she smiled at me and continued, "When you approached the Forest, we thought the Earthkiller must have sent you. And so we sent Danali and the others to greet you. We couldn't have known that you would be wearing the mark of the Ellama."

"What is this Ellama?" I asked her, touching the scar on my forehead.

"The Ellama is the Ellama," she said. "And the lightning bolt is sacred to him. This is the fire that connects the earth to the heavens, where the Ellama walks with the rest of his kind."

"With the Star People?" I asked.

"Some think of them as people," she said. "But just as people such as you and I are also animals, we are something more. And so it is with them who are more than human, the Bright Ones, the Galad a'Din."

"You mean, the *Galadin*?"

"You say words strangely. But yes, I mean they who walk

among the stars. When Danali saw the mark on you, he wondered if it was perhaps the Ellama who really sent you to us."

I smiled at this as I shook my head. Then I related as much about my friends and me as I thought it prudent to reveal. I even told Pualani and the others about my encounter with the Lord of Illusions and the stone-faced gray men who had nearly driven us mad.

When had I finished speaking, Pualani bowed her head to me and said, "Thank you for opening your heart to us, Sar Valashu."

She went on to say that the world of castles and quests and old books full of tales were as unknown to the Lokilani as the stars must be to us. She had never heard of the Nine Kingdoms, nor even of Alonia, in whose great forests the Forest abided. In truth, she denied that any king could have a claim upon her woods or that it might be a part of any kingdom, unless that kingdom be the world itself. As she said, the Lokilani were the first people, the true people, and the Forest was the true world.

"Once, before the Earthkiller came and men cut down the great trees, there was only the Forest," she told us. "Here the Lokilani have lived since the beginning of time. And here we will remain until the stars die."

I sat quietly for a moment, then asked her, "But do you not fear that, in the end, the Red Dragon will find a way to destroy your woods?"

Again, a dark look fell over Pualani's face; I was reminded of winter storm clouds smothering a bright blue sky.

"The Earthkiller has great power," she admitted. "And great allies, too. These Stonefaces of yours have tried to enter the Forest in our dreams even as they entered yours."

I nodded my head at this and said, "There are things here that the Lord of Lies would give a great deal to know: how you grow trees to such great heights and grow gems from the very ground."

"You seem to know a great deal of what he would wish to know."

Truly, I *did* know much more of Morjin's mind than I wanted to. I knew that if he could, he would crush these secrets from the Lokilani as readily as he would grapes beneath his boots.

"There is one thing he seeks above all else," I said.

"This is the Lightstone that you spoke of, yes? But what *is* this stone? Is it an emerald? A great ruby or diamond?"

"No, it is a cup—a plain golden cup."

Here, Master Juwain broke in to tell of the gelstei and of how the great crystals had been made through many long ages of Ea's history. And the greatest of all the gelstei, he said, was the gold, which most men believed had been created by the Star People and brought to earth at the beginning of the Lost Ages. But he admitted that many thought that the Lightstone had been forged and cast into the shape of a cup in the Blue Mountains of Alonia sometime during the Age of Swords. Whatever the truth really was, the Lord of Lies sought not only the Lightstone itself but the secret of its making.

"He would certainly create a Lightstone of his own, if he could," Master Juwain said. "And so he would certainly steal from you any knowledge of growing and shaping crystals that might help him."

Pualani sat very straight, pulling on the emeralds of her necklace. She looked at Master Juwain for a long moment, and then at Atara, Maram, and me. She asked us why we sought the Lightstone. We each answered as best we could. When we had finished speaking, she said, "The gold gelstei brings light, as you say. And yet this lord of darkness seeks it above all other things. Why, we want to know, why, why?"

"Because," Master Juwain said, "the gold gives power over all the other gelstei except perhaps the silver. It gives immortality, too. And perhaps much else that we don't know."

"But it is light, you say, pure light bound into a cup of gold?"

"Even light can be used to read good or evil words in a book," Master Juwain told her. "Just as too much light can burn or blind."

I sat thinking about this for a moment, and then I added, "Even if this cup brought the Red Dragon no light at all, he would take joy in keeping others from it."

"Oh, that is bad, very, very bad," Pualani said. She bent forward to confer with Danali. After looking at Elan in silent understanding, she told us, "There is great danger here for the Lokilani. A danger we never saw."

"My apologies," I said, "for bringing such evil tidings."

"No, no, you mustn't apologize," Pualani said. "And you've brought nothing evil into our woods, so we hope, so we pray. It may be that you're an emissary of the Ellama after all, even if you didn't know it."

I looked down at the ground because I didn't know what to say.

"The Ellama still watches over the Forest," she told us. "The Galad a'Din haven't forgotten the Lokilani, they would never forget."

I smiled sadly at this, because I supposed the Galadin had looked away from the ways and wars of Ea long ago.

"And we haven't forgotten them, we must never forget," Pualani said to us. "And so we celebrate this remembrance and their eternal presence among us. Will you help us celebrate, Sar Valashu Elahad?"

She looked straight at me then, and I felt something inside her light up all green and blazing like life itself.

"Yes, of course," I told her. "Even as you've helped us."

"And you, Prince Maram Marshayk—will you help us, too?"

Maram eyed his empty cup and the jug of wine that had found its way to the end of the table. He licked his lips and said, "Help you *celebrate*? Does a bear eat honey if you hold it to his face?"

"Very good," Pualani said, nodding at him. Then she smiled at Atara and asked, "And what about you, Atara of the Manslayers? Will you celebrate the coming of the Galad a'Din?"

"I will," Atara told her, nodding her head.

Pualani now turned to Master Juwain and asked him the same question, as if reciting the words to a ritual. And he replied, "I would like very much to celebrate with you, but I'm afraid my vows don't permit me to drink wine."

"Then you may keep your vows," Pualani said, "for it's not wine we drink in remembrance of the Shining Ones."

At this news, Maram looked crestfallen. "What *do* you drink, then?"

"Only fire," Pualani said, smiling at him. "But it might be more precise to say that we eat it."

"Eat?" Maram groaned as he held his bulging belly. "Eat *what*? I don't think I can eat another bite."

"Does a bear eat honey when it's held to his face?" Pualani asked him with a coy smile.

"You have *honey*? I thought the Lokilani didn't eat honey."

"We don't. But we have something much sweeter."

So saying, she pulled off a silvery cloth from a bowl at the end of the table. Inside were piled many small golden fruits about the size of plums. She took one in her hand and then passed the bowl to Elan, who did the same. The bowl quickly made its way around the table. I noticed that although Danali's three children all seemed quite interested in the bowl's gleaming contents, none of them touched the fruit. I gathered that just as a child in Mesh would never participate in our rituals of toasting and drinking beer, so the Lokilani children were forbidden to participate in what was to come.

"The fruit has probably fermented," I said to Maram as I took one in my hand. "You'll probably find all the wine inside that you wish."

"Now *that* would be a miracle," he said as he picked up one of the little fruits and regarded it doubtfully. He looked at Pualani and asked, "What do you call this thing?"

"It's a timana," she said. She pointed up at the golden-leafed tree above us. "Once every seven years, the astors bear the sacred fruit."

Maram held the timana to his nose for a moment but said nothing.

"Long ago," Pualani explained, "the Shining Ones walked the Forest and planted the first astors. The trees were their gift to the Lokilani."

She sat looking at the timana in her hand as I might look at the stars. Then she told us that the Galadin were angels and this was their flesh.

"We eat this fruit in remembrance of the brightness of being," she explained. "Please join us in our celebration today."

Now the whole glade fell very quiet as the Lokilani at the other tables put down their cups of wine or water to watch us eat the timanas. I wondered why none of them had been given any fruit. I thought that it must be quite rare and used by only a few Lokilani at any one ritual.

Without any more words, Pualani bit into her timana, and all the men and women at our table did the same. As my teeth closed on the fruit, a waterfall of tastes exploded in my mouth. It was like honey and wine and sunlight all bound up into the most fragrant of juices. And yet there was something bittersweet about the fruit as well. Beneath its succulent sugars was a flavor I had never experienced: it recalled mighty trees streaming with spring sap and the fire of a greenness that no longer existed on earth.

The fruit's savor was exquisite and lingered on my tongue. Along with Pualani and Maram and everyone else, I took a second bite. The timana's flesh was reddish-orange and studded with a starlike array of tiny black seeds. It glistened in the waning light for an endless moment before I put the fruit in my mouth and ate the rest of it.

"We're so glad you've joined us," Pualani said as the others finished theirs as well. "Now you'll see what you'll see."

"*What* will we see?" Maram asked, licking the juice from his teeth.

"Perhaps nothing. But perhaps you'll see the Timpum."

"The Timpum?" Maram asked in alarm. "What's that?"

"The Timpum are the Timpum," Pualani said softly. "They are of the Galad a'Din."

"I don't understand," Maram said, rubbing his belly.

"The Galad a'Din," Pualani said, "are beings of pure fire. When they walked the earth in the ages before the Lost Ages, they left part of their being behind them. So, the fire, the beings that men do not usually see—the Timpum."

"I don't think I *want* to understand," Maram said.

Pualani looked from him to Master Juwain and Atara, and at last at me. She said, "It's strange that you seek your golden cup in other lands when so much is to be found so much closer. Love, life, light—why not look for these things in the leaves of the trees and along the wind?"

Why not indeed? I wondered as I looked up at the soft lights dancing along the trees' fluttering golden leaves.

"Am I to understand," Maram said, breathing heavily, "that this fruit you've fed us provides visions of these Timpum?"

"Yes," Pualani said gravely, "either that or death."

We were all silent for as long as it took my heart to beat three times. Then Maram gasped out, "What? What did you say?"

"You've eaten the angels' flesh," Pualani explained. "And so if it's meant to be, you'll see the angel fire. But not all can bear it. And so they die."

At this news, Maram struggled to his feet, puffing and groaning. He held his big belly as he cried out, "Poison, poison! Oh, my Lord—I've been poisoned!"

He bent and stuck his fingers down his throat to purge himself of the dangerous fruit. Pualani stopped him with a few soft words. She told him that it was already too late, that he would have to live or die according to the grace of the Ellama.

"Why have you done this?" Maram shouted at her. His face was now almost as red as a plum. "What have we done to deserve this?"

"Nothing that others haven't," Pualani said. "All the Lokilani, when we become women and men—we eat the sacred fruit. Many die, sad to say. But it must be so. Life without sight of the Timpum would not be worth living."

"It would be to me!" Maram cried out. "I'm not a Lokilani! I don't want to die!"

"We're sorry this had to be, so sorry," Pualani told us. She looked at Master Juwain, who sat frozen like a deer surrounded by wolves, and then she smiled at Atara and me. "There are only two paths for you. You may remain with the Lokilani and become as one of us. Or you must return to your world."

My breath came hard and fast now as the woods about us seemed to take on the tones of the waning sunlight. It was a yellow like nothing I had ever seen, a waiting-yellow over the trees and through them. A watching-yellow that was very close and yet somehow far away.

"Please forgive us, please do," Pualani said. "But if you *do* return to your world, we must be utterly certain of who you are. The Earthkiller's people could never bear the sight of the Timpum. And no one who has ever seen the Timpum could ever serve the Earthkiller."

I noticed that the children at our table, and every table throughout the glade, were watching us with awe coloring their small pale faces. It came to me that awe was nothing less than love and fear, and I felt both of these swelling inside me. Everyone was looking at us in fear for our lives, watching and waiting to see what we would see.

Suddenly, Maram threw his hands to the side of his face and let loose a wild whoop of laughter. He fell to his knees, all the while shaking his head and laughing and crying out that he was dying but didn't care.

"I see them! I see them! Oh, they're everywhere!"

Master Juwain, who had been sitting as still as a statue, leapt to his feet and waved his hands about his bald head. "Astonishing! Astonishing!" he shouted. "It's not possible, it can't be possible. Val, do you see them?"

I did not see them. For at that moment, Atara let out a terrible cry and fell backward to the ground as if her spine had been cut with an axe. She screamed, once, before her eyes closed. Then she grew quiet. The movement beneath her doeskin shirt was so slight that I couldn't tell if she was breathing. I fell over toward her and buried my face in the soft garment. Her whole body seemed as still as stone and colder than ice. I understood too well what it felt like for another to die; I would have died myself rather than feel this nothingness take Atara. I knew then with an utter certainty that I *did* love her—as much as I loved anyone who had ever lived and breathed.

The cold suddenly grew unbearable, and I realized with a deep despair that she was leaving me. There was nothing but darkness inside her and all about me. I could see nothing because my eyes were tightly closed as I gripped the soft leather of her shirt and wept bitterly.

Then I, too, let out a terrible cry. My heart beat so hard I thought it would break open my chest. Everything poured out of me: my love for her, my tears, my whispers of hope that burned my lips like fire.

"Atara," I said softly, "don't go away."

The pain inside me was worse than anything I had ever known. It cut me open like a sword, and I felt the blood streaming out of my heart and into hers. It took forever to die, I knew, while the moments of life were so precious and few.

And then, as if awakening from a dream, her whole body started. I looked down to see her eyes suddenly open. She smiled at me as her breath fell over my face. "Thank you," she said, "for saving my life again."

She struggled to sit up, and I held her against me with her head touching mine and my face pressing her shoulder. My breath came in shudders and quick gasps, and I was both weeping and laughing because I couldn't quite believe that she was still alive.

"Shhh," she whispered to me, "be quiet, be quiet now."

As I sat there with my eyes closed, I became aware of a deep silence. But it was not a quietening of the world; now the songs of the sparrows came ringing through the trees, and I could almost hear the wildflowers growing in the earth all around me. It was more a silence within myself where the chatter of all my thoughts and fears suddenly died away. I could hear myself whispering to myself in a voice without sound; it seemed the earth itself was calling out a name that was mine but not mine alone.

"Oh, there are so many!" Atara said to me softly. "Look, Val, look!"

I opened my eyes then, and I saw the Timpum. As Maram had said, they were everywhere. I sat up straight, blinking my eyes. Above the golden leaves of the forest floor, little luminous clouds floated as if drawing their substance from the earth and returning to it soft showers of light. Among the wood anemone and ashflowers, swirls of fire burned in colors of red, orange, and blue. They flitted from flower to flower like flaming butterflies drinking up nectar and touching each petal with their numinous heat. Little silver moons hovered near some cinnamon fern, and the ingathering of white sparks beneath the boughs of the astors reminded me of constellations of stars. From behind rocks came soft flashes like those of glowworms. The Timpum seemed to come in almost as many kinds as the birds and beasts of the Forest. They flickered and fluttered and danced and glittered, and no leaf or living thing in the glade appeared untouched by their presence.

"Astonishing! Astonishing!" Master Juwain called out again. "I must learn their names and kinds!"

Some of the Timpum were tiny, no more than burning drops of light that hung in the air like mist. Some were as huge as the trees: the trunks of a few of the astors were ringed with golden halos that brightened and deepened as they spread out to encompass the great crowns of leaves. Although they had forms, they had no faces. And yet we perceived them as having quite distinct faces—to be sure, not of lips, noses, cheeks, and eyes, but rather colored with various blendings of curiosity, playfulness, effervescence, compassion, and other characteristics that one might expect to find on a human countenance. Most marvelous of all was that they seemed to be aware not only of the trees and the rocks, the ferns and the flowers, but of us.

"Look, Val!" Maram called to me. He stood above the table as he brushed the folds of his tunic. "These little red ones keep at me like hummingbirds in a honeysuckle bush. Do you see them?"

"Yes—how not?" I told him.

All about him were Timpum of the whirling fire variety, and their flames touched him in tendrils of red, orange, and violet. I turned to see a little silver moon shimmer in front of Atara for a moment as if drinking in the light of her bright blue eyes. And then I blinked, and it was gone.

"They seem to want something of me," Maram said. "I can almost hear them whispering, almost see it in my mind."

The Timpum seemed to want something from all of us, though we couldn't quite say what that might be. I looked at Pualani to ask if it was that way for the Lokilani, too.

"The Timpum speak only the language of the Galad a'Din," she told us. "Even so, we *do* understand the Timpum sometimes. They warn us if outsiders are approaching our realm or of when we have hate in our hearts. On cloudy nights of no moon, they light up our woods."

I looked off into the trees for a moment, and the shimmering spectacle before my eyes dazzled me. To Pualani I said, "Do your people then see the world like this all the time?"

"Yes, this is how the Forest *is*."

She told me that so long as we dwelled in the Forest, we would see the Timpum. If we someday chose to eat the sacred timanas again in remembrance of the Shining Ones, even as she and the others had eaten them, our vision of the Timpum would grow only brighter.

"If you decide to leave us," she said, "it will now be hard for you to bear the deadness of any other wood."

Just then an especially bright Timpum—it was one of the ones like a swirl of flickering white stars—fell slowly down from the tree above me. It spun about in the space before my eyes as if studying the scar cut into my forehead. It seemed to touch me there with a quick silver light; I felt this as a surge of compassion that touched me to my core and brightened my whole being as if I had been struck with a lightning bolt. Then, after a moment, the flickering Timpum settled itself down on top of my head. Maram and the others saw it shimmering in my hair like a crown of stars, but I could not.

"How do I get it off me?" I asked as I brushed my hand through my hair.

"Why would you want to?" Pualani asked me. "Sometimes a Timpum will attach itself to one of us to try to tell us something."

"What, then?"

"Only you will ever know," she said as she gazed above my head. Then she told me, "I think the 'why' of your coming to our woods has been answered, however. You are here to listen, Valashu Elahad. And to dance."

And with that, she smiled at me and rose from the table. This seemed a signal that Elan and Danali—and all the Lokilani at the other tables—should rise, too. Along with Pualani, they came over to Atara, Master Juwain, Maram, and me. They touched our faces and kissed our hands and congratulated us on eating the timanas and surviving to see the Timpum. Then Danali began singing a light, happy song while many of his people clapped their hands to keep time. Others began dancing. They joined hands in circles surrounding circles and spun about the forest floor as they added their voices to Danali's song. I found myself clasping hands with Atara and Maram and turning with them. Although it was impossible to touch a Timpum, their substance being not of flesh but the fire of angels, there was a sense in which they danced with us and we with them. For they were everywhere among us, and they never stopped fluttering and sparkling and whirling about golden-leafed trees.

Much later, after the sun had set and the Timpum's eyeless faces lit up the night, I took out my flute and joined the Lokilani in song. The Lokilani marveled at the slender piece of wood, for they had never imagined music could be made in such a way. I taught a few of the children to play a simple song that my mother had once taught me. Atara sang with them, and Maram, too, before he took Iolana's hand and stole off into the trees. Even Master Juwain hummed a few notes in his rough old voice, though he was more interested in trying to ferret out and record the words of the Timpum's language.

I, too, wished to understand what they had to tell me. And so, even as Pualani had said, I stayed awake all night playing my flute and dancing and listening to the fiery voices that spoke along the wind.

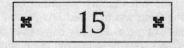

OUR VISION OF the Timpum did not fade with the coming of the new day. If anything, in the fullness of the sunlight, their fiery forms seemed brighter. It was impossible to look at them very long and imagine a life without them.

After a delicious breakfast of fruits and nutbread, Atara and I held council with Master Juwain and Maram. We stood by a stream not far from our house, inhaling the fragrance of cherry blossoms and marveling at the miracle of the woods that we could not explain.

"Well, there's one miracle that I *would* like explained," Master Juwain said to me. "What happened last night between you and Atara?"

I looked at Atara, and she returned my gaze for a long moment before she answered him: "After I ate the timana, I saw the Timpum almost immediately. It was like a flash of fire. It was so beautiful that I wanted to hold it forever—but can one hold the sun? I felt myself burning up like a leaf caught in the flames. And then I couldn't breathe, and I thought I was dying. Everything was so cold. It was like I had been buried alive in a crystal cave, so cold and hard, and everything growing darker. I *would* have died if Val hadn't come to take me back."

"And how did he do that?" Master Juwain asked.

Again, Atara looked at me. "I'm still not sure. Somehow I felt what he felt for me. All his *life,* his desire that I live—I felt it breaking open the cave like lightning and burning into me."

Now Master Juwain and Maram looked at me, too, as the bluebirds sang and the Timpum glittered all about us. And Master Juwain said, "That sounds like the *valarda*."

Master Juwain's use of this word, utterly unexpected, fell out of the air like lightning and nearly broke *me* open. How did he know the name of my gift that Morjin had spoken to me out of the land of nightmare? For many miles, I had wondered about this strange name, as I wondered about Master Juwain now. But he just smiled at me in his kindly but proud way, as if he knew almost everything there was to know.

It seemed that the time had finally come to explain about my gift, which they had already suspected lay behind my sensing of the Stonefaces and the other strangenesses of my life. And so I told them everything I knew. I said that I had been born breathing in others' sufferings and their joys as well. I revealed my dream of Morjin and how he had prophesied that one day I would use my gift to make others feel my pain.

"You should have come to us long ago," Master Juwain told me. "I read about the *valarda* in a book once. I'm sure that there must be other books that could instruct you in its development and use."

"Does one learn to play the flute from a book?" I asked him. I shook my head and smiled sadly. "No, unless there is another who shares my affliction, there is only one thing that can help me."

"You mean the Lightstone, don't you?"

"Yes, the Lightstone—it's said to be the cup of healing."

If I could feel the fires that burned inside others and touch them with my own, then surely that meant there was a wound in my soul that allowed these sacred and very private flames to pass back and forth. This one time, perhaps, they had touched Atara and brought her back from the darkness. But what if the next time, through rage or hate, whatever was inside me flashed like real lightning and struck her dead?

Maram, who always understood so much without being told, came up to me and placed his hand above my heart. "I think that this gift of yours must be like living with a hole in your chest. But Pualani healed you of the wound that Salmelu made. Perhaps she can heal this wound, too."

The following morning, I went to Pualani's house to ask her

about this. And there, inside a long door garlanded with white and purple flowers, she took my hand and told me, "In the world, there are many sights that are hard to bear. Would you wish to be healed of the holes in your eyes so that you didn't have to see them?"

She went on to say that my wound, as I thought of it, was surely the gift of the Ellama. I must learn to use it, she said, as I would my eyes, my ears, my nose or any other part of me. If finding the Lightstone would help me in this, then I should seek it with all my heart.

Later that day, after walking the woods deep in wonder, I gathered my friends together and told them that I must leave for Tria the next morning. "By my count," I said, "tomorrow will be the first of Soldru, and that gives us only seven more days to reach Tria."

Master Juwain and Atara agreed that we must set out, and soon. Maram, when he saw that our minds were made up, reluctantly said that he would come with us as well. "If you go without me," he said, "I'll never find either the strength or courage to leave these woods."

"But what about Iolana?" I asked him. "Don't you love her?"

"Of course I do. I love the wine that the Lokilani serve, too. But there are many fine wines in the world, if you know what I mean."

Maram's fickleness obviously vexed Atara, who said, "I know little of wines. But there can't be another fruit on all of Ea like the timana."

"And that is my point exactly," Maram said. "When I find the one wine that is to lesser vintages as the timana is to the more common fruits, I shall drink it and no other."

At last it came time for me to put on my cold armor. After we had burdened the packhorses with a good load of fruit and freshly baked nutbread that the Lokilani provided us, we saddled Altaru and our other mounts. And then there, in the apple grove where they were tethered, the whole Lokilani village turned out to bid us farewell.

"It's sad to say good-bye," Pualani told us. She stood beneath a blossom-laden bough with Elan, Danali, and Iolana, who was weeping. Around them were hundreds of men, women, and children. And around all the Lokilani—everywhere in the grove—flickered the forms of the Timpum. "Yet maybe some-day you'll return to us as we all hope you will."

From the pocket of her skirt, she removed a green jewel about the size of a child's finger. She pressed it into Master Juwain's gnarly old hand and said, "You are a Master Healer of your Brotherhood. And emeralds are the stones of healing; they have power over all the growing things of the earth. If you should take wounds or illness, from the Earthkillers or any others, please use this emerald to heal yourselves."

Master Juwain looked down at the gleaming emerald, mystified. Then Pualani touched him on his chest. "There is no book that tells of this. To use it, you must open your heart. It has no resonance with the head."

Master Juwain's bald head gleamed like a huge nut as he bowed and thanked her for her gift. Then she kissed him good-bye, and all the Lokilani, one by one, filed passed us to touch our hands and kiss us as well.

"Farewell," Pualani told us. "May the light of the Ellama shine always upon you."

Danali, with twenty or so of the Lokilani, had prepared an escort for us. As before, they each carried bows, but this time no one spoke of binding our hands. Because I thought it would be unseemly to mount our horses and sit so high above them when we already towered over them merely as we stood, we agreed to walk our horses through the Forest.

It was a lovely morning, and the canopies of the astors shined above us like a dome of gold. The air smelled of fruits and flowers and the leaf-covered earth. Many birds were singing; their music seemed to pipe out in perfect time with the tinkling of the little stream that Danali followed. I thought that he was leading us west, but in the Forest I found my sense of direction dulled as if I had drunk too much wine.

We walked as quietly as we could in the silence of the great trees. No one spoke. An air of sadness hung over the woods, and we breathed its bittersweet fragrance with every step we took away from its center. The Timpum, so brilliant in their swirls of silver and scarlet, seemed less bright as we passed from the stands of astors into the giant oaks. There were fewer of them, too. We all knew that the Timpum could not live—if that was the right word—outside of the Forest. But to see them diminishing in splendor and numbers was a sorrowful thing.

Around noon, Danali left the stream and led us by secret paths through a more thickly growing wood. Here the predominance of the oaks gave way to elms, maples, and chestnuts, which, though still very tall, seemed stunted next to the giants of the deeper Forest. We walked along the winding paths for quite a few miles. The sun, crossing the sky somewhere above us, was invisible through the thick, green shrouds of leaves. I couldn't tell west from east or north from south.

After some hours, Danali finally broke his silence. He gave us to understand that the Forest could be almost as difficult to leave as it was to enter. Unless the Lokilani pointed themselves along certain fixed paths, they would find themselves wandering among the shimmering trees and being drawn back, always toward its center.

"But it has been many years since any us has left the Forest," he said. "And many more since anyone, having left, found his way back in."

Another couple of miles brought us to a place beyond which Danali and his people would not go. Here, in a stand of oaks sprinkled with a few birch trees, we felt a barrier hanging over the Forest like an invisible curtain. There were only a few Timpum about, lingering among the oaks and shining weakly. It was hard to look beyond them into the dense green swath of woods. For, only a few hundred yards from us, we could see nothing—only leaves and bark and ferns and other such things.

"We'll say good-bye here," Danali said. He pointed down the narrow path cutting through the trees. "Follow this, and do not look back. It will take you into your forest."

The Lokilani embraced each of us in turn. After Danali had pressed his slender form against Maram's belly, he smiled at him and said, "Take care, Hairface. I'm glad, so very glad, that we didn't have to kill you."

And with that, the Lokilani stepped off into the trees to allow us to pass.

After only a few hundred yards, the air lying over the woods grew heavier and moister. The leaves of the trees suddenly lost their luster, as if clouds had darkened the sky above them.

Everything looked duller. The colors seemed to have drained from the woods and flattened out into various shades of gray. Even the birds had stopped singing.

The path ended suddenly about half a mile farther on. Despite Danali's warning, we turned to look back along it. We knew well enough that it should lead back into the Forest. But the scraggy scratch in the earth, crowded with bushes and vine-twisted trees, seemed to lead nowhere. In gazing through the thick greenery behind us, I felt repelled by a strong sensation pushing at my chest. It was as if I should proceed in any other direction but that one. And so I did. I walked Altaru through the woods toward what I thought to be the northwest. After a few hundred yards, the path vanished behind the walls of trees. A mile farther on, where the trees opened up a little and some dead elms lay down like slain giants, I would have been hard-pressed to say exactly where the unseen Forest lay.

"We're lost, aren't we?" Maram said when we had paused to take our bearings. He turned this way and that toward the dark woods surrounding us. "Why did we have to leave the Forest? No more sweet wine for Maram. Not an astor to be seen here. Nor any Timpum."

But this last proved to be not quite true. Even as Maram stood pulling nervously at his beard, a little light flashed in the air above us. It seemed to appear out of nowhere. Suddenly, framed against the leaves of some arrowwood, the little Timpum that had attached itself to me floated in the air and spun about in its swirls of silver sparks. We all saw it as clearly as we could the leaves on the trees.

"Look!" Maram said to me. "How did it come here?"

Atara took a step closer to it, fixing the little lights with her wide blue eyes. "Oh, look at it!" she said. "Look how it flickers!"

Maram, inspired by her words, took this opportunity to give a name to the Timpum. "Well, then, little Flick," he said, "look around you and you won't see any of your kind. Sad to say, you're all alone in these dreary woods."

Master Juwain pointed toward Flick, as I now couldn't help thinking of him. He said, "Pualani was quite clear on this matter: the Timpum can't live outside of the Forest."

"Nevertheless," I said, looking at Flick, "here he is, and here he lives."

"Yes—but for how long?"

Master Juwain's question alarmed me, and I suddenly let go Altaru's reins to step forward toward the shimmering Timpum.

"Go back!" I said, waving my hands at Flick as if to shoo him away. But Flick just floated in front of my eyes, spinning out sparks at me.

"Maybe he's lost," Maram said. "Maybe he can't find his way back."

He proposed that we should return to the Forest in order to rescue Flick and spend at least one more night drinking wine with the Lokilani.

"No, we must go on," Atara said to him. "Even if we *could* return to the Forest, there is no certainty that Flick would follow us. And if he did, there is no reason why he wouldn't just follow us out again."

Her argument made sense to everyone, even to Maram. But it saddened me. For I was sure that as soon as we struck off into these lesser woods that covered the earth before us, Flick would either die or slowly fade away.

"Do you think he might follow us toward Tria?" Maram asked.

"We'll see," I said as I pulled myself up onto Altaru.

"But *where* is Tria? Val—do you know?"

"Yes," I said, pointing off northwest into the woods. I smiled with relief because my sense of direction had returned to me. "Now let's ride while we still have some light left."

For the rest of that day and the ones that followed, we rode more or less along a straight course. We all dreaded the return of the Stonefaces, especially at night when we made camp, and we looked for them to come out of the blackened trees to attack us. During the hours of dim sunlight, we pushed deeper into stands of maple and elm. Against my memory of the Forest's splendor, the trees here seemed ashen and stunted, and the animals all moved about dully and listlessly, as if drained of life. On the second day it rained, all through the afternoon and into dusk. I watched with little hope for the sky to clear and the stars to shine, even as I looked for Flick. But in the dark, dripping woods, I couldn't find the faintest glint of light. By the time dawn came, I was sure that he was dead.

What is despair, really? It is a dark night of the soul and the remembrance of brighter things. It is a silent calling out to them. But the call comes from the darkest of places and is often heard by dark things instead.

On the third night out from the vild, in an endless expanse of trees shagged with mosses and reeking of mushrooms and rotting wood, I had dreadful dreams: of worms eating at my insides, bats biting me open, and mosquitoes smothering me in black clouds and sucking out my blood. I came sweating and sobbing out of sleep to an unsettling sense that men were listening for me as from many miles away. I heard Atara, Maram, and even Master Juwain moaning, too. When morning came, misty and gray, we spoke of our nightmares and discovered they were very much the same.

"It must be the Stonefaces," Maram said. "They've found us again."

That day we rode hard for the Nar Road through swaths of grayish-green trees that blocked out the sun. We came upon the highway without warning, just before dusk. As our tired horses clopped onto the broad band of stone, I ventured a guess that we must have bypassed Suma by quite a few miles. After some miles more—perhaps as few as eighty—we would find Tria down the road to the west.

"We're saved, then!" Maram cried out. He climbed down from his horse, and collapsed to his knees as he kissed the road's stones in relief. "Shall we ride on until we find a village or town?"

I dismounted Altaru and stood beside him along the curb of the road. The day was dying quickly, and for the first night in many nights, we had a clear view of the sky. Already Valura, the evening star, shined in the blue-black dome to the west. In the east, the moon was rising: a full moon, as we could all see from its almost perfect circle of silver. The last time I had stood beneath a moon so bright had been in the Black Bog.

With the coming of night, the pain in all our heads grew suddenly worse. I looked at Master Juwain slumped on his horse and at Atara forcing a smile to her worn-out face. We were all exhausted, I thought, and growing weaker by the hour. I doubted whether we could ride half the night to the next village, and I told Maram this. "It seems to me that the Stonefaces, whatever they are, take their greatest strength and boldness from the dark," I added. "It would be very bad if they were waiting on the road to ambush us at night."

"All right," Maram said wearily. "I'm too tired to argue."

We remounted our horses and retraced our steps to a meadow that we had passed half a mile back. It was a grassy expanse perhaps a hundred yards in diameter. Copses of mulberry and oak surrounded it. We hauled some deadfall from these woods to the center of the meadow, where we built around our camp a sort of circular fence. It took many trips back and forth to gather enough wood to construct the rudimentary fortifications. But when we were finished, we were glad to go inside it and lay out our bearskins.

It was full night by the time we finished our dinner. The moon had climbed above the meadow and silvered it with its cold light. Long, grayish grasses swayed in the wind blowing in from the east. In the eerie sheen of the earth, the many rocks about us seemed as big as boulders. We had a clear line of sight fifty yards in any direction toward the rim of dark trees that surrounded us. Unless it grew very cloudy, no one could steal upon us unseen. Atara stood up against the breastwork of the fence as she practiced drawing her great bow and aiming arrows over the top of it. She seemed satisfied that we had done all we could. After bidding us goodnight, she slipped down to the ground to sleep, holding her bow as a child might a blanket.

I took the first watch while the others slept fitfully. I knew they must be having evil dreams: Maram sweated and rolled about, while Master Juwain's small body twitched and started whenever he let out a low moan. Several times Atara murmured, "No, no, no," before falling into the ragged rhythms of her breathing.

When it came my turn to sleep, I couldn't bear the thought of closing my eyes. And so I walked in a slow circle behind the fence, looking out across the meadow. The horses, tethered to the fence, were silently sleeping. So still did they stand that they looked like statues. As did the trees of the surrounding woods. In their dark shadows, I could see nothing. I listened for any telltale that men might be coming to attack us, but the only sounds were the crickets in the meadow and the distant howling of some wolves. Wherever the great, gray beasts stood, I thought, they must look upon the same moon as did I. I watched the pale disk climb the starry heavens inch by inch. I might have measured out the moments of its rise and fall by the painful beating of my heart, but the night seemed to deepen into a timelessness that had no end.

And so I let my friends sleep in place of standing their watches. Despite the pain in my head, which drove through my eyes like nails, I was wide awake. The night was very warm, and I sweated beneath my armor. For many hours, I stared out across the meadow, listening and waiting. I walked around and around our camp, trying to catch the sense of whoever might be hunting us.

Near dawn, without warning, Atara started out of her sleep and rose to stand by my side. When she saw the angle of the moon, she chided me for staying awake nearly all night. Then she sniffed the wind as might a tawny lioness and said, "They're close, aren't they?"

"Yes," I said, "they are."

For a while we spoke of little things such as the direction of the wind and the grimness of the gray face of the moon. And then I looked at her and asked, "Are you afraid to die?"

She thought about this for a long moment before saying, "Death is like going to sleep. Should I be afraid of sleeping, then?"

I looked at Master Juwain as he lay against the ground moaning softly. I almost told Atara that death is cold, death is dark, death is an evil dream full of empty black nothing. But I kept myself from voicing such despair.

Even so, she sensed my doubts. She smiled at me and said, "We take our being from the One. How can the One ever stop being? How can we?"

Because I had no answer for her, I looked up at the black spaces between the stars.

I felt her hand touch my face, and I turned to look at her as she asked me, "Are you afraid?"

"Yes," I told her. "But most afraid for you."

She smiled at me in a silent understanding that had been awakened in the Lokilani's wood. Then her face fell serious as she said a strange thing: "I can see them, you know."

"See who, Atara?"

"The men," she said. "The gray men."

"You mean, you saw them in your dreams?"

"Yes, that of course. But I can see them here, now."

I looked at the gray trees standing in a circle all about us with their leafy arms raised toward the sky, but I saw no men standing with them.

Then Atara pointed out across the moonlit meadow and said, "I can see them walking toward us with their knives."

I shook my head because if the Stonefaces came to attack us, then surely they would stand behind the trees shooting arrows at us or charge us on horses with drawn swords.

"Once, when I was a child," she said, "I saw a spider weaving a web in a corner of my father's house a month before she actually did. I can see the gray men the same way."

I continued looking out around the meadow; other than the wind-rippled grasses, nothing moved. The moon seemed like a silver nail pinning still the sky. In between the soughs of Atara's breaths, I could almost feel each beat of her heart as it hung in the air like a boom of a great red drum.

And then Altaru came violently awake and let out a tremendous whinny, and I saw them, too. They suddenly appeared next to the trees as if the dark shadows had given them birth. Tall men they were, with grayish cloaks covering them from head to knee. As Atara had said, there were at least eleven of them. Although we couldn't see their faces, they stood around the circle of trees watching us and waiting for something.

I quickly drew my sword.

Again, Altaru whinnied and stomped the earth as he pulled and rattled the fence. His noise shook Master Juwain and Maram awake.

"What is it?" Maram grumbled as he struggled to his feet. Then he looked across the meadow and cried out, "Oh, Lord— it's them!"

When pressed, Maram could move quickly, big belly or no. It took only a moment for him to grab up his bow and join Atara and me by the fence. His voice bellowed out toward the gray men: "Who are you? What do want of us?"

But their only answer was a silence that came with the sudden dying of the wind.

"Go away!" Maram called to them. "Go away or we'll shoot you!"

But still the gray men didn't move, and the silence in the meadow grew only deeper.

"I'm going to give them a warning," Maram said, nocking an arrow to his bowstring. "I'm going to shoot this into a tree."

Without waiting for me to say yea or nay, he drew his bow. But his hands and arms suddenly started trembling; the arrow, when it came whining off his string, buried itself in the ground only forty feet from the fence.

"Hmmph—shooting at moles again," Atara said. Then she too fired off a shot. But at the moment she released her arrow, her bow arm buckled as if broken at the elbow. Her arrow drove into the ground after covering even less distance than had Maram's.

Something moved then in the shadows of the trees. Twigs cracked, and even from fifty yards away, we could hear the rustling of leaves. A very tall man stepped forward into the moonlight. He was dressed as the others in gray trousers and cloak. He had an air of command about him. When he turned toward us as if staring into our souls, the others did too.

"Go away!" Maram cried again. "Go away, now!"

The gray men seemed not to hear him. Following their leader, they all drew forth long gray knives and began walking across the meadow toward us, even as Atara had foreseen.

Atara and Maram fired more arrows at them, but they flew wild. The men advanced slowly as if taking care not to stumble over any branch or rock. Their gray-steel knives glinted dully in the moon's eerie light. When they had covered perhaps half the distance toward our camp, I could better see their leader as he looked straight at me. His face was long and flat, without expression and as gray as slate. There seemed to be something stuck to the middle of his forehead, where it was said one's third eye lies: it looked like a leech or some kind of flat, black stone.

"Go away," I whispered. "Go away, or one of us will have to die."

Just then a swirl of little lights appeared as of stars dropping down from the heavens. It was Flick, spinning about furiously as he streaked back and forth in front of the gray men. So then, I thought, he still lived! It seemed that he was trying to warn them away or perhaps was weaving a fence of light through which they couldn't pass. But the men took no notice of his presence. They walked slowly forward as if nothing stood between them and us.

The urge to flee suddenly overcame Maram and Atara. They began backing away from the gray men, all the while shooting arrows as I joined them in edging up near the rear of the fence. Master Juwain pressed up close to us. And then the gray men's leader stood very still. The black stone on his forehead caught the moonlight and gleamed darkly. At that moment, a crushing heaviness fell across my whole body. I dropped my sword, and my friends let go of their bows. My arms and legs were so weak that it seemed something had drained the blood from them. I wanted desperately to run, to will myself to move, but I could not. A terrible coldness spread quickly through me and froze me motionless like a fish caught in ice. I couldn't even open my mouth to scream.

Neither could my friends. But I sensed them screaming inside for the gray men to go away, and I knew that they could hear the screams of the horses, even as I could. The gray men's leader dispatched two of his confederates toward them. All the horses were now whinnying and rearing and kicking the ground. Altaru aimed a mighty kick at the fence. It splintered the wood, and he pulled free from it, along with the two sorrels and Tanar, who immediately ran off into the woods. Altaru charged straight for the two men closest to the fence. But then they showed him their knives and something worse, and he suddenly changed courses, galloping off into the woods, too. Although he was the bravest of beings, something about the men sent him into a panic.

The two men now closed on the remaining horses. They seemed bothered by their screaming and the beating of their hooves; it was as if the gray men sought silence in the outer world so that they could hear the voices of the inner. And so, moving with great care, they used their long knives to slash open the horses' throats.

No, I cried out in my mind, *no, no, no!*

The other men began pulling at the branches and logs of the fence, dismantling it and making an opening wide enough for all of them to pass. And still I stood with the others at the rear of the fence, watching them but unable to move.

And then the gray men's leader stepped forward. The black stone on his forehead was a dark moon crushing us to the earth. The flesh of his face was gray as that of a dead fish. As Atara had told us, he had no eyes like any man I had ever seen. They were all of one hue and substance: a solid and translucent gray that covered them like dark glass. I couldn't guess how they let in any light. They seemed utterly without pity, utterly empty, utterly cold. The cold struck straight into my heart like a lance and filled me with a wild fear. A steely voice spoke inside me then and told me that I couldn't move. I was nothing, it said to me; I was nothing more than an empty husk of flesh to be used as the gray men wished. I was one with the dead, and would take a long, long time in dying.

Evil, I knew then, is much more than darkness: it is a willful turning away from the light of the One. It is a poison that twists the soul, a madness, a terrible need to inflate one's self at the expense of others, as a tick swells on its victims' blood.

No—go back!

All the men now gathered around their leader at the opening to the fence. Their knives pointed toward us. Although they wore no stones on their foreheads, their faces were as eyeless and stonelike as their leader's. They stood in the cold moonlight, watching us and waiting.

Oh, no! Oh, no! Oh, no!

I felt Atara's terror, and Master Juwain's and Maram's, thundering at me with the wild beating of their hearts. I couldn't close it out. Neither could I close my eyes as the gray men pierced me with theirs and began drinking from inside me that which was more precious than blood.

NO! NO! NO!

I wanted with all my soul to close my eyes and end the living nightmare from which I could not awaken. But then, even as I tried desperately to move my legs and run away, I looked across the meadow to see another cloaked figure break from the trees. The lone man ran as silently as a wraith through the silvery grass. He had a sword drawn: it was longer than a knife, and longer than many swords, for it was a kalama. His powerful strides revealed the gleaming mail beneath his cloak. It took him only a few seconds to reach the wolf pack of men by the open fence. He crashed into them, sending two flying and slicing through the neck of a third. And then, even as the gray men finally realized they were under attack and turned toward him, he stabbed his sword straight through the back of their leader.

"Move!" he cried to us in voice like the roar of a tiger. "Move now, I say!"

And then he drove into the men with his sword, whirling about powerfully yet gracefully, cutting at them with a rare and terrible fury.

With the death of the gray men's leader, I found myself suddenly free to move. A great surge of life welled up inside me and filled my hands with a new strength. Some of the gray men were running from the wild man at the opening of the fence; some were running at Atara and me. One of these aimed his knife at her throat; without thinking, I picked up my sword and chopped off his arm in almost a single motion. Grayish-black blood sprayed into the air. It surprised me that he wore no armor and that the steel of my sword sliced through him so easily. The kalama is a fearsome weapon at any time but most terrible against unprotected flesh. As I was forced to use it now. For in the rush of men coming at us with their gray, slashing knives, even as Maram and Atara drew their swords and laid about them in a wild death struggle, one of the men stole up behind her to stab her in the back. His back was to me, his knife poised to thrust home, and I was faced with a terrible choice: I could cut him down or let him kill her. It was no choice at all. And so, still reeling from the wound I had inflicted on the first man, I swung my sword at him. It sliced into his side and through his chest; I felt its cold steel rip through his heart. Dark blood sprayed into my eyes. I could hardly see as he jumped in agony and turned to regard me for a moment in the strange silence of his hate. And then he died, and I almost died, too. I fell down to the blood-soaked earth screaming like a child as the darkness closed in and the battle raged all about me.

Later, when the last of the gray men had been killed and Maram and Atara stood panting with their bloody swords in their hands, the man who had run to our rescue let loose a howl of triumph. He stood in the moonlight holding his sword up to the stars. I felt his great joy at having slain so many of his enemies. Even through the death-agony covering my eyes like a shroud, I watched him turn toward me. He threw back the hood of his cloak. His face blazed with a terrible beauty, and I gasped to see that it was Kane.

■ **16** ■

WITH MY FRIENDS and I still weak from what the gray men had done to us, Kane took command. He ordered Master Juwain to tend to me while he walked around our camp counting the bodies of the slain. He numbered them at twelve, including the one that I had killed. Maram had managed to send two on to the other world, while Atara had added three more enemies toward her hundred. That meant Kane had accounted for six. As I lay with my head in Master Juwain's lap, I blinked my eyes in disbelief. I had never seen anyone fight with such quickness, skill, and sheer ferocity.

After Kane had completed his tally, he knelt by the gray men's leader on the bloody earth. He used his sword to cut the black stone from his forehead. He studied the flat oval a long time before tightening his fist around it. Then he turned toward us and said, "This is no place to remain, eh? The sun will be up soon. Let's get Val into the shade of the trees before it boils his brains."

With Kane's help, my friends carried me into the trees. They found a nice dry spot beneath an old oak, and there they reestablished our camp. Atara laid out our sleeping skins while Maram got a fire going and Master Juwain went to work on making some tea. Kane brought over the packs from the dead horses. And then he went off into the woods to look for Altaru and the rest of the horses. We heard his sharp whistles through the trees.

Sometime later he returned holding the reins of a big bay, which I took to be his horse. Altaru, Tanar, and the sorrels followed them. Kane, looking down at me, said, "So, Valashu Elahad, I've wandered the wilds of Alonia looking for you. And now that I've found you, you're nearly dead."

He spoke the truth. The coldness cutting through me was worse than that with which the gray men had touched me. I lay against the earth without the strength to rise. Having killed again, I wanted to die. But seeing the concern on Maram's face and the love on Atara's as they gathered around me, I wanted to live even more.

"Few people," Kane said, pointing toward the dead men in the meadow, "survive meeting the Grays."

"But who are these *Grays*?" Maram asked him.

"Servants of the Great Beast," Kane growled out. "They have the gift of speaking to themselves and others without using their tongues."

Maram, Atara, and Master Juwain looked at each other, having never heard of such men before. Neither had I.

"They can see without using their eyes and hear the whisperings of others' minds," Kane went on. "That's how they tracked you from Anjo."

As the wind rose and the night began to fade, he told us that no one knew the Grays' true origins. "It's said that the Great Beast bred them during the Age of Swords from those who had the gift of mindspeaking."

"But their faces, so gray," Atara said, shuddering as she looked out into the field. "Their eyes, too. No men on Ea have such eyes."

"They don't, eh?" Kane said. Then he pointed up at the setting moon. "It's also said that Morjin summoned the Grays from other worlds ages ago. From worlds even darker than this one."

In the dimness of the dawn, I thought that nothing could be darker than the lightless world pulling me down into the cold earth.

"The Grays like to kill," Kane said, "by draining the life of their victims over many days. Then, when they're too weak to move, they come for them with their knives."

Master Juwain had finally finished preparing his tea, which he managed to make me drink with Maram's and Atara's help. Then, to Kane, he said, "But we weren't so weak that we couldn't have fought them off. There was something else, wasn't there?"

Kane looked down at his fist for a while before opening it to reveal the black stone. He said, "So, there *was* something else. The baalstei."

"What's that?" Maram asked.

"The black gelstei," Master Juwain said, staring at Kane's open hand. "Can that truly be one of the great stones?"

Kane gazed at the stone, a crystal like the darkest obsidian. "It *is* a gelstei," he said. "It's known that Morjin keeps at least three of the black stones."

He told us that the black gelstei were very rare and very powerful. Originally created to control the terrible fire of the red gelstei, they had a much darker side. The Grays and some of the priests of the Kallimun used the stones to dampen the life fires of their victims and weaken their wills, mastering their very minds and thus enslaving them. Used ruthlessly, as by the Grays, the black gelstei could blow out the ineffable flame, causing degeneration and ultimately death.

"They would have killed Val outright," Kane said. "Or worse."

"What could be worse than death?" Maram said.

"It may be," Kane said, "that Morjin would have made him a ghul."

His words chilled me even more, and Maram eyed him suspiciously as he said, "You seem to know a great deal about these Grays."

"That I do," Kane said, his black eyes burning. "I know that your friend might very well die if we don't help him."

His words blunted Maram's curiosity for the moment. I, too, had a hundred questions for Kane, but I was too weak to move my lips to ask them.

Master Juwain bent over me then, feeling my forehead and testing the pulse in my wrist. Then he said, "I've given him a tisane of karch and bloodroot. Perhaps I should have added some angel leaf as well."

"That's unlikely to do much good," Kane muttered. "It may warm him a little, but his real problem is the *valarda*, eh?"

Now Master Juwain and Maram—Atara, too—looked at Kane in surprise. No one had said anything to him of my gift.

"Val has had the life nearly sucked out of him," Kane said. "We must help him light the sacred fire again, eh?"

"Yes, but how?" Master Juwain asked. "I'm afraid I've had no experience with this."

"Neither have I," Kane admitted. "At least, not for a long time."

So saying, he bade Master Juwain and Maram remove my armor. As the sun rose over the meadow and the birds brightened the morning with their songs, they laid my body bare. I felt the sun's warm rays touching the skin of my chest. And then I felt my friends' hands there, too, as well as Kane's large, blunt hand. Together, the four of them made a circle of their hands over my heart. I heard Kane telling me that I must partake of the life they had to give me. This I tried to do. But I was too weak to open very far the door that I usually kept closed. Only the faintest of flames passed from them into me to warm my icy blood.

"It's not enough," Kane said. "He's still as cold as death."

Just then, Flick appeared from behind the oak tree and streaked straight toward Master Juwain. He spun about just above the pocket of his robes. The swirls of his little form lit up as of a smiling face.

"Eh, what's this?" Kane said, looking at Flick. "It's one of the Timpimpiri!"

"You can *see* him?" Maram said.

"As clearly as I can see your fat nose. But I never hoped to find one in woods such as these."

Master Juwain, touched by Flick's numinous light, seemed suddenly to remember something. He reached into his pocket and pulled out the sparkling green jewel that Pualani had given him. He said, "The queen of the Lokilani told me that this emerald was to be used for healing."

Kane said nothing as he looked very closely at the emerald.

"She said that I was to use my heart to touch the stone."

"She did, eh? Well, use it then."

Master Juwain held the emerald against his chest for many moments as if meditating. Then he opened his eyes and took out his copy of the *Saganom Elu*. His knotty fingers began dancing through the pages.

"I thought you were supposed to use your *heart*," Maram said, pointing at the book. "Won't all these words cloud your head?"

"Some of us," Master Juwain said with a smile, "must use our heads to reach our hearts. Now be quiet, Brother Maram, while I'm reading."

Maram watched his eyes flicking across the page. "Excuse me, sir, but shouldn't you read the words out loud? Didn't you teach me that the verses of the *Elu* were meant to be recited?"

"Oh, all right!" Master Juwain muttered. "You've paid more attention to my lessons than I'd thought. This passage is from the *Songs*."

He cleared his throat and began speaking in his most musical voice. He fairly sang out the words of *A Warrior's Heart:*

> *A warrior's heart is like the sun,*
> *She shines with golden light,*
> *Her golden sinews brightly spun*
> *With angel-given might.*
>
> *A warrior's heart is like the sea,*
> *Her love is very deep,*
> *She streams and swells with bravery*
> *That makes the waters weep.*

When Master Juwain had finally finished, he again closed his eyes and held the emerald to his chest. He sat beside me as the sun rose and cast its rays into the woods. Atara sat beside me, too. She cupped her warm hand around mine. She remained silent, saying nothing with her lips. But her bright eyes said more than all the words in the *Saganom Elu.*

After most of an hour, Master Juwain opened his eyes and then his hand. We were well-shaded by the leaves of the oak tree; even so, some bit of sunlight fell upon the emerald and set it shimmering a brilliant green. Or perhaps I only imagined this: when I looked more closely, it seemed that the emerald shined with a deeper light. Master Juwain touched the beautiful stone to my chest then. He touched his hand there, and so did Atara, Maram, and Kane, making a circle as before. Something warm and bright passed into me. It made me want to open myself to the touch of the whole world. I gasped, breathing in the sweetness of the air. I breathed in as well the essence of the oak trees streaming with hot spring sap and the very fire of the sun.

For one blazing moment, I felt myself overflowing with the life of the forest—and with that of my three friends and the strange man named Kane.

"So," Kane said to Master Juwain as he touched my face, "this *emerald* of yours has great power, eh?"

As quickly as it had overcome me, the death-cold suddenly left me. Although I was still very weak, I managed to sit up and press my back against the oak tree.

"Thank you," I told Master Juwain. Then I smiled at Maram, Kane, and Atara. "You saved my life."

I pressed my hand to my side where Salmelu's sword had cut me. I remembered Pualani holding a green crystal there and my awakening the next day to find myself miraculously healed.

"I see," Master Juwain finally said. He gazed at the green stone that he held in his hand. "This can't be an ordinary emerald, can it?"

"No—you know it can't be," Kane said. "This is a varistei. A green gelstei."

Master Juwain gripped the green stone as if he were afraid he might drop it and lose it among the leaves on the forest floor. He said, "I thought the green gelstei had all perished in the War of the Stones. This is a treasure beyond price. How could the Lokilani have come by it?"

For a moment Kane fell quiet in reflection. Then he said, "The Lokii were one of the tribes of the Star People sent to Ea ages ago."

He went on to explain that there had been twelve of these tribes: the Danya, Weryin, Nisu, Kesari, Asadu, Ajani, Tuwari, Talasi, Sakuru, Helkiin, Lokii—and, of course, the Valari, headed by Elahad and entrusted with guarding the Lightstone. Each of the tribes had brought with it a single varistei meant to bring the new world to flower. For the green crystals had power over all living things and the fires of life itself. The Galadin and Elijin who had sent the twelve tribes to Ea had intended for them to create a paradise. But instead, Aryu of the Valari had risen up in envy to slay his brother. He had stolen the Lightstone and broken the peace and hope of Ea.

"This much is known everywhere, if not always believed," Kane said. "But what is *not* known is that Aryu also stole the varistei from Elahad."

He told us that Aryu, and many of the Valari who followed him, had set sail from Tria on three ships, fleeing into the Northern Sea. Near the island of Nedu, a storm had driven two of the ships onto rocks, killing everyone aboard them save Aryu. But Aryu had been mortally wounded, and at last, realizing his folly, he crawled ashore a small island and hid the Lightstone in a cave. The Valari on the remaining ship, under his son, Jolonu, found Aryu's body but not the Lightstone. Jolonu then took the varistei from Aryu's dead hand and set sail for the most distant land he could find.

And so the renegade Valari came at last to the island of Thalu in the uttermost west. There they used the green gelstei to slowly change their form to adapt to the cold mists of that harsh and rugged land. The followers of Aryu, or the Aryans, as they came to be called, became a tall, big-boned people, fair of face, with flaxen hair and blue eyes as bright as the sea.

Here Kane paused in his story to look at Atara. She sat on old leaves beneath the oak tree, and her bright, blue eyes were fixed on Kane's face. "Have you never wondered at the origins of your people?" he asked her.

"But my people are the Sarni."

"The Sarni, indeed: descendants all from Bohimir and the other Aryan warlords who conquered most of Ea at the end of the Age of the Mother."

Kane sat looking back and forth between Atara and me. Then he muttered, "It's strange. Very, very strange."

"What is?" I asked him.

He pointed at my hair and then held his hand toward my face as his black eyes burned into mine. "It's said that all the Star People who came to Ea looked like you. Like the Valari. The Valari who settled the Morning Mountains were the only people to have had their varistei stolen. And so they were the only people of Ea to remain true to the Star People's original form."

I looked down at the black hair spilling over my chest and at the ivory tones of my hands. I rubbed my long, hawk's nose and the prominent bones of my cheeks. Then I looked at Atara, whose coloring and cast of face couldn't have been more different.

"The Valari and the Aryans," Kane said, "were once of one tribe. Thus they're the closest of all peoples, and yet, the bitterest of enemies. So, the Aryans, the Sarni—who has warred with the Valari more?"

Only the Valari, I thought, biting back a bitter smile.

"Ah, this is all very interesting," Maram said to Kane. "But what does this have to do with the Lokii?"

"Just this," Kane said. "After Aryu stole the Lightstone and the Valari were broken into their two kindreds, the remaining tribes scattered to every land of Ea. Each tribe carried its own varistei; they used the stones to adapt their forms to the various climes of Ea. The Lokii, being lovers of trees, disappeared into the Great Northern Forest. Over the ages, they came to look even as you've seen them."

The Lokii, he explained, became masters of growing great trees and things out of the earth, and of awakening the living earth fires called the telluric currents. After thousands of years, they learned to grow more of the green gelstei crystals from the earth. They used these magic stones, as they thought of them, to deepen the power of their wood. So changed and focused did these telluric currents become that their wood separated from Ea in some strange way and became invisible to the rest of it. The Lokii called these pockets of deepened life fires "vilds," for they believed that there the earth was connected to the wild fires of the stars. Since the Lokii could not return to the stars, they hoped to awaken the earth itself so that all of Ea became as alive and magical as the other worlds that circled other suns.

"You say 'vilds,'" Maram said. "How many are there?"

Kane nodded his head and told us, "During the Lost Ages, the Lokii tribe split into at least ten septs and bore varistei to other parts of Ea. There, they created vilds of their own. At least five of them remain."

"Remain *where*?"

"Somewhere," Kane said. "They are somewhere."

At this, Flick soared over to him and began spinning in front of his bright eyes. I could almost see the sparks passing back and forth between them. It was the longest I had ever seen Flick remain in one place.

"How is it," Maram wondered, "that Flick can live outside the vild?"

"*That* I would like to know, too," Kane said. He knelt next to me, studying the scar on my forehead. Then he told me, "There is more than one mystery here. This mark of the lightning bolt is why the Lokii spared your life: it's sacred to the archangel they call the Ellama. But others know him as Valoreth. It's strange that you should bear his mark, eh?"

Maram, not liking the look on Kane's face just then, said to him, "What's strange is that you should know so much that no one else knows."

"It's a strange world," Kane growled out.

"How did you know about the Grays? And how did learn to fight as you do? Are you of the Black Brotherhood?"

As Maram waited for an answer, we all looked at Kane, who said, "If I *were* of the Black Brotherhood, whatever you think that is, do you suppose I'd be permitted to tell you?"

Maram pointed at Flick, who now hovered over some flowers like a cloud of flashing butterflies. He said, "If you can see the Timpum, then you must have spent time in one of the vilds."

"Must I have?"

Master Juwain sat holding his book and said, "We of the Brotherhood spend our lives in search of knowledge. But even our Grandmaster would have much to learn from you."

Kane smiled at this but said nothing.

"But how," I asked him, "did you find the vild and enter it?"

"Much the same as you did."

He told us that he had spent much of his life crossing and re-crossing Ea in search of knowledge—and something else.

"I seek the Lightstone," he told us. "Even as you do."

"Toward what end?" I asked him.

"Toward the end of bringing about the end," he growled out again. "The end of Morjin and all his works."

I remembered touching upon his bottomless hatred for Morjin at our meeting in Duke Rezu's castle; I could still feel the anguish that he bore, and I shuddered.

"But what grievance do you have against him?" I asked.

"Does a man need a grievance against the Crucifier to oppose him?"

"Perhaps not. But to hate him as you do, yes."

"Then let's just say he took from me that which was dearer than life itself."

I remembered wondering if the Red Dragon had murdered

Kane's family, and I bowed my head in silence. Then I looked up and said, "Your accent is strange—what is your homeland?"

"I have no home. No homeland that Morjin hasn't despoiled."

"Who are your people, then?"

"I have no people whom Morjin hasn't killed or enslaved."

"You almost look Valari."

"I almost am. Like your people, I'm Morjin's enemy."

As I sat looking at him, I couldn't help remembering the story of the Hundred Year March that a minstrel had once told in my father's hall. After the theft of the Lightstone ages ago, Elahad's grandson, Shavashar, had led the remnants of the Valari tribe into the Morning Mountains. It was said that some of the Valari lost heart along the way and broke off from the rest of the tribe. In what land these lost Valari might have established themselves, not even the legends told. But I wondered if Kane might have been one of their descendants.

"You make a mystery of yourself," I said to him.

"No more than the One has made a mystery of life," he told me. "It's not important who I am—only what I do."

I turned to look at the dead Grays in the sunlit meadow. I still couldn't quite believe that he had killed six of them at close quarters without taking a scratch. I said, "Is *this* what you do, then?"

"As I told you at the duke's castle, I oppose Morjin in any way I can."

"Yes, by slaughtering his servants. How is it that you found them here? Were you following them—or us?"

Kane hesitated while he drew in a breath and regarded me. "I've been looking for *you*, Valashu Elahad, for a year. When I heard that Morjin's assassins had found you first, I set out for Mesh as soon as I could."

"But why should you have been looking for me at all? And how did you hear about the assassins?"

"My people in Mesh sent me the news by carrier pigeon."

"*Your* people?" I asked, now quite alarmed.

"There are brave men and women in every land who have joined to fight the Crucifier."

"Are they of the Black Brotherhood, then?"

As he had when Maram had asked, he ignored the question.

"When I heard that you had fought a duel with Prince Salmelu and were being pursued by the Ishkans along the North Road, I hurried through Anjo to Duke Rezu's castle to intercept you."

"But how could you know that we'd come there? *We* certainly didn't know this until we escaped from the Black Bog."

Now Kane smiled savagely at me and said, "I made a guess. Duke Barwan eats from the Ishkans' hands like a dog, and so how much sense would it have made for you to cross the Aru-Adar bridge into his domain? But where else could you cross into Anjo? It was a good guess, eh?"

I nodded my head as Maram and Master Juwain looked at me in silent remembrance of the terrors of this nighttime passage. Then, with a shudder, Maram asked, "But what *is* the Black Bog? It's like no place on earth I ever wanted to see."

"That it's not," Kane said. "Because the bog isn't wholly *of* the earth."

He went on to tell us that there were certain power places in the earth where the telluric currents gathered like great knots of fire. If they were disturbed, as the ancient Ishkans had done in leveling a whole mountain with firestones, then strange things could happen.

"Other worlds around other suns stream with their own telluric currents," Kane said. "The currents everywhere in the universe are interconnected. And so are the lands of the various worlds: in places such as the bog, it's possible to pass from one world to another."

"Do you mean to say that we were walking on other worlds like earth?" Maram asked.

"No, *not* like the earth, I hope. The bog is known to connect Ea only with the Dark Worlds."

I looked up at the sun pouring its light on the green leaves and the many-colored flowers of our woods; I didn't want to imagine what a Dark World might be. But Master Juwain slowly nodded his head as he squeezed his black book in his little hands and explained, "The Dark Worlds are told of in the *Tragedies*. They are worlds that have turned away from the Law of the One. 'There the sun does not shine nor do men smile or birds sing.' Shaitar was one such world. Damoom is another. Angra Mainyu is imprisoned there."

Even I had heard of Angra Mainyu, the Baaloch, the Dark

Angel—the Lord of Darkness himself. It was said that he had been the greatest of the Galadin before falling and making war against the One. But Valoreth and Ashtoreth, along with a great angelic host, had finally defeated him and bound him to the world of Damoom.

"Do the Grays," I asked Kane, "come from one of these Dark Worlds?"

"It's thought that long ago they *escaped* from Shaitar."

"It seems they're very much of this world, now. They picked up our track somewhere in Anjo."

"Yes," Kane said. "When the assassins failed to kill you, Morjin must have decided to send his most powerful retainers against you."

"You followed us from the duke's castle, didn't you?" I stood up and looked down at Kane. "Did you find the Grays following us, too?"

Kane slowly nodded his head, then stood up beside me. "You were in great danger. I knew they'd kill you if I didn't follow and kill them first."

"If you truly wanted to help us," I said, looking out into the meadow, "you waited a long time."

"That I did. There was no other way. It's impossible to steal upon the Grays and attack them unless their minds are completely occupied."

"So you used us as bait to spring your trap."

"Would you rather I had walked into *their* trap and died with you?"

I shook my head. What he had said made sense. "We should thank you for taking such great risks to save our lives."

"It's not your thanks I want."

"What is it you want, then? You said you've spent a year looking for me—why?"

Now Master Juwain, Maram, and Atara stood up beside me facing Kane. We all waited to hear what he would say.

As the sun rose higher and the woods grew even warmer, Kane began pacing back and forth beneath the oak tree. His grim, bold face was set into a scowl; the large tendons along his neck popped out beneath his sunburnt skin as his jaw muscles worked and he clamped his teeth together. I felt in him a great doubt, and even more, a seething anger at himself for doubting at all.

"I will tell you of the prophecy of Ayondela Kirriland," he said to me. The sounds issuing from his throat just then were more like an animal's growls than a human voice. "Listen, listen well: 'The seven brothers and sisters of the earth with the seven stones will set forth into the darkness. The Lightstone will be found, the Maitreya will come forth—' "

"And a new age will begin," Maram said, interrupting him. "Ah, we already *know* the words to the prophecy. King Kiritan's messenger delivered it in Mesh before we set out."

"*Did* he?" Kane said, fixing his gaze on Maram.

"Yes, we already know that the seven stones must be—"

"Be quiet!" Kane commanded him. "Be quiet, now—you know nothing!"

Maram's mouth snapped shut like a turtle's. He looked at Kane in surprise, and not a little fear, as well.

"There's more to the prophecy than you'll have heard," he told us. He turned to stare at me. "These are the last lines of it: 'A seventh son with the mark of Valoreth will slay the dragon. The old world will be destroyed and a new world created.' "

As his voice died into the deepness of the woods, I stood there rubbing the scar on my forehead. Then Maram turned toward me as if seeing me for the first time, and so did Atara and Master Juwain.

"If this is truly the whole prophecy," I said to Kane, "then why didn't King Kiritan's messenger deliver it?"

"Because he almost certainly didn't know it."

He stared at my face as he told us of the tragedy of Ayondela Kirriland. It was well known, he said, that Ayondela was struck down by an assassin's knife just as she recited the first two lines of the prophecy. But what was not known was that the great oracle in Tria had been infiltrated by Morjin's priests who helped murder Ayondela. Just before she died, she whispered the second two lines of the prophecy to one of these Kallimun priests, who kept them secret from King Kiritan and almost everyone else.

"If the lines were kept secret, then how did you learn of them?" I asked.

"The priest informed Morjin, of course," Kane said. His dark eyes gleamed with hate. "But before the priest died himself, he whispered the whole of the prophecy to *me*."

I looked at the knife that Kane wore sheathed at his side; I didn't want to know how Kane had persuaded this priest to reveal such secrets.

"The priest was an assassin," Kane said to me. "And I'm an assassin of assassins. Someday I may kill the Great Beast himself—unless you do first."

The scar above my eye was now burning as if a bolt of lightning had put its fire into me. I squeezed the hilt of my sword, hardly able to look at Kane.

"You bear the mark of Valoreth that Ayondela told of," he said to me. "And unless I've forgotten how to count, you're Shavashar Elahad's seventh son. *That's* why Morjin sent his assassins to kill you."

Atara came up to me and put her hand on my shoulder. I felt within her a terrible excitement and a great fear for me as well. Master Juwain smiled as if he had found a piece to a puzzle that he had thought lost. Maram bowed his head to me as a swell of pride flushed his face.

To Kane, I said, "Why didn't you tell me all this at the duke's castle?"

"Because you didn't trust me—why should I have trusted you?"

"Why should you trust me now?"

Kane's breath fairly steamed from his lips as he stared deep into my eyes. "Why should I indeed, Valashu Elahad? Why, why? So, I trust your valor and the fire of your heart—and your sword. I trust the truth of your words. I trust that if you set out to seek the Lightstone, you won't turn back. Ha—I suppose I trust you because I *must*."

So saying, he opened his hand to show me the black stone that he had torn from the Grays' leader's head. "This, I believe, is one of the stones told of in Ayondela's prophecy."

He nodded at Master Juwain and said, "And I believe that the varistei that the Lokii queen gave you is another."

Master Juwain took the green gelstei from his pocket and held the sparkling crystal up to the sun.

"The first two of the seven stones have been found," Kane said. "And here we stand, five of the seven brothers and sisters of the earth."

"No, it's not possible," I murmured. "It can't be me that the prophecy told of. It can't be us."

But even as I spoke these words, I knew that it was. I heard something calling me as from far away and yet very near. It was both terrible and beautiful to hear, and it whispered to me along the wind in a keening voice that I could not ignore. I felt it burning into my forehead and tingling along my spine and booming out like thunder with every beat of my heart.

"You can't choose your fate," Kane said to me. "You can decide only whether or not you'll try to hide from it."

Could I hide from my fate? I wondered. Exactly what would it mean to slay the dragon? Did the prophecy refer to *the* Red Dragon? I had no wish to slay anyone, ever again—not even Morjin. Any one of my father's other sons, or my father himself and all his grandfathers' great-grandfathers going back to Elahad, would have been more fit to play the hero's part. Why had *I* been chosen to do this deed?

"So, you are what you are," Kane said as he gazed at me. "And I am what I am. And I will help you, where I can."

I tried to feel my way deep inside him; I sensed in him a whole sea of emotions: wrath, hope, hate, love—and passion for life in all its colors and shades of light and dark. There was a terrible darkness about him that I feared almost more than death itself.

He suddenly drew his sword, which had sent on so many of the Grays. Its long blade gleamed in the sunlight filtering down through the trees. He said to me, "You have the gift of the *valarda*. If you choose to, you can hear the truth in another's heart. Hear the truth of mine, then: I pledge this sword to your service so long as you seek the Lightstone. Your enemies will be my enemies. And I'll die before I see you killed."

There was a darkness about Kane as black as space, and yet there was something incredibly bright about him, too. The same black eyes that had fallen upon his enemies with a hellish hate now shined like stars. It was this light that dazzled me; it was this bright being whom I looked upon with awe.

"Take me with you," he said, "and I'll fight by your side to the gates of Damoom itself."

"All right," I finally said, bowing my head. "Come with us, then."

And with that, I touched my hand to his sword. A moment

later, he sheathed his fearsome weapon, and we grasped hands like brothers, smiling as we tested each other's strength.

It was rash for me to have spoken without the others' consent. But I knew that Master Juwain would welcome Kane's wisdom as would Maram the safety of his sword. As for Atara, she had nothing but respect for this matchless old warrior. She came up to him and clasped hands with him, too. And then she told him, "If fate has brought us together, as it seems it has, then we should go forth as brothers and sisters. Truly we should. I'd be glad if you came with us—though let's hope we won't have to go quite so far as these Dark Worlds that you've told of."

Master Juwain and Maram both welcomed Kane to our company, and we stood there in the shade of the oak tree smiling and taking each other's measure. Then we turned to saddle the horses and begin the last leg of our journey to Tria.

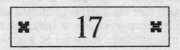

WHEN WE WERE ready to set out, Kane sat atop his big brown horse and told us that one of the Grays must have run off into the woods in the heat of the battle. "I counted only twelve bodies," he said, looking toward the meadow. "But the Grays always hunt in companies of thirteen. So until we reach Tria, we should keep our eyes open."

We quickly found our way through the woods back to the great road. I took the lead, keeping open much more than my eyes as I felt through the forested countryside for anyone who might be lying in wait for us. Atara, her bow at the ready, rode beside me, followed by Maram and Master Juwain. Kane insisted on taking the rear post. He was wise to the ways of ambuscade, he said, and he wouldn't let anyone steal upon us and attack us from behind.

After an hour of easy travel along the straight road, the forest gave out onto broad swaths of farmland. The ground here was flat, allowing a view across the fields for miles in any direction. It was an intensely cultivated land of oats, barley, and wheat—and cattle fattening in fallow fields next to little wooden houses. When I remarked that I had never seen so many people packed so closely together outside of a city, Kane just laughed at me. He told me that the domains along the Nar Road were barren compared to the true centers of Alonian civilization, which lay along the Istas and Poru rivers.

"And as for true cities, you've never seen one," he said. "No one has until he's seen Tria."

That night, in a town called Manarind, we found lodging at an inn, where we had a hot bath, a good meal, and a sound sleep. We awoke the next morning feeling greatly refreshed and ready to push on toward Tria. As we rode out from the inn that morning, we passed the estates of great knights. In the fields surrounding their palatial houses, ragged-looking men and women worked with hoes beneath the hot sun. Kane called them peasants. They slept in hovels away from their masters' houses; Kane said that the knights permitted them to till their fields and let them keep a portion of the crops they cultivated. Such injustice infuriated me. Even the poorest Valari, I thought, lived on his own land in a stout, if small, stone house—and possessed as well a sword, a suit of armor, and the right to fight for his king when called to war.

"It's this way almost everywhere," Kane told us. "Ha, the lands ruled by Morjin are much worse. There he makes his people into slaves."

Around noon, we came to a village called Sarabrunan. To the north stood a low hump of earth topped with a unique rock formation that looked like an old woman's face. Its granite countenance froze me in my tracks and called me to remember.

"Sarabrunan," I said. "Sarburn—this is the place of the great battle."

While Kane stared silently up at the Crone's Hill, as it was called, I found a villager who confirmed that indeed Morjin had met his defeat here. For a small fee, he offered to guide us around the battlefield.

"No, thank you," I told him. "We'll find our way ourselves."

Despite Maram's protests that we had little time to reach Tria before the celebration the next night, I led forth along a stream winding through the estate of some knight who had no doubt gone off to the great city. After perhaps a mile of riding through the new wheat and fallow fields, we came to a place where another stream joined the one flowing back toward the village. I pointed along these sparkling waters and said, "This was once called the Sarburn. Here Aramesh led a charge against Morjin's center. He beat back his army across the stream. It's said that it turned red with the blood of the slain."

We rode up this stream for a half mile and stopped. Five miles to the east, the Crone's Hill rose up overlooking the peaceful countryside. Other than a small knoll half a mile to our west—I remembered that it had once been called the Hill of the Dead—the land in every direction was level as the skin of a drum.

"The armies met in Valte, just after the harvest," I said. "The wheat had been cut, and the chaff lay in the fields when the battle began."

I turned to ride toward the knoll, then. I found its slopes overgrown with a thick woods where once meadows had been. While the others followed behind me, I dismounted Altaru and walked him through the trees. Near an old oak, I began rooting about in the bracken as I listened to a crow cawing out from somewhere ahead of me. I searched among old tree roots and the dense undergrowth for twenty yards before I found what I was looking for.

"Look," I said to the others as I held up a long, flat stone for them to see. It was of white granite and covered with orange and brown splotches of lichen. Two long ages had weathered the stone so that the grooves cut into it were blurred and almost impossible to read.

"It looks like the writing might be ancient Ardik," Master Juwain said as he traced his finger along one of the smooth letters. "But I can't make out what it says."

"It says this," I told him. " 'Here lies a Valari warrior.' "

I handed the stone to him; it was the first time in my life I had ever given him a reading lesson.

"Ten thousand Valari fell that day," I said. "They were buried on this knoll. Aramesh ordered as many stones cut from a quarry near Tria and brought here to mark this place."

Maram and Kane began searching the woods for other death stones, and so did I. After half an hour, however, we had found only two more.

"Where are they all?" Maram asked. "There should be thousands."

"Likely the woods have swallowed them up," Kane said. "Likely the peasants have taken them to use as foundation stones to build their huts."

"Have they no respect for the dead, then?" Maram asked.

"They were Valari dead," I said, opening my hands toward the forest floor. "And the army they fought was mostly Alonian."

This was true. In ten terrible years toward the end of the Age of Swords, Morjin had conquered all of Alonia and impressed her peoples to his service. And in the end, he had led them to defeat and death here on this very ground upon which we stood. And so Aramesh had finally freed the Alonians from their enslavement—but at a great cost. Who could blame them for any bitterness they might feel toward the Valari?

For a long while, I stood with my eyes closed listening to the sounds of the earth. Men might die, I thought, but their voices lingered on almost forever: in the rattling of the oak leaves, in the groaning of the swaying trees, in the whisper of the wind. The dead didn't demand vengeance. They made no complaint against death's everlasting cold. They asked only that their sons and grandsons of the farthermost generations not be cut down in the flush of life as they had.

I took the stone that Master Juwain still studied, and then used my knife to dig a trench in the leaf-covered ground. I planted the stone there and said, "Here lie ten thousand Valari warriors. Now come—it's growing late."

After that we returned to the road. We rode in silence for a few miles toward Tria, even as Aramesh had once ridden following his great victory.

Near sunset, we found another inn where we took our rest. We set out very early the next morning, and rode hard all that day. It was the seventh of Soldru—a day of clear skies and crisp air, perfect weather for riding. Around noon, we entered a hilly country. I would have thought to find there fewer fields, but the Alonians had cut them out of the very land. Except on the steepest slopes, terraces of wheat and barley like green steps ran in contours around the hills. White stone walls supported each terrace and set one level off from another. It was a beautiful thing to see, and a hint of the Alonians' great skill at building things.

A few hours later, the proof of their genius was laid before us. The Nar Road cut between two of these hills; at the notch, where the road rose to its greatest elevation before winding down into lower and flatter lands, we had our first view of Tria. I could hardly believe what my eyes told me must be true. For there, to the northwest across some miles of gentle farmland, great white towers rose high above the highest wall I had ever seen. They sparkled as if covered with diamond dust, catching and scattering the brilliant sunlight, and cut like spears a quarter mile high into the blue dome of the sky. Other, lesser buildings—though still very great—formed a jagged line beneath them. Master Juwain told us that during the Age of Law, these structures had been cast of living stone, a marvelous substance of great beauty and strength. Although the secret of its making had long been lost, its splendor remained to remind men of the glories to which they might attain.

The City of Light, Tria was called. It stood before us in the late afternoon sun shimmering like a great jewel cut with thousands of facets. It was sited at the mouth of the Poru River where it widened and flowed into the Bay of Belen. The blue waters gleamed beyond the city along the horizon. It was my first glimpse of the Great Northern Sea. Jutting out of the bay were the dark shapes of many islands. The largest of these—it looked almost like a skull made of black rock—was called Damoom. Master Juwain said that it had been named after the world where the Dark Angel, Angra Mainyu, was bound. For on this ominous-looking island, Aramesh had imprisoned Morjin after his defeat.

"Why didn't Aramesh," Maram asked, "just execute Morjin and be done with him?"

"Because Morjin threw down his sword and begged for his life," I told him. "According to our warrior codes, Aramesh had to spare him."

At this Kane spat out, "The damn Valari codes! The damn prophecy, too."

We all turned to look at him as we waited for him to say more.

"Have you not heard the prophecy of Katura Hastar?" he asked us. "She has foretold this: 'That the death of Morjin will be the death of Ea.'"

"Can that really be?" I asked him.

"Ha! The future is only what we make of it—who can ever see the damn, bloody future?"

At this, I walked over to where Atara stood by her mount off the side of the road. She stared at the vast city below us as if she did not want to take another step toward it. I felt her heart beating quickly and anxiously inside her.

"It is strange," I said to her. "Kane speaks of accepting fate, or not, and yet I do not think he believes in the prophecies."

"Do *you* believe the future can be foreknown?" Atara asked me.

"Sometimes I do." I fell quiet a moment as I watched her swallow against the tension in her throat. "Do you?"

She laughed coldly and told me, "I'm not sure the *past* can be known—not really."

I sensed that she was speaking about something more than the long history of ageless Tria, and I said, "You've never told me much about yourself. About your father and mother. I don't even know if you have brothers, sisters."

"I'm sure I have brothers," she said. "But we would not call the same woman our mother."

"I see."

"My father thinks of himself as a great warrior. But, as he says, he is reluctant to have to do battle in my mother's bed."

I took her hand in mine, and she allowed me to hold it. I told her, "Your father's tent, your home—it must have seemed very small."

She laughed again, this time with bitterness. "I never called it home. Some have said I must be fearless to have taken my vows, but there are worse weapons in the world to have to face than arrow or sword."

"I'm sorry," I said, squeezing her hand. "I should not have asked."

Her fingers tightened against mine as she smiled at me. I felt her mood suddenly shift, as through the force of her will, and I loved her for that.

"The past is the past," she said to me. "Can I change one moment of it? Truly, I can't. But the future! It is like a tapestry yet to be woven. And each moment of our lives, a thread. Each beautiful moment, everything we do. I *have* to believe that we can weave a different world than this. Truly, truly, we can."

It was a beautiful thing for her to say, and I couldn't help thinking of the spider she had seen weaving its web in her father's house—and of the Grays walking toward us across the moonlit meadow before they actually had. I wondered, then, if she might be gifted with seeing visions of the future. But when I asked her about this, she just laughed in her spirited way, and said, "Twice, only, I've seen these things. I'm no scryer."

After that, we went back to the others. We rode down to the city, crossing fields and estates that led nearly up to the great walls themselves. Nine gates, named after the nine Galadin who had defeated Angra Mainyu, were set into the wall. The Nar Road led straight up to the Ashtoreth Gate, which opened upon the southern districts of the eastern quarters of the city. We rode past its iron doors unchallenged. And so we entered the City of Light late on the day that Count Dario had appointed as the date that his king would call the great quest.

"We'll still have to hurry if we're to be on time," Kane said. "We've the whole city still to cross."

With our cloaks pulled tight to hide our faces, we continued down the Nar Road, which led toward the king's palace across the river in West Tria. Carts drawn by tired horses and laden with wheat grain—and with barrels of beer, bolts of cloth, and a hundred other things—blocked our way. Many hundreds of people crowded the street. Most were dressed poorly in homespun woolens, but there were also merchants wearing fine silks and not a few mercenaries clad in mail, even as Kane and I were. The din of horses whinnying, men shouting, and ironshod wheels rolling along the paving stones nearly deafened me. I had never heard such a noise other than on a battlefield. It came to me then that cities such as Tria, however beautiful, were dangerous places where men had to fight for a few feet of space or to keep themselves from being trampled—if not worse.

As we forced our way through the crowds, I kept my eyes open for the Gray who had escaped Kane's wrath—and for the Kallimun assassin-priests that he might have enlisted as reinforcements. We saw no sign of them, only the endless commerce of the city. Along the street were many stalls selling various viands: roasted breads, sausages, hams, apple pies, and hot cakes sizzling in sesame oil. Maram eyed the stands of the beer sellers and wines from Galda and Karabuk. I stared at a diamond seller, whose sparkling wares might have been looted from dead Valari warriors and reset into brooches and rings. Other shops sold pottery from the Elyssu, Sunguru cotton as white as snow, glasswork blown by the Delian masters—almost anything made by the hand of man.

Everyone seemed eager to take our money. Hawkers shouted at us to enter shops where beautifully dressed women sat inside the windows beckoning to the passersby; would-be scryers offered to read our futures for a few bronze coins while the astrologers did a brisk business casting horoscopes and drawing maps of the stars. Swarms of ragged children bravely darted in between our horses, holding out their hands as they stared at us with their big, sad eyes. Kane called them beggars. I had never seen such poor, gaunt-faced people before. Every few yards, it seemed, I reached into my purse to give one of them a silver coin. Atara, too, gave them coins: *gold* coins, of which she seemed to have many. Kane chided her for attracting attention to us and wasting her money. Atara, however, met his hardened stare with an icy one of her own. She drew herself up straight in her saddle and told him, "They're *children*. Have you no heart?"

Kane muttered something about the softness of women, then smiled secretly as we came upon the Old Sanctuary of the Maitriche Telu—or rather its ruins. I learned that in the year 2284 of the Age of Swords, Morjin had tried to annihilate this sisterhood of scryers and mind readers who opposed him. And so he had ordered their sanctuaries across Alonia torn down and the Sisters crucified. It was said that he had utterly destroyed their ancient order. But it was also said, by Kane and others, that the Sisters of Maitriche Telu still existed, dreaming their impossible dreams and plotting to remake the world from secret sanctuaries, perhaps even in Tria itself.

A couple of miles from the Ashtoreth Gate, the Nar Road led down to the river. Here the air grew moister and smelled of the faint, salt tang of the sea. Along the Poru's muddy banks were many docks, at which great ships were anchored. I gawked at them as we clopped onto a bridge named after an angel called Sarojin. And then, after we had progressed some hundred yards, the curve of the river allowed a view of a much more magnificent sight half a mile to the north. This was the famous Star Bridge. No pylons supported its immense mass. It seemed cast of a single piece of living stone that spanned the river in a great, sweeping, mile-long arch. All golden it was in the light of the setting sun, and Master Juwain called it by its more common name, which was the Golden Band. He said that the High King, Eluli Ashtoreth, had built it to remind his people of the Ieldra's sacred light that fell upon the earth at the end of every age.

When we reached the Poru's west bank, just past the dockyards, we came upon the more splendid districts of the city. I stared in awe at the great palace of the ancient Marshan clan and that of the Hastars. And then, as we turned onto to a broad tree-lined street, Kane directed my attention to a hill a mile to the north. The palace rising from the top of it was larger than my father's entire castle. Built of living stone that gleamed like marble and with nine golden domes surmounting its various sections, it was the most impressive thing I had ever seen.

As we passed the houses of the rich and powerful and drew closer, I felt in Atara a great disquiet. Was she fighting again not to dwell in the past? I wondered if she might feel ill at ease to be traveling toward the seat of power of the Sarni's ancient enemy—or perhaps Tria's splendor overawed this barbaric, manslaying woman. Soon we came to a wall surrounding the palace grounds. The guards at the gate blocked our way with spears until I told them that I was Sar Valashu Elahad of Mesh and that Count Dario had invited us to the king's celebration. As it was now growing dark, the guards' captain, a burly graybeard dressed in a fine tunic, hesitated as he studied my stained cloak and the long sword I wore beneath it. He stared even more dubiously at Kane, and he cast Atara a long look as if deciding whether she was truly a Sarni warrior or only a serving girl whom we had dressed to play the part.

"You're an odd lot," he said to us with the arrogance the Alonians hold for all other peoples. "The oddest yet to pass this gate today. And, I hope, the last. You should have arrived an hour ago so that you might have been properly presented. Now you'll have to hurry if you're to be graced with the king's welcome."

So saying, he waved us through the gate. Inside it we found a city within a city. The palace itself faced east, overlooking the harbor. The grounds were laid out with a temple, a library, two cemeteries, a guards' barracks, armory, stables, and a smithy—and various residences for those who attended the king. The road leading up to the palace, which was lined with magnificent oak trees, passed through great lawns of some of the lushest grass I had ever seen. As well there were gardens, fountains, and long pools of water decked with white marble and reflecting the light of the rising moon.

We rode up to the front of the palace, where grooms waited to take our horses. Kane didn't like it that I had so openly presented myself to the guards; he insisted that we now keep our cloaks pulled tightly around ourselves and make no mention of our names. He seemed more wary of the nobles waiting inside than he had been of the crowds of dangerous-looking men on the streets. As he put it, "The Gray who escaped us must have known we'd come here. There'll be Kallimun priests among the knights here tonight—we can be sure of that. So let's watch each other's backs."

With his dark cloak covering his face, he led the way up the steps to the colonnaded portico. We passed between thick white pillars and through the doorway into the palace proper. There the guards waved us on, and we walked quietly through a magnificent hall. Its white walls shined like mirrors and the high ceiling was inlaid with squares of lapis and gold; it was so large that for a moment I wondered if we hadn't come too late after all and missed the entire gathering. But this proved to be only the entrance hall. Beyond it, through great wooden doors trimmed out in silver and bronze, was the king's great hall. We greeted the guards stationed by the doors, and then we passed one by one into King Kiritan's immense throne room.

Three thousand people stood there beneath a great dome high above them. From a distance, this dome had appeared golden; now, looking up at it past walls of a particularly bright living stone, I could see that it was as clear as glass. It let in the starlight, which fell like a shower of silver among the many people awaiting the king. Kane's quick, dark gaze swept the room, which could easily have held three halls the size of my father's. In a low voice, he identified for us various princes from Eanna, Yarkona, Nedu, an ' the islands of the Elyssu. He pointed out the exiled knights of Galda, Hesperu, Uskudar, Sunguru, and Karabuk. There were a dozen Sarni warriors, too, with their long blond hair and drooping mustaches, and a few Valari from the kingdoms of Anjo, Taron, Waas, Lagash, Athar, and Kaash. I was proud to stand for Mesh, as Maram was for Delu. But most of those present were Alonians: knights and nobles of the Five Families; barons from Alonia's every domain; and not a few adventurers and rogues. Not all would be making the quest, but they wanted to be present at its calling. King Kiritan had invited his people to the greatest celebration in living memory, and the boldest and most powerful of them had taken advantage of his magnanimity.

We crowded into the room, which was circular in shape. An aisle bisected it and was lined on both sides with guards in polished armor. Another aisle, also guarded, cut the room crosswise, thus dividing the crowd of people into four quadrants. Where the aisles gave out at the center of the room, under the apex of the star-washed dome, stood the King's throne. Mounted on a large pedestal, it was a massive construction, all covered in gold and encrusted with precious gems. Six great steps led up to it. On each step, at either side, stood the sculptures of various animals. Master Juwain explained to us that each pair symbolized the various spiritual and material forces than man must reconcile within himself.

To climb to his throne, the king had to pass first between a golden lion and a silver ox. These represented the sun and the moon, or the active and passive principles of life. On the next step awaited a lamb and a wolf, symbols of the pure heart and the devouring passions. A hawk and a sparrow framed the third step while on the fourth stood a goat and a great leopard, cast in bronze. The goat, I guessed, embodied the need for self-sacrifice, a calling that a king must never forget. The fifth step held both a falcon and a cock, reminders of obedience to the highest and the opposing gratification of lust. On the last step, across ten feet of a worn red carpet, there perched a golden eagle facing a peacock, cast of silver but completely covered in various gemstones so as to look like brightly colored feathers.

The eagle spoke of man's striving toward transcendence as Elijin and Galadin, where the peacock represented the earthbound vanity and pride of the self. Set into the very top of the throne, beneath which the King would sit, was a golden dove, the great symbol of the peace to be attained at the end of this ascension. The final symbol, Master Juwain said, which wasn't really a symbol at all, was the starlight that fell upon the throne and called everyone to remember that shimmering place from which men had once come and to which they would someday return.

After we had stood a while pressed back against a great pillar, the doors to our left opened, and the heralds stationed there blew their trumpets to quiet us. Then the king, accompanied by a tall, handsome woman whom I took to be his wife, strode into the room. King Kiritan was himself a tall man; his golden crown, set with a large emerald on the front point, brought him up to about my height. Although his neatly trimmed beard was reddish-gray, his hair was all of silver and gold and fell down to the shoulders of a magnificent white ermine mantle. Beneath this he wore a blue velvet tunic showing the three golden lions of the royal house. He wore a long sword at his side, while in his hand he carried the golden caduceus of power and peace.

He made his way slowly down the aisle toward the throne. Although he walked with a slight limp, there was power yet in his stately gait and not a little pride. His face, cut with an unusual circular scar on his cheek, was as stern and unmoving as a stone, yet seemed ablaze with his devotion to lofty ideals and a strict moral order. He turned his head neither to the left nor right, but he must have been aware of the many people watching him. The most important of these—the princes from the island kingdoms and his barons—stood the nearest the throne. There Count Dario and other nobles of the House Narmada waited for him to mount its six broad steps.

The king, however, paused before the first step while a herald came forward. The Alonians, as I would discover, cherished their rituals. And the most ancient of all rituals in Tria was the reminding the king of his duties and from where his power ultimately came. As the king's foot fell upon the first step, the herald called out to him, and to us, the first law for kings: "You shall not multiply wives to yourself, nor shall you multiply lands, nor silver or gold."

The next step brought the following injunction from the herald, who would never think to speak to the king so boldly on any other occasion: "You shall not suffer your people to live in hunger or want."

And so it went, step after step, until the king passed between the eagle and the peacock and drew up before his throne. Then, as the king lifted up his eyes toward the great dome, the herald cried out the final law: "Know the One before whom you stand!"

Only then did King Kiritan sit upon his throne and prepare himself to act as judge and lord of his people.

Now it came time for the herald to remind the subjects attending the king to whom *they* must bow: "We honor Kiritan Ars Narmada—Duke of Tria, King of Alonia, Emperor of the North, Great Father, Exalted Grace . . ."

For a while, as everyone stood regarding the great throne, the herald continued called out King Kiritan's titles: "Blesser of the Fields, Protector of the Forests, Clearer of the Waterways . . ."

And Maram leaned up close to me and murmured, "This king takes much upon himself, does he not?"

"Guardian of the Past, Champion of the Times, Bringer of the New Age!"

The herald finally finished his accolades and bowed his head to King Kiritan, as did almost all present. Then someone let loose a great cheer, which a thousand other throats immediately caught up and magnified to a deafening thunder that shook the hall: "King Kiritan! King Kiritan! King Kiritan!"

The king seemed in no hurry to silence this acclaim. Finally, though, he held up his hand as he looked down from his throne.

"Welcome," he called out to us in a strong voice. He allowed himself a broad smile that hinted of warmth but failed to convey it. "We welcome all of you with open heart and all the hospitality that we can command."

Here he paused to nod at a Sarni chieftain and at the gold-bearded giant standing next to him, who proved to be Prince Aryaman of Thalu.

"Thirty years now," King Kiritan said, "we have sat upon this throne. And in all that time, there has never been an occasion like this. Truth to tell, Tria hasn't seen such a gathering of such illustrious personages for an entire age. Now, it would be flattering to suppose that you have come here tonight to help us celebrate our birthday. That, however, would be more flattery than is good for any king to bear. Still, celebration *is* the essence of why we are here tonight. What is a birthday but the marking of a soul's coming into life? And what is this quest that we've called you to answer but the coming of all of Ea into a new age and a new life?"

While the king went on about the great dangers and possibilities of the times in which we lived, I marveled at his audacity in conflating a high point in his life with much greater events. I noticed Atara tensing her jaw muscles as she stood next to me watching him. I recalled that the Kurmak and Alonians had often been great enemies, and I sensed in her a great struggle to like or even trust this vain and arrogant king. Kane watched him closely as well. We gathered together with Maram and Master Juwain, pressed close by a group of Alonian knights.

"Now, we must speak of this quest," King Kiritan told us. "The quest for the Cup of Heaven that has been lost for three thousand years."

His square, handsome face fairly shined in the radiance falling down from the walls. There, set into curved recesses around the room, blazed at least fifty glowstones. These were regarded as only lesser gelstei—though to my mind, they were still marvelous enough. It was said that they drank in the light of the sun, held it, and gave it back at night. Master Juwain whispered to me that these same stones had illuminated this hall for much longer than three thousand years.

"Now, if you're all standing comfortably," the king said, "we shall tell you a story. Parts are recorded in the *Saganom Elu* and other books; to those studied men and women who are familiar with these chronicles, we beg your indulgence. The whole story remains unknown, for it is yet unfinished, and we beg of all of you not only your indulgence but your enthusiasm and inspiration in completing it. After all, this *is* the king's birthday, and we can think to ask no finer gift."

So saying, he drew in a deep breath and favored us with another calculated smile. And then, as the stars poured down their light through the dome, as he sat on his immense and glittering throne beneath the golden dove of peace, he told us of many tragic deeds in the long and immensely bloody history of the Lightstone.

■ **18** ■

AND SO WE listened as he told of how the Star People had brought the Lightstone to earth and had founded Tria, the City of Light. The golden cup's radiance, he said, was meant to illuminate the flowering of a great civilization, ordered and led from sacred Tria. But then Aryu of the Valari tribe fell mad and killed his brother, Elahad, and stole the Lightstone only to lose it in death on an island near Nedu. Then the whole Valari tribe fell mad and set out on the Hundred Year March to recover the Lightstone and avenge Elahad—all in vain. And so it seemed that the Cup of Heaven's radiance might be forever lost.

"But it *cannot* be lost!" King Kiritan called out into the hall. "For its radiance blazes forever in the hearts of men, and men— and women—can never forget their ancient calling. And so in the year 2259 of the Age of Swords, our ancestor, King Sartag Ars Hastar, called a quest to recover the Lightstone. Let us honor the heroes of that great First Quest, as we honor ourselves."

In his role as Guardian of the Past, after he had motioned for his herald to bring him a huge old tome entitled the *Damitan Elu,* King Kiritan called out some of the names recorded there: Averin, Prince Garain, Iojin, Kalkin the Great, Bramu Rologar, and Kalkamesh. Then he told of the man once regarded as greatest of the heroes, whose name was Morjin. For Morjin, before he fell into darkness, was renowned for his trueness of heart and was fair to look upon; he was said to be the finest swordsman of the age.

"Little is known of Morjin's origins," King Kiritan said. "But various sources hold that he was himself a Valari of Aryu's line, and therefore as susceptible to pride and covetousness as his forebears."

"That is a lie!" I wanted to shout out. Instead, as Kane's iron hand locked onto my arm, my words came out in a hissing whisper. Several nobles nearby turned to stare at me. "Morjin is no Valari!"

King Kiritan paused as he gazed out into that part of the hall where I stood with my companions. Then he went on with his story: "According to the ancient account, Morjin led his six companions to Yarkona. In the great library they found an ancient map once drawn by Aryu's son, Jolonu, and passed down to his descendants for ages until it finally found its way into the collections. The map showed the location of the island on which Aryu had died and hidden the Lightstone more than ten thousand years before."

King Kiritan's voice grew heavy with sorrow, and I could not determine if this sentiment was real or if he conjured it out of thin air. He went on to tell that after many adventures, the heroes had at last come to this little island near Nedu, where they found the Lightstone still sitting in a dark cave. The seven heroes then passed it from hand to hand as they beheld the intense radiance streaming out of the golden cup. Six of them it had filled with the splendor of the One. But the seventh, Morjin, was unable to bear its brilliant light. He fell mad, as had Aryu and the Valari; he began a long descent into the black caverns of envy and hate that open inside anyone who covets the infinite powers of creation itself. And so, on the voyage home to Tria, he secretly slew the great Kalkin and pushed him into the sea. One by one, he then murdered Iojin, Prince Garain, Averin, and Bramu Rologar, for in touching the Lightstone they had gained immortality even as he had, and he was afraid that one of them would eventually kill *him* and claim the Lightstone for himself. Only Kalkamesh lived to avenge his companions. The *Damitan Elu* told that he had escaped by jumping into the shark-infested waters off the islands off the Elyssu. He had swum to safety, vowing to kill Morjin if it took him a thousand years and to reclaim the Lightstone for himself and all Ea.

"Who of us," King Kiritan's voice boomed out, "does not know of what happened next? Of how Morjin reappeared ten years later and came to power in the Blue Mountains? And then used the Lightstone to conquer Alonia and much of Ea?"

Only the fateful arrival of Kalkamesh at the battle of Sarburn, King Kiritan said, had saved Aramesh and the Valari from utter defeat. For Kalkamesh, having gained illumination in touching the Lightstone, had learned the secrets of the gelstei and had managed to forge a sword of pure silver gelstei. The Bright Sword, men called it. It was said to cut steel as steel does wood. Kalkamesh used it to cut a swath through Morjin's army, and thus Morjin was finally overthrown.

"Kalkamesh was a great hero," King Kiritan said. "Perhaps the greatest ever to arise from our land."

As the crowds of Alonians rumbled their approval, I traded a quick look with Kane. His black eyes were blazing; so, I thought, were mine. I had been taught that Kalkamesh was Valari and of Mesh—hence his honored name. Kane must have thought this, too. He leaned his head close to me and whispered, "Ha, Kalkamesh was no more Alonian than you or I!"

King Kiritan paused to look out into the hall; I had a disquieting sense that he was singling out the few Valari present to bear his opprobrium.

"After Morjin was taken," he said, "Kalkamesh had wanted to execute Morjin, as should have been done. Instead, Aramesh imprisoned him and took the Lightstone for himself. He took it back to Mesh where it was selfishly kept in a tumbledown little castle for all the Age of Law."

At this, my eyes began burning. My father's castle, I thought, might not be especially large, but it had always been kept in excellent repair.

"For all the Age of Law!" King Kiritan thundered. "For three thousand years, while men learned to forge all the gelstei except the gold and built a civilization worthy of the stars, the Valari kept the greatest of the gelstei from being used. And then, when Godavanni the Glorious came forth as that age's Maitreya, Aramesh's descendent, King Julamesh, at last allowed the Lightstone to be brought back here to its proper place. But it came too late, for Morjin escaped from Damoom and murdered Godavanni in this very hall!"

King Kiritan pointed with his caduceus down at the floor as if he could almost see Godavanni still lying there in a pool of blood. Then, as he recounted how the Valari kingdoms had fallen mad over this tragedy and had plunged all Ea into the most terrible of wars, he searched the room as if hoping to find anyone who thought to dispute his rendering of ancient history. Finally his gaze settled on a Valari warrior bearing on his tunic the green falcons of the Rezu clan. I guessed that this must be Sar Ianar, Duke Rezu's son. King Kiritan regarded him scornfully. Great blame he had told of, and blame lived on in his stern countenance almost three thousand years after Godavanni's death.

"And so," King Kiritan continued, "Morjin spirited away the Cup of Heaven to the fastness in Sakai that his priests had made ready for him. Argattha—that is an evil name we all know too well. Just as we know the name of the one who entered Morjin's stone city to once more deliver the Lightstone."

Many of the men and women around me nodded their heads at this, for the tale had spread into all lands as the *Song of Kalkamesh and Telemesh*—the very same song that the minstrel in Duke Rezu's castle had sung for us. Now King Kiritan reminded his listeners of how Kalkamesh had gained the aid of one of Morjin's most trusted priests, the traitor Sartan Odinan. The king told of how together the two had broken into the underground city of Argattha to steal back the Lightstone; and of how Kalkamesh was captured and tortured while Sartan escaped with the Lightstone—only to lose it again or hide it somewhere unknown to history or to any man.

"Where the Lightstone now lies, no one knows," King Kiritan said. "But we *do* know that it will be recovered. Who has not heard the prophecy of Ayondela Kirriland? 'The seven brothers and sisters of the earth with the seven stones will set forth into the darkness. The Lightstone will be found, the Maitreya will come forth, and a new age will begin.'"

He did not, of course, include the missing lines of which Kane had told us. Kane and I—and Atara, Maram, and Master Juwain—all traded knowing looks as a great stir of excitement spread through the hall.

"Ayondela did not live to see this new age," King Kiritan told us, "for she was struck down by an assassin sent by Morjin, who would silence those who speak of hope. But he has no power to silence us now. We must now speak of *our* great hope: and that is the very dream of the Star People who came to Ea ages ago. It was their purpose to create a civilization that would give birth to men and women as we were born to be. Men who would transcend themselves, in body and spirit, and return to the stars as Elijin; immortal women shining like suns who would follow the Law of the One and go on to ever deeper life in the glorious forms of the Galadin themselves.

"But where are these men and women? Where is this great civilization? Where *is* the golden cup that will restore the lands of Ea to their promise and hope? We know that it lies *somewhere* on Ea, and that Morjin at this very moment is seeking it. If it is he that finds it, then not only Galda and Surrapam along with the southern kingdoms will fall, but all Ea will fall. Then the seven brothers and sisters of the earth will go forth into the darkness and not return; the Maitreya will come forth only to be crucified; a new age will begin: the Age of Darkness that will last a thousand times three thousand years."

King Kiritan, who was now breathing hard, paused as if nearly overcome with thirst. And then he cried out, "And that is why it must be *we* who find the Lightstone! We have told you that the story of the Lightstone remains incomplete. Who will help write its ending? Who will join in the great endeavor of creating our civilization anew?"

Now he set down his golden wand of office and picked up the copy of the *Damitan Elu* instead. He thumped this ancient book with his hand. His gaze swept out into the room from the face of one great noble to the next, and he proclaimed, "We see standing here in our ancestors' hall a great gathering of heroes. Whose names will be recorded in the book that will tell of the great Second Quest and the coming of the Age of Light? Whose names will be sung by the minstrels throughout the world to the end of the ages? Who *will* hold the Lightstone in his hands? One of us here tonight! Or seven, or seventy, or a thousand—who will join voices with me and vow to make this quest?"

For a moment, no one in the hall moved. Then Count Dario, with his flaming red hair and burning eyes, put his hand to his sword as he cried out, "I will seek the Lightstone!"

Behind him, two more Alonian knights touched hands to swords and shouted, "I will!" as well. And then five knights from the Elyssu called out their promise, and all at once, like a fire shooting through dry wood, the fervor to regain the lost cup spread through the hall as hundreds of voices began crying out as one: "I will! I will! I will!"

There was magic in that moment, and I found myself calling out the same pledge I had made in the hall of my father's castle. Atara and Master Juwain joined me, and Maram, despite his doubts, added his booming voice to the clamor. Even Kane seemed swept away by the great passion of it all and growled out his assent.

After a while, when the multitude had quieted and the stones of the hall grew silent again, King Kiritan drew forth his sword and held it by the blade for all to see. He said to us, "Swear this oath, then. By your swords, by your honor, by your lives—swear that you will seek the Lightstone and never rest until it is found. Swear that you will seek it by road, by water, by fire, by darkness, by the paths of the mind and the heart. Swear that your seeking will not end unless illness, wounds, or death strike you down first. Swear that you will seek the Cup of Heaven for all of Ea and not yourselves."

It was a harsh oath that King Kiritan called us to make, and more than one knight present bit his lip and shook his head. But many more called out that they would do what was asked of them. Atara, Kane, and I did; Master Juwain, though no knight, did as well. I was afraid that Maram might balk at speaking such binding words. But he surprised me, and himself, by vowing to seek the Lightstone to his very death.

"Maram, Maram, my friend," I heard him muttering to himself a moment later, "what have you done?"

Now the time had come for King Kiritan to bless those who had made vows. These numbered perhaps a thousand. King Kiritan called for them to move toward his throne. Even as my friends and I began pressing through the crush of people in the hall, King Kiritan stepped down from his throne. Then ten of his grooms came forth bearing a golden chest between each pair of them. They set the five chests at King Kiritan's feet near the first step of his throne. King Kiritan smiled as he bowed toward the handsome woman I had presumed to be his wife. And so she was. She had golden hair almost the color of Atara's and a haughty manner, and the king presented her as Queen Daryana Ars Narmada.

The queen opened one of the chests and removed a large gold medallion suspended from a golden chain. She held it high above her head for everyone to behold. The medallion was cast into the shape of a sunburst with flames shooting off of it. As I would soon see, a cup stood out in relief at its center. Seven rays, also in relief, streamed out of the cup toward the medallion's rim. There, around the rim, were written words in ancient Ardik that those making the quest should never forget: *Sura Longaram Tat-Tanuan Galardar.*

Queen Daryana gave this medallion to King Kiritan, who then draped it over the head of Count Dario, the first knight to have called out his pledge. After the king had given his blessing, Queen Daryana reached into the chest for another medallion, even as another knight stepped up to the king. And so it went, the queen removing the medallions from the chest one by one as the king gave them with his own hands to the many questers lining up before him. As there were a thousand of us, however, this gift-giving took a long time. My friends and I were the last to enter the hall, and so we would be the last to receive our medallions.

While we stood waiting among the multitude in the hall, various knights announced their plans for finding the Lightstone. Many would journey to Ea's many oracles in hope of receiving prophecies that might direct them. Some would search the islands off Nedu, for they believed that perhaps the Lightstone that Morjin claimed at the end of the Age of Law was only one of the many False Gelstei and that the true and only Gelstei remained somewhere on the island where Aryu originally left it. I heard knights vowing to seek the cup in old sanctuaries or museums or in the ruins of ancient cities. A few decided to set forth alone, but many more were forming into bands of seven, for good luck and protection, but also because the prophecy spoke of "the seven brothers and sisters of the earth with the seven stones."

With Master Juwain pressed against my side, I thought of the varistei that Pualani had given him and of the black stone that Kane had cut from the Gray's forehead. But Kane seemed to care nothing for lesser treasures, even gelstei. He nodded toward King Kiritan and the chests of medallions and said, "That's a pretty piece of gold that the King's handing out, and a thousand of them must have cost him dearly. But gold's only gold—it's the true gold that we're after. We've made our vows to find it. Now why don't we leave before something keeps us from our quest?"

"But we haven't received the king's blessing," I whispered to him.

"If it's a blessing you want," he grumbled, "I'll give you mine."

"Thank you," I said. "But you're not a king."

At this, Kane ground his teeth together as he stared at me. Master Juwain said that we should certainly stay to receive King Kiritan's blessing while Maram, in his own mind, was likely already strutting before the ladies with his new golden medallion shining from his chest. As for Atara, she hadn't come all this way from the Wendrush and fought two battles to turn aside now. Each time Queen Daryana handed a medallion to the King, I felt Atara burning with a fierce desire.

The greatest nobles of Alonia were the first to receive their medallions that night. I heard them call out their names one by one: Belur Narmada, Julumar Hastar, Breyonan Eriades, Javan Kirriland, and Hanitan Marshan. These were all scions of the ancient Five Families that had fought among themselves for the Alonian throne ever since the invasion of the Aryan warlords who had once sailed with the great Bohimir Marshan. Next came Baron Narcavage of Arngin and Baron Monteer of Iviendenhall and various dukes and counts. Some of them were descendants of lords who had opposed the reconquest and unification of Alonia by King Kiritan's grandfather only two generations earlier; some of them had recently opposed King Kiritan himself. King Kiritan, it seemed, had spent almost his entire reign riding at the head of his knights into one rebellious domain or another. Just two years before, the last of the lords had knelt before him and called him sire. And so Alonia had been restored to her ancient borders: from the Dolphin Channel in the north to the Long Wall in the south; and from the Blue Mountains in the west six hundred miles east all the way to the Alonian Sea. Many there were who had begun calling him King Kiritan the Great. It was said that although he hadn't sought this honorific for himself, neither did he discourage it.

It was also said—I heard these whispers and grumblings from various knights around me—that the king had more than one reason for calling the quest. No one doubted that he loved Ea and wished to see her restored to her ancient splendor. None doubted that he opposed Morjin with all his will and might. But neither did anyone doubt his need to check the power of his barons. And so he had called them to make vows: those who accepted his medallion would have to go forth upon the quest and leave their domains and intrigues behind them. Those who refused would shame themselves and mar their honor, thus diminishing their ability to mount any opposition to the king. As for King Kiritan, he would make *his* quest by seeking the Lightstone solely within Alonia's various domains. He would ride at the head of his knights into Tarlan or Aquantir as he always had, and so keep watch upon his realm. A cunning man was King Kiritan Ars Narmada, and a deep one, too.

Finally, after the lesser lords of smaller domains and common knights had received their shining medallions, it came time for my friends and me to stand before the king. As a great feast had been promised following this ceremony, everyone was now waiting for us to receive the king's blessing. Everyone grew quiet and watched as we approached the throne. Master Juwain was the first of us to throw back his cloak and call out his name: "Master Juwain Zadoran," he said, "Greetings, King Kiritan."

"Master Juwain Zadoran of what realm?" the king asked him as he studied his plain woolens doubtfully.

"Formerly of the Elyssu," Master Juwain said. "But for many years of that landless realm known as the Brotherhood."

"Well, this *is* a surprise," the king said with a smile. "A master of the Brotherhood will dare to undertake the quest! We are honored."

"The honor is mine, King Kiritan."

King Kiritan nodded at Queen Daryana, who reached into the fifth golden chest and removed a medallion. The king draped this over Master Juwain's bald head and told him: "Master Juwain Zadoran, accept this with our blessing that you might be known and honored in all lands."

Master Juwain bowed to the king and backed away as Maram now stepped up to him. With a flourish, he loosened his cloak to reveal the red tunic beneath. Then he called out: "Prince Maram Marshayk of Delu."

This announcement caused a great stir among the nobles in the room. At least forty knights present were from Delu's various dukedoms or baronies, and they looked at Maram with the shock of recognition.

"Now, this is an even greater surprise," the king said. "We were hoping that King Maralah might send one of his own to honor us this day. How is it that his son happens to be traveling with a master of the Brotherhood?"

"*That* is a long story," Maram said as he stared much too boldly at Queen Daryana. "Perhaps I could tell it to you and your lovely queen later over a goblet of your finest wine."

"Perhaps you could," King Kiritan said, forcing a thin smile. And with that, he bestowed upon Maram his much-desired medallion.

Next Kane approached the king. With great reluctance, he uncloaked himself. And then, in a quietly savage voice, he gave his name.

"Just 'Kane?' " the king asked as he gazed at him disapprovingly.

"So, just Kane," Kane growled out. "Kane of Erathe."

The king seemed as curious to learn of his homeland as I was, and he asked, "Erathe? We have never heard of that realm. Where does it lie?"

"Far away," Kane said. "It is very far away."

"In what direction?"

But in answer, Kane only stared at him as his eyes grew bright with the starlight pouring down through the dome.

"Who is your king, then? Tell us the name of your lord."

"No man is my lord," Kane said. "Nor do I call any man king."

King Kiritan bit his lip in distaste and then said, "You're not the first lordless knight to make vows tonight. But you *have* made vows, it seems. And so we will give you our blessing."

As quickly as he could, the king took the medallion from Queen Daryana and dropped it over Kane's head. He looked away as Kane pressed his finger to the cup at the center of the medallion and stepped over to me.

"It's your turn," he snarled out. "Let's get this over and be done."

It *was* my turn, and some three thousand knights, nobles, and ladies were waiting for me to take it. And so I stepped up to King Kiritan, pulled back my cloak and told him my name: "Sar Valashu Elahad of Mesh."

For a moment, King Kiritan's face looked as if it had been

slapped in front of everyone quietly watching us. Then he recovered his composure; he nodded toward Count Dario as he said, "We had heard that the son of King Shamesh would make this quest. But it is a great distance between Silvassu and Tria. We had supposed you had lost your way in coming here."

"No, King Kiritan," I said as I glanced at Kane, "we were delayed."

"Well, then, we should rejoice that the Valari have sent a prince upon the quest," he said joylessly. "We're honored that Shavashar Elahad sends us his *seventh* son."

I winced as he said this, and so did Kane. I felt many eyes upon me. Who knew which pair of them had heard the words of the last two lines of Ayondela's prophecy?

"It is good," King Kiritan continued, "that a prince of Mesh will seek to put aright the great wrong done by his sires in ages past."

Great pain the kirax in my blood still caused me, but it seemed slight against the burning I felt there now. King Kiritan knew nothing of my purpose in making the quest. And it was wrong for him to say that the kings of my line had done wrong. Even so, I did not gainsay him. I thought it more seemly to respect the decorum of the moment even if he did not.

"By my sword, by my honor, by my life," I told him, "I seek the Lightstone. For all of Ea and not myself."

"Very good, then," King Kiritan said, looking at me closely. He held out his hand for a medallion, which he placed over my head. It seemed a great weight pressing against my chest. "Sar Valashu Elahad, accept this with our blessing that you might be known and honored in all lands."

I bowed and backed away, glad to done with him. And then Atara stepped forward.

"Look, it's the princess!" I heard someone exclaim as Atara threw back her cloak.

I thought it a strange thing to say. The granddaughter of Sajagax she might be, but I had never heard the chiefs of the Sarni tribes called kings nor those of their lineage called princesses.

Atara, clad in her bloodstained trousers and black leather armor studded with steel, caused the assembled nobles to wag their fingers and begin talking furiously. Other Sarni warriors, similarly attired, had already stood before the king. But they had been men; it seemed that no one present had ever seen a woman warrior, much less one of the Manslayer Society.

She stepped straight up to the king and looked him boldly in the eyes. Then she said, "Atara Manslayer of the Kurmak."

The king's ruddy face paled with shock; his lips moved silently as he fought for words. Queen Daryana, too, stared at Atara, as did Count Dario and all the other nobles near the throne.

"You," the king said as he held his trembling hand out to Atara, "have another name. Say it now so that we may hear it."

Atara looked at me as if to beg my forgiveness. Then she smiled and called out: "Atara Ars Narmada—of Alonia *and* the Wendrush."

I gasped in astonishment along with a thousand others. How it had come to be that this wild Sarni warrior was also a princess of the Narmada line, I couldn't understand. But that she was King Kiritan's daughter couldn't be denied. I saw it in the set of their square, stubborn faces and in the fire of their diamond-blue eyes; I felt it passing back and forth between them in fierce emotions that tasted both of love and hate.

"It's his daughter," someone behind me whispered. "She's still alive."

"*Is* she still our daughter?" King Kiritan asked, looking at Atara.

"Of course she is," Queen Daryana said as she dropped the last medallion back into its chest. She hurried past the king and threw her arms around Atara. Not caring who was watching, she kissed her and stroked her long hair with delight. Tears were streaming from her eyes as she laughed out, "Our brave, beautiful daughter—oh, you *are* still alive!"

King Kiritan stood very straight as he scowled at Atara. "Six years it's been since you fled our kingdom for lands unknown. Six years! We had thought you dead."

"I'm sorry, Father."

"Remember where you are!"

"Excuse me . . . sire."

"That's better," King Kiritan snapped. "Are we to presume, then, that you've been living with the Kurmak all this time?"

"Yes, sire."

"You might have sent word to us that you were well." The

king stared in distaste at Atara's garments. "And now you return to us, on *this* night, in front of our guests, attired as . . . as what? A Sarni warrior? Is this how women dress on the Wendrush?"

Across the room I saw several Sarni warriors, with their drooping blond mustaches and curious blue eyes, pressing closer.

"Some of them do," Queen Daryana said. Standing next to her daughter, it was clear to see that they were of the same height and strong cast of body. They were both strong in other ways, too. The queen seemed as unafraid of her husband as Atara had been of the hill-men. To King Kiritan she said, "Did you not hear her name herself as a Manslayer?"

"No, we tried *not* to hear that name. What does it mean?"

"It means she is a warrior," Queen Daryana said simply. Then a great bitterness came into her voice. "You take little interest in my people beyond seeing that they remain outside your Long Wall."

My father would have thought it beneath him to bicker with his family in public—or, indeed, at all. It seemed, however, to be King Kiritan's way ever to strive for predominance in the sight of others and to fight battles everywhere, even in his own hall, where he contended with envoys from hostile monarchs and with rebellious barons—to say nothing of his own daughter and wife.

"*Your* people," he reminded the queen, "are Alonians and have been for more than twenty years."

In the heated words that followed, I pieced together the story of Atara's life—and some of the recent history of Alonia. It seemed that early in King Kiritan's reign, to protect his southern borders, he had felt compelled to cement an alliance with the ferocious Kurmak tribe. And so he had sent a great weight of gold to Sajagax in exchange for his daughter Daryana's hand in marriage. The Kurmak had made peace with Alonia, and more, had checked the power of the equally ferocious Marituk tribe who patrolled the Wendrush between the Blue Mountains and the Poru, from the Long Wall as far south as the Blood River. But there had been little peace between King Kiritan and his proud, fierce, headstrong queen. As she would tell anyone who would listen, she had been born free and would not be ruled by any man, not even Ea's greatest king. And so for every command or slight the king gave her, she gave him back words barbed like the points of the Sarni's arrows. It was said that King Kiritan had once dared to strike her face; to repay him, she had cut the scar marking his cheek with her strong, white teeth.

"The king," she said to Atara, "has told me that your grandfather and grandmother, and your mother's brothers and sisters and their children—all the warriors and women of the Kurmak—are not *my* people. If he cut out my heart, would he not see that my blood remains as red as theirs? But he is the king, and he has said what he has said. And this on a day when he has invited all the free peoples of Ea into our home to go forth on a great quest as one people. Is this worthy of the great man you love and revere as your sire?"

It was also said that for many years, King Kiritan had given Daryana coldness in place of love. And so she had given him one daughter only and no sons.

I wondered why Daryana hadn't fled back to the Kurmak as Atara had done. Almost as if she could hear my thoughts, she said, "Of course, some might say that since gold has been paid in dower to my father, I now belong to him who paid it. A deal is a deal and can't be broken, yes? But I hadn't heard that the Alonians had entered the business of buying and selling human beings."

At this, the king flashed her a look of hate as he said, "No, you're right—that is not our business. And you're also right to say that a deal cannot be broken. Especially one that was agreed upon freely, and as we remember, enthusiastically."

Queen Daryana's eyes were full of sadness as she looked at Atara and said, "Choices must always be made; seldom can they be unmade. I might have joined the Manslayers even as you have. But then I wouldn't have lived to bear such a beautiful daughter."

Atara, who was blinking back tears, bowed her head to her mother and then looked down at the floor.

"Yes, a *daughter*," the king said as if he had bit into a lemon. "A daughter who must kill a hundred of her enemies. When none of even my finest knights have dispatched so many."

"They haven't been trained by the Manslayers," Atara said proudly.

The king ignored this slight against Alonian arms and said,

"Then none of these women may marry until they've reached this number? Are there no exceptions?"

"No, sire."

"Not even for one who is also the daughter of the Alonian king?"

"I have made vows," Atara told him.

"Do your vows then supersede your duty to your lord?"

"And what duty is that?" Atara asked as she looked at Prince Jardan of the Elyssu. With his curled brown hair, he was a handsome man and a tall one—though the webwork of broken blood vessels on his red nose hinted of weakness and craving for strong drink. "The duty to be sold in marriage to the highest bidder?"

It was well, I thought, that Atara had fled her home at the young age of sixteen. I saw that she vexed King Kiritan even more sorely than did her mother. How could he ever overawe his subjects into calling him Kiritan the Great, Emperor of the North and Righteous Conqueror, when he couldn't even rule his own daughter? Now his hand closed into a fist as he ground his teeth and his whole body trembled with rage. Because I couldn't allow him to strike her, I readied myself to rush forward and stand between them. But the king's guards saw my concern and readied themselves to stop me. King Kiritan saw this, too.

"When did the sanctity of marriage come to be so little regarded?" he said to Atara. He cast me a dismissive look, then glowered at Maram and Kane. "Is it right that you should forsake such a blessed union to take up with a ragtag band of adventurers?"

"Hmmph," Atara said, "you may call them that, but my friends are—"

"A bald, old man, a fat lecher, a mercenary, and a knight of little name."

Atara opened her mouth to parry his careless words. But warrior of the Manslayers though she might be, I could not allow her to fight my battles for me. I threw off my cloak then so that the king could see my surcoat and the silver swan and seven stars shining from it.

"My sires were kings, even as yours were, King Kiritan," I said. "And *their* sires were kings when the Narmadas were still warlords fighting the Hastars and Kirrilands for the throne."

Now the hands of Count Dario and Baron Belur Narmada

snapped toward the hilts of their swords. Other knights grumbled their resentment of what I had said. It was one thing for the
king's wife and daughter to dispute with him, but quite another
for an outland warrior to shame him with the truth.

"Sar Valashu Elahad," the king huffed at me. "It's said that
your line is descended, father and son, from *the* Elahad. Well, it's
also said that the Saryaks claim descent from Valoreth himself."

"Many things are said, King Kiritan. And one of these is that
a wise king will be able to tell what is true from what is false."

"*We* tell you this then. *You* Valari are as prideful as you ever
were." He glanced at Atara, and he added, "And as bold."

"It's boldness that wins battles, is it not?"

"We haven't heard of any notable battles you've won of late,"
he said. "It would seem that you're too busy fighting yourselves
over diamonds."

"That might be," I said bitterly. "But once we fought for other
things."

"Yes, for a golden cup that does not belong to you."

"At least the cup was won," I said, recalling the white stones
I had found on the Hill of the Dead the day before. "At the
Sarburn—you will have heard of that battle."

"Indeed we have. Eighty-nine Narmada knights fell there
that day."

"Ten *thousand* Valari are buried there!" I said. "And their
graves aren't even marked!"

"That is not right," the king said with surprising softness.
And then a note of bitterness crept back into his voice. "But you
can't blame my people for not wanting to honor outland warriors who invaded their land for plunder."

"The Valari did not die for plunder," I said.

"Nevertheless, Aramesh *did* claim the Lightstone. And then
took it back to Mesh and kept it for himself behind his mountains."

"That is not true," I said. "He invited all to come and behold
it. And in the end, Julamesh surrendered the cup to Godavanni,
even as you have told of here tonight."

"We have told of how the cup was lost. By Valari selfishness
and pride."

"The cup *was* lost. Which is why some of us have vowed to
regain it."

"We do not see many Valari here tonight," the king said, looking out at the masses of people packed into the hall. "And why is that?"

Because our hearts have been broken, I thought.

The king, answering his own question, said, "Your land is long past its time of greatness. Now you Valari care for little more than your diamonds and your little wars. It's almost savage the way you glorify it: every man a warrior; your duels; meditating over your swords as if they were your souls. No, we're afraid that the Valari's day is done."

Because I had nothing to say to this, I stared up through the dome at the stars. Then Atara touched my shoulder, and we looked at each other in a deep understanding.

"Well, what's this, then?" the king said, glaring at us.

But neither Atara nor I answered him; we just stood there before three thousand people looking into each other's eyes.

"You," the king said to Atara, "will remain here, now that you've returned."

"But, sire," Atara said, turning toward him, "I've made vows to seek the Lightstone. Would you have me break them?"

"You'll do your seeking in Alonia, then."

Atara looked at me as she sadly shook her head. Then, to her father, she said, "No, I'll go on the quest with Val, if he'll have me."

"If he'll *have* you!" the king thundered. "Who is he to take you anywhere? To take you off to oblivion or death?"

"He has saved my life, sire. Twice."

"And who has given you life?" the king shouted. Quick as cat, he turned to me and pointed his finger at my chest. "Tell us the truth about what you want of our daughter!"

The first thing a Valari warrior is taught is always to tell the truth. And so I looked at King Kiritan and told him what my heart cried out, even though I had never said the words to anyone, not even myself: "To marry Atara."

For a moment, King Kiritan did not move. It seemed that no one in the hall dared breathe. And then he shouted, "Marry *our* daughter?"

"If she'll have me," I said, smiling. "And with your blessing."

King Kiritan laughed at me then: a series of harsh, cutting sounds that issued from his throat almost like the barking of a dog. Then his face purpled and he began raging at me: "Who are *you* to marry her? An adventurer who hides himself in a dirty cloak? A seventh son who has no hope of ever becoming a king? And a king of what? A savage little kingdom no bigger than many of my barons' domains! You think to marry *our* daughter?"

In that moment, as King Kiritan's outraged voice echoed from the stone walls of his hall, I pitied him. For I saw that he resented having had to marry beneath himself, as he surely thought of his union with Daryana. And now he hoped to ennoble his line more deeply by marrying Atara to the crown prince of Eanna or possibly Prince Jardan of the Elyssu. Even Maram, I supposed, as a prince of the strategically important Delu, would have been considered a more suitable match than I if not for his lustful ways and friendship with me.

I saw another thing, too: that the king, unlike lesser men, was not at the mercy of his terrible rages. Rather, he summoned them from some deep well inside him like a conjurer, and more, wielded his wrath precisely as he might a sword to terrify anyone who stood against him. But I had lived with swords all my life. And I had one of my own.

"I love Atara," I said to him. My eyes were now wide open, and much else as well. "Will you bless our marriage, King Kiritan?"

In answer, he laughed at me again. And then, as his eyes filled with malice, in a mocking voice, he said, "Yes, you may marry our daughter—when you have found the Lightstone and have delivered it here to this room!"

I was sure he expected me to cringe like a beaten dog or perhaps protest that the Cup of Heaven might be found only by the One's grace. Instead, I grasped the hilt of my sword and rashly told him, "This I vow then."

While he stared at me in disbelief, I took Atara's hand and kissed it. I said, "If you won't yet bless our marriage, then will you at least give Atara your blessing so that we may set out on the quest?"

"You dare too much, Valari!" he snapped at me. "Should we then give her my own dagger so that she can stab me in the back?"

"Please, King Kiritan—give her your blessing."

From somewhere to our side, a woman called out, "Your blessing, King Kiritan!" Others picked up this cry so the hall rang with the sound of many voices, "Give her your blessing!"

But the king was the king, and would not be so easily swayed. He stood before his jeweled throne, staring at both Atara and me as if we were rebellious barons who had dared enter his own hall to defy him.

How is it that we set out with so much love for our fathers, daughters, or brothers, ready to make great sacrifices or even die for them—only to see this most sacred gift transmuted by an evil alchemy so that we cause them the greatest hurt and bring them its opposite instead?

As I stood there holding Atara's hand, I felt both her anguish and adoration for her father surging through her. It was strange, the sense I had that I could touch King Kiritan with either of these. In my dream, Morjin had told me that I would one day strike out at others with the black dagger of my hate; it hadn't occurred to me that I might also thrust the bright sword of another's love straight into their hearts.

"Don't look at me that way, Valari," King Kiritan whispered to me. "Damn your eyes—don't look at me!"

But I couldn't help looking at him. And he couldn't help turning toward Atara as a great tenderness softened his face. Few were close enough to see the tears welling in his eyes. And only Atara and Daryana—and I—could feel the great love pouring out of him.

"We were afraid you were dead," he said to Atara.

"There have been many who tried to make me so," Atara told him. "But as you always said, sire, we Narmadas are hard to kill."

"Yes we are," he said with a grateful smile. "And by the grace of the One, as we set out on this quest, may we continue to be."

So saying, he nodded at Daryana, who reached into the chest to hand him a medallion. With a gentleness few would have suspected he possessed, he placed it over Atara's head and told her, "Atara Ars Narmada, accept this with our blessing that you might be known and honored in all lands."

To the cheers of almost everyone in the hall, he clasped her to him, kissed her fiercely on the forehead and stood there weeping softly. But it took him only a few moments to compose himself and put the steel back into his countenance. And the anger, too. He glared at me darkly as he called out to the knights and nobles around us: "All who have wished have made their vows and have received our blessing. Now please join us outside that you might help us celebrate this great occasion and our birthday as well."

And then, with a last, cutting glance at me, he turned and stormed from the hall.

■ **19** ■

FOR SOME TIME after that, I stood off to the side of the throne with Atara as we watched the immense hall empty. Still stunned by what had just happened, I could think of nothing to say. And then Atara made a fist as she pounded the air and fairly shouted at me: "How *dare* you ask my father for my hand in front of everyone? Before you'd even asked *me*?"

I took a step toward her to touch her arm, but she backed away from me. And so I said, "My apologies if what passed with your father caused you embarrassment. But I thought—"

"You *didn't* think. You told my father that you loved me. But you never told *me*."

"I'm sorry—I couldn't even tell myself. Will you forgive me?"

I stood gazing at her, and I felt something warm and bright build into an unbearable pain inside me. And suddenly, her anger went away.

"I *didn't* know, Val. I should have, but I didn't." She opened her fist and glanced down at the little cuts that her fingernails had made in the palm of her hand. "But you *can't* love me. That is, you shouldn't. I can't help who I am."

"But why didn't you *tell* me who you really are?" I asked her.

"I was afraid that if you knew, you'd look at me differently," she said as she lifted up her head toward me. "As I'm afraid you're looking at me now."

That deep, brilliant light that had dazzled me from our first moment together seemed to pour itself out through her eyes, and I said to her, "There is only one way I could ever see you."

"As your *wife?*" she said bitterly. "To be bound by yet another vow?"

"No," I said, as I reached out to touch her hand, "to be joined in love."

Her fingers clasped mine, and she smiled at me. "But I haven't said anything about love."

"You didn't need to," I told her. "I've always known—even if I didn't *know* that I knew."

"Yes, with this gift of yours. I don't think I could ever keep anything from you, could I? But this is no time for love."

For a moment, I could see my grandmother's beautiful face shining through hers, and I told her, "Some would say that nothing else really matters."

"This is no time for marriage, then. I've made other vows, and I must keep them."

"But if someday you fulfill them, then—"

"This is not the time for *anyone* to marry," she said. "Should I bear your children only to see them slain in the wars that must surely come?"

"But if the Lightstone were found and the Red Dragon defeated, war itself brought to an end, then—"

"Then it would be then," she told me. "Then you may ask me about marriage—if that is still what you desire."

She squeezed my hand, and we stood there looking at each other for what seemed forever.

Then Master Juwain, Maram, and Kane, who were fighting the throngs streaming toward the doors, came up to us with their gold medallions showing beneath their cloaks.

"What a night this is!" Maram called out. He cupped his hand beneath his medallion. "And what a kingly gift this is! I never thought to be given anything so magnificent."

"And I never thought to hear you vow to seek the Lightstone," Master Juwain told him. "But you seem to have a fondness for making vows."

"Ah, I do, don't I?" Maram said.

"I seem to remember you were to forsake wine, women, and war."

"Well, I suppose I'm not very good at forsaking, am I? And that's just the point—I *won't* forsake this quest."

Maram's sudden earnestness made me smile. I clapped him on the shoulder and said, "But why make vows at all? Didn't you set out only so far as to to see Tria?"

"True, true," he said. "And I *have* seen Tria. And a great deal else."

"We've vowed to seek the Lightstone until it is found," I reminded him. "We can't do very much of that seeking in taverns or boudoirs."

"No, perhaps we can't, my friend. But maybe we'll find a few glasses of beer along our way." Here he paused to eye a beautiful Alonian woman dressed in a blue satin gown. "And perhaps great treasures as well."

"We also vowed to go on seeking unless we're struck down first."

"I *am* mad, aren't I? But someone is bound to find this cup, and it might as well be us. Do you think I'd let you have all the fun yourself?"

With a brave smile, he clapped me on my shoulder. "Now, I'm hungry as a bear. Why don't we go out and help the king celebrate his birthday?"

"I think the king has seen enough of us for one night, eh?" Kane said. "Others have seen us, too. We should find a quiet inn to take our meal."

Kane's was the voice of prudence, but I didn't want to have to slink away like a whipped dog. And so I said, "If King Kiritan has gone to so much trouble to honor us, then we should accept his hospitality."

I led the way out of the north door of the hall. There we found a broad corridor giving out onto a vast lawn. The king's thousands of guests easily might have become disoriented on it if not directed by a line of torches toward a long pool where many tables had been set with food. Against the backdrop of fountains lit up with glowstones, the tables fairly groaned beneath the weight of mutton joints, beef roasts, and whole roasted pigs. There were cheeses and breads, too, and pastries and puddings and fruits. This being Tria, the king's cooks had also set before us braised salmon, smoked herring, mussels, and various other creatures that lived within shells. I couldn't believe that human beings could eat such things, but the Trians seemed used to feasting on them.

It was a clear, beautiful night. The city spread out in all directions below us. Little lights like those of fireflies flickered from the many houses and buildings. To the south, the great Tower of the Sun stood between the Hastar and Marshan palaces, while to the north, arising from Narmada Hill, gleamed the Tower of the Moon. The silvered pillars of stone seemed to hold up the heavens like a star-studded canopy over the whole of Tria.

Following Maram's lead, we all filled our plates with mounds of food and found an empty table near some lilac bushes where we could take our meal in peace. But peace we could not have, for even as we finished eating and stood around the table drinking wine, various men and women began coming up to us and presenting themselves. The first of these I was very glad to see for he was a Valari knight whom I knew from my childhood: Sar Yarwan Solaru of Kaash, king Talanu's third son and my first cousin by my mother, who was sister to the king. Sar Yarwan, a striking man with a great hawk's nose, clasped hands with me warmly and then told me the names of the six knights who accompanied him. Sar Ianar, the son of Duke Rezu, had his father's sharp features and sharpness of eye. He looked at some Alonians milling about nearby and said, "Sar Valashu, it's good to see another Valari here—so few of us made the journey."

Sar Yarwan rested his hand on my shoulder and said, "We all appreciate what you said to the king."

"The truth is the truth and must be told," I said.

"Nevertheless, it takes courage to tell it—especially when few wish to listen." He bowed his head to me and continued, "We didn't know you would be coming to Tria. It's too bad you arrived so late."

Although he was my cousin, I didn't tell him about the Grays and that we'd had to fight for our lives to arrive at all.

"You would be a welcome addition to our company," he said to me. His bright eyes seemed to be searching for something in mine. "We are seven, and that is good luck and accords with the prophecy. But we're all agreed that it would be even better luck to have you with us."

"You honor me," I said. Then I nodded at Kane, Maram, Atara, and Master Juwain. "But these are my friends, and we'll journey on together."

"As you wish, Sar Valashu," he said. "It's strange company you've chosen, but we wish you well. May you walk in the light of the One."

I said the same to him, and Atara did, too. Then she looked over toward one of the fountains and her face brightened. I turned to see Queen Daryana walking toward us accompanied by a large knight bearing the crest of two oaks and two eagles on his green tunic.

"Mother," Atara said, "may I present Sar Valashu Elahad? I was hoping you might be able to meet him in less difficult circumstances."

I bowed to Queen Daryana, who glanced at the fountain where the king stood talking with two of his dukes. Then she smiled and said to me, "It seems that all circumstances will be difficult so long as you remain in Tria."

And with that, she motioned toward the knight standing next to her. "This is Baron Narcavage of Arngin. The king has sent him with me to make sure that you don't attack me."

I nodded my head to the baron, who reluctantly returned the bow. He had a deep chest and great arms, and his large head was sunk down into a neck swollen with muscle or fat—it was hard to tell which on account of his thick blond beard. His little blue eyes seemed the only small thing about him; they were almost lost beneath his overhanging forehead and bushy eyebrows. But they peered out at me with a sharp intelligence all the same. There was cunning and resentment there—and the wit to hide them as well.

"Sar Valashu Elahad, the king sends his regrets that he is too busy to further make your acquaintance. But he has also sent his best Galdan wine to thank you for honoring him tonight." So saying, he showed everyone a large green bottle that he had held. "May I pour you a glass?"

"Perhaps in a moment. We haven't finished the presentations."

I told the queen the names of my friends, then presented Sar Yarwan and the Valari knights. She cast them, and me, a wary look. We were Valari, after all, and she was still the daughter of a Sarni chieftain.

As the moon rose over the cool lawns and bubbling fountains, we stood talking about the quest. Sar Yarwan announced his plan to journey to Skule in the wilds of northern Delu. He would search the ruins of that once great city for any sign that Sartan Odinan might have brought the Lightstone there.

"Skule lies on the other side of the Straits of Storm," Baron Narcavage said to him. "If you'll be crossing them from Alonia, you'll have to pass through Arngin. Which you may do with my blessing."

"Thank you, that would be the most direct route," Sar Yarwan agreed.

"And the safest—you wouldn't want to cross Delu, which is now nothing more than a dozen savage provinces practically ruled by their warlords."

"No, you're wrong about Delu," a strong voice called out. Here Maram stepped forward and looked Baron Narcavage in the eye. "Delu is certainly much more than you have said."

"Forgive me, Prince Maram, but I've journeyed through what is left of your father's kingdom while you've been off learning your dead languages at the Brotherhood's school."

"Delu has its troubles," Maram admitted. "But it wasn't so long ago that Alonia had worse."

To cool their rising tempers, I came between them and said, "We live in a time of troubles."

"We do indeed," Baron Narcavage said, smiling at me. "We've all heard that we can expect war between Ishka and Mesh."

"That hasn't been decided yet. We can still hope for peace."

"How can there ever be peace in the Nine Kingdoms when each of your so-called kings insists on coveting his neighbors' lands?"

"What do mean, 'so-called'?"

"Is the King of Anjo truly a king? Or Anjo a kingdom? And what of Mesh? My own domain is bigger than your entire realm."

Now I felt my temper rising, too, and Maram gripped my arm to steady me. To Baron Narcavage, he said, "That might be true, but at least his, ah, *sword* is longer than yours."

Being well-pleased with his repartee, Maram grinned broadly and then winked at Queen Daryana.

Baron Narcavage shot him a dark look and then said, "Yes, the famed Valari swords—used mostly to cut each other to pieces."

Queen Daryana seemed to like neither the baron nor his usurping the conversation. To distract us all from squabbles almost as old as time, she called out, "We live in a time of swords, and it's said that the Valari *do* have long ones. But this is a night of peace. Celebration and song. Who knows the Song of the Swan? Who will sing it with me?"

As I touched the silver swan embroidered on my tunic, she smiled at me, and I loved her for that. Then we all started singing the song. It was mostly a sad song, telling of a king who falls in love with a great white swan. To gain her love in return, he builds a magnificent castle in which to keep her, and feeds her delicacies even as he dresses her in the finest silks. But the swan soon sickens and starts singing her death song. The grief-stricken king then goes among the people of his realm offering a great measure of gold to anyone who can tell him the answer to the riddle of how he may heal her without letting her go.

As we worked through the verses, Maram and the Valari knights joined us, and then other knights and their ladies came over and began singing, too. One of the women caught my eye: she had iron-gray hair and a pretty, pleasant face, and around her neck she wore the same gold medallion as did Atara and I. I remembered her earlier giving her name to King Kiritan as Liljana Ashvaran; she was one of the few Alonian woman to have vowed to make the quest. Although obviously no knight, she had an air of courage about her. She pressed in closer toward Queen Daryana, all the while singing with a measured assurance. When she thought I wasn't looking, she stole quick glances at me.

We stood there singing beneath the moon and stars for quite a while, for the song was a long one. When we reached the part of it where the king asks his people for advice, I took note of a new voice added to the chorus. Although in no way overpowering any other, it distinguished itself in subtle harmonies with its clarity and perfection of pitch. It came from a slender man whose black, curly hair gleamed in the light of the glowstones. He had the large brown eyes and the brown skin of a Galdan, those comeliest of people; his fine features seemed in perfect accord with the great beauty of his voice. His age was perhaps thirty: the only lines I could make out on his face were the crow's-feet around his eyes—I guessed from smiling so much. He struck me as being spontaneous, gifted, guileless, and wild, and I liked him immediately.

I cocked my head, listening as we sang out the words to the king's terrible dilemma:

> How do you capture a beautiful bird
> without killing its spirit?

And then the answer came, from this man's perfectly formed lips and those of many others:

> By letting it fly;
> By becoming the sky.

The song ended happily with the king tearing down the walls of stone that he had built to imprison his beloved swan—and himself. For he realized that his true realm was not some little patch of earth but was of the heart and spirit and was as vast as the sky itself.

When we had finished, the queen, who obviously had a good ear, called the Galdan over to her. He gave his name as Alphanderry. Although no noble, with his silk tunic trimmed in gold and elegance of carriage he managed to look more distinguished than any of the princes there. He was a minstrel, he said, exiled because his songs had offended Galda's new rulers. At the queen's request, he lifted up his mandolet and sang for us.

No bird, I thought, not even a swan, had a voice so beautiful as his. It spread out across the lawn and seemed to touch even the grasses with dewdrops of light. As we all grew quiet, it was much easier to appreciate its power and grace. His words were beautiful, too, and they told of the anguish of love and the eternal yearning for the beloved. As with the Song of the Swan, its themes were bondage and the freedom that might be attained through the purest of love. Like the ringing of a perfect golden bell, his verses carried out in the night—so sweet and clear and full of longing that they were both a pain and a pleasure to hear.

And as he made his music, Flick suddenly appeared above

him and whirled about like a tiny dancer raimented in pure light. Alphanderry, I thought, couldn't see him, nor could any of the nobles gathering around him. But I felt Maram's hand squeeze my shoulder as Atara flashed me a look of relief almost as sweet as Alphanderry's singing.

At the end of his song, he lowered his mandolet and smiled sadly. I, like everyone else, was filled with a sense that he had been singing just for me. We looked at each other for a moment, and he seemed to know how deeply his music had touched me. But there was no pride or vanity in him at this accomplishment, only a quiet joy that he had been gifted with the voice of the angels.

"That was lovely," Queen Daryana said to him as she wiped the tears from her eyes. "Galda's loss is Alonia's gain. And Ea's, as well."

Alphanderry bowed to her, then gripped the medallion that King Kiritan had given him. Now his smile was happy and bright; like a butterfly among flowers, he seemed able to flit easily from one color of emotion to another.

"Thank you, Queen Daryana," he told her. "I haven't had the privilege of singing before such an appreciative audience for a long time."

Baron Narcavage stepped forward and raised the wine bottle that he still held. He said, "Allow us then to show our appreciation with some of this. I think you'll like the vintage—it's Galdan, from the king's special reserve. I was just about to pour Sar Valashu and the queen a glass."

So saying, he motioned to a groom, who brought over a tray of goblets. The baron uncorked the wine, then poured the dark red liquid into eight of them. He handed the goblets one by one to me and my friends, and to Alphanderry and the Queen. The last one he took for himself. I thought it rude of him to ignore Sar Yarwan and the Valari knights—and everyone else who gathered around looking at us. Liljana Ashvaran seemed especially watchful of this little ceremony. She stood with her little nostrils sniffing the air as if any wine not offered to her must be sour.

"To the king!" the baron called out, raising his glass. He nodded at King Kiritan, who was still talking with his dukes near the fountain while a dozen of his guards kept watch nearby. I gripped my goblet tightly in my hand as I looked down into the blood-red wine.

"It's not poison, Sar Valashu," the baron said to me.

I looked into the wine, which smelled of cinnamon and flowers and the strange spices of Galda.

"Do you think *I* would drink poison wine?" he said. Then he put the rim of the goblet to his thick lips and took a long drink. "Come now, Sar Valashu, drink with me. All of you—drink!"

I sensed in him no intention to harm me, only a sudden exuberance and desire to win my good regard—most likely to atone for his previous unkindness. And that, I thought, was a noble thing indeed. Kane and my friends were watching to see what I would do. The queen and Alphanderry, and Liljana Ashvaran—everyone was waiting for me to take a drink of the king's wine.

Just as I was lifting the goblet to my lips, however, Liljana suddenly rushed toward me, crying out, "No, it *is* poison— don't drink it!"

The certainty in her voice shocked me; I whirled around toward her to see if she might have fallen mad. Many things happened then almost in the same moment. Baron Narcavage, standing to the other side of me, looked toward King Kiritan and cried out, "To me!" He drew a long dagger and lunged at my throat even as Liljana knocked the goblet from my hand. Alphanderry, who was nearer to me than any of my friends, jumped between me and the baron. He grabbed at the baron's knife arm with both hands and stood locked in a desperate struggle with him. If not for the minstrel's courage, the knife would have torn open my throat.

For that was surely the baron's intention. I saw it clearly now in the way his face fell into a fury of hate as he clubbed Alphanderry's head with his other hand, ripped free his knife, and lunged at me again. Now, however, Liljana was close enough to grab his arm. She held onto it with all the tenacity of a hound, even as he cursed at her, beat at her with his other arm, and knocked her about. Then I struck out with my fist straight into his bearded face. I felt my knuckles almost break against his thick jawbone. But he seemed invulnerable to pain and possessed of an insane strength. He shook his knife arm free and aimed another lunge toward my throat. He would have killed me if Kane hadn't come up then and run him through with his sword.

The baron fell dead to the grass. Alphanderry stood dazed, shaking his bleeding head. From the trees planted across the palace grounds, the nightingales sang their songs.

Then I became aware of a great clamor toward the fountains. Spears clashed against shields; swords crossed with swords, and the sound of outraged steel rang out to a great chorus of curses and shouts. Lords and ladies were running away in great numbers, even as the king's guards fell upon one another. At first, I thought they had fallen mad. And then I saw the king slash his sword toward one of his dukes while five of his guards fought fiercely to protect the king from his murderous guards. And other men—all wearing green tunics bearing the oaks and eagles of House Narcavage—were running toward us to kill the queen.

Or so I thought, for it didn't occur to me that they might be coming to kill me. There were nearly thirty of these knights; they appeared out of the throngs of panicked people like vultures from the clouds. Their swords were drawn and gleaming in the moonlight. "To me!" the baron had called out, and now I understood to whom he had been calling.

Queen Daryana cried out as she saw her husband fighting for his life; she positioned herself near Alphanderry, as did Liljana and Master Juwain. The rest of us stared at our attackers as we decided what to do.

We had no one to lead us, or rather too many: Sar Yarwan and the other six Valari knights—and Kane, Maram, Atara, and myself. The leading of others into battle, my father once told me, is a strange thing. It depends not so much on rank or authority, but rather on the courage to see what must be done and the mysterious ability to communicate one's faith that victory is not only possible but inevitable. For a only moment, we stood there confused by the violence that Baron Narcavage had unleashed. And then I looked at the two diamonds shining like stars from my ring. A light flashed in my eyes, and in my heart, and I called out: "Form a circle! Protect the queen!"

For another moment, my command hung in the air. And then, as on the drill field, Sar Yarwan and the other Valari knights formed up into a circle around Queen Daryana. Savages, the

king had called us, and savages we were: savages whose swords
were our souls, and we called kalamas.

We drew them now just in time to meet the attack of Baron
Narcavage's men. Kane stood to my right, Atara and Maram to
my left—all of us facing outward. Sar Yarwan guarded the
point of the circle directly across and in back of me. We were
only eleven against some thirty knights. And yet when our
swords were done flashing and stabbing and rending flesh, all
of them lay dead or dying in the grass.

As I stood gasping for breath, I realized that a good number
of the baron's knights had come directly at me. And there,
within a few yards of me and Kane's bloody sword, they
sprawled in twisted heaps. I was almost certain that I had slain
four of them myself. Their death agonies built inside me like
great, cresting waves. But strangely, they never crushed me
down into the icy dark. Perhaps it was because I remembered
how Master Juwain had healed me after the battle with the
Grays; perhaps I was able to open myself to the life fires blazing through Kane and Atara and everyone around me. Or perhaps I was only learning to keep closed the door to death and
others' sufferings.

Even so, the great pain of it drove me to my knees and then
caused me to collapse moaning. Queen Daryana must have
thought the baron's men had run me through, for she called out,
"Over here! A man is wounded!"

I couldn't imagine to whom she might be calling. Then,
through the cold clouds of death touching my eyes, I saw many
of the king's guards running toward us. The queen cried out to
them that my friends and I had saved her life. She called for
everyone to put aside their swords, and this they did.

For what seemed an eternity, confusion reigned across the
blood-spattered lawns of the palace grounds. Trumpets sounded
while horses thundered across the grass some distance away. I
heard women wailing and men screaming that the king had
been killed. Then Queen Daryana took charge, calling out commands with a coolness that stilled the panic in the air. She de-
ployed guards to see that the palace gates were closed to
prevent any of the plotters from slipping away. Other guards
she sent to hunt down any of the baron's men who might be hiding around the palace. She ordered that the bodies of the slain

be taken away and their blood washed with buckets of water into the earth. And she sent messengers to call up many new guards from the garrison that manned the city walls.

Word soon came that the king had only been wounded and borne away into the palace. He had called for Queen Daryana to come to his side. And so the queen gathered up five guards and hurried off to join him.

Other guards drew up in a protective wall around us. King Kiritan's thousands of guests still milled about the fountains; despite their panic over Baron Narcavage's plot, they had nowhere to flee. But it seemed that most of the baron's knights had died in attacking our circle. As for the traitorous guards, they had all been killed, too—or so it was hoped.

While the Valari knights gathered some yards away, Alphanderry and Liljana drew in closer above me. They watched Kane, Atara, Maram, and Master Juwain kneel in a circle by my side. My friends removed my armor and lay their hands upon me. So great was the power of their touch that I immediately felt a familiar fire warming me inside. Then Master Juwain drew out his green crystal and placed it over my chest. He and the others positioned their bodies to shield the sight of the healing from the guards and others looking on.

Very soon, I was able to stand up and move about again. I nodded to each of my friends. "Thank you, all of you," I said as I put on my armor.

I noticed Alphanderry looking at me curiously as if wondering why I had needed my friends' ministrations at all. He smiled at me in great relief and said, "I think you follow a lucky star, Valashu Elahad."

"And I think you're a man who follows his heart," I told him. "You risked your life for me as would my own brother!"

His smile deepened as he replied, "All men are brothers."

Master Juwain's order, of course, taught this ideal of a higher love for all beings, even strangers. But Alphanderry's selfless act was the first time I had seen it embodied so unrestrainedly.

"Thank you," I said to him. Then I turned to Liljana Ashvaran, whose courage had been no less than his. "Thank you, too."

Liljana bowed her head to me and smiled. Then she pointed at Master Juwain's pocket, to which he had returned his green gelstei. In a voice pitched soft and low so that none of the guards or other onlookers might hear, she said, "I think you have one of the stones told of in the prophecy."

"What do you know of *that*?" Kane said sharply. He took a step closer to her; I was afraid he was about to draw his dagger and hold it to her throat. "And how did you know the wine was poisoned?"

Liljana folded her hands together as she stood there considering her answer. Her round face, I thought, was given to sternness as easily as kindness, and she seemed a thoughtful, unhurried, and even relentless woman. She looked at Kane with her wise old eyes and told him, "I smelled it."

"You *smelled* it?" he said. "You must have the nose of a hound."

"It was poisoned with wenrock. Its scent is almost like that of poppy. I've been trained to detect such things."

"Trained by whom?"

"By my mother and grandmother. They were master tasters to King Kiritan's father and grandfather."

"Then are you King Kiritan's taster, too?"

"I was," she said, "when I was a young woman. But he insisted I leave his service when *I* insisted on marrying."

"And your husband?"

"Count Kinnan Marshan—five years dead now. My children died in infancy. When the king called the quest, I decided it was time for me to leave Tria and all its plots and poisons behind me."

As she turned into the light of moon, the medallion that she wore glowed with a soft golden light. Kane's black eyes bored into her as if drilling for the truth.

"What *I* don't understand," Maram said, stroking his beard, "is why Baron Narcavage was willing to drink the wine if it was poisoned."

"That should be clear enough," Kane snapped. He nodded at Liljana and said, "Tell him."

Liljana nodded back at him, then explained, "Certain men and women, when they use poisons such as wenrock—they take minute quantities of it over a period of years to build an invulnerability to it."

"And who are these men and women?" Kane demanded.

Liljana looked at him and said, "They're priests of the Kallimun."

At the mention of this dreadful name, Alphanderry shuddered and said, "Before Galda fell to the Kallimun, they poisoned many. And crucified many more. My friends. My brother."

Kane seemed to forget himself for a moment and laid his hand gently upon Alphanderry's head. "So, the baron was certainly Kallimun."

"A priest, then?" I said. "But when he served the wine, I was sure he wanted to celebrate with me."

"Celebrate, ha! He wanted to celebrate your death." As if troubled by his own tenderness, Kane suddenly snapped his hand away from Alphanderry's head and stared at me. "The baron's plot must have been hastily planned—even so, it nearly succeeded."

"In Galda," Alphanderry said, "there were many such plots before the king was brought down." He looked at me and asked, "But why would the priests also want to kill you?"

Kane flashed me a warning glance then. Liljana, who was staring at my forehead, said softly, "Because he has the mark."

At this, Kane whirled upon her. "What do you know of *that*?"

We waited to hear what she would say, but she would not be hurried. She drew in a breath, then said, "Earlier, I overheard the baron whispering to one of his knights that Val had the mark. I didn't know what he meant."

"He meant that Val was marked out for death. Nothing more."

But Liljana clearly did not believe Kane. Her gaze fell upon my face as if searching for the truth.

"You saved my life," I said to her. "Is there anything you would ask in return?"

"Do you think I told you about the wine in hope of gain?"

"No, of course not," I said. "But in so doing, you've gained much, even so. My gratitude—my trust."

"That is a great deal," she said. "You honor me, Prince of Mesh."

"Please—call me Valashu. And it is you who honor yourself. In risking so much to help me. And in vowing to make the quest. Where did you hope to seek the Cup of Heaven?"

"I don't know," she told me. "I don't have any idea of where to search, not really, and so I've been looking for a company to join. It's not easy for a woman to take to the roads alone."

Alphanderry smiled at me as well. "I've been looking for companions myself. Would you consider adding two more to your company?"

"We've too many as it is," Kane growled out. "The greater the numbers, the greater the chance of someone falling ill and slowing down the others."

"But what is your hurry?" Alphanderry asked him. "If we are to honor our vows, we have our whole lives to complete this quest."

"Yes, your *lives*," Kane said, looking from Alphanderry to Liljana. "If you value them, you'd do best to look for other companions."

Since Kane's dark scowl seemed not to discourage either of them, I said to them, "As you've seen tonight, there are those who would hunt me. If you joined us, you'd be hunted, too."

"Hunted . . . why?" Alphanderry asked. "And by whom?"

"Those are things that you don't need to know," Kane said.

"We do, if we are to go with you, wherever we are going," Liljana said.

Because I trusted them both—and because they *did* need to know—I told them how Morjin had sent assassins to kill me in Mesh; I told them of the Grays and of our battle in the woods. Finally, I gathered in all my faith and told them the full prophecy of Ayondela Kirriland.

"You do have the mark, then," Liljana said, looking at me in wonder. "If what you say is true, you'll need *more* companions to help you."

Alphanderry looked happy, as if he were setting out on a great epic that he would one day sing about. All that he said to me was, "Please, take me with you."

And then Maram said, "The prophecy told of the seven brothers and sisters of the earth. We have need of two more to make seven."

"Yes—two more *warriors*," Kane said.

"Warriors we already have," I said, looking at Atara and Kane. "Ours are not the only skills we might need on a long journey."

"The seven brothers and *sisters*," Master Juwain said. He smiled at Alphanderry and Liljana. "It seems that this was meant to be."

We all stood looking at each other. And then Atara whispered, "Val—I can *see* them with us. On the road. In the forest by the sea."

I turned to Kane and asked, "Will you have them join us?"

"Is this what you truly want?"

"Yes," I said, "it is."

Kane touched his sword and told me, "I pledged this to your service in seeking the Lightstone. And that your enemies would be my enemies. Well, I suppose I should pledge that your friends will be mine as well."

So saying, he held his hand out and laid it on top of mine. Then Atara covered his hand with hers, and so with Master Juwain and Maram. Then Liljana carefully placed her hand on top of Maram's, while Alphanderry laughed happily as he slapped his hand down upon all of ours.

"Very good, then," Maram said. "Let us make a toast."

He went off to gather up glasses and a new bottle of wine. When we all stood holding goblets full of the dark, red liquid, he looked at Liljana. And she sniffed her glass and said, "I think *this* wine is fine."

"Excellent," Maram said. He raised his glass and called out, "To the finding of the Lightstone in the best of company a man could ever hope to find!"

I clinked goblets with my friends and took a sip of the wine. We all stood about drinking and laughing with that nervous relief that comes after a narrow escape from death.

Soon after that, King Kiritan and Queen Daryana, accompanied by many guards, strode from the palace and rejoined the celebration. The guards from the garrison stood about with their shields and spears to provide a sense of enforced safety at odds with the gaiety that the king wished to encourage. After all, this was still the night of his fiftieth birthday and the calling of the quest, and he wasn't about to let a little poison and death spoil it for him.

As he stood upon the lawn's dark grass, he held up his arm as if to reassure everyone that he was all right. Apparently this was also a signal, for just then the sky over the gardens below the palace filled with a booming like thunder. All at once, fireworks burst into the air like lightning splitting the night. Flowers of blue light opened outward in perfect spheres; millions of red and silver sparks spun through space and outshined the very stars. Flick, perhaps mistaking these lights for Timpum, spun with them. I saw him as a swirl of silver against the line of trees at the edge of the palace grounds. Farther to the east, in the districts of the city running down to the river and beyond it, more fireworks were exploding: from the rooftops of buildings and above the various great squares and out above the dark islands at the mouth of the river. Soon the sky above the whole of the city blazed like a fiery umbrella of light.

As I stood there with my friends, Maram admitted that he had never seen such a sight in all his life. None of us, I thought, had. It called us to hope that the Lightstone might someday be regained, even as we had vowed it would. Toward that end, we began discussing our dreams of finding it.

"When I set out from Mesh," Maram said, looking out at the fireworks, "all I wanted was to reach Tria safely. I never really thought about the Lightstone as existing somewhere, ah, you know, in a place where someone could actually go and fetch it. But now it's now. And now I suppose we *do* have to go looking for it. But who has any idea of where to look?"

At this, Alphanderry smiled at us and said, "I know where."

We all turned toward him as his large eyes lit up with a different kind of fireworks. He said, "You see, I know where Sartan Odinan hid the Gelstei."

And then, as great, red flowers of fire burst in the air above us and my heart boomed like thunder, he smiled again as he told us where the Lightstone might be found.

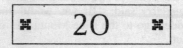

NEAR SENTA IN the faraway reaches of the Crescent Mountains, there is a series of caverns whose walls are lined with colored crystals. Some are violet or emerald and hang like pendants from the caves' glittering ceilings; some shine like sapphires and arise in great blue pillars from the floors. All the crystals, whatever their shape or hue, vibrate like chimes in the wind. In truth, they sing.

For centuries, it is said, men and women from across Ea have come to the caverns to listen to these singing crystals and add their own voices to the music that pours out of them. For it is also said that the crystals will record any words that fall upon them so long as they are true and sung with the fire of one's soul.

Upon entering the caverns, all but the deaf hear a million voices trolling out the words of living languages and those long dead. The seven caverns resonate with ancient ballads, love songs, canticles, carols, and the death songs of those who have come to say good-bye to the earth that bore them. Their walls, ashimmer with a radiance that also pours from the crystals, echo with plaints and whispers, with cries and exaltations and prayers. The great sound of it has been known to drive men mad. But others have found there a deep peace and an answer to the great mystery of life. For in the Singing Caves of Senta, people hear only what they are ready to hear. Even a deaf man, it is said, might hear the Galadin speaking to him, for the voices of the angels are not carried upon the wind alone and can sometimes be heard as a soundless music deep inside the heart.

All this Alphanderry told us on the lawn of King Kiritan's palace as we watched the fireworks. He told as well of an old Hesperuk minstrel named Venkatil who had journeyed to Senta to learn the secrets of the caves. There, almost by chance, Venkatil had listened in wonder to the words of an ancient ballad that told of where Sartan Odinan had brought the Lightstone. And Venkatil, before he died, had sung this ballad to Alphanderry.

"The words were in Old Ardik but their meaning was clear enough," Alphanderry said: "'If you would know where the Gelstei was hidden, go to the Blue Mountains and seek in the Tower of the Sun.'"

That particular Tower of the Sun, as Alphanderry told us, was also known by its more ancient name: the Tur-Solonu. Once the greatest of Ea's oracles, it had lain in ruins since Morjin had destroyed it in his first rise to power during the Age of Swords.

"Just so," Kane muttered upon hearing what Alphanderry had to say. "The Tur-Solonu *is* destroyed. There's nothing there but a heap of burnt stones. Why should we waste our time there?"

"Because," Alphanderry said, "the Singing Caves have never been known to tell anything but the truth."

"Ha, it's gobbledygook they tell!" Kane said with inexplicable vehemence. "If there *is* truth in the babble you hear there, who could ever tell what it is?"

We debated the course of our journey long into the night. Kane and Maram both doubted the wisdom of exploring a dead oracle, and Master Juwain seemed inclined to agree with them. But Liljana pointed out that Sartan Odinan might indeed have brought the Lightstone to the Tur-Solonu, which even Morjin might not think to search. For the site was said to be accursed and haunted by the ghosts of the many scryers murdered there.

Atara, standing beneath the night's brilliant stars, spoke the name of the Tur-Solonu in a strange voice. She looked to me for affirmation that we should journey there. But I hesitated a long time while I listened to the wind sweeping above the lawn's soft grasses.

"If we can't decide," Maram said, "perhaps we should make a vote."

"No, there's to be none of that on this quest," Kane said. "We must agree, as one company, what we should do. And if we can't all agree, then one of our company must set our course."

He proposed then that I lead us. It was I, he said, who had drawn our company together. It was I whom Morjin sought and would be killed first if he found us. And it was I who bore the mark of Valoreth.

To my surprise, everyone agreed with him. At first I protested this decision, for it seemed to me that as elders, either Kane, Liljana, or Master Juwain should more properly bear the burden of leadership. But something inside me whispered that perhaps Kane was right after all. I had a strange sense that if I did as he said, I would be completing a pattern woven of gold and silver threads and as ancient as the stars. And so I reluctantly bowed my head to my six friends and accepted their charge. And then we set the rules for our company.

These were simple and few. At all times, I was to ask the counsel of my friends in reaching any decision that must be made. And at any juncture in our journey, either along roads winding through dense forests or the even darker paths that lead down through the soul, any of us would be allowed to leave the company at any time. For freely we had come together as brothers and sisters, and freely we must all follow our hearts.

With my friends all looking at me to decide where we should go, I searched *my* heart for a long while. At last I said, "We'll journey to the Tur-Solonu, then. Liljana is right: it is as good a place to begin as any."

We then agreed on our most important rule: that whoever first saw and laid hands upon the Lightstone, either at the Tur-Solonu or some other place, would be its guardian and decide what should be done with it.

When it came time to leave, Atara led us over to where King Kiritan and Daryana were bidding their various guests farewell. Our turn came, and we drew up close to the king; he stood stiffly and sternly, as if in great pain. I noticed that he seemed unable to use his right arm. His gaze fell upon me with a great heaviness as he said, "Sar Valashu Elahad, we wish to thank you and your friends for saving the queen's life. We had heard that the traitors wounded you."

"They did," I said, bowing my head. "But it was nothing that Master Juwain couldn't take care of."

The king smiled as if he didn't quite believe me. Then he turned to Liljana and said, "It seems we should have kept you in our service after all. Perhaps you would have sniffed out the baron's plot even as you did the poison in his wine."

"I'm sorry, sire," she told him, "but I had to follow my heart."

"As you now follow Valashu Elahad and my daughter to lands unknown?" The grinding of his jaws told me that, gratitude or no, he would never relent in his pronouncement that I must bring the Lightstone into Tria if I ever hoped to marry Atara.

"The heart finds its own way," she said to him. "Can we not hope that *ours* will lead us to the Lightstone?"

"Hope, indeed," King Kiritan said. His lips pulled up into a thin smile as if life's ironies and cruelties amused him. "Then we suppose that *we* must hope that the Elahad finds his golden cup, else how will our daughter ever come back home?"

Then he turned to Atara, who said, "Of course I'll come home again, sire. I *will*."

But despite her brave words, she looked upon King Kiritan as if she were seeing him for the last time. Something inside him seemed to soften, as of old snow crusts warming, and I could feel him fighting back tears.

"You are welcome to stay here tonight," he told her. "Every other room is full, but we've kept yours waiting for you."

"Thank you," she told him. She glanced at me, and then at Liljana and the others. "But I should go on with my friends."

"As you will. Then let us say goodnight. And good-bye."

He embraced her and kissed her, and she told him, "Good-bye, Father."

So it went with Atara's leave-taking of Queen Daryana. Without further ado, King Kiritan gathered Daryana's arm and led her back into the palace. It almost seemed that he was disappearing into a tomb.

We were among the last to leave the palace grounds that night. We retrieved our horses and tromped wearily through Tria's dark and deserted streets to an out-of-the-way inn down by the docks. After an hour of sleep, we arose early the next morning and began preparing for our journey to the Tur-Solonu. Atara went off to the horse market by the river, where she purchased a fine roan mare to replace the mount that she had lost fighting the hill-men. Inspired by the red hairs of the mare's flowing mane, she named her Fire. As well, she bargained for four more packhorses. These would bear the supplies we would need to reach the Blue Mountains: dried apples, dried beef, salt cod as thin and hard as wooden planks—and much else.

Kane insisted that we pack as much weaponry as possible. Arrows especially we might lose along the way, and so he and Atara went to an arrow maker's shop, and they laid in a great store of long feathered shafts. Kane said that Master Juwain, Liljana, and Alphanderry should be able to defend themselves, and toward that end, he went to the sword maker's and selected three cutlasses that they might find easy to wield. Master Juwain, upon beholding his gleaming yard of steel, shook his head sadly and informed us that he would keep his vow to renounce war. Liljana, too, seemed chagrined at Kane's gift. She stood holding her cutlass as she might a snake and then said a strange thing: "Am I a pirate that I should begin carrying a pirate's sword? Well, perhaps we're *all* pirates, off to take the Lightstone by force. And this age, whatever men may call it, is still the Age of Swords."

We set out at midnight on the tenth of Soldru. It was a dark hour to begin our journey but safer than departing during the day: since the city's gates were closed after sunset, it would be unlikely that any of our enemies would be watching them. Kane proposed to unlock one of these gates with a golden key: a purseful of coins, with which he bribed the guard of the Urwe Gate at the northwestern corner of the city. And so the great iron gate opened as if by magic, and we left Tria and her towering walls behind us.

It was a night of intense moonlight showering down upon the fields and hills of Old Alonia. I led forth, feeling the surge of Altaru's muscles beneath me as I gazed out at the road to the west. Atara, astride Fire, rode next to me, followed by Master Juwain and Maram on their sorrels, with the packhorses trailing them. Then came Liljana on a gelding a little past his prime; Alphanderry rode one of the magnificent Tervolan whites, which were famed for their fine heads and proud, arching necks. He called him by the strange name of Iolo. Kane, atop his big bay, took up the point of greatest danger at the very rear.

We had fine, clear weather for travel. With the world opening out before us toward the starry horizon, I felt wild and free as I hadn't for a long time. The wind off the unseen sea to the north carried the scent of limitless possibility while the moon in the west called with its great silvery face. I could almost hear my fate whispering to me, and I wanted to embrace it, whatever it might be, as I did the very world. The road that led onward, though not quite so broad as the Nar Road, was a good one, with paving stones set at a contour to shed the rain and with mile markers along our way. It took us northwest, along the Bay of Belen, where there were many fishing villages and little towns. These were our first miles on the road together as a whole company and the first true night of the quest.

For a long while, we spoke nothing of it. Even so, I felt my friends' excitement crackling like lightning along a rocky crag. The moon fell toward the earth as the white towers of Tria grew ever smaller behind us and we rode deeper into the beautiful night. Although each of us might have his or her own reasons for seeking the Lightstone, we moved as with one purpose, as if our individual dreams were only part of a greater dream, as old as the earth and indestructible as the stars.

About an hour before dawn, we stopped to take a little rest. We lay wrapped in our cloaks atop a grassy knoll overlooking the ocean. The sight of the shimmering water thrilled me and loosed inside me deep swells of hope. I fell asleep to the sound of waves crashing against rocks. I dreamed of the Lightstone: it sat on a pinnacle arising from the surf. There, from this still point above the world, it poured out its radiance as from a bottomless source. I wanted to open myself to this flowing light, to drink it in until I was full and vast as the ocean itself. I dreamed that I could hold whole oceans inside me, and more, perhaps even the sufferings and joys of those I loved.

When I awoke, the sun was a red disk glowing above the Poru valley behind us, and the sky was taking on the bright blue tones of morning. I sat on the grass looking out at the sea as I remembered my dream. It led me to realize that I must keep myself open to my companions, for I had something vital to give them.

And I couldn't *not* give. I felt my grandmother's deep love for all my family come alive inside me. My companions were as my brothers and sisters, and each of them was close to my heart in a different way. Each had weaknesses and even greater strengths that I was beginning to see ever more clearly. This was my gift, to see in others what they couldn't see in themselves. And in Kane and Atara, no less Maram and Master Juwain, was buried a finer steel than they ever knew.

Maram, my fat friend, lived in fear of the world and all that might come growling out of its dark shadows to harm him. But he also *lived,* passionately and with great joy, as few men dared to do, and I believed that someday his love of life would overcome his fright. Master Juwain might dwell too much in his books and his brain, but I knew that someday, and soon, he would find the door to his own heart and emerge from it as a healer without equal. Atara might be overzealous in striving to make the world and everything around her perfect. But in her, more than anyone I knew, blazed a brilliant light that was already perfect in itself and needed no refinement to touch others with its beauty. As for Kane, his hate pooled black and bitter as bile. But his rage at life was all the more terrible for concealing something sweet and warm and splendid. I prayed that someday he would remember himself and behold the noble being he was born to be.

Liljana and Alphanderry were harder for me to read, for I had known them only a few days. Already, however, on this very morning, Liljana's caring for others was obvious in the way she surprised us with a breakfast of bacon, eggs, and some delicious crescent bread that she managed to coax out of a stone oven that she had painstakingly built while we had slept. She insisted on keeping our plates full while she waited to eat. And Alphanderry, when we had finished our meal, picked up his mandolet and sang us a song with all his heart. He was incapable, I thought, of singing any other way. His music made our spirits soar and our feet eager to set out on the road before us.

I believed in my friends as I did the earth and the trees, the wind, the sky, the very sun. In their presence I felt more fully human, more alive. Often it seemed that I longed for their smiles and kind words as I did food and drink; the beating of their hearts reminded me of the power and purpose of my own. I loved the sound of Maram's deep voice, the smell of Atara's thick hair, even the wild gleam bound up in the darkness of Kane's black eyes. Their gift to me was greater than anything I could ever give to them. For it fed the fire of my *valarda;* it made me want to touch all things no matter the passion or pain, to burn away and be reborn like a great silver swan from the flames.

We resumed our journey that morning with great good cheer. We rode without time pressing at us—and neither were we harried by wounds or men pursuing us with swords or knives. The country through which we passed, with its little farms and fishing villages, was as peaceful as any I had ever seen. There was no smell of danger in the air, only the scent of the sea that blew over us in soft breezes and cooled the sundrenched land.

We stopped to take our midday meal in a village called Railan. From a stand near the boats by the beach, we bought some fried fish and slices of potatoes all crisp and redolent with strangely spiced oils. I stood a long time staring out at the shining ocean and marveling at its size. And then Kane growled out that it was growing late and we should be on our way.

We left the coast road where it continued along the headland to the ancient town of Ondrar, built at the point of a peninsula sticking out into the ocean. Kane was expert at maneuver and believed in always misdirecting the enemy: Ondrar was famed for its museum housing many artifacts from the Age of Law, and in setting out toward this town, which lay northwest of Tria, we had hoped that anyone following us would suppose we would begin our quest there. The Tur-Solonu, to the southwest, remained our objective. And so we finally turned toward it on a little dirt road leading out of Railan. It was scarred with potholes and wagon tracks, but so long as the weather held good, it would suit our purpose well.

"We're free," Maram said to me that evening as we made camp on a farmer's field by a stream. "No one is following us, are they, Val?"

"No, they're not," I said, smiling at him. I looked at the farmland spread across the green hills around us and the occasional stands of trees along the streams. "It's likely that there aren't even any bears."

The following morning we continued on into the fine spring sunshine. Away from the coast, the air grew warmer, but never so hot that we suffered, not even Kane and I in our steel armor. All that day and the next our horses walked down the dry road. Fifty miles, at least, we covered with our steady plodding, and every mile was full of birds singing or bees buzzing in the flowers in the woods by the road. Along our way, the farms grew ever smaller and were separated by ever greater stands of trees.

On the fourth day of our journey, we passed from Old Alonia into the barony of Iviunn. A woodcutter that we met along the road told us that we had crossed into Baron Muar's domains. He also told us that we would find few farms or towns thereabout. We had entered a forest, he said, that so far as he knew went on to the west for a good seventy miles.

"So," Kane told us later, "the forest goes on a *hundred* and seventy miles, all the way to the Tur-Solonu—and beyond, across the mountains into the Vardaloon. *That's* the greatest forest in all Ea."

The thought of such an unbroken expanse of trees awed me

almost as much as had the sight of the ocean. And it frightened Maram. He stared off into the darkening swath of oaks and elms crowding the road—now reduced to a dirt track—and he said, "I don't like *this* forest."

"You're thinking of your bears again, aren't you?" Kane asked him.

"Well, what if I am?"

"You've seen bears and you've seen Morjin's men. Which do you prefer?"

"Neither," Maram said, shuddering. "But we don't *know* that we'd find the Kallimun along the king's roads, do we?"

"We won't find them here," Kane snapped at him. Then, as if remembering that Maram was now his sworn companion, his voice softened and he said, "At least, it's much less likely."

That night we made camp under the cover of the trees. We laid out our sleeping furs near some thickets full of baneberry, with their tiny white flowers that looked like clumps of snow. The coming into our company of Kane, Alphanderry, and Liljana had changed our daily routines—for the better, I thought. Atara had a talent for finding good clear water, and so she set herself the task of filling our canteens and pots and bearing them back and forth from a nearby stream to our camp. I took charge of tending the horses: tethering and combing them down and feeding them the oats that the packhorses carried. It gave me some moments to be alone with Altaru beneath the tree-shrouded stars. Maram gathered wood for his fires, while Kane worked furiously to fortify our camp, sometimes cutting brush or thornwood to place around it, sometimes hiding dry twigs among the bracken so that whoever stood watch might be warned of approaching enemies by hearing a sudden snap. Master Juwain took to helping Liljana prepare our meals. Although he had acquired some skill with the cookware since Mesh and could turn out a good plate of hotcakes, he had much to learn from Liljana, who immediately commandeered the food supply and practically turned him into her servant. But we were all grateful that she did. That night she conjured up a savory fish stew out of the ugly planks of salt cod and some roots, herbs, mushrooms, and wild onions that she found in the forest. For dessert we had raspberries, accompanied by a little brandy. And then, while Master Juwain washed the dishes, Alphanderry played his mandolet and sang to us before we slept.

He did little other work. To be sure, he might wander about the camp, joining me to brush the horses or helping Kane cut sharpened stakes to be driven into the earth—until Kane grew exasperated with his desultory axework and growled at him to be left alone. Set him loose in the woods to find some raspberries, and he might wander about for hours before returning with a handful of pretty flowers instead. He flitted from one task to another, sometimes completing it, sometimes not, but always having a good time talking with whomever he chose to help. And we took delight in his company, for he was always cheerful and responsive to others' moods or remarks. If he saw it as his charge to keep our spirits uplifted, no one disputed that. In the end, despite whatever fine foods we found to put into our bellies, sharpened stakes or no, it would only be by strengthening our spirits that we would ever find the Lightstone.

That night, as we sat on top of our furs sipping brandy, while Alphanderry's beautiful voice flowed out into the night, Flick appeared and spun about to the music. This gladdened our hearts, for we hadn't seen much of him since we entered Tria. But ever since leaving the city, he had become ever more active and visible, and now the darkness between the trees filled with tiny, twinkling stars. I laughed to see him dancing among the flowers as he had in the Lokilani's wood. Even Kane smiled when Flick pulsed with little bursts of light to the rhythms of Alphanderry's song. He pointed off into the trees and said to me, "Your little friend is back."

Alphanderry, sitting toward the fire, put down his mandolet and turned to look into the woods. Then he looked around the fire at Atara, Maram, Master Juwain, and me, and asked, "What are you all staring at?"

Strangely, although Flick had been with us since the fireworks, we hadn't yet remarked his presence. Does one make mention of the stars that come out every night?

"It's one of the Timpimpiri," Kane told Alphanderry. "He's followed us through most of Alonia."

Now Alphanderry blinked his eyes and stared hard toward the trees. Liljana did too. But neither of them saw anything other than shadows.

"You're having a joke with me, aren't you?" Alphanderry said as he smiled at Kane.

"A joke, is it?" Kane called out. "Do I look like one to joke?"

"No, you don't. And we'll have to change that before this journey is through."

"You might as well try changing the face of the moon," Maram put in.

Again, Alphanderry smiled as he studied the woods and suddenly said, "Hoy, yes, I *do* see him now! He's got ears as long as a rabbit and a face as green as the leaves we can't see."

"Ha—foolish minstrel," Kane muttered as he took a sip of brandy. But his glass couldn't quite hide the smile that touched his lips.

"Here, Flick!" Alphanderry called to the trees. "Why don't you come here and say hello?"

Alphanderry began whistling then, and this high-pitched sound was as sweet as any music that ever flowed from a panpipe. To our astonishment, and Kane's most of all, Flick came whirling out of the trees and took up position in front of Alphanderry's face.

"Oh, Flick," Alphanderry said to the air in front of him, "you're a fine little fellow, aren't you? But it's too bad we've eaten all of Liljana's good stew and have only bread to share with you."

So saying, he found a crust of bread and held it out as he might to feed a squirrel.

"You really *can't* see him, can you?" Maram said to him.

"How could he," Master Juwain asked, "if he never ate the timana?"

"Of *course* I can see him," Alphanderry said. "He's a shy little one, isn't he? Come, Flick, this bread won't hurt you."

To prove this, he ate most of it and left a large crumb between his lips. And then he held out his hand as if beckoning Flick to hop onto it and take the crumb from his mouth.

Once again, it astonished us when Flick moved onto the palm of his hand. The swirls of his form flared with sparks and little purple flames.

"Ha!" Kane said, "he must understand more than we thought. It would seem that there's more to the Timpimpiri than *anyone* thought."

"Of course there is," Alphanderry said, after swallowing the breadcrumb. "They are magical beings, known to live only in the deeper woods. If they've taken food from you, they must grant three wishes."

"But Flick can't take food at all," Maram said.

"Of course he can!" Alphanderry said. "Didn't you *see* him?"

"I suppose I must have been looking away," Maram said, grinning. "What are your three wishes, then?"

"My first wish, of course, is that Flick grant all my future wishes."

"That's cheating!" Atara called out.

"And my second wish," he said, ignoring her, "is that we accomplish the impossible and find the Lightstone."

"That's better," Atara said, smiling.

"And my third wish," he continued, "is that we accomplish the *truly* impossible and make our grim Kane laugh."

Kane sat by the fire staring at Alphanderry with his hard eyes; a stone statue couldn't have been more still.

"Now, then," Alphanderry said, rising to his feet, "the, ah, Timpimpiri are capable of many feats, magical and otherwise. Please watch closely, or you'll miss this."

Alphanderry, it turned out, was skilled not only in music and singing but in the art of pantomime. He stood looking at his open hand and talking to Flick as if trying to persuade his invisible friend to entertain us. And all the while, his face took on different moods and expressions, and seemed as easily molded as a ball of Liljana's bread dough. The extreme mobility of his face, no less the sudden and comical deepening of his voice, made us all laugh a little—all of us except Kane.

"Now, Flick," Alphanderry said in a voice arrogant and stern like King Kiritan's, "you've eaten our food and must obey us. At my command, you'll jump into my other hand."

Alphanderry now held his left hand out and away from his body. He looked down toward Flick in his right hand, and said, "Are you ready?"

Just then his face underwent a sudden transfiguration and fell softer. His voice softened, too, becoming fully feminine, and when he spoke, its tone was unmistakably that of Queen Daryana. As if speaking to himself, this new voice called out, "Is he a Timpimpiri or a slave? Why don't you set him free?"

Again, Alphanderry's face took on the manner of King Kiritan. And he called out in his deep voice, "Who rules here, you or I?" He looked down at his hand and continued, "When the king says jump, you jump."

But before he, as King Kiritan, could get another word out, his face fell through yet another change. And speaking with Queen Daryana's voice, he said, "The king has said you must jump, Flick. All right then, jump!"

All at once, Flick shot up off Alphanderry's hand and streaked up in a fiery arc to land on the other. And Alphanderry, who had yet again returned to his King Kiritan persona, pretended to watch this feat with outrage coloring his face. His eyes opened wide at his queen's defiance and bounced like balls as they turned toward his other hand.

Now Kane's stony visage finally cracked. The faintest of smiles turned up his lips. Alphanderry's antics amused him much less, I thought, than did his utter blindness to Flick.

Alphanderry, still speaking as Queen Daryana, said, "Quick, Flick—jump! Jump again, jump now!"

Each time he said this, Flick streaked from Alphanderry's one hand to the other, back and forth like a blazing rainbow. And with each jump, Alphanderry's face returned to the stern lines of King Kiritan as his eyes bounced up and down.

Maram and I—everyone except Kane—were now laughing heartily. Alphanderry's failure to move Kane must have distressed him, for he stopped his pantomime, looked at Kane, and in his own voice, he said, "Hoy, man, what will it take to make you laugh?"

Kane didn't blink as he said, "Make him spin on your nose."

Alphanderry again became King Kiritan as he replied, "*That* would be beneath our dignity. A king cannot allow—"

"Enough!" Kane called out, holding up his hand. He stood up facing Alphanderry and pointed at Flick, who was spinning above Alphanderry's hand. "The Timpimpiri *are* real. They dwell in the woods of the Lokilani."

"And who are the Lokilani?" Alphanderry asked.

"They're the people of the woods," Kane said. He held out his hand just below his chest as if measuring a man's height. "The little people."

"Oh—and I suppose they have ears like a rabbit's and green faces." Alphanderry turned to wink at Maram. "You see, I *have* gotten him to joke."

Kane pointed again at Flick and said, "This is no joke. Although I can't understand it, the Timpimpiri seems to hear you and do as you bid."

"Really? Then will he spin on my finger?" Alphanderry held up his finger as if pointing at the stars. "I suppose he's spinning there now?"

No sooner had he spoken these words, then Flick flew up and turned about above his finger like a jeweled top.

Alphanderry abruptly took away his hand, and then bent to retrieve his personal kit from the foot of his furs. From it he removed a needle, which he held up to the light of the fire.

"And now," he said, "I suppose he's dancing upon this needle?"

And lo, in a flash, with perfect equipoise, Flick spun wildly about the point of the needle.

"Hoy, yes, and now, of course, he's spinning on my nose!"

To emphasize the foolishness of what he had said, his eyes suddenly crossed as if fixing on a fly on the tip of his nose. And there, unseen by him, Flick appeared doing his wild, incandescent dance.

This last proved too much for Kane. The crack in his obduracy suddenly widened into a bottomless chasm. His face broke into the widest smile I had ever seen as he let loose a great howl of laughter. He couldn't stop himself. He fell to his knees, laughing hard and deeply, tears in eyes, his belly heaving in and out as he sweated and gasped and his whole body shook. I thought the earth itself cracked open then, for the laughter that shook his soul was more like an earthquake than any human emotion. Out of him erupted blasts of smoke and fire, thunder and lightning—or so it seemed. He lay on the ground laughing for a long time as he held his belly, and we were all so awed by this sudden outburst that we didn't know what to do. In truth, there was nothing *to* do except laugh along with him, and this we did.

Finally, however, Kane grew quiet as he sat up breathing hard. Through his tears, his bright, black eyes seemed to shine with great happiness. I saw in him, for a moment, a great being: joyful, open, radiant, and wise. He smiled at Alphanderry and said, "Foolish minstrel—perhaps you *are* good for something."

And then he regained much of his composure. The harsh, vertical lines returned to his face; flesh gave way before stone.

He stared at Flick, who was now wavering in the air a few feet from Alphanderry.

Then came a time for explanations. While the fire burned down and the great constellations wheeled about the heavens, we took turns telling of our stay in the Lokilani's wood. Alphanderry came to see that we were not having a joke with him after all. I spoke to him of my first glorious vision of the many Timpum lighting up the forest, and he believed me; trust came easy to him. When Atara, with tears in her eyes, told of how she had almost died upon eating the timana, Alphanderry looked at me and said, "You saved her life, then. With this gift that Kane calls the *valarda*. Is that why your Flick followed you out of the vild?"

Flick came over to me and hovered above my shoulder. I could almost feel the swirls of fire that made up his being. "Who knows why he followed me?" I said.

"Perhaps for the same reason we all do," Alphanderry said thoughtfully. "Well, perhaps someday I'll be able to see him with you."

All this time, Liljana had remained silent when she hadn't been laughing. Now, as it became clear that a great mystery had been set before her, she said simply, "I'd like a taste of this timana, too."

The following morning we made our way through a forest wide and thick enough to hide ten of the Lokilani's vilds. As we moved away from Old Alonia deeper into Iviunn, the gentle hills gave out onto a forested steppe. We made good progress along the winding track through the trees. And then the following day, gray clouds moved in from the sea, and it began to rain. By late afternoon, our track had turned into a slip of mud. Although the deluge didn't slow us very much, it made the going miserable, for it was a cold, driving rain that soaked our cloaks and found its way into our undergarments. It didn't stop that day, nor even the next or the one following that. By the fourth day of the wet weather, we were all a little on edge. We had all lost sleep, twisting and turning and shivering on the sodden earth.

"I'm cold, I'm tired, I'm wet," Maram complained. "But at least I'm not hungry—and we have Liljana to thank for that. Dear woman, no one else could prepare such delicious meals in such foul weather!"

Liljana, riding her tired gelding through the squishing mud, beamed at his compliment. I noticed that just as she thrived on sacrificing herself and serving others, she relished their appreciation at least as much.

Her selflessness was an example to us all. Twice, she volunteered to stand the exhausted Alphanderry's watch in his place; as she put it, some people needed more rest than others, and we had all observed that Alphanderry's talent for sleeping was almost as great as for making music and song.

On the fourth night of rain, we were all awakened to the din of Kane shouting. I immediately grabbed my sword and sprang up from my wet furs, as did Atara and Liljana, followed more slowly by Maram and Master Juwain. We rushed to the edge of our camp, where Kane had piled some brush. He stood glowering above Alphanderry, who sat in the drizzling rain looking bewildered. If not for the fire that Maram had made earlier—and the radiance pouring out of Flick—it was so dark that we wouldn't have been able to see them at all.

"He fell asleep!" Kane accused as he shook his fist at Alphanderry.

"I don't know what happened," Alphanderry said as he rose to his feet. He yawned, then looked at Kane as he smiled sheepishly. "I just wanted to rest my eyes, and so I closed them and—"

"You fell asleep!" Kane thundered again. "While you rested your damn eyes, we might all have been killed!"

His whole body tensed then, and I was afraid he might raise his arm to Alphanderry. So I clamped my hand around his elbow. He turned toward me and glared at me; again his body tensed with a wild power. I knew that if he chose to break free, I couldn't stop him. Could I hold a tiger? And yet, for a moment, I held him with my eyes, and that was enough.

"So, Val," he said to me. "So."

As I let go of him, Liljana came up to Kane and poked her finger into his chest. Her pretty face had now grown as hard as Kane's. In her most domineering voice, she told him, "Don't you speak to Alphanderry like that! We're all brothers and sisters here—or have you forgotten?"

Her admonishment so startled Kane that he took a step backward and then another as her finger again drove into his chest. Her zeal to defend Alphanderry completely overwhelmed Kane's considerable anger. I was reminded of something I had once seen near Lake Waskaw, when a wolverine, through the sheer ferocity, had driven off a much larger mountain lion trying to take one of her cubs.

"Brothers and sisters of the earth!" Liljana said again. "If we fight with each other, how can we ever hope to find the Lightstone?"

Kane looked to me for rescue as he took yet another step backward. But for a few moments I said nothing while Liljana scolded him.

"All right!" Kane said at last, smiling at her. "I'll mind my mouth, if it bothers you so. But something must be done about what happened."

He nodded toward Alphanderry, then looked at me. "What befalls a Valari warrior caught sleeping on watch in the land of the enemy?"

Alphanderry ran his hand through his curly hair as he looked about the dark forest. "But there are no enemies here!"

"You don't know that!" Kane snapped.

"Well, at least I don't *see* any enemies," Alphanderry said, looking Kane straight in the eye.

I thought that the usual punishment meted out to overly sleepy warriors—being made to stay awake all night for three successive nights beneath the stinging points of his companions' kalamas—would do Alphanderry little good. He would likely wind up looking like a practice target—and then fall asleep in exhaustion during his next watch anyway. And yet something had to be done.

"It's not upon me to punish anyone," I said. "Even so, if everyone is agreeable, we might change the watches."

I turned to Kane and said, "Perhaps *you* can teach our friend to stay awake. Why doesn't Alphanderry join you on your watch?"

Truly, it was my hope that, like a stick held to a furnace, Alphanderry might ignite with something of Kane's fire.

"Join me, eh?" Kane growled again. "Punish *him,* I said, not me."

With a bow of his head, Alphanderry accepted what passed for punishment. Then he smiled at Kane and said, "I haven't had Flick's company to help keep me awake, but I'd welcome yours."

The yearning in his voice as he spoke of Flick must have touched something deep in Kane, for he suddenly scowled and muttered, "I suppose you *can't* see him, can you?"

Alphanderry shook his head sadly then said, "I'm sorry I fell asleep—it won't happen again."

The utter sincerity in his voice disarmed Kane. It seemed impossible for anyone to remain angry with Alphanderry very long, for he was as hard to pin down as quicksilver.

"All right, join me then," Kane said. "But if I catch you sleeping on *my* watch, I'll roast your feet in the fire!"

True to his word, Alphanderry kept wide awake during his watches after that. It surprised us all that he and Kane soon became friends. None of us saw very much of what passed between them each night. But Alphanderry hinted that Kane was teaching him tricks to stay awake: walking, watching the stars, keeping the eyes moving, and composing music inside his head. As for Kane, he listened closely whenever Alphanderry sang his songs, especially those whose words were of a strange and beautiful language that we had never heard before. And it gladdened all our hearts to hear Kane laughing in Alphanderry's presence— more frequently, it seemed, with every day and night that passed.

On the morning following Alphanderry's failed watch, the rain finally stopped, and we had our first glimpse of the Blue Mountains. Through a break in the trees, we beheld their dark outline above the haze hanging over the world. They were old mountains, low to the earth with rounded peaks. Another two days' march, perhaps, would bring us to the ancient Tur-Solonu. And if the words that Alphanderry had heard relayed from the Caves of Senta proved true, there, among the ancient ruins, we would find at last the golden cup that held so many of our hopes and dreams.

■ 21 ■

AS WE DREW closer to the mountains, the land through which we rode rose into a series of low hills running north and south. Kane told us that we had entered the ancient realm of Viljo; some seventy miles to the southwest, he said, near the headwaters of the Istas River, Morjin had begun his rise to tyranny. His usurpation of Viljo's throne, however, had not gone unopposed. A rebellion led by outcast knights had nearly succeeded in defeating him. For a time, Morjin had brought the Lightstone to the Tur-Solonu and had gone into hiding. But the scryers who dwelt at the oracle there had betrayed him; Morjin had barely escaped the Tur-Solonu fighting for his life. In revenge, four years later, when he had crushed the rebellion and captured the Tur-Solonu, he had ordered the scryers to be crucified and the Tower of the Sun destroyed.

"It's said that the scryers' blood poisoned the land about the Tur-Solonu, that nothing would ever grow there again," Kane told us.

We had paused to eat a quick lunch on the side of a hill. From its grassy slopes, we had a good view of the mountains, now quite close to us in the west. Kane pointed at a spur of low peaks. If we followed the line of this spur, he said, we would find the ruins of the Tur-Solonu in the notch where it jutted out from the main body of the Blue Mountains.

"It can't be more than forty miles from here," Kane said. "If we ride steadily, we should reach the ruins by sunset tomorrow."

"Sunset!" Maram cried out. "Just in time to greet the scryers' ghosts when they come out to haunt the ruins at night!"

We rode hard that day and the next into the notch in the mountains. Their wooded slopes rose to our right and left; in places bare rock shined in the sun to remind us of their bones, but they were mostly covered with trees and bushes all the way up their slopes. Like a huge funnel of granite and green, they directed us toward the notch's apex, where the Tur-Solonu had been built late in the Age of the Mother, nearly a whole age before its destruction. I kept looking for the remnants of the tower through the canopies of the trees around us. All I saw, however, was wild forest everywhere. If men had ever lived in this country, there was no sign of them, not even a gravestone to mark their lives and deaths.

And then, through a break in the trees, we saw it: the tower rose up above the notch's floor like a great chess piece broken in half. Even in its destruction, it was still a mighty work, its remains standing at least 150 feet high. The white stone facing us was cracked and scarred with streaks of black; in places, it seemed to have been melted and fused into great glistening flows that hung down its curved sides like drips of wax. I wondered if Morjin had used a firestone to destroy it.

After some more riding, we crested a little hill, and there the trees about us gave way to barren ground. We came out onto a wedge-shaped desolation some three miles wide—but growing ever narrower toward the point of the notch where the spur met the main mountains. Walls of rock rose up on either side of us; the Tur-Solonu was now a great broken mass directly to the north at the middle of the notch. Little grew about this scorched-looking land except a few yellowish grasses and some lichens among the many rocks. As we drew closer to the tower, waves of heat seemed to emanate from the ground; Flick flared more brightly while Altaru suddenly whinnied, and I felt a strange tingling run up his trembling legs and into me. I had a sense that we were coming into a place of power and treading over earth that was both sacred and cursed.

The first ruins we crossed occupied an area about a half mile south of the tower. Much of the blasted stone there lay upon the ground in rectangular patterns or still stood as broken walls. We guessed it to be the remains of buildings, perhaps dormitories and dining halls and other such structures that the ancient scryers must have used. We dismounted and began walking slowly among the mounds of rattling rock.

"There is no reason that Sartan Odinan would have hidden the Lightstone *here*," Master Juwain said. He pointed toward the Tur-Solonu to the north, and then due east a quarter of a mile where stood the scorched columns of what must have been the scryers' temple. "Surely he would have hidden it *there*. Or perhaps inside the tower itself."

"The tower is empty," Kane said. "As I saw the first time I came here."

"You never *did* tell us why you came here," Atara said, fixing her bright eyes upon him.

"No, I didn't, did I?" Kane gazed at the tower, and it seemed he might retreat into one of his deep, scowling silences. Then he said, "When I was younger, I wanted to see the wonders of the world. Now I've seen them."

Maram was walking slowly among the shattered buildings; he paused from time to time and looked back and forth toward the tower, as if measuring angles and distances with his quick brown eyes. After a while, he said, "Well, there's still much of the ruins *we* haven't seen. Why don't we begin our search before it grows too late?"

"But where should we begin?" Master Juwain asked.

"Why don't we walk around the tower," I said, "and take a look?"

The others agreed to this, and so we began leading the horses in a wide spiral around the tower. Soon we came to a circle of standing stones. That is, some of the stones were still standing, while most were scorched and lying flat on the grass as if some impossibly strong wind had blown them over. Each stone was cut of granite and was twice the height of a tall man.

The area was also peppered with smaller stones, likewise melted, which we took to be the broken remains of the tower. There were many of them, all of a white marble nowhere visible in the rock of the surrounding mountains.

"Look!" Maram said, pointing at the ground closer to the tower. "There are more stones over there."

A hundred yards closer in toward the tower, we found another circle of the larger stones half-buried in the grass. Only a few of these were still standing. They were covered with splotches of green and orange lichens that seemed to have been growing for thousands of years.

No sooner had we begun walking around these stones than Maram descried yet a third circle of them fallen down closer still to the tower. We moved from stone to stone around toward the east in the direction of the temple. Neither I nor any of the others was sure what we might be looking for among them, if not the Lightstone itself. But their configuration was intriguing. Master Juwain believed they had been set to mark the precession of the constellations or some other astrological event. Liljana, however, questioned this. With one of her mysterious smiles that hid more than it revealed, she said, "The *ancient* scryers, I should think, cared more about the earth than they did the stars."

Maram, who was in no mood for learned disputes, continued leading the way around the circle. Soon we found ourselves to the north of the Tur-Solonu, directly along the line leading toward the apex of the notch. Without warning, Maram began walking toward the second circle as he studied the fallen stones and the scorch marks on the few standing ones with great care. When he reached the wide ring of stones, he stopped to point at a huge stone overturned and sunken into the ground. It lay by itself exactly at the midpoint between the second and third circles. It was thrice as long as any of the other stones and must have once stood nearly forty feet high.

"Look, there's something about this stone!" he said. Again, he stood measuring distances with his eyes. He was breathing hard now, and his face was flushed. Inside, he was pure fire. "This is the place—I know it is!"

So saying, he hurried over to one of the packhorses and unslung the axe that it carried. With the axe in his hands and a wild gleam in his eyes, he rushed back to the end of the great stone and there fell upon it with a fury of motion most unlike him.

"Hold now! What are you doing?" Kane yelled at him. He rushed over and grabbed Maram from behind. "You fat fool—that's good steel you're ruining!"

Maram managed one last swipe with the axe before Kane's grip tightened around him. By then it was too late: the axe's edge was already notched and splintered from chopping into cold hard stone.

"Let me go!" Maram shouted, kicking at the ground like a maddened bull. "Let me go, I said!"

And then the impossible happened: he broke free from Kane's mighty armlock. He raised the axe above his head, and I was afraid he might use it to brain the astonished Kane.

"It's here!" Maram shouted. "I know it is!"

"*What* is here?" Kane growled at him.

"The gelstei," Maram said. "The firestone. Can't you see that when this stone was still standing, the Red Dragon must have mounted the red gelstei on top of it to burn down the Tower?"

Suddenly, we all *did* see this. Looking south toward the Tur-Solonu and all the other structures and stones in the notch, we could all see in our minds the blasts of fire that must have once erupted from this spot.

"Even if you're right," Kane said to him, "why should you think the firestone is still here?"

"How do I know my heart is here?" Maram said, thumping the flat of the axe against his chest. Then he pointed at the end of the stone, which was all bubbled and fused as if it had once been touched by a great heat. "It *is* here. Can't you see it must have melted itself into the stone?"

Again, he raised up the axe, and again Kane called to him, "Hold, now! If you must have at it, don't ruin our axe beyond all repair."

"What should I use then—my teeth?"

Kane strode over to the second packhorse, where he found a hammer and an iron picket-stake. He gave them to Maram and said, "Here, try these."

With his new tools, Maram set to work, panting heavily as he hammered the stake's iron point against the stone. Little gray chips flew into the air as iron rang against iron; dust exploded upward and powdered Maram all over. Twice, he missed his mark, and the hammer's edge bloodied his knuckles. But he made no complaint, hammering now with a rare purpose that I had seen in him only in his pursuit of women.

We were all keen to see what this furious work might uncover. But it was growing dark, and Maram was bent close to the stone, using his large body for leverage. So that we wouldn't be blinded by the flying stone chips—as we were afraid Maram might be—we stepped back to give him room.

"Ha—look at him!" Kane said as he pointed at Maram. "A starving man wouldn't work so hard digging up potatoes."

All at once, with a last swing of the hammer and a great cry, Maram freed something from the rock. Then he held up a great crystal about a foot long and as red as blood. It was six-sided, like the cells of a honeycomb, and pointed at either end. It looked much like an overgrown ruby—but we all knew that it must be a firestone.

"So," Kane said, staring at it. "So."

"It *is* a tuaoi stone," Master Juwain said, gazing at it in wonder.

Alphanderry, ducking as Maram carelessly swung the point of the crystal in his direction, laughed out, "Hoy, don't point that at *me!*"

I stood beneath the night's first stars and watched as Flick appeared and described a fiery spiral along the length of the gelstei. With such a crystal, I thought, Morjin had once burned Valari warriors even as he had destroyed the Tur-Solonu.

"The seven brothers and sisters," Liljana said quietly, "with the seven stones will set forth into the darkness."

The words of Ayondela Kirriland's prophecy hung in the falling darkness like the stars themselves. Seven gelstei Ayondela had spoken of, and now we had three: Master Juwain's varistei, Kane's black stone, and a red crystal that might burn down even mountains.

"Prophecies," Kane muttered. "Who can believe the words of scryers?"

Despite his bitterness, the light in his eyes told me that he desperately wanted to believe them.

"Is this," he asked, pointing at the firestone, "the reason we've journeyed half the way across Ea to a dead oracle?"

His deep voice rolled out as if he were speaking his doubts to the wind. And it seemed that the wind answered him. A different voice, deeper in its purity if not tone, poured down the mountain slope to the west and floated across the field of stones: "And who is it who has journeyed half the way across Ea to tell us that our oracle is dead?"

We all whirled about to see six white shapes appear in the darkness from behind the standing stones. Kane and I whipped free our swords even as Maram shouted, "Ghosts! This place *is* haunted with ghosts!"

His eyes went wide, and he held out his crystal in front of him as he might a short sword.

Then the "ghosts" began moving toward us. In the twilight, they seemed almost to float over the grass. Soon we saw that they were women, all wearing plain white robes that gleamed faintly: the robes of scryers.

"Who are you?" their leader said again to Kane. She was a tall woman with dark hair and a long sad face. "What are your names?"

"Scryers," Kane spat out. "If you're scryers, you tell me, eh?"

Kane's rudeness appalled me, and I quickly stepped forward and said, "My name is Valashu Elahad. And these are my companions."

I presented my friends in turn. When I came to Kane, he practically cut me off and asked the scryer, "What is *your* name, then?"

"I'm called Mithuna," she said. She turned to the five women who accompanied her and said, "And this is Ayanna, Jora, Twi, Tira, and Songlian."

All of us, even Kane, bowed to the women one by one. And then Mithuna looked at Kane with her dark eyes and said, "As you can see, the oracle of the Tur-Solonu is not dead."

"Ha—I see a broken tower and scattered stones. And six women dressed up in white robes."

"It's said that men and women see what they want to see. Which is why they don't truly *see*."

"Scryer talk," Kane muttered. "So it is with all the oracles now."

"We speak as we speak. And you hear what you will hear."

"Once," Kane said, "this oracle spoke the wisdom of the stars."

"Indeed, it did," Mithuna said. "Indeed, it still does."

She told us then what had happened in this place in an age long past. After Morjin had destroyed the Tower of the Sun with the very crystal that Maram held in his hands, he had ordered the scryers who served the oracle to be crucified. But a few of them had eluded Morjin's murderous priests and had escaped into the surrounding mountains. There they had built a refuge in secret. And when Morjin and his men had finally abandoned the Tur-Solonu, the scryers had returned to the ruins to stand beneath the stars. The scryers grew old and died as all must do, but as the years passed, others had joined them. Thus had Mithuna's predecessors established a true and secret oracle in the ruins of the Tur-Solonu. And so, century after century, age after age, scryers from across Ea had come to this sacred site to seek their visions and listen for the voices of the Galadin on the stellar winds.

"But how would they know to come here?" I asked her.

"How did *you* know to come, Valashu Elahad?"

A savage look from Kane warned me to say nothing of our quest, and so for the moment I kept my silence.

"Surely," she said, "you came because you were called."

I closed my eyes and listened to my heart beating strongly. Deeper, beneath my feet, the very earth seemed to beat like a great drum calling men to war.

"There *is* something about this place," I said as I looked at her.

"Something, indeed," she said. "There is no other like it in all Ea."

Here, she said, beneath the ground upon which we stood, the fires of the earth whirled in patterns that burned away time. Nowhere else in the world did the telluric currents well so deeply and connect the past to the future. "This is why the Tur-Solonu was built, to draw up the fires from the earth."

As Mithuna told of this, Master Juwain rubbed his bald head thoughtfully. Then he said, "The Brotherhood has suspected that there was a great earth chakra in the Blue Mountains. We should have sent someone to search it out long ago."

"And now they have sent you," Mithuna said. "But I'm sorry to tell you that only scryers ever see visions here."

Here she smiled at Atara, and her gaze filled with a strange knowingness. "Thank *you* for making the journey, dear child."

Atara looked at me, and I looked at her, and then to Mithuna she said, "But I'm no scryer!"

"Aren't you?"

"No, I'm of the Manslayers; I'm Atara Ars Narmada, daughter of—"

"It's all right," Mithuna said, reaching out to grasp Atara's hand. "Few know who they really are."

A wild look flashed across Atara's face then. She turned to me as she said, "I saw the spider spinning her web, and there were the gray men, too, but that must have all been chance. It *must* have been, mustn't it?"

I said nothing as I looked at her in the failing light.

"You speak of chance," Mithuna said, "but why is it, do you think, that you came here?"

"I came here to look for the Lightstone," Atara said simply.

Although Kane scowled at this indiscretion, Atara ignored him. She touched her gold medallion and spoke of the great quest upon which many knights had set out. Then she nodded toward Alphanderry and told Mithuna what his dead friend had heard in the Singing Caves.

"The Lightstone," Mithuna said. She traded quick looks with Ayanna, who had white hair and a deeply lined face and was the oldest of the scryers. "Always the Lightstone."

Here Kane smiled savagely and said, "Ha—you didn't *see* that, eh?"

"No scryer has ever seen the Lightstone," she said, staring back at him. "At least, not in our visions."

"But why not?" Atara asked her.

Now Mithuna favored the young and almond-eyed Songlian with one of her faraway gazes before turning back to Atara. "Because, dear child, all that is or ever will be flows out of a single point in time, and there the Lightstone always is. To look there is like looking at the sun."

"Paradoxes, mysteries," Kane spat out. "You scryers make a mystery of everything."

"No, it is not we who have made things so," Mithuna reminded him.

In the light given off by Flick's twinkling form, Kane's face filled with both resentment and longing.

"The Singing Caves," Alphanderry said to Mithuna, "spoke these words: 'If you would know where the Gelstei was hidden, go to the Blue Mountains and seek in the Tower of the Sun.'"

"The Singing Caves always speak the truth," Mithuna said. She pointed at Maram's red crystal and smiled. "There is the gelstei."

"Hoy, there it is," Alphanderry agreed. "But it is not *the* Gelstei."

"It is difficult, isn't it, to know of which gelstei the Caves spoke?"

Kane, who was growing angrier by the moment, scowled as he looked about the starlit ruins and the dark mountains that towered above us.

"Are you saying that the Lightstone *wasn't* hidden here?" I asked.

"No," Mithuna said, shaking her head, "I wouldn't say that. Morjin hid it here long ago."

"But it is not hidden here now?"

"No, I wouldn't say that either," she said mysteriously. "The Lightstone still *is* here. But if you truly want to recover it and hold it in your hands, you'll have to journey somewhere else."

"So," Kane muttered to the wind. "Scryers."

But I wasn't about to give up so easily. To Mithuna, I said, "So the Lightstone is here, somewhere, somehow—but it isn't here, as well?"

"Is the Tur-Solonu here?" she asked, pointing at the broken tower above us. "Are *you* here, Valashu Elahad? What would a scryer have said to this ten thousand years ago? What would she say ten thousand years hence?"

I took a deep breath as I asked, "If the Lightstone is here, have you seen it, with your eyes?"

"No one sees the Lightstone with just the eyes," Mithuna said. "The eyes won't hold it any more than hands will light."

"But how do you know it isn't somewhere among these ruins, then?"

"Because, although I cannot see where it is, I can see where it is not."

"But I thought you said it was everywhere."

"That is true—it is everywhere and nowhere."

I was beginning to see why Kane hated scryers. Was Mithuna, I wondered, willfully confounding us? Talking with her was like trying to eat the wind.

"We've come a very long way, Mistress Mithuna," I told her. "A great deal may depend on our finding the Lightstone. Would you mind if we searched the ruins for it?"

Mithuna's face fell sad; almost as if speaking to herself, she said, "Should I mind the rising of tomorrow's sun? What should be shall be."

She turned to Atara and said, "It is growing late—will you sit with us beneath the stars tonight?"

It seemed that she was ready to steal Atara away to some secret rite, which prompted Maram to hold up his hand and say, "No, don't go just yet! We've brandy and beer and Ea's finest minstrel to help us appreciate it. Won't you share this with us?"

He held his crystal carelessly so that it stuck straight out from his body. All his attention was now turned on Mithuna.

Mithuna looked at him a long time, then said, "It was foretold that a man in red would find the firestone that destroyed the Tur-Solonu. I, myself, saw you in one of my visions."

"Ah, you saw me, did you?" Maram said. "And what did you *see?*"

"What do you mean? I saw you with the firestone."

"And is that all?"

"Should there be more?" Mithuna asked as her eyes brightened.

"Oh, yes, indeed there should be," Maram said as he gripped his crystal more tightly. "Did you see my heart filling up with the fire of the sun? Did you see this fire pouring out of the gelstei?"

"I saw it melting the hardest rock," she said with a smile.

"Did you? And did you see the earth shake, volcanoes erupting?"

"It is said that the firestones of old caused such cataclysms," Mithuna admitted. "They were very powerful."

"Powerful, yes," Maram said, holding his crystal pointing almost straight up. "I suspect none of us knows just how powerful."

"*That* is a dangerous thing," Mithuna said, stretching her finger toward the firestone. "We do know that."

"Yes, but surely one can learn how to use it."

"Perhaps some can. But can you?"

"Do you doubt me?" Maram said with a hurt look. "Perhaps I should leave it where I found it?"

"No, surely it is yours to do with as you will."

"Should I give it to you, then, Mistress Mithuna?"

"And what would I do with a firestone?"

"I wish I could, ah, give you *something*."

Mithuna's face suddenly fell serious, as if the whole weight of the world were pulling at it. In a sad voice, she said, "Then give me your promise that you will learn to use the stone wisely."

"I *do* promise you that," Maram said, glancing at the broken Tur-Solonu. Then his eyes covered her as he smiled. "More wisely than did the Red Dragon."

"Don't joke about such things," she told him. Now she pointed fiercely at the firestone. "You should know that a doom was laid upon this crystal: that it would bring Morjin's undoing. That is why he left it here."

We all looked at the firestone in a new light as Maram held it out and marveled at it.

"It's growing late," Mithuna said again. "Will you come with us, Atara?"

"No," Atara said, "I'll stay with my friends."

"Then we'll return tomorrow," Mithuna said. "Good night." And with that, she gathered her sister scryers around her, and they walked off into the deep shadows of the mountains.

"A beautiful woman," Maram said to me after she was gone.

"How long do you think it's been since she did more than just *look* at a man?"

"She's a scryer of an oracle," I told him. "Therefore she must have taken vows of celibacy."

"Well, so have I."

"Ha!" Kane said to him. "You might as well try to love this crystal as love a scryer!"

We camped that night by the stream where the ancient scryers had built their baths. It was a long night of dreams and brilliant stars. The wind blew unceasingly down from the mountains to the north. Altaru and the other horses were restless, more than once whinnying and pulling at their picket-stakes. In the dark notch of the Tur-Solonu, the ruins gleamed faintly in the starlight like broken bones defying time.

Atara, lying on top of the inconstant earth with its whirling and numinous fires, sweated and turned in a sleep that wasn't quite sleep. Her murmurs and cries kept me awake most of the night. Nightmares I had suffered through with her before, as she had with me. But this was something different. I felt something vast and bottomless as the sea pulling her down into its onstreaming currents. There, in the turbid darkness, Atara screamed silently in fascination and fear, and I wanted to scream, too.

We were all grateful for the rising of the sun. When I asked Atara what she had seen in her sleep, she looked at me strangely as an uncharacteristic coldness came over her. Then she told me, "If I had been blind from birth and asked you to describe the color of the sky to me, what would you say?"

I looked above the mountains, with their silvery rocks and emerald trees sparkling in the sun. There the sky was a blue dome growing bluer by the moment. "I would say that it is the deepest of colors, the softest and the kindest, too. In the blue of morning, we find ourselves soaring with hope; in the blue of night, with infinite possibilities. In its opening out onto everything, we remember who we really are."

"Perhaps you should have been a minstrel instead of a warrior," she said with a wan smile. "I'm sure I can't do as well."

"Why don't you try?"

"All right, then," she said. The sleeplessness that haunted her face convinced me that she had seen something much worse than ghosts. "You spoke of remembrance, but who are we *really*? Infinite possibilities, yes, but only one can ever *be*. The one that shall be is the one that should be. But all of them *are*, always, and we are . . . so delicate. Like flowers, Val. Which is the one you will pick for me and tell me that you love me? And which is the one that can stand beneath the light of the sun?"

Already, I thought, she was beginning to talk like a scryer, and I didn't like it. And then she fell quiet as she looked over at the Tur-Solonu where it rose up a few hundred yards away. Her eyes grew as clear as diamonds and gleamed with a wild light. She pointed at the tower and said, "Inside there is the future. I should have seen that all along."

Without another word she leaped to her feet and began walking quickly toward the tower. The others, now rising up from their sleeping furs, gathered themselves together, and we all followed her. It didn't take very long for us to wind our way among the standing stones and those lying down in the grass. When we reached the foot of the tower, we found Mithuna and the other scryers mysteriously waiting for us there.

"It's *dangerous* for you to enter the tower," Mithuna said to Atara. She held out her palm as if to stop her.

"Yes," Atara said, "but I must *see*."

And with that, she swept past Mithuna and entered the tower's crumbling open doorway. I rushed in after her, and Mithuna and Kane followed me, with Maram puffing just behind him. Then came Liljana, Alphanderry, and Master Juwain. The five scryers waited for us outside.

It was cool and dark inside the broken tower, and if not for the faint radiance streaming off Flick's spinning form, we wouldn't have been able to see very much. As it was, there was nothing much to see—nothing more than a few cobwebs and the bones of some poor beast who had dragged itself inside the door to die there in peace. The tower held no rooms that might be explored, for it was only a series of steps winding up inside a tube of marble. The ancient scryers had used it only as means of standing closer to the stars. I saw immediately that Kane was right, that there was nowhere in its stark interior that Sartan Odinan could have hidden a golden cup.

But Atara sprang straight for the cracked stone steps and began racing up the winding stairway. She was as lithe as a mountain lion, bounding up the steps three at a time, and I couldn't quite catch her. When she reached the broken opening that was now the top of the tower, she paused on the highest step to gasp for air. I stood just below her gasping, too. For there, poised on the melted marble of the outer wall, was the Lightstone.

"Atara," I said, "look!"

I lunged forward to grasp the shimmering golden vessel, but it suddenly winked into nothingness before my hands could close around it.

"Atara, come down!" Mithuna suddenly called. She was standing with Kane and Maram just below me. In the narrow space of the stairwell, there was room for three people on any step, but no more. Now Master Juwain, Liljana, and Alphanderry crowded in behind Maram and looked up at Atara.

"The Singing Caves *did* speak the truth," Atara said. She carelessly rested her hand against the tower's broken outer wall as she looked out at the mountains and sky.

"If you would know where the Gelstei was hidden," Alphanderry reminded us, "go to the Blue Mountains and seek in the Tower of the Sun."

"If we would *know*," Atara said. She stood with the wind whipping her hair about her face. "If *I* would."

She suddenly held her hands out toward the earth as she lifted back her head and gazed straight up into the sky. If her third eye was a door, she flung it wide open then. I felt her do this. And so, it seemed, did Mithuna.

"No, Atara—you don't know what you're doing!" Mithuna said.

But Atara was a warrior and as wild as the wind. She opened herself utterly to the invisible fires that streamed up through the Tur-Solonu. And then she let out a soft cry as her eyes rolled back into her head. She lost her balance and teetered at the edge of the tower's wall. I moved quickly to grab her back and clasp her to me; if I hadn't, she would have fallen to her death.

"Take her down from here!" Mithuna told me. "Please!"

I lifted Atara in my arms and followed the others down through the tower. Atara's eyes were now staring out at nothing, and she was breathing raggedly. The tower's steps seemed endless. By the time we reached the bottom of them, my arms were trembling with the weight of her body.

"Bring her over there!" Mithuna said, pointing at a standing stone in the direction of the temple. I and the others followed her a hundred yards over the swishing grass, where we sat Atara back against the huge stone.

"Atara!" Mithuna said, as she knelt beside her.

I knelt by her other side and tried to call her back to the world even as I had after she had eaten the timana. But the trance into which she had fallen, it seemed, was too deep.

Now Mithuna reached into the pocket of her robe and removed a clear, crystalline ball the size of a large apple. She pressed it into Atara's hands. The crystal, which sparkled like a diamond, caught the light of the sun and cast its brilliant colors into Atara's eyes.

"What's the matter with her?" Maram asked. He stood with Kane and the others peering above the half circle that the scryers made around Atara. "Will she be all right?"

"Quiet now!" Kane barked at him. "Quiet, I say!"

At that moment, Flick appeared above Atara's head and spun about with a slowness that I took to be concern.

And then little by little, as all our breaths came and went like the whooshing of the wind, the light returned to Atara's eyes. She sat staring deep into the crystal.

"What *is* that?" Maram whispered to Master Juwain as he pointed at the crystal. "A scryer's sphere?"

"A scryer's sphere indeed," Master Juwain whispered back. "Usually they're made of quartz—and more rarely, diamond."

"That's no diamond, I think," Liljana said as she pressed closer to look at the sphere. She seemed to be sniffing at it as she might a glass of wine.

Just then a shudder ran through Atara's body, her eyes blinked, and she finally looked away from the crystal. She nodded at Mithuna and smiled.

"That is a kristei, isn't it?" Liljana said to Mithuna, pointing at the crystal. "A white gelstei."

"It *is* a kristei," Mithuna said. "It was brought here long ago and has been passed down among us from hand to hand."

The white gelstei, I remembered, were the stones of seeing. Through the clarity of such crystals, a scryer might apprehend things far away in space or time. It was said that during the Age of Law, each scryer had her own kristei. But now, only a very few did.

"Looking into the future," Mithuna explained, "is like gazing up into a tree that grows out toward the stars. The possibilities are infinite. And so it is easy to become lost in the branches of such visions. The kristei helps a scryer find the branch she is seeking. And find her way back to the earth."

That was as clear an explanation of scrying as I was ever to hear from a scryer. Everyone looked at Atara then as I asked her, "What did you see?"

"The Sea People," she told me. "Wherever I looked for the Lightstone, I saw them."

"Do they have the Lightstone, then?"

"That is hard to say. I couldn't see that. I only know that all the paths I could find led toward them."

"Yes, but led *where*?"

Atara didn't know. The paths to the future, she said, were not like those that led through the lands of Ea. Although she'd had a clear vision of the Sea People, she couldn't tell us where we might find them.

"I'm afraid that no one knows anymore where the Sea People live," Master Juwain said.

"*We* know," Mithuna said. "You'll find them at the Bay of Whales."

We all looked at her as Maram let loose a long groan. The Bay of Whales lay at the edge of the Great Northern Ocean at least a hundred miles northwest across the great forest known as the Vardaloon.

"Are you *sure* they're there?" Maram asked Mithuna. "Have you *seen* them?"

"Songlian has," Mithuna said. She nodded at the shy young woman next to her. "We've known about the Sea People for some time."

Atara turned toward me and smiled, and I traded a knowing look with Kane. And Maram groaned again and said, "Oh, no, my friends, please don't tell me that you're thinking of journeying to this Bay of Whales!"

We were thinking exactly that. It now seemed certain that we wouldn't find the Lightstone here.

"But I'd hoped we would end our quest in this place!" Maram said. "We can't just go tramping all over Ea!"

"Courage, my friend, and remember your vow," I told him. "And we need not journey *all* over Ea—only a few more miles."

We were all disappointed that we had gained nothing more in the tower than the firestone and a vision as to where the Lightstone might still be found. But none of us—not even Maram—was ready to break his vows and abandon the quest so soon. And so we held a quick council and decided to set out for the Bay of Whales the next day.

"I believe that would be your wisest course," Mithuna told us.

Atara, who had now gained the strength to stand up, held out the crystal sphere toward her and said, "Thank you for lending me this."

Mithuna reached out her hands and squeezed Atara's fingers the more tightly around the sphere. "But, dear child, this is our gift to you. If you really hope to find the Cup of Heaven, you'll need this more than I."

The sunlight glazing off the crystal was so bright that it dazzled all of us. For a moment, it seemed that Atara might disappear through its sparkling surface. And then she said, "No, this is too much."

"Please take it," Mithuna insisted. "It's time the kristei passed on."

"If so, then it should pass to a true scryer."

"I know of none truer," Mithuna said, smiling.

"But I've *seen* so very little."

Mithuna took Atara's empty hand, stroked it, and told her, "You *have* seen so very little of what there is to see. If you had been trained . . . Oh, dear child, you've sacrificed much to forsake such training."

Atara withdrew her hand and looked at it, as if trying to understand her fate from its many lines.

"It is *dangerous* to look into the future without being trained," Mithuna said. "Dangerous to look at all. Will you not consider remaining with us so that we can teach you what you must know?"

Atara drew in a long deep breath as she gazed at the crystal sphere nestled in her hand. Then she turned to look at me.

"No, I must go on," she told Mithuna.

"Then please, accept the kristei as our gift. It will help you where we cannot."

Atara continued staring at the stone. I felt strong sentiments washing through her like waves: exhilaration, pride, gratitude, fear. At last, she bowed her head to Mithuna and said, "Thank you—I think you have given me a very powerful thing."

This made Mithuna smile. She cast a long, sad look at the broken tower and told us, "It's said that when the Lightstone is found, the kristei will come into its *true* power, which is not merely to see the future but to create it. Then the Tur-Solonu will be raised up again. Then a new age will begin: the Age of Light we have all seen and yet feared could never come to be."

With that, she leaned forward and kissed Atara upon the forehead. She told us that she and the other scryers would come to say good-bye to us later that morning, and then she walked off with them into the mountains.

For a while, as the sun rose in the east, we all stood staring at Atara's crystal sphere. There I saw the reflection of the ruined tower. But there, too, in the shimmering substance of the white gelstei, in my deepest dreams, flickered the form of the tower as it had once been and might be again: tall and straight and standing like an unbroken pillar beneath the brilliant stars.

22

WHEN WE HAD packed up the horses and stood gathered by the stream, Mithuna arrived with the other scryers as promised. They brought cheeses and fresh bread to sustain us on our journey. Although we were grateful for their gift, we needed oats for the horses even more, and this they could not provide. Where we would be going, I thought, we would find no grain and precious little grass.

"I can't believe we're setting out to cross the Vardaloon," Maram said, shaking his head as he adjusted the saddle of his sorrel.

As I stood by Altaru, Mithuna came up to me and whispered, "There *are* dangers in the great forest. There is something in there."

"What is it, then?" I whispered back.

"I don't know. We've never quite been able to see it—it's too dark."

A shudder rippled through my belly then, and I told her, "Please say nothing of this to my friends."

But Maram needed no fell words from Mithuna to feed the flames of his imagination. He looked off toward the mountains to the west as he muttered, "Well, if any bears come for us, we've cold steel to give them. And if the forest grows too deep, we can always burn our way through the trees." Here he held up his firestone, which gleamed a dull red in the weak morning light.

Mithuna walked over to him and pointed at the crystal. "You have a great fire in your heart, and now a great gelstei to hold it. But you must use it only in pursuit of the Lightstone—not for burning trees or against any living thing, if you can help it. This we have all seen."

To our astonishment, Maram's most of all, she leaned forward and kissed him full upon the lips. Then she laughed out, "I hope you won't mind leaving me with a little of this fire."

Then she stepped up to me and said, "Only after you have gained your gelstei will you be ready to truly seek the Lightstone—if what we have seen comes to pass and you survive what is to come."

"I *will* live," I said to her. "I must. As the seven brothers and sisters must gain the seven gelstei."

For a moment, she only smiled at this. And then she said, "Prophecies are strange, as we should know. We believe that seven with seven stones *will* set forth into the darkness. And that the Lightstone will be found. But will it be found by *these* seven? Or the seven I see here today? *Are* they truly the same? Not even the One can see that."

Upon these troubling words, she pointed out a path along the stream that led up into the woods surrounding the Tur-Solonu. "If you follow this west, it will take you over the mountains into the Vardaloon. Now good-bye, dear man—and good fortune find you."

We went among Mithuna and her sister scryers, embracing them and making our farewell. Then we mounted our horses. We left the scryers standing almost in the shadow of the Tur-Solonu as they watched us with their cold, clear eyes that seemed as old as time.

For a few miles, we wound our way along the stream through the rising woods. Then the path veered off to the right, where the trees grew thickest in an unbroken swath of gleaming leaves. It was a good path that Mithuna had shown us: wide enough for the horses to keep their footing, if a little overgrown. Its pitch was long and low, cutting as it did along the gentle slopes of one of the long, low Blue Mountains. High passes such as we had crossed from Mesh into Ishka we would not find here. Our greatest obstacle, I thought, would be the forest itself, for it grew thickly all around us, and shrubs such as virburn and brambles made for low, green walls between the trees. If the path hadn't cut through this dense vegetation, we would have had to cut through it with our swords. Or burn through it with the firestone that Mithuna had said we must not use.

We traveled all that day through the peaceful mountains. It was quiet in the woods, with little more to listen to than the tapping of a woodpecker or the calls of the occasional thrush or tanager. Our failure to gain the Lightstone drove us all inside ourselves, there to ask our souls if we really had the courage to keep on seeking unless illness, wounds, or death struck us down first. And yet, I thought, we had cause for much faith. Atara's newly found gift gave us to hope that she might see our way through to the end of our quest. And we had not left the Tur-Solonu with empty hands. Maram had his firestone and Atara her kristei; with Kane's black stone and Master Juwain's healing crystal, that made four of the seven gelstei told of in Ayondela's prophecy—if indeed *we* were truly the ones she had told of. But could this be nothing more than the rarest of chances? How could I not believe, with all my heart, that we *were* the ones destined to set forth into the darkness and win the Lightstone?

We all knew that it was not enough simply to have gained these four gelstei. Somehow we must learn how to use them. Toward that end, Master Juwain continued his own private quest of moving the dwelling of his soul from his head to his heart. As we rode through the thick greenery, he would take out his green crystal and hold it up to the swaying leaves as if trying to capture their life fire and hold it within himself. Atara, lovely woman of flowers and sun, would gaze into her glittering scryer's sphere as she turned inward toward that dark land where only scryers could go. And there brought what light she could.

As for Maram, he regarded his firestone as might a child who has been given a long-desired birthday present. He studied its dark, red interior with a diligence he had never applied to the *Saganom Elu* or the healing arts. Late that afternoon, as we made camp by a stream running through a pretty vale, he managed to coax the first fire from his stone. We all watched as he knelt over a pile of dry twigs and positioned the gelstei so that it caught what little light the sun drove through the forest's thick canopy. And it was good that the crystal drank in only a little light. For just as Maram's whole body trembled excitedly and he let loose a great gasp of wonder, the pointed end of the crystal erupted with a bolt of red flame. It shot like lightning into the firepit, instantly igniting and consuming the tinder, turning it to black ash. The pit's stones cast the fire straight back into Maram's face so that it burned his cheeks and scorched his eyebrows. But he seemed not to mind this chastisement or even to feel it. He jumped away from the pit and thrust his crystal toward the sky as he cried out, "Yes! Yes—I've done it!"

After that, we decided that Kane should stand over Maram whenever he summoned the fires of the red gelstei, and this Kane did. The next morning, Maram tried to burn holes in an old log just for the fun of it. Then Kane drew forth his black stone, and his whole being seemed to touch upon a place that utterly devoured light. The coldness that came over him chilled my heart and reminded me of things that I wished to forget. But it also seemed to cool the fires of Maram's crystal. In truth, Maram managed to call from it scarcely more than a candle's worth of flame. If Maram chafed at having to work with Kane and having his best efforts at fire making dampened, Kane was wroth. When Maram complained that Kane had gone too far, Kane practically shoved the black gelstei in Maram's face and growled out, "Do you think I *like* using this damn stone? Too far, you say, eh? What do you know about too far?"

His words remained a mystery to me until that night when we made our second camp in the mountains. Our two days of traveling had taken us almost all the way across the narrow range; just to the west, below us, gleamed the sea of green that was the Vardaloon. We found a shelf of earth on the side of a mountain overlooking it, and there we made our firepit and set out our furs. Around midnight, Kane and I stood together gazing at Flick's whirling form against the backdrop of the stars.

"Too far," Kane said again in a low voice, "always too far."

"*What* is too far?" I asked, turning toward him.

He looked at me for a long moment as his face softened. "*You* might understand. Of all men, you might."

He smiled at me, and the warmth that poured out of him was a welcome tonic against the chill of the mountains. Then he opened his hand to show me the black gelstei and said, "There is a place. One place, and one only, eh? All things gather there; there they shimmer, they whirl, they tremble like a child waiting to be born. From this place, all things burst forth into the world. Like roses, Val, like the sun rising in the morning. But the sun must set, eh? Roses die and return to the earth. The source of all things is also their negation. So, this is the power of the black gelstei. It touches upon this one place, this utter blackness. It *touches*: red gelstei or white, flowers or men's souls. And whatever fire burns there is sucked down into the blackness like a man's last gasp into a whirlpool."

He stared down at his stone, even as Flick spun faster and flared more brightly. I waited for him to go on, but he seemed caught in silence.

"To use this gelstei," I said, "you must touch upon this place, yes?"

"Yes—I must. I cannot, but I must."

"It is dangerous, yes?"

"Dangerous—ha! You don't know, you don't know!"

"Tell me, then."

His voice fell strange and deep as he looked at Flick and said, "This place I have told of—it's darker than any night you've ever seen. But it's something else, too. Out of it come the sun, the moon, the stars, even the fire of the Timpimpiri. The fire, Val, the light. There's no end to it. *This* is why the black stones are the most dangerous of the gelstei. Go too far, touch what may not be touched, and there's no end. Then instead of negation, its opposite. So, a light beyond light. If a black gelstei is used wrongly in controlling a firestone, then out of it might pour such a fire as hasn't been seen since the beginning of time."

He looked over toward Maram where he slept by the fire holding his red crystal in his hand. Then he stared out at the blazing stars for a long time and said, "No, Val, it's not the darkness I fear."

We stood there on the side of the mountain talking of the gelstei as the sky turned and the night deepened. After a while, because he was Kane, the man of stone who also held a deep and brilliant light, I told him of Mithuna's last words to me.

"There is something there," I said as I looked off toward the dark hills of the Vardaloon. "Some dark thing, Mithuna said."

"Stories are told of the Vardaloon," Kane muttered.

"Tell me."

"They're just stories."

"Perhaps," I said.

"You fear this thing, eh?"

I continued staring into the night and said, "Yes."

"So it always is," he said. "It's fear that's the worst, eh? Well, let's at least slay this one enemy, if we can."

Without other warning, he suddenly whipped his sword from its sheath. So quickly did he move that it seemed to burn the air. I heard its steel hissing scarcely inches in front of my face.

"What are you doing?" I asked him.

"Draw! Draw now, I say! It's time we had a little practice with these blades."

"Here? Now? It must be nearly midnight."

"So?"

"So it's too dark to see."

"Of course it is—that's the point! Now draw before I lose my patience!"

"But we'll wake the others."

"Let them wake, then, dammit! Now draw your sword!"

I looked over at our friends sleeping soundly by the fire. There was little enough ground between them and the wall of thistles and branches we had cut to surround our camp. I looked back at Kane, and the change that had come over him chilled me. He stood glaring at me with his kalama held at the ready. The stars gave off just enough light that I could see it glinting behind his head in silhouette.

"All right then," I said, freeing my kalama from its sheath.

I should have been grateful that he deigned to fence with me. In all the battles I had fought, in all the duels I had ever watched, I had never seen his like with the sword. He knew things that even Asaru and my father's weapons master, Lansar Raasharu, did not. And it was his way to hold onto his secrets more tightly than a miser does gold. But now, it seemed, he was willing to share them with me.

"Ha!" he cried out. "Ha, now, Valashu Elahad!"

His long steel blade leaped out of the dark like lightning from a blackened sky. I barely had a moment to raise up mine to parry it. The clash of steel against steel rang out across the side of the mountain. As I had feared, it brought Atara and the others flying out of their sleep. While Maram waved his crystal wildly in front of his face, Atara made a quick grab for her sword and might have charged toward us if Kane hadn't called out: "It's only us, now go back to sleep! Or stay up and watch, if that's what you want!"

Again, his sword flashed out at me, and again I parried it— by inches, by the shrieking sound of it as much as sight. We stared at each other through the darkness as we each waited for the other to move.

And move Kane did, suddenly, explosively, attacking me in a fury of slashing steel. For several moments, we whirled about the dark ground, feinting and cutting at each other. Something dark came over him then—or came howling out of him like a tiger who hunts at night. It knew little of fellowship and nothing at all of the conventions of a friendly fencing match. I stood before Kane with drawn sword, and that was the only thing that mattered to him. In the madness of the moment, in the wildness of his black eyes that I could barely see, I had somehow become his enemy. And I wondered if he had become mine: had Morjin somehow suborned him? His sudden and utter viciousness terrified me, for I knew that he would destroy me, if he could.

"Ha!" he cried out gleefully. "Ha—again!"

If not for my gift of sensing his movements—and the skills

that my father had taught me—he might have killed me then. He struck out with his sword straight toward me again and again, and I managed to dance out of his way or parry his ferocious blows only by the narrowest of distances.

"Again!" he called to me. "Again!"

And again we circled each other, watching and waiting and exchanging slashes of our swords in a flurry of motion. We dueled thus for a very long time—so long that sweat soaked through my mail and the cool air that I gasped burned my lungs like fire. I lunged about the starlit earth looking for an opening that I couldn't find. At last, I retreated toward the fire where the others sat watching us. I held up my hand as I shook my head and leaned forward to catch my breath.

"Again!" Kane cried out. The fire cast its red light over his closely cropped white hair and harsh face.

"What are you doing?" Atara asked him as she gripped her sword.

"Fight, Valashu!" Kane roared at me. "Don't hide behind others! Now fight, damnit—fight, I say!"

I had no choice but to fight. If I hadn't raised my sword to parry his blow, he would have sent me on to the otherworld. Not even Atara could have moved quickly enough to stop him. The fury of his renewed attack caught me up like a whirlwind. His eyes flashed in the fire's glow to the lightning strokes of his sword, and I felt my eyes flashing, too. I felt something else. His whole being burned with one purpose: to cut, to thrust, to tear and rend, to survive—no, to thrive, always and only to live deeply and completely, exultantly, destroying with joy anything that stood ready to destroy him. To *know* with utter certainty that he couldn't fail, that a light beyond light would always show him where his sword must strike and an infinite fire pooled always ready to fill his wild heart. His sword touched mine, and I suddenly felt this terrible will blazing inside me. I knew then that the light of it could always drive away any darkness that I feared. This was his first lesson to me, and the last.

"Good!" he cried out. "Good!"

Zanshin's timeless calm in the face of extreme danger, I thought, was one thing; but this was quite another. I suddenly found the strength to spring forward and attack him with all the fury he had directed at me. The steel of my kalama caught up the starlight as I whirled the long blade at him. For a moment, it seemed that I might cut through his defenses. But he was more cunning than I. He slipped beneath my blow and leaped forward with an unbelievable speed. And I suddenly found the point of his sword almost touching my throat.

"Good!" he cried out again. "Very good, Valashu! That's enough for one night, eh?"

After that, he put away his sword and came forward to embrace me. Then I stood back, looking at him.

"You would have killed me, wouldn't have you?" I asked him.

"Would I have?" he said, almost to himself. Then his gaze hardened, and he growled, "So—I *would* have, if you hadn't fought with all your heart. This quest of ours is no practice session, you know. We may only have one chance to gain the Lightstone, and we'd damn well better be ready to take it."

I went to sleep thinking about what he had said to me—and taught me. I awoke the next morning strangely eager to cross blades with him again. But it was a day for travel into an unknown land. Kane promised another round of swordplay that evening if I were willing, and I had to content myself with that.

And so we went down into the Vardaloon. The path we had been following took us into a hilly country at the very edge of it. But soon the ground leveled out into a lowland of little streams and still ponds. Although the forest was rather thick here, we had no trouble making our way through it. The elms and oaks were familiar friends; birds sang in their branches, while beneath them shrubs such as lowbush blueberries were heavy with fruit and promised a welcome addition to our meals.

And yet, there was something disquieting about this wood. The air was too warm and close, and too little light found its way through the unbroken cover of leaves. The squirrels who made their home here were sluggish in their motions and seemed too thin. A doe that crossed our path bounded out of the way much too slowly. That there should have been a path at all in a woods where no one had lived or gone for thousands of years disturbed us all. Perhaps, I thought, it was only an ancient game trail.

"Perhaps," Maram said as we rode along, "it is used by people."

"I doubt that," Kane said. "I've never heard of people living here."

"They must," Maram said as he slapped a mosquito that had landed on the side of his sweating neck. "How else are these bloodsuckers fed?"

We continued our journey, riding down the path as it wound its way west through the trees. We saw no people but there were plenty of mosquitoes, even in the full warmth of the day. They clung to the leaves of the bushes and took to the air in whining swarms as we brushed by them. They bedeviled our mounts as well, biting their ears and choking their nostrils. The dark woods soon filled with the sounds of slapping hands and horses snorting.

"I was wrong, Val," Maram called from behind me. His big voice filled the spaces between the tall trees around us; it almost drowned out the *whumph* of Altaru's hooves and the whine of the mosquitoes biting us. "No one could live here. Perhaps we should turn back."

"Be quiet!" Kane called from behind him farther down the path. "No one ever died from a few mosquitoes!"

"Then I'll be the first," Maram complained. He sighed and said, "Well, at least they can't get any worse."

But that evening, as we made camp near some pretty poplars, they got worse. With the bleeding away of the thin sunlight from the forest, the mosquitoes came out like demons from hell. They sought us out in swarms of swarms, and now I began to fear that they might really kill us, draining us of blood or filling our noses and mouths so that we couldn't breathe.

"I've never seen mosquitoes like these!" Maram said, waving his firestone and slapping at his face. "They can't be natural!"

He sat with the rest of us between three smoky fires that he had built. We were all hunched over with our cloaks pulled tightly around our faces as we now choked on the thick streams of smoke that wafted this way and that. But it was better than being stung by the mosquitoes.

"They're just hungry," Kane muttered to Maram. "If you were that hungry, you'd carve up your own mother for dinner."

At any other time, Maram might easily have found a riposte to Kane's jibe. But now it seemed to drive him into a sullenness and self-pity that he couldn't shake. He was so miserable that he even refused the cup of brandy that Atara brought him to cheer him up. And so I came over and knelt by his side. I touched his arm and said, "Things will get better."

"No, no, they never will," he moaned. "Well, what can I do?"

I reached toward the nearest firepit and picked up a round rock. I handed it to Maram and said, "This is a beautiful thing, don't you think?"

"It's a rock, Val," he said, looking at it dubiously.

"Yes," I said, "it is. But don't you think it has a beautiful shape?"

"I suppose so."

"It lacks only one thing, though."

"And what is that?"

"A hole."

"A . . . hole?" He looked at me as if my head were full of holes.

"Yes, a hole," I told him. "Someday, when we return home with the Lightstone and tell of our journey, we'll show this as well. And everyone will marvel at the rocks of the Vardaloon that have holes in them."

Maram's face shined with a sudden understanding as he hefted the rock in his hand and tapped it with his firestone.

"Make me a hole," I said, smiling at him.

"All right," he said, smiling back. "For you, my friend, I'll make the most beautiful hole you've ever seen."

And with that, he bent over it and went to work. There was just enough light left in the woods to bring his gelstei alive and summon forth a thin stream of flame. It melted out a little bit of rock before the light failed altogether, and with it the firestone. But Maram had the beginnings of a hole to show for his efforts, and this pleased him greatly. And it distracted him, for the moment, from the murderous mosquitoes.

When it grew dark, Kane and I further entertained him with another round of swordplay. Then it came time for sleep, which none of us managed very well. The merciless whining in our ears, I thought, was the song of the Vardaloon, and it kept us turning and slapping at the air far into the night.

We arose the next morning in very low spirits. All of our hands and faces were puffy from mosquito bites—all of us except Kane. He gazed out at the forest from behind his tough, unmarked face and explained, "These little beasts drink blood for breakfast. Well, some blood is too bad even for them, eh?"

After we had saddled the horses, we held council and decided it was time we left the path. It was taking us ever farther into the Vardaloon toward the west, whereas we needed to cut off northwest to reach the Bay of Whales.

"The going will be rougher," I said, looking off at a wall of green. "But there may be higher ground that way, and so fewer mosquitoes."

"Then let's go," Maram called out as he waved his hand about his head. "Nothing could be worse than these accursed mosquitoes."

We rode as hard as we could. But the horses, drained of blood, moved slowly, and we couldn't bring ourselves to drive them faster. As I had hoped, the ground rose away from the path, and it seemed that the swarms of mosquitoes grew thinner. The undergrowth, however, did not. We forced our way through some hobblebush and thickets of a dense shrub with pointed leaves. These scratched the horses' flanks and pulled at our legs. In a few places, we had to hack our way through with swords to keep the branches out of our faces.

Thus we endured the long morning. It was dark beneath the smothering cover of the trees—darker than in any woods I had ever been. The shroud of green above us nearly blocked out the sun.

"It's almost as dark here as the Black Bog," Maram grumbled as we paused to take our lunch in a relatively clear space beneath an old oak tree. "But least the mosquitoes aren't so bad here. I think the worst is . . ."

His voice died off as a look of horror came over his swollen face. His hand darted toward his other wrist, where his fingers closed like pincers, and he plucked something off of him and cast it quickly to the ground. Then he jumped to his feet as he shuddered and began brushing wildly at his trousers and feeling with his panicked hands through his thick brown beard and hair.

"Ticks!" he cried out. "I'm covered with ticks!"

We all were. The undergrowth here, it seemed, was infested with the loathsome insects. They were rather large ticks, flat and hard with tiny black heads. They clung to our garments and worked their way through their openings to find flesh to attach themselves. They crawled along our scalps beneath our hair.

We all jumped up then and beat at our clothes to drive the ticks off us. Then we paired off to search through each other's hair. Atara carefully ran her fingers through my hair. She found seven ticks, which she pulled off me and threw back into the bushes. Then I parted her soft blond hair lock by lock and returned the favor. Master Juwain tended Liljana (for once I was envious of his bald head), while Alphanderry and Maram groomed each other like monkeys. Only Kane, the odd man out, seemed unconcerned with what might be hiding on his body. But he had great care for the horses. He went among them, laying his rough hands on their jumping hides, and combing through their hair as he began pulling off ticks by the tens and twenties.

"Let's ride," he said when we had finished. "Let's get out of here."

I led the way through the woods, trying to keep a more or less straight line toward the northwest. But this way led through yet more undergrowth. We all looked down at the leaves of the bushes for more ticks. It was thus that our attention was turned in that direction. And so we did not see what hung from the branches above us until it was too late.

"What was *that*?" Maram shouted. He clapped his hand to his neck and sat bolt upright in his saddle. "Val, did you throw something at me?"

"No," I said, "it must be—"

"I can *feel* it," Maram said, now pulling frantically at the collar of his shirt. "Oh, no, no—it can't be!"

But it was. Just then, as Maram looked up into the trees to see what had fallen on him, a dozen leeches dropped down upon his face and neck. They were black, wormy things at least four inches long—segmented, with bloated bodies thick in the middle but tapering off toward their sucking parts at either end. They fell upon the rest of us as well. They hung lengthwise from the branches above us in the hundreds and thousands like so many swaying seedpods. And as we passed beneath them they rained down upon us in streams of hungry, writhing flesh.

"I've got to get this off!" Maram shouted as he pulled at his shirt. "I've got to get *them* off me!"

"No, not here!" I called back. Even as I felt something smooth and warm moving down my neck beneath my mail, I pulled my cloak around my head to cover myself from the leeches. "Ride, Maram! Everyone ride until we're out of this!"

We pressed our horses then, but the undergrowth caught at their legs and kept them from moving very fast. They were weak, too, from being eaten by mosquitoes, as were we. We rode as hard as we could for a long while, perhaps an hour, and in all that time the leeches in the trees never stopped falling on us and trying to find their way inside our clothes. They drummed against my cloak and bounced off Altaru's sides—those that didn't fasten to his sweating black hide. After a while, I forgot to check the bushes for ticks. And I almost didn't notice the mosquitoes that still danced around my face.

"This is unbearable!" Maram called out from beside me. We had long since broken order and now we rode as we could, strung out in a ragged line beneath the trees. "I've *got* to get my clothes off! I can feel these bloodsuckers attached to me!"

We all could. I could feel the shuddering skin of my companions as my own. This was my gift and my glory—now my hell. Their horror of the leeches and their other sufferings only multiplied mine. Maram was fighting back panic, and everyone except Kane was near to despair.

"Atara," I said as we stopped to catch our breaths, "can you see our way out of this?"

She sat on her big roan mare, looking down into the crystal sphere that she held in her hands. For all of our journey from the mountains, she had struggled with her newly found skills of scrying. More than once, I thought, she had gazed with terror upon futures that she did not wish to see. But away from the time-annihilating fires of the Tur-Solonu, these visions seemed to come at their own calling, not hers. And so she looked up from her gelstei and smiled grimly. "I see trees and leeches. But I didn't need to be a scryer to see that."

"These damn trees," Maram grumbled. "We'll never find our way out of here!"

His despair nearly overwhelmed me. And then, as I touched the hilt of my sword, I felt something terrible and beautiful blazing inside me, driving away the darkness. I said to Maram, "Do you still have the stone?"

He nodded his head as he reached into the pocket of his robe and removed the stone. His efforts with his gelstei had succeeded in burning a hole clean through it.

"Look through it, then," I said, "and tell me what you see."

With a puzzled expression, he held the stone to his eye and said, "I see trees and yet more trees. And leeches, leeches everywhere."

I held out my hand and said, "Give me the stone."

He placed it in my hand, and then I looked through it at him and said, "I see a glorious thing. I see a man in the likeness of the angels who burns so brightly even stone melts before him. Don't tell me that such a man can't make his way out of the woods."

Maram stared at me as if looking for something. Then he said, "But, Val, these leeches will kill us if we don't get them off."

"No, they *won't* kill us," I said. I climbed down from Altaru and asked the others to dismount as well. "Kane, Alphanderry, Master Juwain—please come here."

While they approached me across the damp bracken, I whipped off my cloak and shook it out. Then, holding one corner of it above my head, I asked my three friends each to take a corner while Maram stood under it to disrobe.

"But, Val, your cloak!" Maram said. "You've nothing to cover yourself!"

"Hurry!" I told him. I stood with my eyes closed as a leech dropped down the back of my neck. "Please hurry, Maram!"

I thought that Maram had never moved so quickly to take off his clothes in all his life, not even at the invitation of Behira or other beauties. In a few moments, he stood bare to the waist, his big hairy belly and chest bare to the world. But my cloak, like a shield, protected him from the falling leeches. And so Liljana was able to join him beneath the makeshift canopy to cut away those that had already attached themselves along his sides and back. When she had finished, she rubbed one of Master Juwain's ointments into the half dozen wounds, which oozed copious amounts of blood. That was the strange thing about leech bites, the way they wouldn't easily stop bleeding.

"All right, Atara," I said, "you next."

As Maram dressed himself, Atara took his place and silently bore the torment of Liljana cutting at her with her knife. I tried not to look upon the splendor of her naked body. And so it went, each of us taking our turns one by one. At last it came my turn. While Maram held up my corner of my cloak, Liljana cut more than a dozen leeches from me. Then I quickly dressed, and when I had finished, my friends let my cloak fall around me so that I was well-covered against further assault.

"That was kind of you," Maram said to me. He smiled at me as his despair melted away.

Master Juwain, looking around at the many leeches that still hung from the trees, shook his head and said, "This can't be natural."

"Perhaps it's not," Kane admitted.

"What do you mean?"

Kane's gaze swept the walls of green around us. "There's a rumor that once Morjin went into the heart of the Vardaloon. To breed things. Leeches, mosquitoes, ticks—anything that drinks blood as do his filthy priests. It's said he had a varistei, that he used it in essays of this filthy art."

"Are you saying Morjin made these things?" Maram asked.

"No, not *made,* as the One makes life. But made them to be especially numerous and vicious."

"But why would he do that?"

"Why?" Kane snarled. "Because he's the filthy Red Dragon, that's why. It's always been his way to torment living things until they find the darkest angles of their natures. And then to use them in his service."

That night we made camp on the side of a low hill, which I had thought might catch a bit of breeze to drive away the mosquitoes. It seemed that there were fewer leeches there, too. As I pulled off Altaru twenty ticks swollen as big as the end of my thumb, I prayed that the worst of the Vardaloon was behind us. And then, as I struggled to sleep beneath my smothering cloak, I sensed something smelling for my blood, which ran from the leech bites and stained my clothes. It was a dark thing that sought me through the forest, and it had the taste of Morjin.

I said nothing about this dread sense the next morning, nor for most of the next day as we drove the horses through the sweltering woods. I waited for it to attenuate or go away, but it only grew worse. I felt its hunger like a gigantic leech wrapped around my spine. Finally, late in the afternoon, as Maram complained for the thousandth time about the ticks and mosquitoes, I said, "There is more here to worry about than vermin." Then I took a deep breath and told them of what I had sensed.

"But this is terrible!" Maram said. "This is the worst news yet!"

We held council then and decided to go no farther that day. And so we gathered wood for the night's fires; we cut brush to fortify our camp. When we had finished it was growing dark. We all stood together near the rude fence we had made. And then Kane walked over toward his horse and slid his bow out of its sling.

"What are you doing?" I asked him.

He stared out at the woods with hate-filled eyes as he strung his bow and slung on his quiver of arrows. Then he said, "I'm going hunting."

"Do you know what it is, then?"

"No—I only suspect."

"You should have told me," I said, staring at the shadows between the trees.

"And you should have told *me*," he said, catching me up in the dark light of his eyes. "You should have told me if it was this close."

And with that, he carefully parted the brush surrounding our camp and stole off into the woods.

And so we waited. While Atara stood ready with an arrow nocked in her bowstring, Maram put aside his firestone in favor of his more reliable sword. Alphanderry and Liljana drew their cutlasses, and I my kalama, and we joined Master Juwain in gazing out through the curtains of green all around us.

After what seemed many hours, I noticed Atara staring into the woods as if the whole world were a scryer's sphere. I stepped up to her and said, "You've seen something, haven't you?"

"Yes," she said, "so many *people* here. In the forest, where the oaks grow along a stream. They were slaughtered. They *are* being slaughtered, or will be—oh, Val, I don't know, I don't know!"

I cupped my hand around the back of her neck as I touched her eyes with mine and she returned, for a moment, to this world. After that, we all stood watching the woods in silence. I was only dimly aware of the mosquitoes whining about and biting me; birds chirped and chittered from far off, but I was listening for other sounds. I gazed past the hanging leeches and the insect-eaten leaves, looking for something that was looking for me.

And then, out of the darkening woods, a terrible scream shook the trees. We all started at the anguish of it. I gripped my sword with sweating hands, while Atara drew her bow and sighted her arrow in the direction from which it had come. A second scream ripped through the air, and then came the sound of something large crashing through the bracken around our camp.

"What *is* it?" Maram whispered to me. "Can you see—"

"Shhh!" I whispered back. "Get ready!"

At that moment, a young woman broke from the cover of the trees running as fast as she could. Her long brown hair seemed torn, as was the homespun dress that barely covered her torn and bleeding body. She ran in a panic, now casting a quick look over her shoulder, now turning her head this way and that as if seeking an escape route through the woods. She stumbled past us barely fifty yards from our camp. But so great was her terror to flee whatever was pursuing her that she seemed not to see us.

"What shall we do?" Maram whispered to me.

"Wait," I said, feeling my fingers curl around the hilt of my kalama. Next to me, Atara aimed her arrow at the trees behind the woman. "Wait a few moments more."

But Maram, who was now trembling with anger, had suffered through too many days of waiting. He suddenly waved his sword above his head and shouted, "Over here! We're over here!"

At the sound of his huge voice, the woman stopped and turned toward us. The look of relief on her pretty face was that of a lost child who has found her mother. She ran straight for our camp, and we pulled aside the brush fence to let her in.

"Thank you," she gasped from her bloody lips as we gathered around her. "It . . . killed the others. It almost killed me."

"*What* did?" I asked her.

But she was too spent and frightened to say much more. She stood near Maram trembling and weeping and gasping for air. Maram, overcome with pity, opened his cloak to gather in the woman next to him. He wrapped it around her and asked, "What is your name?"

"Melia," the woman sobbed out. "I'm Melia."

Liljana sniffed at the bruised and beautiful woman as if jealous of Maram's gentleness toward her. And gentle Maram was, but I could also feel his desire rising like hot sap in a tree. It surprised me to feel as well a fierce desire for him burning through Melia's bleeding body.

"They're all dead," Melia said, pointing into the woods. "All dead."

I turned to peer through the trees, as did Atara, Liljana, Alphanderry, and Master Juwain. Behind me I heard Maram making strangled sounds as if his desire for Melia had caught in his throat.

"Ah," he groaned, "ah, ah, ahhh!"

I turned back to see Melia's face pressed into the curve of Maram's neck. Her hand was clutching there, too, as she pulled closer to him. It took me a moment to credit what my eyes knew to be true. Maram's eyes, I saw, were almost popping from his head as he struggled to scream. And all the while, Melia squeezed harder and harder as she fastened her teeth into him and bit open his neck.

"Ah," Maram gasped through a burble of blood, "ah, ah, ahhh!"

"Hold, there!" I shouted. "What are you doing?"

I moved over to pull her away from the stricken Maram, but she raised an arm and knocked me to the ground with a shocking strength. As I was rising back up, Maram's cloak fell open to reveal Melia's changing shape. Now I couldn't credit what my eyes reported to me, for in only a moment Melia had transformed into a large, black, growling bear.

"Val," Maram gasped as he struggled helplessly, "ah, Val, Val!"

The bear—or whatever Melia really was—pushed its snout against Maram as it growled and bit and lapped his blood. Its black claws dug into his back, pulling him deep into this killing embrace. I swung my sword at it then. I expected to feel the kalama's razor edge bite through fur and flesh. Instead, it fell against the bear's hunched back as if striking stone. With a scream of tortured steel, it broke into two pieces. So broke the noble blade that my father had given me. I stared down at the jagged hilt-shard as if it were I who had been broken.

"Val, help us!" Liljana called to me.

I looked up to see her and Alphanderry futilely strike their blades against the bear. Atara shot an arrow point blank at the bear's back, but it glanced off the furry hide. Master Juwain finally found his heart and beat at the bear with his leather-bound book; but he might as well have beaten at a mountain. Suddenly the bear swiped out with one of its paws and knocked him off his feet. It struck out at Alphanderry and Liljana, too, bloodying and stunning them. It didn't take long for it to rip apart the fence surrounding our camp. Then it carried Maram off into the woods.

"Val, they're getting away!" Atara shouted at me. She fired off another arrow, to no effect.

For only a moment, I hesitated. Then, gripping my broken sword, I sprang after them. I ran crashing and screaming like a wild man through the thick bracken. My feet pounded against the green-shrouded earth as I followed the black, shaggy thing pulling Maram through the bushes with an unbelievable strength. It seemed impossible that I could hurt this unnatural creature in any way. Yet I suddenly knew with an utter certainty that I couldn't fail, that a light beyond light would show me where my broken sword must strike. And so as I closed with them and the bear-thing raised its paw to brain me, I ducked beneath it and stabbed out with all my strength. The splintered steel drove deep into the bear's armpit. It howled in a sudden rage as blood spurted and I wrenched my sword hilt free. Then the bear's paw swiped out again, striking the side of my head and knocking me nearly senseless.

"Val!" Atara screamed from behind me. "Oh, Val!"

I rose to one knee, breathing hard as I blinked and looked out upon an amazing sight. For the beast was shifting shapes and changing yet again—this time into what I took to be its true form. It had two legs and arms, even as I did, and two hands, each ending in five thick fingers. It was entirely naked and hairless and covered with a thick, black carapace more like the burnt iron of a meteor than skin. It couldn't have moved at all except for the joints in this stone-hard armor. Into one of these, between its mighty arm and blocky body, I had chanced to drive my sword. Although blood flowed from it, it seemed that it was not a fatal wound. The beast now dropped Maram onto the ground as it turned to regard me. It was a man, I thought, surely it must be a man. But only its eyes—large and lonely and full of malice—seemed human.

"Val!" Atara shouted. "Get out of the way!"

This hideous man suddenly moved forward, growling and cursing at me. The blazing intelligence of his eyes told me that this time he didn't intend to present his more vulnerable parts to what was left of my sword. He would kill me and then have his way with Maram. And so, sensing the unbearable tension in Atara behind me, I dropped to the ground. I heard her bowstring twang as an arrow shrieked through the air above my head. It drove straight into the beast-man's eye. This stopped him dead in his tracks, though strangely he did not fall. And then another arrow, fired off with the blinding speed of which only Sarni warriors are capable, took him in his other eye.

"Father!" he cried out in a terrible voice that seemed to shake all the world. In this one sound were many deep emotions: astonishment, longing, relief, and bitter hate. For only a moment, it seemed that a howl of grief answered him from far away. And then he died. He toppled backward to the ground like a tree and lay still among the ferns and flowers.

I was very weak, as if it had been my blood that he had drunk. Yet I managed to get up and go over to Maram. Atara and the others joined me there, too. Master Juwain found that the wounds to Maram's neck were not as grave as we had feared. It seemed that the beast-man had only pierced the vein there to take his meal. Maram, he said, had most likely fainted from the loss of blood.

"I hope that is the worst of it," Master Juwain said, looking at the body of the beast-man. "Human bites are more poisonous than a snake's."

He brought out his gelstei and reached deep to find its healing fire. After a while, Maram opened his eyes, and we helped him sit up.

"Atara, you killed him!" Maram said as he looked into the woods.

The beast-man's last word troubled us, for he was so fell and hideous that we did not wish to see his father. And so when we heard something else crashing through the trees behind us, we jumped to our feet and took up our weapons with trembling hands.

But it was only Kane. He came running at us through the bushes, gripping his bow and arrows. He stopped before the body of the creature Atara had killed and stared down at it for a long moment. And then he growled out, "I came upon his spoor a mile from here. But I was too late."

Enough strength had returned to me that I was able to walk up to Kane and touch his shoulder. I asked, "Do you know who this is?"

Kane nodded his head. "His name is Meliadus. He's Morjin's son."

At this news, Atara shuddered, and so did I. Atara's gaze turned inward as if she were seeing some private vision that terrified her.

Master Juwain stepped up to Kane and cleared his throat. "A son, you say? The Red Dragon had a son? But no one has ever told of that!"

"I myself thought it only a rumor until today," Kane said, pointing at Meliadus. "He's an abomination. You can't begin to understand how great an abomination."

He went on to tell us what was whispered about Morjin: that long ago he had gone into the Vardaloon to breed a race of invincible warriors from his own flesh. Meliadus had been the first of this race—and the last. For Meliadus, upon growing to manhood and beholding the hideousness of his form, had conceived a terrible hate for his creator and had risen up against him. According to Kane, he had nearly killed Morjin, who had fled the Vardaloon and had left the vast forest to the vengeance of his mighty son.

"Once," Kane said, waving his hand at the dark trees around us, "the Vardaloon was a paradise. It's said that many people lived here. Meliadus must have hunted them down, man by man, tribe by tribe."

Maram, sitting back against Liljana and Alphanderry, managed to cough out, "But how is that possible? He can't have lived all that time!"

Master Juwain rubbed his bald head and told him, "There's only one explanation: Morjin must have bestowed upon him his own immortality."

"Immortality—ha!" Kane said. He moved over to Meliadus, and with the help of his knife, pried apart the fingers of his left hand. There he found a stone, which he brought over for us to see.

"What is it?" Maram asked.

The stone was a crystal, like in shape to Master Juwain's green gelstei. But its color was brown, and it was riven with many cracks so that it looked more like a withered leaf.

"It's a varistei," Kane said. "Possibly the same one that Morjin used to make his mosquitoes and leeches—and Meliadus."

We all stared at the ugly crystal. And then Maram said, "But that can't be a gelstei!"

"Can it not?" Kane said to him. "You think the gelstei are immortal, but only the Lightstone truly is. The varistei especially are living crystals. And they can die, even as you see."

"But what killed it?" Maram asked.

"He did," Kane said, pointing again at Meliadus. "He took the blood of men and women for hundreds of years, and that sustained him, in part. But he also took the life of this crystal."

I looked at Kane and asked, "You said the Lord of Lies was Meliadus's father. But who was his mother, then?"

"That is not told," Kane said. "Likely Morjin got his son out of one of the tribeswomen who used to live here."

The memory of the bleeding young woman whom Maram had taken beneath his cloak still burned in my mind. As did the growling bear. I told Kane about this, and we all looked at him as he said, "Morjin must have bestowed upon Meliadus one thing at least. And that is his power of illusion. Or some small part of it, anyway. It would seem that Meliadus was able to shape only the image of how he appeared to you."

Maram blushed in embarrassment at the way Meliadus had fooled him. But he was glad to be alive, and he said, "I don't understand why Meliadus didn't just kill all of us once we had taken him inside our camp."

"*That* should be obvious," Kane snapped at him. "Meliadus needed the blood of the living to go on living himself. After he had finished with you, he would have come for the rest us one by one."

The question now arose as to what we should do with Meliadus. Maram favored leaving him for the wolves. But as Master Juwain observed, they would only break their teeth against Meliadus's iron-hard hide.

"Why don't we bury him?" I said. "Whatever else he was, he was a man first, and should be buried."

We all agreed that it would be best to put him into earth and so at least return him to his mother. Liljana went to get the shovels then, and we dug at the tough, root-laced ground of the forest until we had a hole big enough to lay him in. We all stood for a moment looking at the feathered shafts embedded in what seemed the only human part of him. Arrows were dear to Atara, but these she did not retrieve. Then we covered him with dirt so that no one would ever have to see what a monster Morjin had made from a man.

Much later, as we gathered between the fires breathing in smoke, I sat holding the hilt-shard of what had once been my sword. It almost seemed that the ruin of the magnificent weapon had been too great a price to pay for my life. For a moment I felt as if it hadn't been a piece of steel that had broken against Meliadus but my very soul. And then I looked off into the woods toward Meliadus's grave. There I saw the Lightstone shining out of the darkness and reminding me that the deepest fire that burned inside everyone was as inextinguishable as the light of the stars.

THAT NIGHT, I had my first dream of Morjin in nearly a month. He appeared to me with his unearthly beauty and golden dragon's eyes; he told me that he had found me again and would never leave my side. A price, he said, must be paid for the slaying of his son. He would send other fell beings to hunt us down, and if they failed to take us, he would come for us himself.

I awoke drenched in sweat and reaching instinctively for my sword. But when I drew it, I could only stare in mourning at its broken steel. My kalama was irreplaceable, I knew, for only the smiths of faraway Godhra made such wondrous swords. When

Kane saw my distress, he approached me through a cloud of the morning's mosquitoes and said, "I'd give you my sword, if you wish. It's a kalama, too."

"Thank you, but no," I said to him. His concern astonished me. "Your sword is your soul, and you can't just give it to anyone."

"But you're not *anyone*, eh?"

I looked down at the long blade buckled to his waist and said, "No, Kane, we'll all ride more easily knowing that Ea's greatest swordsman still has his."

And ride we did, all that day and the next morning through the thick trees. I tried to shake off the sickening sense that Morjin rode with me. And then, as we crested a line of hills, the Vardaloon suddenly ended. The woods gave way to fields and flats of hawthorn, elderleaf, and highbush blueberry. After six or seven miles of such country, we topped another hill; below us windswept dunes were piled up east and west as far as the eye could see. Beyond them shined the blue waters of the Great Northern Ocean.

"We did it!" Maram said as we rode down to the dunes. When we reached the castlelike mounds of sand, he practically fell from his horse and kissed the ground. "We're saved!"

After whooping like a wild dog and throwing up handfuls of sand, he remounted, and we rode across the dunes toward the sea. Soon we came out upon a wide sandy beach. There were many shells and much seaweed along the high-tide line. The air smelled of salt and carried the sound of the crashing surf. It beckoned us to plunge into the water. Maram, I saw, was still exhausted from what Meliadus had done to him, and all of our faces were haggard and cut from our passage through the Vardaloon. I had seen warriors, after months of siege and starvation, who had looked better than we did. And so we spent a few hours in the shallows washing the blood from our clothing and bathing our wounded bodies. Master Juwain said that sea salt was good for mosquito bites and other hurts of the skin. The water was cold and rimed our clothing, but we all welcomed its healing touch. By the time we had finished, the sun was a great golden chariot rolling down the blue sky in the west. Because it was growing late, we laid out our sleeping furs on the soft sand and made camp.

Atara and I helped Maram gather driftwood for a fire. Kane,

foraging farther down the beach for logs with which to fortify our camp, came upon many blue crabs trapped in tide pool between two belts of sand. He gathered up a hundred of these strange-looking beasts in his cloak and brought them back for Liljana to cook. Master Juwain dug up some clams from the hard-packed sand near the ocean, and these he presented to Liljana as well. She added them to the stew already cooking in her pot. Many of the crabs, however, she saved to be roasted on spits over the fire. It seemed to take hours for her to prepare this unusual meal. But when she had finished, all our mouths were watering. We sat around the fire cracking the crabs with stones and devouring the succulent meat. We mopped up the stew with some bread that Liljana made and washed it all down with mugfuls of brown beer. In all my life, I had never had a finer feast.

As the fire blazed up into the star-studded sky, Kane called for a song. Then Alphanderry brought out his mandolet and began singing of the Cup of Heaven, of how the Galadin had forged it around a distant star long before it had come to Ea. At first, his words were Ardik, which we all knew fairly well. But soon he lapsed into that strange tongue that none of us understood. Its flowing vowels poured out of him like a sweet spring from the earth; its consonants filled the night like the ringing of silver bells. It seemed impossible to grasp with the mind alone, for it changed from moment to moment like the rushing of a moonlit river. It was musical in its very essence, as if it could never be spoken but only sung.

"That was lovely," Atara said when he had finished.

We all agreed that it was—all of us except Kane, who sat staring at the fire as if he longed for its flames to burn him away.

"But what does it *mean*?" Maram asked. He watched as Flick did incandescent turns nearby. "Where did you learn this language?"

Alphanderry strummed his mandolet and then smiled. He said, "But I'm still learning it, don't you see?"

"No, I don't," Maram said, taking another pull of his beer.

Again, Alphanderry smiled. "As I sing, if my heart is open, my tongue finds its way around new sounds. And I know the true ones by their taste. Because there is really only one sound and one taste. The more I sing, the sweeter the sounds and the closer I come to it. And that is why I seek the Lightstone."

He went on to say that he believed the golden cup would help him recreate the original language and music of the angels, both Elijin and Galadin. Then would be revealed the true song of the universe and the secret of singing the stars and all creation into light.

It was a beautiful thought to take with us into sleep and to arise with the next morning. As we stood up one by one to stretch out our stiff bodies, I knew that we were all afire with dreams of the Lightstone.

The question now came up as to whether the body of water gleaming before us really *was* the Bay of Whales. As we stood studying the coastline, Master Juwain worried that our nightmare journey through the Vardaloon might have brought us out either east or west of it. Then Liljana laughed at him as if he had no sense. "Of *course* this is the Bay," she told him.

"But how do you know?" Maram asked, looking at her in surprise.

"Because," she said, her nostrils quivering as she gazed out at the sea, "I can smell the whales."

We all smiled at this wild claim. But after remembering how she had saved me from Baron Narcavage's poisoned wine, I wasn't so sure.

And so we walked up and down the beach as we looked out across the ocean for the Sea People. All we saw, however, were sparkling waters broken only by waves. Master Juwain brought out his varistei and pointed it at the rolling blue swells in the hope of sensing any kind of life. But all he found in the water were more crabs. Atara looked into her crystal sphere for a long time, but if she saw anything there resembling those we sought, she didn't say. Alphanderry took up his mandolet and sang to the sea in the sweetest of voices, but no one sang back.

"Perhaps this *isn't* the Bay of Whales after all," Maram said. "Or perhaps the Sea People don't come here anymore."

His words were as heavy as the sea itself. We stood staring out at the horizon as we thought about them. No one seemed to know what to do.

And then a strange look fell over Liljana's face. With great excitement, she began stripping off her tunic. When she had uncovered herself, she began walking quickly down toward the water. I was afraid that her usual good sense had left her, for I felt in her an urge to swim far out into the surf. I watched her dive into the breaking waves. She was a stocky woman, big-breasted with wide hips, and quite strong for her years. She swam straight out to sea with measured strokes, and I marveled at her skill and power.

"Liljana, what are you doing?" Maram called to her. But the booming surf swept away his voice, and she seemed not to hear him. We all watched as she swam farther out to sea.

"Ah, shouldn't you do something?" Maram asked me.

"What, then?"

"Swim after her!"

I saw Liljana pulling and kicking at the water, and I slowly shook my head. In truth, I was a poor swimmer. It took all my courage even to jump into a mountain lake.

"But she'll drown!" Maram said.

Atara came up and smiled at him. "Drown, hmmph! She seems as likely to drown as a fish."

"But the ocean is *dangerous,*" Maram said. "Even for strong swimmers."

"Then perhaps you should go after her."

"I? I? Are you mad? I can't swim!"

"Neither can I," Atara admitted.

And neither could any of us, I thought, swim as Liljana did. We all watched from the beach as she made her way far out past the line of the white-crested breakers.

And then Maram's puffy mosquito-bitten face went as white as if another monster had drained him of blood. He pointed toward Liljana as two grayish fins suddenly cut the water near her, and he cried out, "Sharks! Sharks! She'll be eaten by sharks!"

As I held my breath, another ten or twelve fins appeared in a circle around Liljana. They were closing on her quickly, like a noose around a neck.

And then, without warning, a bluish shape leaped straight out of the water only a few yards from Liljana and fell back in with a terrific splash. Two more broached the surface and blew out their breaths in steamy blasts while others raised their heads out of the water and began talking in a high-pitched, squeaking language stranger even than the songs that Alphanderry sang for us. They had long, pointed snouts that seemed cast in perpetual smiles, and Master Juwain called them dolphins. He said that once they had been the most numerous, if the least powerful, of the Sea People.

For a long time, the dolphins swam near Liljana. They jumped out of the water, doing flips seemingly just for the fun of it. They nudged her with their noses and buoyed her up with their sleek, beautiful bodies. And all the while, they never stopped whistling and clicking and speaking to her. But what words or wisdom they imparted to her, none of us could tell.

After perhaps half an hour of such frolic, Liljana turned back toward the land. Two dolphins, one on either side of her, swam with her as far as the line of the breakers. They appeared to watch as she caught herself up in a gathering wave and let it carry her a good way toward the beach. As Liljana stood up in the shallows and streams of water dripped from her olive skin and brown hair, the dolphins gathered offshore as if holding a council of their own.

"How did you know the Sea People were here?" Maram asked Liljana after she dressed herself and rejoined us. "Did you really smell them?"

"Yes, doubtful prince," she said, "in a way, I did."

She cast a quick look at the squeaking dolphins, and so did we.

"Did they speak to you?" I asked her.

"Yes, they did," she said. Her hazel eyes fell sad and dreamy. Then she continued, "But I'm afraid I didn't understand them."

"So it's been for thousands of years," Kane said. "No one can speak to the Sea People anymore."

Liljana looked out to where Flick spun like a silver wheel over the water in the direction of the dolphins. Then she said, "They *want* to speak with us. I know they do."

"Ha—why should the Sea People speak with us?" Kane asked. "It's said that ever since the Age of Swords, men have hunted them like fishes."

"We have much to tell each other," Liljana said. "I know we do."

Liljana quickly redressed and we stood on the beach for quite a while staring out at the immense barrier of water that separated us from the whales. Then Alphanderry suddenly stuck out his arm and said, "Look, they're swimming away!"

Indeed, the whole dolphin tribe was now swimming slowly

parallel to the shore toward the west. Liljana slowly nodded her head, watching them. And then she said, "They want us to follow them."

"But how do you know?" I asked her.

"I just know," she told me. My doubt seemed to wound her, and she said, "Now will you please help me discover what these people want from us?"

Her sweet, imploring smile called to mind all the kindnesses she had done for me on our journey and suggested that I would be churlish to refuse her. Without waiting for me to answer, she began striding down the beach, all the while keeping her gaze fixed upon the dolphins. It was left to me to gather up the others and break camp as quickly as we could.

We caught up with her about two miles down the beach. For the fun of it, Alphanderry and I raced our horses along the water's edge. Altaru snorted and shook with a joyous power as I gave him his head. His hooves pounded against the wet, hard-packed sand leaving great holes in it. But although he was the strongest of the horses, he could not quite keep up with Alphanderry as he sang to Iolo and urged his white Tervolan forward. What the dolphins made of us as we galloped clear past Liljana before wheeling about was impossible to say. For they just kept swimming a few hundred yards offshore as if they had all the time in the world to lead us toward some secret place.

"Perhaps they know where the Lightstone is," Maram said as he and others caught up with Liljana. He handed her the reins of her horse. "Perhaps Sartan Odinan fled north from Argattha and died on this forsaken shore."

What Maram had suggested seemed unlikely—but no more so than any other speculation as to the Lightstone's fate. We grew silent after that, each of us holding inside the image of the sacred golden cup. Our hopes fairly floated in the air like the puffy white clouds above the bay. We were all a little excited, and we rode our horses at a bone-jarring trot as we tried to keep pace with the dolphins.

For hours, as the sun crossed the sky to the south, we made our way along the beach. The dunes gradually gave way to a headland of water-eaten limestone while the beach narrowed to a ribbon of rocky sand scarcely twenty yards wide. The horses hurt their hooves on the rough shingle. If we pressed them much harder, I thought, they would pull up lame. As it was, they were still weak from what the Vardaloon had taken from them, and they could not continue this way for long.

And then, just as I feared the beach would vanish to nothing between the headland to our left and the crashing surf, we came upon a cove cut into the stark white cliffs. Great rocks broke from the shallows and the sand. There was little beach there, and most of it was covered with driftwood, pebbles, and heaps of shells. I did not think we could take the horses across it. It seemed that we could follow the dolphins no farther. Then I saw Liljana looking out to sea, and I looked, too. The dolphins had ceased their tireless swimming and were now gathered together in the rippling water. They whistled and clicked at us with great urgency. All their long smiling faces were pointed straight toward the cove.

Liljana needed no further encouragement to dismount and begin searching along the beach. Neither did the rest of us. After we tied the horses to a couple of logs, we walked among the piles of shells, crunching them with our boots. Here and there, upon catching a glimpse of a pretty pebble or a golden shell, we would pause and drop to our knees as we dug at the beach. With every passing moment, as our breaths rushed in and out and the surf pounded wildly, it seemed more and more likely that Sartan Odinan had died here after all. Time and the relentless wash of the waves, we supposed, had buried his bones beneath layers of shells and sand. If we dug in the right place, we might find his remains—and the Lightstone.

All that long afternoon we searched there. Twice I thought I'd caught a glimpse of it. But we found no golden cup nor any other thing made by the hand of man—or the angels. And then at last, with the sun falling down toward the ocean like a flaming arrow, Liljana let out a little cry. She bent down and plucked something from the carpet of shells. She held it up in the slanting light for us all to see.

"What is it?" Maram asked, drawing near her. "It looks like glass."

"Driftglass," Master Juwain said, looking at it. "I used to collect such things when I was a boy."

The driftglass, if that it truly was, was deep blue in color and about the size of Liljana's thumb. It was old and chipped and scoured smooth by the sea.

"It looks like a whale," Maram said. "Don't you think?"

As Liljana turned it over and over in her tapering fingers, we saw that it was cast into a little figurine shaped like a whale. What it had been used for or how it had come here, no one could say.

And then Liljana suddenly made a fist around the glass and pressed it against the side of her head. Her eyes glazed as they stared out at the dolphins and then closed altogether.

"Liljana," Master Juwain said to her, "are you all right?"

But she didn't answer him. She stood utterly still, facing the sea.

Curiously, the dolphins also fell silent. The only sounds about us were the cries of the seagulls and the ocean's long dark roar. We were all concerned for Liljana, but we knew not to speak lest the spell be broken.

At last Liljana opened her eyes and smiled as she nodded her head. She looked down at the figurine gleaming dark blue in the palm of her hand. And then she said, "This is no driftglass."

Master Juwain held out his hand and asked, "May I see it?"

Liljana rather reluctantly gave it to him. His bushy eyebrows pulled together as he turned it beneath his sparkling gray eyes.

"Surely it is a gelstei," Liljana said. "I spoke with the Sea People—I could hear their words inside me."

The blue gelstei, I recalled as I looked at the figurine, were the stones of truthsaying, languages, and dreams. In certain gifted people, they also quickened the power of speaking mind to mind.

"I see, I see," Master Juwain said, giving back the figurine. "I believe it *is* a blue gelstei."

We all crowded close to Liljana to get a better look at the stone. Kane looked at Liljana strangely. He said, "It *is* one of the witches' stones."

I noticed the puzzled looks on Atara's and Alphanderry's face, and so I asked, "Why do you call it that?"

"Because once, long ago, in the Age of the Mother," Kane said, "the witches of the Maitriche Telu were among the first to use these stones—they used them to rape men's minds."

"I'm afraid you malign the Sisterhood," Master Juwain said. "Their history is very complex, and so are their deeds."

"Malign, you say? The witches are still weaving their plots.

Assassins, they are. Poisoners of minds. Makers of spells that capture men's souls."

"But it's not known if the Maitriche Telu even still exists."

"Ha, it exists!" Kane barked out. His eyes flashed toward Liljana as he pointed at her gelstei. "You should be very careful, Liljana. The Sisters would kill you for this crystal, you know."

Liljana smiled mysteriously and told us that she was very good at keeping secrets; she promised that the gelstei would be safe with her. And then Master Juwain looked at her and said, "I didn't know you had the power of mindspeaking. It's very rare these days."

"I didn't know myself," Liljana told him. "I've never been good at much more than cooking and sniffing out poisons."

She spoke with modesty and little pride. Yet something in her quiet composure gave me to suspect that finding the blue figurine and speaking with the dolphins had confirmed a secret sense she had of herself.

"Ah, but you are *very* good at sniffing out poisons," Maram said to her. He studied the blue figurine in her hand and then eyed her suspiciously.

"Well, you've nothing to worry about," she told him.

"Did I *say* I was worried?" Maram turned to Alphanderry and then me. "Did anyone hear me say this?"

"Well, you didn't have to. I saw the way you looked at me."

"You did, did you? But did *you* by chance happen to look into *my* mind?"

Liljana's round, pleasant face reddened as if she had been slapped. "No, Prince Maram Marshayk, I did not!"

It was strange, I thought, that although my friends rather welcomed my being able to sense their moods and emotions, none of them wanted Liljana listening to their thoughts. And neither did I.

"Are you *sure* you couldn't hear what I was thinking?" Maram asked.

I walked across the shell-strewn beach and placed my hand on Maram's shoulder. "If Liljana says that she wasn't listening to your thoughts, you shouldn't doubt her."

"Oh, shouldn't he?" Liljana said to me. "And why shouldn't he, young prince, since you doubt me yourself?"

"Did you hear me say anything about doubting you?" I asked.

Maram smiled to hear me echo his words, and he said, "Do you see, Val? She *can* hear your thoughts! It's that damn stone of hers."

Liljana held up her blue gelstei and said, "I don't need *this* for *that* when I have my eyes and nose! Your eyes say it all."

She turned toward me and said, "What have I done to make you doubt me so? Do you think I haven't learned from bitter necessity to read the motives of powerful men, Valashu Elahad?" She squeezed the whale-shaped figurine. "Before I ever dreamed of finding this, I knew that your thoughts have been turning in one direction."

"And which direction is that?"

"From the hate in your voice, I would guess toward the Lord of Lies."

Now everyone was looking at me, and I said, "This is true."

"He's found you in your dreams again, hasn't he?" Liljana asked.

"In my dreams, yes."

"And this makes you furious, doesn't it?"

"Yes," I admitted, "it does."

"And you're afraid of this terrible fury of yours, aren't you? You think about ways of not being afraid, don't you?"

"That is so," I said, staring out away from the beach.

"And so you think about the Lightstone—all the time."

In truth, most of my waking hours—and many of my dreams—were spent looking for the golden glow of the Lightstone inside myself. As I now looked for it on the beach and above the streaming waters of the sea.

Liljana touched my hand and reassured me. "I don't think I can go inside anyone's mind unless they let me. I don't think I could hear their thoughts unless they spoke them to me."

"No, you don't have that power," I said, looking at her. "Not yet."

Maram had kept his eyes fixed on her and her gelstei, and now he said, "Well, the Sea People *did* speak to you. What did they say, then? Did they tell of the Lightstone? Is it here?"

He looked farther down the beach at the shells piled up against a jutting rock. He looked at the driftwood, at the cliffs, and his face lit up with hope.

"No, they know nothing of the Lightstone," Liljana said. "They don't even understand what such a thing might be."

"Well, I hardly understand myself," Maram said. "But surely if they knew about your gelstei, they would know about the Lightstone."

"You're thinking like a man," she said to him. "But the Sea People don't think like we do."

"Then they can't help us, can they?"

"Don't you give up so easily, my dear," she scolded him. "The Sea People are kind creatures, and they like puzzles as much as play. They've called others of their kind to come and talk with me."

"Other dolphins?"

"I don't know," she said. "They called them the Old Ones."

We looked out away from the land where the dolphins still swam in lazy circles around each other. Now the sun had disappeared into the ocean, and the blueness had left the water as if suddenly sucked away. Long dark waves moved upon the darker deeps as the light bled from the horizon. In the dusky sea, the dolphins waited, as did we. We stood on the windy beach looking out at the edge of the world where the evening's first stars blazed out of the immense blue-black sky. They cast their silver rays upon the onstreaming waters and the great gray shapes rising up from them. There, in the cold ocean, in that strange time that is neither day nor night, six immense whales suddenly broke the surface and blew their spray into the air. Master Juwain, who knew about such things, named their kind as the mysticeti. But I thought of them as Liljana did and called them simply the Old Ones.

For a while, they spoke with one another in their long, mournful songs that were more like moans than music. Their great voices seemed to still the whole world. And then, as Liljana again pressed the blue gelstei against her head, they too fell silent. The stars filled the heavens and slowly turned above the shimmering sea.

This time, Liljana did not open her eyes. She stood nearly motionless on the shell-strewn beach. If not for the slow rise and fall of her breath, we would have thought that she had turned to stone.

"Master Juwain," Maram said softly after some minutes had passed, "what shall we do?"

"Do? What is there to do but wait?" Master Juwain said. Then he sighed and told him, "I'm afraid the gelstei are dangerous stones. I've always said that the knowledge to use them has long been lost."

But this was not good enough for Atara. She came up to Liljana and brushed the wind-whipped hair away from her face.

"We shouldn't just leave her like this," she said, nodding at me. "Horses can stand all night, but not a woman. Val, will you help me?"

I was afraid to touch Liljana just then, but together Atara and I, with Maram's help, managed to sit her down against a large rock facing the sea. Atara joined her there on the sand. She sat holding Liljana's free hand while Liljana continued holding the gelstei tightly to her head.

"Now we can wait," Atara said.

And wait we did. At first, none of us thought that Liljana would sit there entranced all night. We kept looking for some sign that she might open her eyes or that the whales might grow tired and swim away. But as a yellow half moon rose in the east and the hours passed, we resigned ourselves to watching over Liljana for as long as it took. Maram got a fire out of some driftwood that he piled up nearby, and Master Juwain managed to make us a meal of steamed clams and hotcakes. It was midnight by the time Alphanderry and Kane washed the dishes by the water's edge, and still Liljana did not move.

"I'm afraid for her," Maram said to me as the fire burned lower. It cast its flickering light over Liljana's stricken face. "You met minds with Morjin in your dreams, and it nearly drove you mad. What must it be like to speak this way with a whale?"

"Here, now," Master Juwain said crabbily. He knelt in front of Liljana, testing the pulse in her wrist. "To name the Lord of Lies in the same breath as the Old Ones—well, *that* is madness."

He went on to say that the Sea People had never been known to make war or take their vengeance upon men, not even when men put their harpoons into them. Indeed the Sea People, through many long ages, had often rescued shipwrecked sailors from drowning, swimming up beneath them so that they could breathe and taking them toward land.

"That is true," Kane said in a faraway voice. "I've seen it myself."

I thought about this as I sat on the cool sand and watched the great whales floating on the luminous surface of the sea. How was it, I wondered, that the Sea People had forsworn war where men had not? Had the Galadin sent them from the stars before even Elahad and Aryu and the stealing of the Lightstone? What would it be like to talk to such beings, who obeyed the Law of the One so faithfully?

I waited there on the dark beach for Liljana to look at me and answer these questions. The wind blew across the water, from what source no one knew. The waves pounded against the shore like the beating of a vast and immortal heart. And the stars rose and fell into the blackness beyond the world and made me wonder if they were really distant suns or some kind of light-giving crystals created every night anew.

It was nearly dawn when Liljana opened her eyes and looked at us. As if saying good-bye, the whales sang their unfathomable songs and struck the water with their great tails. Then, along with the dolphins, they dove into sea and swam away.

"Well," Master Juwain said, as he knelt near Liljana, "did you understand them? What did they tell you?"

But Atara, still sitting by Liljana, held up her hand protectively and said, "Give her a moment, please."

Liljana slowly stood up and walked back and forth along the water's edge. And then she turned and said, "They told me many things."

It was impossible for her to recount all that had passed between her and the Old Ones in their hours of conversation together. Nor, it seemed, did she wish to. She liked keeping secrets to herself almost as much as she delighted in bestowing upon others her cooking and her care. But she did admit that the Sea People were very doubtful of men.

"They said we were free," she told us. "They said that we were free but didn't know it. And not knowing this, that we weren't. They said we made chains—this is my word—out of our harpoons and ships and swords, and everything else. They said that wanting to master the world, we are made slaves of it. And so thinking ourselves cursed, we are. A cursed people bring death to themselves, and to the world. And worse, we bring forgetfulness of who we really are."

She grew silent as the ocean sent its waves breaking against the shore. And then Master Juwain said, "They must hate us very much."

"No, my dear, it is just the opposite," she said. "Once, in the Age of the Mother, there was a great love between our kinds. They gave us their songs and we gave them ours. But at the end of the age, the Aryans came. Their wars destroyed all that. They hunted down all the Sisters who could speak mind to mind to oppose them. Then they gathered up the blue gelstei and cast them into the sea."

The Aryans, of course, had brought their swords to Tria— and the Age of Swords to all Ea. They had prepared the way for the rise of Morjin, who hated the Sea People because he could find no way to make them serve him.

"It was the Red Dragon," she said, "who first began the hunting of the whales. The Old Ones told me that it had something to do with blood."

"So," Kane said in his grimmest voice, "I've seen whale blood, too bad. It's darker than ours, redder and richer. To the Kallimun priests, it must be like gold."

"To the Sea People," Liljana said, "our hunting of them is as much an abomination as if we hunted and ate our own kind. They think we've fallen mad."

"Perhaps we have," I said as I touched the hilt of my broken sword.

"Ours is a dark age," Kane said. "But there will be others to come."

Liljana scooped up a handful of wet sand and held it to the side of her face as if to ease a burning there. Then she said, "The Old Ones spoke of that. They remember a time before we came to Ea. And they've told of a time when we will leave again, too."

I stood a few yards from the crashing waves as I wondered how human beings could ever return to the stars when we spent the precious gift of life in slaughtering each other. As if Liljana were reading my thoughts, she said, "The Old Ones say we *will* leave the earth—either in glory or death. They are waiting to see which it will be."

I gazed toward the horizon to see if I could catch one last sight of these great beings whose souls must be as deep as the ocean. But the waters were empty, and it seemed that the whales had gone. I said to Liljana, "Did you ask them about the Lightstone?"

Everyone moved a little closer to Liljana. And she said, "Of course I did. I think it amuses them that we're seeking a *thing*, true gold or not, however powerful it might be."

"But do they know where it is?"

"They know where *something* is. They told me of a stone that gives much light."

"Many stones give light," Master Juwain said. "Even the glowstones and the lesser gelstei."

"This is no glowstone, I think," she said. "The Old Ones told of an island to the west where there is a great crystal. It is the most powerful gelstei they've ever sensed."

"Yes, but is it *the* Gelstei?"

"I wish I knew." She paused a moment as she looked at me. "There was something else. The Old Ones also told that the seventh son would find his fate on that island."

Shells and sand shifted beneath my feet as I gazed back at Liljana. What, I wondered, might the whales have meant by "finding my fate"? The Lightstone? My death? Or one of the great gelstei that might complete the first part of Ayondela's prophecy? I asked Liljana this, but she only gripped her crystal more tightly and said that she did not know.

Master Juwain held out a trembling finger to touch the blue figurine. Then he asked, "Did the Old Ones tell what island this is?"

We all awaited the answer to this question as we held our breaths and looked at Liljana.

"Almost, they did," she said. "But their words are not our words. Understanding their names is like trying to grab hold of water."

"I see," Master Juwain said. "But did they say *where* this island is?"

"It must be west of here—they said the evening sun sets upon it."

"Very good, but how would anyone get to it? The whales must know."

"Of course they do," she said. "But they don't steer by the stars, as we do. I think they . . . make pictures of the land and sea with sounds. With their words. When they speak to each other, they see these maps of the world. But I couldn't."

"You couldn't see anything, then?"

"Only the shape of the island. It looked something like a sea horse."

At this news, Master Juwain grew silent as he gazed out at the ocean.

Maram, still the student of the Brotherhood despite his failings, said, "Nedu and Thalu lie to the west of here. And so do ten thousand other islands. Who would ever know if any of them were shaped like a sea horse?"

As it happened, Master Juwain did. The knowledge that he had gained from old books always astonished me. As did his memory.

"When I was a novice," he told us, "I read of a little island off Thalu where great flocks of swans gathered each spring. It was called the Island of the Swans, though it was said to be shaped like a sea horse."

Now I, too, stared out at the ocean to the west. The sun was rising behind me; in the touch of its golden rays upon the world, I saw the Lightstone gleaming beyond the wild blue waters.

"We must go there, then," I said.

I looked at Atara and Kane; I looked at Maram, Master Juwain, Alphanderry, and Liljana. I couldn't hear the words of affirmation they spoke to themselves. But I didn't need a blue gelstei to know that their thoughts were mine.

"But, Val," Master Juwain said to me, "the account of this island that I read was *old*. There have been great wars since then. The firestones opened up the earth, you know. And the earth took back its own, in cataclysm and in fire. Many of the islands off Nedu and Thalu were blasted into rocks, utterly destroyed. Now the sea covers them."

"The Old Ones told of this island," I said. "So it must still exist."

A troubled look came over Liljana's face, and she said, "The

Old Ones told of this island, yes. But I think they don't see time as we do. For them, what has been still is—and always will be."

"They sound like scryers," Maram said, smiling at Atara.

Atara smiled back at him. "No, a scryer would say what will be always was. And never quite *is*."

"And what does *this* scryer say?" I asked, smiling at her, too.

"Why, that we should search for this island. Of course we should."

There was really nothing else we could do. We each assented to this new course. I felt the events of our life rising up like an immense, unstoppable wave and sweeping us all along toward our fate.

We decided to celebrate our passage of the Vardaloon and Liljana's great feat of speaking with the Sea People. We filled our cups with brandy, clinked them together, and drank to our resolve to find the Island of the Swans. As the fiery liquor warmed my throat and the sun warmed the world, I looked down at the silver swan shining from my surcoat. The name of the island, I sensed, was a good omen. For the swan was not only sacred to the Valari but a sign of bright things to come.

▪ 24 ▪

OUR PLAN WAS to journey west along the coast bordering the Vardaloon until we chanced upon some fishing village or town where we could hire a vessel to take us to the great port of Ivalo in Eanna. There, if our purses hadn't emptied of coins, we might find an oceangoing ship to cross the seas to the Island of the Swans. But none of us—not even Kane or Master Juwain—knew if there were any habitations on this desolate coast. And so we had to prepare ourselves to ride the entire five hundred miles to Ivalo, if that proved to be our fate.

We traveled all that day toward the west. After retreating a few miles back down the beach, we found a path that led up along the headland overlooking the sea. This we followed for many more miles. It was rough terrain, broken by many cliffs and coves, and we found that we could best traverse it by keeping inland where the ground was somewhat level and covered with elderleaf and pepperbush and other such shrubs. Late in the afternoon, when the ground grew lower and we came upon a mead rippling with long green grass, we decided to make camp. We picketed the horses along the mead so that they could eat their fill, then we spread out our furs on the beach just below it.

The next day—the first of Marud—found us hugging the coast as nearly as we could. But with its many cliffs, we often had to veer quite a few miles inland where the goldenrod, fleabane, and other shrubs gave way to a forest of oaks and tall pines that reeked of pitch. The two days after that found us still working our way to the northwest along the Bay of Whales. On our fifth day since Liljana's talk with the whales, we made camp above a rocky prominence that pointed out toward the Northern Ocean. There the coast turned sharply toward the southwest. We journeyed in this direction for about fifty miles. And then, at the mouth of a river flowing out of the Vardaloon, we came across the town that we had been hoping to find.

Varkall, as it was named, was an assemblage of muddy streets and miserable houses eaten with wormholes or altogether rotten. Its main industry being the repair of ships unfortunate enough to have to dock there, the whole city smelled of tar and turpentine. We hurried down to the harbor as quickly as we could. We might have despaired of finding any kind of suitable vessel in such a place, for the harbor was nothing more than four rickety docks sticking out into the river. But there we had a stroke of fortune that almost made up for the torments of the Vardaloon. For tied to one of the docks was a vessel that Master Juwain called a bilander. This stout, two-masted ship had pulled into the harbor to take on a cargo of furs and was bound for Ivalo that very night.

We rode our horses right down onto the dock to which it was tied. Then Kane called for the captain to come down the gangplank and meet us. The dozen sailors who had stopped their work to look at us made way for him. Captain Kharald was a burly man, dressed, like the men he commanded, in a wool shirt, wide black belt, and bright blue pantaloons. He had the red hair of a Surrapamer and eyes as green as the sea. His face, burnt red from years of sun and wind, was creased with many lines, like an old piece of leather. When he saw that we intended to take passage with him, it lit up with greed.

"Well, it's a clear hundred and fifty leagues from here to Ivalo," he said, looking us over. "And there are seven of you and eleven horses, two of them heavily laden."

The captain, I thought, was a man who liked numbers and sums—and calculating profit to the thinnest piece of silver. I told him then that we wished not only to journey to Ivalo but on to the Island of the Swans.

"The Island of the Swans, you say?" he grumbled, looking aghast. "Why would you want to go there? It's cursed."

"Cursed how?" I asked him.

"No one knows for certain. But it's said there are dragons there. No one ever sails to that place."

I told him that we must reach this island, and soon. I told him about the vows we had made and our hopes of regaining the Lightstone.

"The Lightstone, the Lightstone," Captain Kharald sighed out. "I've heard talk of little else in all the ports from Ivalo to the Elyssu. But surely your golden cup no longer exists. It must have been melted down into coinage or jewelry long ago."

"Melted, ha!" Kane called out. "Can the sun itself be melted? The Lightstone is no ordinary gold."

"Perhaps it's not," Captain Kharald said reasonably. "But I've only ever known gold of one kind."

Here he smiled significantly at Atara, whose gold medallion gleamed from beneath her cloak. In the end, after an hour of hard negotiating, it took her entire purse of gold coins—and nearly our medallions as well—to persuade Captain Kharald to take us all the way to the Island of Swans.

After that we set about boarding the ship. There was some trouble getting the horses up the gangplank and then down into the stables in the hold. Altaru, especially, did not want to be taken down into the dank, darkish place. Three of the sailors assured me that they had shipped horses before, and they tried to take his reins from me. This was a mistake. Altaru kicked out at them, missing their heads by inches and almost splintering the topsides above the deck. Captain Kharald's jaws clenched as he inspected the divots that Altaru's hooves had left in the wood. He said nothing, but I could almost hear him tallying up the damage and determining to add it to the cost of our passage.

Finally, I took it upon myself to lead Altaru down the walkway into the hold. Atara and the others did the same with their horses. After making sure that their stables were spread with fresh straw, we fed them oats from the ship's store and then went up to lay out our sleeping furs on the deck.

An hour later, with the ebbing of the tide and the night's first stars pointing our way west, the ship sailed out from the mouth of the Ardellan River into the Great Northern Ocean.

There was a full moon that night, and it rose over a world that was nothing but water in all directions. Long past the time that I should have been sleeping with my companions back near the stern, I stood alone at the bow, gripping the railing there as I watched the ship splitting the waves of the moon-silvered sea. Sailing out of sight of the land terrified me. Merely looking out at the ocean threatened to drown me in its bright black vastness. To the south and west, east and north, I saw no bit of land upon which I could fix my gaze or hope of setting foot should a sudden storm take us under. My life, I realized, and those of my companions and everyone else aboard, was utterly tied to the fate of a rolling and pitching clump of wood that men had nailed together.

Captain Kharald had named his ship the *Snowy Owl,* and this gave me at least a little courage. Owls can see through the darkness, as could our red-bearded captain. He walked the deck for hours that first night of our voyage, now casting his eyes up at the wind-filled sails, now checking with the pilot who steered the ship to make sure that we held our course. This, I thought, he set by the stars. They were very bright that night. Their millions of points of light streaked out of the black sky like diamond-tipped spears and almost outshined the moon itself. At no time in my life since I had climbed the mountains of my home had I felt so close to them.

I might have remained there all night gazing out into the unnerving splendor and smelling the salty spray of the sea. But then I heard steps behind me, and I turned, expecting to see Captain Kharald or one of his crew of fifty sailors who worked the ship. Instead, a stranger stood limned in the moonlight. Or so I thought at first, for he wore neither the rough wool shirt and pantaloons of Captain Kharald's men but rather a long traveling cloak with a deep hood that covered most of his face. And then he spoke, and I knew he was no stranger.

"Valashu Elahad," he said, "why are you trying to run from me?"

His voice was sweeter than Alphanderry's; when he threw back his hood, the moon's light fell across the most beautiful face I had ever seen. His hair gleamed like gold, and his eyes were like twin suns pouring a golden light into the darkness. Across the chest of his tunic, which was trimmed with black fur, there coiled a great red dragon.

I tried not to look at him, but my eyelids seemed pinned open as with nails. I tried not to listen to him, but his voice rose above the creaking of the ship's timbers and the howling wind: "I know you murdered my son."

I started to deny this, but then I remembered that I mustn't speak to him at any cost.

Morjin then reached out his finely made hand and touched the scabbard where my broken sword was sheathed. He said, "I told you that you would slay with this sword again, and so you have."

"No," I whispered, "it was he who—"

"*My son!*" Morjin suddenly roared at me. So great was this shout that I thought the force of it might crack the ship's masts. And so terrible was the anguish in Morjin's voice that I was afraid it might crack *me* apart.

"My son," Morjin said in softer tones that slid into me like silken knives. "My only son."

I threw my hands up over my ears to shut out his words. I closed my eyes to blind myself to the immense suffering I saw on his face.

But then Morjin touched my hands with his hands; he touched my forehead, pressing his finger against the scar there. His thumbs brushed against my eyelids as he smiled. I saw his eyes seeking me out and looking where no man should look.

"The last time we met," he said, "we agreed that you must die. But now that you have murdered Meliadus, you must die a thousand times. Shall I show you these deaths?"

Without waiting for me to answer, his hand lashed out, catching me full in the chest. The force of his blow propelled me over the railing, and I fell through black space. And then I plunged into the even vaster blackness of the sea. I sank into the churning waves like a stone. I gasped for air, choked, breathed water. The salt burned my lungs even as the cold took me deeper and crushed the life from me.

And then the darkness of the sea gave way to a stinging glister, and I realized that I was not falling into its depths after all but rather caught in the cleft between two mountains as a blizzard raged all about me. Still I struggled to breathe as the liquid wind froze my limbs and needles of ice pierced my flesh. The pain of it grew so great so that I was sure that cold steel knives were tearing into me.

And then I *was* being torn open—with the shouts of fierce blue-skinned warriors who had somehow surrounded me and forced me up against a mountain wall. Their gleaming axes beat aside my father's shield and chopped through my armor into my belly. I opened my mouth to scream at the incredible agony of it all, but then another axe caught me in the face, and I had no mouth with which to utter any sound, not even the faintest whisper of how terrified I was of death.

So it went. The Lord of Lies had promised me a thousand deaths. But as I stood there on the bow of the rolling ship with Morjin's hand touching my forehead, it seemed that I died a thousand times.

"Do you see, Valashu?" he said to me. "Do you see?"

For what seemed hours, as the moon dropped its chill radiance down upon us, I fought not to behold the terrible visions that Morjin gave me. But I didn't fight hard enough. Not even the will to battle that I had learned from Kane was enough to drive them or him away.

Finally, Morjin took his hand away from me. He stood beneath millions of stars that hung like knives above our heads. And in the saddest of voices, he said to me, "Now you have seen your fate. But know that there is one, and only one, who can change it. And only one way that I will be persuaded to let you live."

So saying, he looked down at my hands, which I saw were grasping a plain golden cup. Before I could blink at my astonishment, he took this cup from me and held it so that I could look inside.

And there, in its shimmering depths that were deeper than the sea, I saw myself standing on top of the world's highest mountain before a golden throne. Morjin, sitting on top of the throne, came down off it and extended his hand toward me. Then he pointed east and west, north and south, at Delu and Surrapam, at Sunguru and Alonia and all the other kingdoms of the world. All these, he said, he would give me to rule. He would give me Atara as my queen, and I would reign for a thousand years as Ea's high king.

For a long time, I stared into the golden cup he held before me. I saw the Red Desert bloom with flowers and the Vardaloon changed into a paradise. I saw warriors in the thousands laying down their swords and peace brought to all lands.

When I finally looked up, I saw that Morjin had changed as well. If possible, he was even more beautiful than before. His face had softened with an immense compassion, and in place of his dragon-embroidered tunic, he seemed clothed in an unearthly radiance of many colors. Without his telling me so, I knew that he had been made from a man into one of the Elijin themselves.

"For three ages," he told me, "in a hard and terrible world, I've had to do terrible things. Many times I've slain men, even as you have, Valashu Elahad."

The suffering I sensed in his soul burned straight through me like a heated iron.

"But soon the Lightstone will be found," he told me as he looked down into the golden cup. "The old world will be destroyed and a new one created. And you and Atara—all your children and grandchildren—will live your lives in a world that knows only peace."

Only Morjin knew how badly I wanted the things that he showed me. But it was all a lie. The most terrible of lies, I thought, is that which one desperately wants to be true.

"You're close, aren't you?" Morjin said to me.

I shut my eyes as I slowly shook my head back and forth.

"Yes, so very close now to finding it," he said. "Open your eyes to me that I might see where you are."

I wanted with a terrible longing to open my eyes and see the world transformed into a place of beauty and light.

"Open your eyes, please—it's growing late and the morning will soon be upon us."

I stood at the bow of the heaving ship, trying to listen to the wind instead of his golden voice. I knew that I couldn't fight him much longer.

"The stars, Valashu. Let me look at the same stars that you see."

My hand closed about the hilt of my sword, but I remembered that it was broken. And so, at last, I opened my eyes to look upon the stars rising in the east. Master Juwain had once told me that darkness couldn't be defeated in battle—it was defeated only by the shining of a bright enough light. And there, just above the dark line of the horizon, blazed a white star that was brighter than any other. I fixed my eyes upon the single shimmering light that was called Valashu, the Morning Star. As I opened myself to its radiance, it suddenly filled the sky like the sun. It consumed me utterly. And I vanished into it like a silver swan soaring into that sacred fire that has no beginning or end.

"Damn you, Elahad!" I heard Morjin's voice cursing me as from far away. But when I turned to look at him, he was gone.

I gripped the railing along the topsides as I gasped and gave thanks for my narrow escape. I breathed in the smell of the sea and the pungency of pitch that sealed the seams of the creaking ship. Although the night's constellations still hung in the sky like twinkling signposts, there was a red sheen in the east that heralded the rising of the sun.

When I returned to my companions where we had spread out our furs along the deck, I found that Kane was awake. He was always awake, it seemed. Or perhaps it was more true to say that he seldom slept.

"What is it?" he murmured to me as I sat down on my fur. "You look like you've seen a ghost."

"Worse," I whispered back to him. "Morjin."

Many times, Master Juwain had warned me not to say this accursed name; now the mere utterance of it seemed to rouse him from his sleep. Of course, he liked to rise early anyway, and the ship's open deck was now glowing in the day's first light.

I told them both what had happened. And Master Juwain said, "You did well, Val. The Morning Star, you say? Hmmm, an interesting variation of the light meditations I've taught you."

Kane peered along the deck and behind the towering masts as if searching for Morjin. His seething hatred seemed to wake the others even more surely than did the rising sun. When my friends learned of Morjin's visitation, they gathered around me with great concern.

"But how did Morjin find you here?" Maram said, looking over his shoulder as if for spies or the cloaked figures of the Grays.

And then Kane said, "It disturbs me how much he knows of his son's death. He's growing stronger, I think. And surely with the aid of one of the damned blue gelstei."

Now Liljana drew forth her blue figurine and sat holding it protectively. I said to Kane, "Why are you so certain that Morjin has such a stone?"

Kane stared at her gelstei for moment, then looked at me and said, "The Lord of *Illusions* has great powers, eh? What could be greater than the power to make others see what is not? But even he can't cast these illusions and nightmares all over Ea. For that he would surely need a blue gelstei."

"He has seen my mind, then," I said. "He has seen me."

Kane moved closer to me so that he could grab my arm and shake some courage into me. "He's seen your mind, and that's too bad. But he hasn't seen your soul, I think. *That's* beyond any blue gelstei to reveal, even the most powerful."

The strength of his hand reassured me a little. But his words disturbed Maram, who said, "But can he see Val, in his body? See where he is? If he can see him, then he can see us."

"If he *could* see us," Kane said, "he wouldn't have been so insistent that Val show him the damn stars to fix our position."

"I'm sure that must be true," Liljana said. "So long as Val keeps from speaking to his mind, I would think that the Lord of Illusions would be able to do nothing more than sense his presence somewhere—but not know where."

"This accords with what is known of the blue gelstei," Master Juwain said. "But we mustn't forget the poison that his man put into Val. I'm afraid that the kirax speaks for Val whether he wills it or not."

"So, it speaks," Kane said. "But speaks *how*? Surely not to the mind. As we've seen by Val's most recent dream."

"How so?" Master Juwain asked. "Aren't dreams *of* the mind?"

"Ha, the mind!" Kane coughed out. "I say that dreams are of the soul. But no matter. Val was free from Morjin's dreams and illusions after we killed the Grays. Why did the dreams return, then?"

Master Juwain thought for a moment and then said, "Meliadus."

"Just so," Kane said. "When Meliadus died, both Val and Morjin felt his death—and much else as well. It's the *valarda* that truly joins Val to Morjin. This is Val's greatest vulnerability, eh?"

As the rising sun drove away the last remnants of the night, we sat there speaking of the gifts of mindspeaking and the *valarda*. Master Juwain believed that the kirax exacerbated my gift, leaving me even more open to Morjin's sorcery. Finally, Kane held up his hand as if to ward off our most fearful speculations. And then he told us, "No one knows everything about the Great Beast's powers. But this much we can take courage from: he can be fought. So, he casts illusions, but not all are maddened by them. He sends terrible dreams, but those there are who refuse to make them their own. He turns men and women into ghuls—but never the strongest, eh? In the end, I have to believe that each of us has the will to turn away from him."

He went on to say that one's will must be tempered like the toughest of steels and sharpened so that it cut through all fear; it must be polished to a mirrorlike finish so to cast back to Morjin all his illusions, nightmares, and lies.

"Isn't this what I've always said?" Master Juwain asked, turning toward me. "Have you been doing the exercises I taught you, Val?"

I remembered him telling me how I must create an ally who would watch over me in my sleep and guard me from evil dreams. I shook my head as I told him, "After the Grays' deaths, there seemed no need."

"I see. Then perhaps it's time for some new lessons."

"Yes, perhaps it is, sir."

"And the dreams are the least of it," he went on. "While you're awake, you must try to turn your thoughts away from the Lord of Lies."

I bowed my head in acknowledgment that this was so.

"And so must you, Liljana," Master Juwain said, pointing at

her blue crystal. "Of all of us save Val, you must be the most careful."

"Of *course* I will," she told him. "Have you known me to be otherwise?"

Master Juwain sighed as he rubbed the back of his head. "Will you promise that if you *do* use your gelstei, you'll refrain from trying to see what is in the Red Dragon's mind?"

"Of *course* I will," she said again. "I think I know too well what is in such men's minds."

Her offhand dismissal of Morjin as merely a man like any other alarmed me. As it did Atara. She suddenly looked up from her clear crystal and said, "Beware, Liljana—on the day you touch Morjin's mind, you'll smile no more, nor will you laugh again."

And that, I thought, was a warning we all should heed.

After that, Kane took me aside and told me that it was not enough for me merely to continue my meditations and guard the doorway to my dreams. "We must practice swords, eh? Not all our battles against Morjin, I think, will be with his damned illusions and lies."

When I pointed out that I had no sword to cross against his, he said, "Why don't you make one? I'm sure Captain Kharald can spare a bit of wood."

As it happened, Captain Kharald was only too glad to provide me with a piece of a broken old spar that one of his men fetched from the hold—for a price. He said that good oak was valuable, broken or not, and demanded a silver piece in payment. But silver we had none, only a few coppers left in Kane's purse, and Captain Kharald decided to settle for two of these. I spent most of the morning whittling the hard oak spar. While the sails above me filled with a good following wind and the *Snowy Owl* fairly flew through the water, I shaved off long strips of wood with my dagger—the same blade that I had put into Raldu's heart. It wasn't the best tool for such work, but its Godhran steel cut well enough. By the time the fierce Marud sun was high above us and heating up the deck, I had a wooden sword as long as a kalama. Wood being lighter than steel, I had made it thicker than the blade I was used to in order to preserve its heft. But its balance was good and it handled quite well—indeed, so well that I held my own against Kane for most of our first round of swordplay. Although he finally cut through my defenses, it seemed that he was having to work ever harder to do so.

We sailed all that day and next night into the west beneath fair skies. A hundred miles we made from sunset to sunset, Captain Kharald told us. By the second morning of our voyage, we had reached a point just south of Orun off Nedu. There some clouds came up upon a rising wind as the sea grew rougher. The ship rocked and heaved to the swelling of ten-foot waves, and so did our bellies. A strange malady called seasickness stole upon us like a fever that comes from eating rotten meat. It grabbed hold of Maram and me the most tightly, while Atara, Alphanderry, and Liljana were less troubled. Master Juwain, who had grown up around boats, said that he hardly felt sick at all. As for Kane, the ship might have rolled over on its side and cast us all into the ocean before he complained of any distress.

By the next morning, however, the sea had quieted somewhat and so had our bellies. I found myself able to stand and fix my gaze upon the wavering blueness of the horizon. One of Captain Kharald's men, another redbeard named Jonald, pointed out a hazy bit of land to the starboard and said that it was one of the Windy Isles. This was a long chain of rocky outcroppings that ran for more than three hundred miles between Nedu and the coast of Eanna to the south. We had made good speed, he said, coming some 250 miles since setting sail from Varkall. Another 150 should find us pulling in to the great harbor at Ivalo.

Later, as I joined Maram near the bow, we gazed out at the sheeny waters to the west. And Maram asked me, "How many people throughout the ages, do you think, have sought the Lightstone?"

"Many," I said, looking at the ripples on the sea.

"Too many," Maram agreed. "Sometimes it seems impossible that the Lightstone really *could* be found. And yet, right now at least, I have a strange hope that we are nearing the end of our quest."

"Yes—it is that way with all of us."

Maram looked back along the deck at where our friends gathered. As his gaze settled on Alphanderry, I felt a sadness welling up within him. And he said to me, "If by some miracle we *do* claim the golden cup, I suppose Alphanderry will journey on to other lands to sing of it. Liljana will certainly return to Tria, and Kane, I suppose, will go off by himself into some dark land—only the stars know where. And you. . . ."

His voice died into the wind as I laid my hand on his massive shoulder and looked at him. The claiming of the Cup of Heaven, I thought, *would* spell the disbandment of our company. And we were all sorry for that, for we had come to love and trust each other as do the fingers of one's hand.

"It's strange," he said to me. "When I lived in Mesh and even growing up in my father's palace, I always felt that I was seeking *something*. In a way, always wandering, do you see? And now that we really *are* wandering the world, for the first time, I feel like I'm home."

That night, after dinner, we sat with the others on the *Snowy Owl*'s deck looking out on the stars in a strange melancholy. The cool, groaning wind off the waves carried murmurs of lamentation from distant corners of the world. Even the waning moon seemed saddened to lose slivers of itself night after night.

Alphanderry, pulled by the weight of the pale orb, took out his mandolet and began to sing. At first his words were of that impossible language it seemed no man could ever understand. There was a great pain in the sounds that poured from his throat but a great beauty, too. I had never heard him sing so well. Perhaps, I thought, his song had been made purer and clearer by listening to that of the whales. Even Flick, that magical being who chose to join us on this journey, seemed to apprehend this new quality of Alphanderry's music, for he hovered just above the minstrel and flared up like a cluster of shooting stars with every note.

Captain Kharald's men gathered around us then to listen to Alphanderry play his mandolet. I knew that they had never heard anything like it before. Then Captain Kharald came out of his cabin and stood staring at Alphanderry, as if seeing him for the first time.

After Alphanderry had finally finished his song, he looked up and realized that he had an audience. "Hoy," he said, "I'm getting closer, I think. Maybe someday, maybe someday."

"What *was* that song?" Jonald asked in a rough voice. "I couldn't understand a word of it."

"I'm not sure I could either," Alphanderry said, laughing along with Jonald and the other sailors.

"Well, do you know any songs we *can* understand?"

"I don't know—what would you like to hear?"

Captain Kharald suddenly stepped forward and said, "What about 'The Pilot King'? That's good song for a night such as this."

Alphanderry nodded his head agreeably and began tuning his mandolet. Then he smiled at Captain Kharald as he began to play:

> *A king there was in Thaluvale,*
> *His name was Koru-Ki,*
> *He built a silver ship to sail*
> *The heavens' starry sea.*

It was a sad song, full of wild longing and great deeds; it told of how King Koru-Ki, in the Age of Law, had sailed out from Thalu in search of the streaming lights of the Northern Passage, which was said to lead off the edge of the world up to the stars. It was a long song, too, and Alphanderry played for a long time. The moon was high in the sky by the time he finished.

"Thank you," Captain Kharald told him politely. His men began drifting off, to their duties or beds. But he stood there a long while, staring at Alphanderry strangely. "Thank you, minstrel. If I had known you had such a voice, I wouldn't have let you pay your passage."

Then he, too, went off to bed, and so did we.

We reached Ivalo late the next morning. We caught our first sight of it just as we rounded a hump of land along Eanna's northern coast. Like Varkall or Tria, it was a river city, built at the mouth of the Rune. But it had none of Tria's splendor and too much of Varkall's squalor. Too many of its houses and buildings were of wood and seemed jammed together in dirty, fetid districts that crowded the river. Unlike ancient Imatru a hundred miles farther up the Rune, it was a new city, scarcely a thousand years old. No great towers graced the muddy banks upon which it was sited. No gleaming bridges of living stone spanned the muddy Rune. Neither were there walls to catch the light of the midday sun. The Eannans, who were perhaps the greatest mariners in the world, liked to say that they were better protected with wooden walls, and these were their ships.

Many of them were docked in the harbor into which we sailed. We saw luggers, barks, and bilanders—and, of course, the galliots and warships of the Eannan fleet. These were lined up along the docks jutting out from the Rune's western bank. The eastern bank was given over to Ivalo's many warehouses and shipyards—and taverns and inns that served its sailors.

Here the *Snowy Owl* found berth along a wharf owned by one of Captain Kharald's friends. We tied up across the way from another bilander, commanded by a Surrapamer named Captain Toman. Both he and Captain Kharald were old friends. Like Captain Kharald, he was a thickset man with a shock of fiery hair—though his beard had gone gray. When he saw the *Snowy Owl* strike her sails, he came on board and greeted Jonald and others whom he knew. Then Captain Kharald showed him into his cabin so that they might drink a bit of brandy and speak of their homeland.

An hour later, Captain Kharald came back out and his face was grave. He walked over to me and my companions and said, "I've had bad news from Surrapam. The Hesperuks have broken the line of the Maron River and are laying waste the countryside. And their warships have closed the Dragon Channel."

Our dreams of finding the Lightstone, so bright only the day before, seemed suddenly blackened as if by angry storm clouds.

"So, the barbarians have closed the channel, too bad," Kane said to him. "What will it take to open it again, eh?"

"What *would* it take, then?" Captain Kharald said.

He looked at our medallions and then the two diamonds sparkling in my ring. His gaze outraged me. Was I a diamond seller that I would peddle away that which may not be sold? Would I give up my hand to gain the Lightstone? Would I give my arm?

"Not *this!*" I said, clenching my fingers tightly around my ring.

I felt Kane trembling to draw his sword and run him through; if my kalama hadn't been broken, I would have trembled thusly as well.

"No, no, you misunderstand me," Captain Kharald said, suddenly holding up his hand. He pointed at Atara's medallion and then looked at my ring again. "These things are dear to you, and you should keep them."

I could not quite believe what I was hearing. I looked at Captain Kharald more closely.

"You see," he told us, "there is much hunger in my homeland. I've decided to take on a cargo of grain and sail for Artram as soon as we're loaded. The Hesperuk warships be damned. I'm still willing to put in to the Island of the Swans along the way."

Kane was the next one to surprise me as he growled out with as much politeness as he could muster: "Thank you, Captain Kharald—you're an honorable man."

"Now I must excuse myself," Captain Kharald said as he turned toward the ship's stern. "There's much to do before we sail."

He walked off and left us there, wondering at his change of heart.

"I don't understand," Maram said, watching the sailors and wharf hands swarm the deck in preparation for unloading and loading cargo.

And then Master Juwain explained: "Their whole lives, men fight battles inside themselves. And sometimes, in a moment, the battle is suddenly won."

It took the wharf hands most of three days to unload the bales of sealskins and barrels of whale oil from the *Snowy Owl* and then to take on the many hundreds of canvas bags bulging with wheat berries. When the holds were finally full again, Captain Kharald walked the decks inspecting the rigging and the balance of the ship. And then, on the tide, we sailed for Surrapam by way of the Island of the Swans.

The first hundred miles of our voyage were easy enough, with fair skies and good wind. On the following day, however, as we rounded the Cape of Storms at the very northwest corner of the continent, the seas grew much rougher. The skies darkened, too, though strangely there was no rain. With the great island of Thalu ahead of us somewhere to the west, we sailed south, into the Dragon Channel.

Here the wine-dark waters pitched the *Snowy Owl* up and down as if testing her timbers and the skills of those who sailed her. These, as I saw, were as great in their own way as any of my brothers' prowess with arms. Captain Kharald came alive with the rising of the wind and seas; often he stood near the bow grinning fiercely with his red hair blowing back behind him. At the sharp commands he barked out above the ocean's roar, Jonald and the other sailors turned the ship back and forth against the wind and made progress across the waves even so. The magic of this maneuver amazed me; Captain Kharald called it tacking. We spent most of the next three days tacking back and forth along a line leading mostly south toward Surrapam.

On our fifth day day out from Ivalo, we came upon a sight that chagrined us all: the wreckage of a merchantman, listing badly and dead in the water. As we drew closer to the stricken ship, we saw that it had not run aground on the numerous rocks and reefs off Thalu as Captain Kharald first supposed. Fire had taken her to her doom: the shreds of blackened sails still hanging from her spars and the charred wood there gave sign of this. There was also sign of battle. Black arrows stuck from the masts like a porcupine's quills, and the hacked corpses of many sailors lay about the bloodstained deck. The terrible stench issuing from the ship told us that none had survived the devastation. Captain Kharald wanted to board her to make sure this was so, but the rough seas about us prevented any such maneuver.

"Who do you think did this?" Maram asked him as everyone gathered along the *Snowy Owl*'s port side to look at the death ship.

"Pirates, we can only hope," Captain Kharald said. "There are many pirate enclaves on Thalu."

Maram shuddered at this and muttered that nothing could be worse than such lawless, marauding men. And then the sea turned the black ship slowly about, and what we saw told of something much worse. For there, nailed to the main mast, hung the burned and tormented body of a man.

"I've heard the Thalunes are without mercy," Kane said. "But I've never heard that they are crucifiers."

"No, they're not," Captain Kharald admitted. "This is certainly the work of a Hesperuk warship. It's said the Hesperuks have taken to crucifying in the Red Dragon's name."

"They'll crucify *us* if they catch us carrying wheat to Surrapam," one of Captain Kharald's men said. "Or feed us to the sharks."

After that, Captain Kharald gave orders for an extra sailor to go aloft and stand watch on the crow's nest high on the fore-mast. We all cast nervous looks about the gray ocean as the wind drove the *Snowy Owl* ever farther south and we left the wrecked ship behind us.

But it is one thing to sail away from such sights on a fleet ship built of stout oak; it is quite another to leave them behind in one's soul. That night, terrible dreams nailed me to the deck of the ship. For what seemed hours, I tried to shield myself from Morjin's fell words that burned me like dragon breath. It took all my will finally to fight myself awake. I sat up trembling and sweating and peering through the darkness for any sign of land. And then Atara came over to touch a dry cloth to my face.

"Here," she said, wiping my forehead. "You were dreaming again."

"Yes, dreaming," I said.

The sea beneath us swelled and fell as the ship's wooden joints groaned like an old man. The wind off the cold water chilled me to the bone. It seemed that I could still smell the stench of the blackened ship we had passed.

"Of what were your dreams?" Atara asked me.

I looked at Maram snoring on top of his furs nearby and our other companions stretched out peacefully on the deck. And I said, "Death. My dreams were of death."

She nodded her head at this. "Sometimes, I dream of that, too. But I mustn't."

"We are both warriors," I said to her. "My father once told me that a warrior must always live with death breathing on the back of his neck."

"I would rather feel the breath of life on my face," she said as she pressed her fingers to my lips. "To feel *your* breath, telling me that you won't let yourself be taken down."

"All men die," I said to her softly.

"No, I won't let you." Her hands wrapped around behind me, and she pulled my head against her belly. "Not *you*—not so soon!"

I wanted to reassure her then that I would fulfill all my vows, as she would hers, and that we would marry and live to see our many grandchildren playing happily in the sun. Instead, I could only stare at her in silence as a dark and dreadful thing ate at my soul.

An immense sadness fell over her then. She sat down facing

me and wrapped her arms around my sweat-soaked back. She held me tightly against her warm body as she began weeping. And then, through her tears, she murmured, "No, no, you can't die. You mustn't—don't you see?"

"See what, Atara?"

"That if you died, I'd want to die, too."

For a long time she sat there kissing the tears from my own eyes as she stroked my hair. The ship rolled and dipped along the rising waves. Above us, the stars poured down a fierce white radiance.

And then, to comfort herself as much as me, she told me, "Surely the Lightstone can take away these terrible, terrible dreams of yours."

"The Lightstone," I said. I gazed out at the stars. "Have you seen it, then?"

"No, I think Mithuna was right," she told me. "No scryer can ever behold it. But I know we're getting close to it, Val. We *must* be."

I prayed that what she said was true. I felt my fate, like the moaning wind, calling to me. As I held her against me, I looked over her shoulder, out into the darkness of the sea. And there, many miles to the south, beyond the black and rolling waves, I thought I saw a bit of golden light breaking through the clouds and drawing us on.

The next morning at sunrise, the lookout in the crow's nest called out that he had sighted the distant rocks of the Island of the Swans.

▓   **25**   ▓

IT WAS NEARLY noon by the time we had sailed close enough to the island to get a good look at it. This western part of the world was a realm of clouds and mists that lay low over the land and often obscured much of it. The rocks that the lookout had espied proved to be the highlands of four smaller islands just to the east of the Island of Swans. The island itself, like a sea horse with its head pointed west and tail curling southeast, was a much greater prominence about fifty miles in length. Along its central spine, three conical mountains pushed their peaks toward the sky. From the centermost and tallest of these, it seemed that a great plume of smoke issued forth and fed the gray-black clouds above it. Captain Kharald's men feared that this must be dragon smoke; they called for the *Snowy Owl* to flee the accursed waters before the dragon descended upon us and burned us with his fire.

"Dragons, hmmph," Atara said as we all stood near the rail looking at the island. "There hasn't been a dragon in Ea for two thousand years."

We sailed clear around the island looking for a safe place to land. The next day, along the island's gentler southern coast, we saw beaches giving way to the misty, green-shrouded heights beyond. About a quarter mile offshore, the *Snowy Owl* dropped anchor, and Captain Kharald directed the lowering of the skiff that would take us to the island.

"One day we'll wait, but no more," Captain Kharald told us. "Then we'll have to sail for Artram. My people are hungry."

"Yes, they are," I agreed. I stared off at the wall of green rising up beyond the beach, hoping I might catch a gleam of gold there. "But hungry for more than bread."

After Jonald and the others had put us ashore and set out to sea again, I gathered with my friends on the beach. I stood armored in my mail, wearing my black and silver surcoat and my helmet with the silver swan wings projecting upward from the sides. I held the throwing lance that my brother Ravar had given me and my father's gleaming shield. Kane bore his long sword and Maram his shorter one; Atara had her saber and her deadly bow and arrows. Liljana and Alphanderry had strapped on their cutlasses, even though they had chipped them badly on Meliadus's rock-hard hide. And Master Juwain, of course, would carry no weapon. In his gnarly old hands, he clutched his copy of the *Saganom Elu* as if it contained whole armories within its pages.

The island stretched out twenty-five miles to the west and as many to the east. We guessed that it must be at least ten miles wide at its widest part. In listening to the wind pour over this considerable length of land, I realized that I had no idea where the Lightstone might be found. And neither did my friends. Why did we think that we had even a glimmer of a chance of finding it?

Maram looked past the squawking seagulls flying above us and said, "Well, Val, what do we do now?"

I turned to Atara to ask her if she had seen anything in her crystal sphere. But in answer Atara held out her hands and shook her head.

Four points there are to the world, and three of these were land while the fourth was ocean. I stood with my back to the gray water as I gazed at the smoking mountain to the north. When I looked in that direction, my heart beat more quickly. And so I began walking toward it.

The others followed close behind me across the beach. Soon its brownish sands gave out onto the wall of forest that had seemed so forbidding from the water. And forbidding it was, but I immediately liked the feel of this ancient wood. Its giant trees, towering far above the carpets of bracken along the forest floor, were hung with witch's hair and icicle moss as if arrayed in enchanted garments. Every living thing about us seemed soft and glowing with greenness; even the air smelled sweet and good.

I felt strangely at home here although there were many types of trees and plants that were strange to me. Master Juwain put names to a few of them: he pointed out the great cedars with their long strips of red bark and the yew trees and big leaf maples. Others he had never seen either. But it turned out that Kane had. He showed us the sword ferns and the horsehair lichens, the lovely pink rhododendrons and the blue hemlocks shagged with old man's beard. Each name he spoke as if reciting that of an old friend. And each name Master Juwain dutifully recorded. I thought that it was part of his own private quest to remember the name of each and every thing in the world.

"I've never seen a woods so lush," Maram said as he puffed along behind me. "If the Lightstone *is* here, it could be *anywhere*. How are we to find it? I can't even find my own feet beneath me."

Liljana came up to him and said, "Don't you give up hope just yet, young prince. No one would have hidden the Lightstone in this forest. But perhaps we'll find a cave in one of the mountains we saw."

These three peaks were now obscured by the wall of vegetation before us. But we tried to keep a straight line toward the smoking mountain. And so we fought our way up across the densely wooded ground that led toward it. And then, after perhaps a mile, the headland we were climbing came to a crest. The forest suddenly changed and thinned, and gave way to many more yews and maples. Through the gaps between them, we looked down into the most beautiful valley I had ever seen.

"Well!" Maram called out. "There *are* people here!"

We saw signs of them everywhere. Between the crest on which we stood and the mountains some five miles away were many patches of green that could only be fields. Small stands of trees divided them from each other in darker green lines. Pastures covered the long slope leading down to the valley's center. There a sparkling blue lake pooled at the base of the three mountains, which curved around its northern shore like a crescent moon. There, too, near the lake's southern shore, surrounded by what seemed to be many streets and colorfully painted houses, stood a great square building whose white stone caught the sunlight streaming out of a break in the clouds. Liljana said that it reminded her of the ruins of the Temple of Life in Tria.

"Whoever lives here," Kane said to me, squinting as he looked about the valley, "may not want us here. We should be careful, Val."

"Careful we'll be, then," I said. "But when one walks into the lion's lair, there's only so much care that can be taken."

And with that, I led off, walking warily down toward the valley. Soon the woods gave out onto a wide pasture on which only a few isolated trees grew. Here the grass was long and lush, and as green as grass could be. Many day's-eyes, with their sunlike yellow centers and long white petals, made a show of themselves; bees buzzed from flower to flower in their slow but determined way, gathering up nectar peacefully. From somewhere ahead of us, across the lines of rolling and gradually descending ground, came the baahing of some sheep. If this was a lion's lair into which we were walking, I thought as I gripped my lance and shield, then surely we were the lions.

Another quarter mile brought us out onto a pasture smelling of sweet blue flowers and sheep droppings. We saw the flock ahead of us, fifty or sixty fat sheep spread out over the soft green grass, their white fleeces gleaming in the sun. We saw their shepherd, too. And he saw us. The look on his face as we suddenly appeared over a low rise above him was one of astonishment. But strangely, he showed no sign of fear.

"*Di nisa palinaii,*" he said, holding out his hand as if in greeting.

The words he spoke made no sense to me. Nor did any of the others seem to understand him, not even Alphanderry, who held the seeds of all languages upon his fertile tongue.

"My name is Valashu Elahad," I said, pressing my hand to my chest. "What are you called, and who are your people?"

"*Kilima nisti,*" the man said, shaking his head. "*Kilima nastamii.*"

The shepherd wore a long kirtle that seemed woven of the same white wool that covered his sheep. He was tall, almost my height, with ivory skin and a long, high nose that gave great dignity to his noble face—and a hint of fierceness, too. But there seemed nothing fierce about him. His manner was gentle, curious, welcoming. He wore no weapon on his brightly colored cloth belt, and his hand held nothing more threatening than his shepherd's crook. This surprised me almost as much as did his appearance. For with his thick black hair and eyes like black jade, he might have been my brother.

"Amazing!" Maram said to me. "He looks Valari!"

My friends, gathering around the shepherd, stared at him and remarked the resemblance as well. Master Juwain said, "There's a mystery here: a lost island upon which stands a Valari warrior who seems no warrior at all. And who doesn't speak the language that all men do."

If he was a mystery to us, we were an even greater one to him. He approached me as one might a wild animal; he slowly extended his hand and traced his finger along the swan and seven silver stars of my surcoat. He touched the steel links of my armor, too. Finally, he tapped his fingernail against my helmet as he slowly shook his head.

"*Di nisa, verlo,*" he murmured. "*Kananjii wa?*"

It seemed pointless, and a little rude, to continue talking with him from behind my helmet's curving steel plates. And so I took it off. The shepherd stood staring at me as if looking into a mirror for the first time.

"Di nisa," he said again. *"Wansai paru di nisalu?"*

"What language is this?" Maram asked, shaking his head. "I can't understand anything of what he says."

"I can *almost* understand," Alphanderry said. "Almost."

"It sounds something like ancient Ardik," Master Juwain told us. "But, I'm afraid, no more than a pear is like an apple."

Kane had now lost patience, perhaps with his own ignorance most of all. He nodded at Liljana and said, "You spoke with the Sea People, eh? Can't you speak to this man?"

All this time Liljana had been clutching her little carved whale in her hand. Now she brought it to her head. The blue gelstei, I recalled, were not only the stones of mindspeaking but also quickened the powers of truthsaying and apprehending languages and dreams.

"Nomja?" the shepherd said, looking at the figurine.

A quick smile suddenly split Liljana's round face as if she were very pleased with herself. And then she opened her mouth and surprised us all by saying, *"Janomi . . . io di gelstei. Di blestei, di gelstei . . . falu."*

After that, she began speaking the shepherd's language more rapidly. She paused only to allow him to return the discourse and ask her questions. And then, with a smile that lit up her whole being, she found her tongue again and managed to keep up a continual stream of conversation. The strange words poured out of her like a waterfall.

After a while, she took the gelstei away from her head and told us, "He says his name is Rhysu Araiu. And his people are called the Maii."

"And this island?" Kane asked her. "Does it have a name as well?"

"Of course it does," Liljana said, smiling at him. "The Maiians call it *Landaii Asawanu.*"

"And what does that mean, then?"

"It means," she said, "the Island of the Swans."

We asked Rhysu who ruled his land; Liljana, translating for him, told us that on the Island of the Swans there was no king, nor duke nor master nor lord. Their most prominent personage seemed to be a woman named Lady Nimaiu: a sort of priestess who was also called the Lady of the Lake.

"As it was in the ancient days," Liljana told us.

Rhysu, now very excited, insisted on presenting us to this Lady Nimaiu. He left his sheep grazing contentedly and motioned for us to follow him. And so we set forth, with Rhysu leading the way. Soon we came to a little road that led down the valley's center. It was paved with smooth stones cut so precisely that they showed only the narrowest of seams. Flowers of various kinds lined the sides of the road, which wound through the meadows and fields. With the soft sun providing just enough heat to warm us nicely and the many birds singing in the orchards to either side of us, it was one of the most pleasant walks I had ever made.

We stopped more than once to greet other shepherds and farmers curious as to the strange sight that we must have presented. After they had eyed my armor and studied my friends with amazement, more than one of them joined us. By the time we reached the edge of the city, we made a party perhaps thirty strong. And there, from the neat little houses painted yellow, red, and blue, many more of the Maii stepped out to behold us. All of them had the look of my countrymen back in Mesh. Cries of *"Nisa, Nisa!"* sang out as Maiians emptied out of the shops and houses and lined the streets before us. As we passed, they closed in behind us and formed up into a procession of hundreds of excited men, women, and children.

Rhysu, walking now with great dignity, led the way straight toward the temple. From this massive structure, which appeared made of marble, bells began ringing and sent their silver peals out over the city. And now it seemed the whole of the city had been alerted to our coming, for thousands of people crowded the streets before us. In bright streams of kirtles and flowing garments dyed every color, they converged upon the temple from the south, west, and east. There, in a tree-lined square beneath the temple's gleaming pillars, they gathered to greet us and witness what to them must have been an extraordinary event.

A tall woman, perhaps forty years of age, accompanied by six younger women, emerged from between the temple's two centermost pillars and slowly made her way down the steps toward us. She was as beautiful of face and form as my mother, and she wore a long white kirtle trimmed with green along the sleeves and hem. A filigree of tiny black pearls was sewn into the kirtle's front, and a fillet of much larger white ones had been set around her forehead and over her long black hair. She stopped immediately in front of us. Then Rhysu stepped forward, knelt, and kissed the woman's hand. Upon straightening again, he said, *"Mi Lais Nimaiu—talanasii nisalu."*

He turned toward me and my companions and continued, *"Talanasii Sar Valashu Elahad. Eth Maramei Marshayk eth Liljana Ashvaran eth. . . ."*

And so it went until he had presented us all. Then he spoke to Liljana, who stepped closer with her blue gelstei to translate for him. Liljana pressed her little figurine to her head as she smiled at the tall women. To us, she said, "This is Lady Nimaiu. She is also called the Lady of the Lake."

Lady Nimaiu, as Rhysu had, spent quite a few moments examining us. Atara's golden hair seemed to hold wonders for her, as did Master Juwain's complete absence of it. But she reserved her greatest curiosity for me and my accouterments. She took in the lineaments of my face, and then she rapped her fingernail against the steel of my helmet, which I held in the crook of my arm. With my leave, she touched this same elegant finger to the silver swan and stars embroidered in my surcoat. She gasped as if these shapes might be familiar to her. Her breathing quickened as she examined the hilt of my broken sword. She spent another few moments running her hand over the steel links of my mail and the swan and stars embossed on my father's shield. Finally, she wrapped her fingers lightly around my throwing lance before stepping back and regarding me warily.

With Liljana translating for us, she began conversing with me: "You bring strange things to our land. Are suchlike common in yours?"

"Yes," I admitted, "most warriors, at least the knights, are accoutered thusly."

Liljana hesitated a moment in her translation because she could find no words in Lady Nimaiu's language for knight or warrior. And so she simply spoke them as I did, leaving them untranslated.

"And what is *warrior*?" Lady Nimaiu asked me.

"A warrior," I said, hesitating as well, "is one who goes to war."

"And what is *war*?"

Now the six women attending Lady Nimaiu pressed closer to hear my answer as did Rhysu and many other of the Maii. I traded swift, incredulous looks with Master Juwain and Maram. Then I said, "That might be hard to tell."

I looked around at the gentle Maii, who stood regarding us with great curiosity but no fear. Could it be possible that they knew nothing of war? That the bloody history of the last ten thousand years had completely passed by their beautiful island?

As I stood there wondering what to say to Lady Nimaiu, she again touched the hilt of my sword. "Is this an accouterment of *war*, then?"

"Yes," I said, "it is."

"May I see it?"

I nodded my head as I drew what was left of my sword. Its broken hilt shard gleamed brightly in the light of the late afternoon sun.

"May I hold it, Sar Valashu?"

I did not want to let her hold my sword. Would I so readily give into her hands my soul? Nevertheless, upon remembering why we had come to her island, I fulfilled her request in order to engender a little goodwill.

"It's heavy," she announced as her fingers closed around the hilt.

I did not explain that if the blade had been whole, it would have been heavier still. But Lady Nimaiu, whose bright eyes missed very little, seemed to understand this as she gazed at the broken end of my sword.

"Of what metal is this made?" she asked me, tapping the blade.

"It's called steel, Lady Nimaiu."

"What is this thing called, then?"

"It is a sword," I said.

"And what is *sword* for?"

Before I could answer, she moved her finger from the flat of the blade and started to run it across its edge. "Be careful!" I gasped. But it was too late: the kalama's razor-sharp steel sliced open her finger.

"Oh!" she exclaimed, instinctively clasping the wounded tip

against her breast to stanch the bleeding. "It's sharp—so very sharp!"

She gave me back my sword while one of the women close to her tended her cut finger. To the murmurs of grave disapproval spreading outward among the crowds around us, she explained that although the Maii used their bronze knives to shape wood and shear their sheep, none were so keen of edge that they cut flesh at the faintest touch.

"Oh, I see," she said sadly as she held up her finger. The white wool of her kirtle was now stained with her blood. "*This* is what *sword* is for."

I felt my own blood burning my ears with shame. I tried to explain a little about warfare then; I tried to tell her that all the peoples of Ea stood ready to protect their lands by going to war.

She spoke her amazement to Liljana, who continued to make her words understandable: "But what do your lands need protecting *from*?" she asked me. "Are the wolves that fierce where you live?"

Behind me Maram muttered, "No, but the Ishkans are."

Liljana either didn't hear this or chose to ignore him. And then I took upon myself the task of trying to explain how we Valari had to protect ourselves from our enemies—and each other.

I spoke for quite a while. But what I said made no sense to Lady Nimaiu—and, in truth, little to me. After I had finished my account of the world's woes, she stood there shaking her head as she said, "How strange that brothers feel they must protect themselves from each other! What strange lands you have seen where men take up swords because they are afraid their neighbors will as well."

"It . . . is not as simple as that," I said. "What would your people do if two neighbors disputed the border of their lands and one of them made a sword to claim his part?"

While Liljana translated this, Lady Nimaiu looked at me thoughtfully. And then she said, "We Maiians do not claim land as your people do. All of our island belongs to all of us. And so there is always enough for all."

"As it was in the ancient days," Liljana said quietly, pausing a moment in her translating duties.

I took a breath and asked Lady Nimaiu, "But what if one of your men coveted one of his neighbor's sheep? What if he slew his neighbor, and then threatened others as well?"

What I had suggested plainly horrified Lady Nimaiu—and the other Maiians, too. Her face fell white, and her jaw trembled slightly as she gasped out, "But such a man would be *shaida!*"

Now it was my turn to be puzzled as Liljana mouthed this Maiian word that had no simple translation into our tongue. After some further discussion between Lady Nimaiu and Liljana, I was given to understand that *shaida* meant something like the madness of one who willfully disregards the natural harmonies of life.

"But what would you do with such a *shaida* man?" I asked. "Slay him with his own sword then?"

I told her that once war between peoples had begun, it was very hard to stop. Then Lady Nimaiu said, "But it could never come to *war,* don't you see? Such a man would be given to the Lady, and all would be restored."

I stood there confused. I didn't know what she meant by "given to the Lady." Wasn't *she* Lady Nimaiu, the Lady of the Lake?

After some rounds of Liljana passing our words back and forth to each other, Lady Nimaiu smiled sadly and said to me, "I am the Lady of the Lake, as you've been told. But I am not *the* Lady, of course. It is to her that we would give your sword-making man."

She pointed above the temple at the smoking mountain across the lake. She said that anyone who fell *shaida* would be dropped into its fiery cone.

"The Lady takes back everyone into herself," she explained. "But some sooner than others."

"Is this Lady the *mountain,* then?" I said, trying to understand.

My question seemed to amuse her, as it did many of the other Maii, who gathered around laughing softly. And then Lady Nimaiu smiled and told me, "Oh, no, the mountain is only the Lady's mouth—and only her mouth of fire at that. She has many others."

She went on to explain that the wind was the Lady's breath and the rain her tears; when the ground shook, she said, the

Lady was laughing, and when it quaked so violently that mountains moved, that was her anger.

"The Maii," she said, stretching out her wounded finger toward her people, "are the Lady's eyes and hands. And that is why none of us would ever make a sword."

I paused to look at the many men and women all around us. And then I asked, "And does this Lady have a name?"

"Of course she does. Her name is Ea."

At the utterance of this single word common to both our languages, the earth seemed to tremble slightly. Smoke continued pouring out of the cone of the mountain above us, but whether this signaled the Lady Ea's gladness at our arrival or displeasure, I couldn't tell.

We had a hundred questions for Lady Nimaiu and the Maiians, as they had for us. They wanted to know everything about our peoples and the lands from which we came. They were fascinated with Liljana's blue figurine and her ability to shape the words of one language into that of another. But they saved their greatest wonder toward the answering of a single question.

"Why," Lady Nimaiu said to me, "have you come to our island?"

My first impulse was to blurt out that we had joined the great quest to find the Lightstone. But Maram, fearing my artlessness, moved up behind me and whispered in my ear, "Be careful, Val. If the Lightstone *is* here, it's surely inside the temple. If we tell them we're seeking what must be their greatest treasure, they'll likely give *us* to this bloodthirsty Lady of theirs."

He advised telling Lady Nimaiu that we had stopped on the Island of the Swans to hunt for fresh meat to replace our ship's dwindling stores. We should wait, he said, and contrive a way to enter the temple. Then we could determine if it really did house the Lightstone and devise a plan for its taking.

Maram was more cunning than I, yet not every situation called for this virtue. The Maiians, sensing something devious in Maram's quiet speech, which Liljana failed to translate, began murmuring among themselves and shifting about the square restlessly. I was reluctant to tell Maram's little lies and even more so to say anything that might get us pushed into a pool of fire. And so I looked at Lady Nimaiu and said, "We're on a quest . . ."

A groan from Maram made me pause in my answer. Then I continued, "We're on a quest to find truth, beauty, and goodness. And the love of the One that is said to find its perfect manifestation somewhere in the world."

My words, after Liljana had rendered them into the Maiians' tongue, seemed to please them. Although I had spoken only vaguely of the Lightstone's essence, what I had said was true enough.

"It may be that your quest will soon be fulfilled," Lady Nimaiu said, smiling at me. "There is a place that we would show you. A place sacred to the Maii. Will you come there with us?"

I looked up at the temple with great hope and excitement, and Maram and my friends looked that way, too. "Yes, we will come," I said.

Lady Nimaiu beckoned for us to follow her. And then she turned, not back toward the temple, but in the direction of the lake's eastern shore. Lady Nimaiu's intention puzzled me, as it did my friends, but it seemed that we had no choice but to do as we had promised. And so, with Lady Nimaiu and her six attendants in the van, and the thousands of Maii in the square spread out behind us, we formed a vast procession as we made our way down to the lake.

The beauty of their island almost quenched my desire to find the Lightstone. We passed by gardens full of oak trees and cherry, where little streams ran through stone-lined channels into the lake. They were so artfully tended and arrayed against the land that they hardly seemed gardens at all. To my astonishment, I saw that two of the trees growing atop a low rise were astors, with their silver bark and golden leaves. Though not so magnificent as those that grew in the Lokilani's wood, their long, lovely limbs spread out beneath the blue sky as if to embrace it and catch its light. The fire mountain, just beyond the quiet lake, perfectly framed their shimmering crowns. It came to me then that the transformation of the island into this earthly heaven was not an altering of nature but rather its finest and fullest expression: for what could be more natural than the Maii, the Mother's eyes and hands, happily working their art upon the earth? I suddenly realized that I did not wish to leave this place. It was as if I had journeyed across the whole length of Ea only to find my real home.

As I walked along with my friends behind Lady Nimaiu, I listened to the hundreds of happily chatting Maiians all about us. They were, I thought, a contented people. It seemed that they found their joy neither in remembrance of the glories of ages past nor in dreams of future redemption, but rather in rock and leaf, wind and flower. The glint of the sun off the marble of their beautiful temple pleased them more than gold; the laughter of their children playing in their pastures or in the square was to them a finer music than even Alphanderry could make. They were wholly wedded to the earth, and they took great delight in that marriage.

"This is a fine place," Maram said, as he ambled along eyeing one of Lady Nimaiu's attendants. "I've never seen a fairer land. So rich, so sweet."

"Yes," I said bitterly, "the Maiians have time for creating such beauty since it seems they spend none of it waging war."

Kane, walking next to me, growled out, "It's a pretty paradise they have made for themselves. But if the Red Dragon ever sends a warship here, it will all be ashes."

His words almost dampened Maram's growing ardor for the voluptuous but rather homely attendant walking just behind Lady Nimaiu. And then Maram asked the question that puzzled all of us: "Who *are* these people? They certainly *look* Valari."

"They certainly are Valari," Master Juwain said, drawing in closer. "The question is, of which tribe? That of Aryu? Or that of Elahad?"

He went on to say that the Maiian's ancestors must be of the Lost Valari: either the followers of Aryu after he had stolen the Lightstone or the companions of Arahad who had set out on the Hundred Year March to search for it.

"The Lost Valari, yes, that seems possible," I said to Master Juwain. "But how could they be of the tribe of Aryu?"

Here Kane caught my eyes and said, "Do you remember what I told you after we killed the Grays? How Aryu had also stolen a varistei, which his people used to change their forms to suit Thalu's cold and mists? So, what if some of *his* tribe repented Aryu's crime? What if they fell out with their brethren before the varistei was used? If they fled Thalu to the south and came to land here, they would still look Valari, eh?"

"That seems the most likely explanation of the Maiians' origins," Master Juwain agreed.

All about us were many Maiians, with the same high noses and exquisitely sculpted face bones of my people; I didn't quite want to admit that they were really Aryans who still retained the Valari form.

"If what you say is true," I said to Master Juwain, "then how is it that the Aryans let the Maiians live here in peace so many thousands of years?"

"I think I might know," Maram said, still staring at the attendant, whose name was Lalaiu. "I think perhaps the Aryans *did* come here to conquer. And the Maiians conquered them."

Lady Nimaiu led us down to the lake's shore, where we stood with her on soft green grass as the thousands of Maiians gathered around us. Though now late in the afternoon, it remained a fine, clear day with only a few clouds in the sky. Its almost perfect blueness was reflected in the calm, mirrorlike waters of the lake. Farther out upon it floated hundreds of swans, their folded wings snowy white, their long arched necks as lovely as the curve of the heavens themselves.

Now the many Maiians, joined by others from across the island, sat about the low shelves of lawn sculpted into the earth along the shore. I had a practiced eye, tutored in battle for taking in large numbers of men, and I counted at least six thousand of them. We stood on the lowest shelf of lawn with this multitude behind us and the lake almost directly in front of us. Only a series of white marble steps, following the contours of the lake's edge and actually leading down into it so that they were half-submerged, stood between us and the lapping waters of the lake itself.

Scarcely ten yards in the direction in which these steps led, three pillars arose out of the lake's shallows. They seemed the remains of a much greater structure that must have once stood there. Liljana, after speaking in hushed tones to one of the temple attendants standing with us, told us that once the lake had been lower but over the ages had risen as it had filled with the

Lady's tears. I sensed then that Lady Nimaiu intended to submerge *us* in these icy-looking waters as part of some ancient rite.

Soon Lady Nimaiu arrived with her six attendants following closely. The kirtle covering her long, graceful body was as white as the swans and embroidered with red roses. She stood with her back to the lake, facing us and the thousands of her people behind us on the lawn. She began speaking of the sorrows that all must suffer, and that only the Mother's even greater sorrows could wash clean. For many ages, she said, since nearly the beginning of time, the Mother's tears had gathered into this lake that the Maii might taste the bitter pain of the world and rejoice in its splendor upon reemerging from it. "For this is why," she told us, "we were born in pain from the Mother's womb: we are that we might know joy."

She asked me and my friends if we were willing to be cleansed in order to experience this joy. I hesitated only a moment. Then, with a quick glance at the temple, I said that I was, and the others did, too.

With no further words, Lady Nimaiu led us down the steps in turns into the lake. One by one, she held us beneath its rippling surface. As I had feared, the water was very cold. In truth, it was bitter. But a short while later, as we stood yet again on the lawn above the steps, the sun warmed us and poured its golden radiance upon our soaked garments and dripping hair. Its light was incredibly sweet; as we looked out into the long, green valley, we saw that the world was incredibly beautiful and good.

The Maii sitting on the grass all applauded our feat. In their front ranks, I noticed Rhysu and others smiling at us.

Then Lady Nimaiu came forward and addressed us, saying, "Only in purification can there be truth, beauty, and goodness. And the love from which they flow. Do you still seek these qualities, Sar Valashu Elahad?"

Although she directed this question to me, it was clear that she expected me to speak for all of us. The soft wind just then found its way through the armor and underpadding plastered to my body; it seemed as cold and bracing as the lake itself. I gave thanks that the Godhran armorers had made my mail of a stainless steel that would never rust.

"We do seek them," I said. I sensed that Lady Nimaiu was

testing me, or rather calling me to embrace the truth that the lake's waters had set so clearly before me. "We seek the gold gelstei that is called the Lightstone. We seek the Cup of Heaven that is said to hold these things inside it."

At this, Maram began moaning. Liljana was reluctant to translate my words, but I nodded at her to do so, and she did. Then I showed Lady Nimaiu my medallion and explained the meaning of the various symbols cast into it.

"It is good that you've given us the truth so freely," Lady Nimaiu said, walking among my friends to examine their medallions as well. "Allow me to return the favor: three days ago, the Sea People told us that strangers would come to our island seeking this shining thing you call a *gelstei*."

That the Maii seemed able to speak with the Sea People astonished me, as it did Liljana. She stared at Lady Nimaiu, her hazel eyes full of wonder. She glanced at her figurine and muttered, "As it was in the Age of the Mother—then they needed no gelstei to talk with the whales."

Although she left this untranslated, Lady Nimaiu seemed to understand her all the same. She nodded at her and said, "But the Sea People know nothing of a golden cup here. Nor do we. There is none such on this island."

I sensed that Lady Nimaiu was telling the truth, at least so far as she knew it. The disappointment I felt then was a palpable thing, as if an acid fruit had lodged in my throat.

"Perhaps the Lightstone was hidden here long ago," I said, "and the Maii have forgotten it."

I couldn't help but glance at the temple, so great was the bitterness burning inside me.

"I can tell you that you *won't* find it there," she said.

The Old Ones had told us that we would find a great gelstei here. Were they wrong? Or had they misled us for some deep purpose of their own?

I looked at my companions: at Atara, whose dashed hopes came flooding into me; at Maram, now lost in the depths of Lalaiu's eyes; and at Master Juwain, Liljana, and Alphanderry. I saw Kane drop his gaze and scowl his frustration at the earth. We had journeyed too long and too far, I thought, and now it seemed that our quest must end here, on this lost island at the edge of the world—or somehow we must find a way and a will to go on.

"Now that you have tasted the Mother's tears," Lady Nimaiu continued, "it might be that you could remain here."

I had no power of mindspeaking, but I knew that my friends were all thinking of the vow we had made that our seeking the Lightstone would not end unless illness, wounds, or death struck us down first. But couldn't the body, while not exactly stricken, grow exhausted of a succession of life-draining wounds? Couldn't the soul sicken? Couldn't hope die?

I knew that we all desperately wanted to remain on this beautiful island. I was ready to strip off my armor and cast my sword into the lake. Then I heard inside myself the undying voice, whispering in fire. I saw Atara looking at me with her lovely blue eyes that burned away time. The same flame, I knew, blazed inside Atara—and in my other friends.

"I can't remain here," I told her.

Atara looked at me with a terrible sadness as she said, "Nor I."

"Nor I," Liljana said, glancing at Master Juwain.

"Nor I," he said as well. "I'm afraid the Lightstone *will* be found—if not by us or others who stood with us in Tria, then by the Red Dragon."

And so it went, each of our company passing the ineffable flame back and forth as we remembered our purpose and reforged our wills to fulfill it. Even Maram broke off gazing at Lalaiu and said, "I hate to leave this island, but it seems I must."

I turned to Lady Nimaiu and said, "This is the most beautiful place we have seen on earth. But we must continue our quest."

"To find this gelstei that you call the Lightstone?"

"Yes, the Lightstone," I said.

"But why would you risk your life for such a thing?"

I heard in her words a question beneath the obvious question, and I sensed that I was somehow being tested again. And so I asked myself for the thousandth time why the golden cup must be found. The answer, I was now certain, lay *not* in pleasing my father or brothers nor even winning Atara as my wife. As for my being healed of the *valarda* and the kirax that quickened my gift, what did the sufferings of a single man matter? If only I could find the strength, I would accept all the pain in the world and pass on the Lightstone to one more worthy if that meant such monsters as Meliadus would never be born and evil places like the Vardaloon would never blight the world again.

At last I looked at Lady Nimaiu and said, "I would find the Lightstone to heal the lands of Ea and make them like yours. I'd fight all the demons of hell that this might be."

After Liljana had translated this, a sad smile broke upon Lady Nimaiu's face. She bowed her head as if acknowledging the purity of my purpose and finding it distressful even so. And then, as the many people behind us on the lawn began murmuring words of approval, she looked deep into my eyes.

"You *would* fight, I think," she said to me. "But would you die for your dream?"

Would I die, truly, to see the Lightstone placed in Atara's hands, or Master Juwain's, and kept safe from Morjin? I gazed at Lady Nimaiu, and said a single word: "Yes."

I felt her whole being grow cold as if encased within ice.

"You are of the sword," she said to me, glancing down at the hilt of my kalama. "And your fate is your fate."

She took my hand then and led me down the steps to the lake's edge. I had no idea what her intentions were; perhaps, I thought, she wanted to cleanse me of blood that I must someday spill in pursuit of this dream.

After taking many deep breaths, she suddenly let go my hand. And then she turned to walk down the steps into the water.

"What is she doing?" Maram cried out.

I, too, wondered this, as it seemed did everyone else. Many of the Maiians stared at Lady Nimaiu as she took one final breath and disappeared into the lake. Their cries of concern told me that this was no part of any purification ceremony they knew.

My heart began beating quickly as if it were I who was holding my breath. I peered into the water and thought that I saw Lady Nimaiu swimming down toward a stone altar covered with silt and swaying with strands of lake moss. But then the mountains moved, casting a glow of fire into the sky and causing the earth to tremble. Gleaming ripples cut the lake's surface, making it impossible to see very far into its icy depths.

"*Quiwiri Lais Nimaiu?*" a young man behind me half shouted. Now he and many of his people were on their feet, pointing at the lake and murmuring, "*Quiwiri Lais Nimaiu?*"

The pressure in my chest grew into a pain almost too great to bear. I couldn't move, so keen was the cold in my limbs that froze me to the shore gazing at the deep blue water.

And then, even as the swans suddenly cried out and leapt toward the sky with a great thunder of beating wings, a hand holding a sword broke the lake's surface. A moment later, Lady Nimaiu's face appeared as water streamed from her glistening black hair and she gasped for breath. Her feet found the marble steps, and she climbed them one by one, arising out of the lake while she held the sword high above her.

"The Sword of Flame," I heard Alphanderry whisper behind me. "The Sword of Light!"

Although I didn't dare believe that he might be right, I saw that the sword was bright enough to be called that and more. It was long and double-edged like the swords of the Valari; its blade shined more brilliantly than silver, and its edges seemed to cut the very rays of the sun.

"It *is* of gelstei!" Master Juwain exclaimed.

Lady Nimaiu looked at me strangely, and a thrill of fear shot through my veins. She asked me, "Would you like to hold it?"

"Yes," I told her, nodding my head.

While all the Maii and the temple attendants stirred excitedly, while my friends looked on and Kane shook his head in wonder, Lady Nimaiu approached to give me the sword. My hands closed around a hilt of black jade that was carved with swans and set with seven starlike diamonds; a much larger diamond, cut with many sparkling facets, formed its pommel stone. At the sword's first touch, fire leaped inside me. I sensed a sort of numinous flame, invisible to the eye, running along its silvery blade from the upswept guard to its incredibly sharp point. I couldn't take my eyes from it or let it go. It was very heavy, as if truly wrought of silver or other noble metal, and yet strangely light, as if the sun itself were filling it with its radiance and drawing it toward the sky. I sliced the air with it a few times to get the feel for wielding it; its balance, I thought, was perfect. How such a marvelous weapon had come to be kept beneath the waters of the Maii's lake I couldn't imagine.

Now it came time for Lady Nimaiu to tell of this. Having shaken the water from her dripping kirtle and caught her breath, her hand swept out toward the sword as she recounted the story: long ago in another age, she said, a Maiian fisherman named Elkaiu had cast out his net hoping to catch some of the silver salmon that swim off the coast of their island. But instead his net snagged on something heavy, and he hauled it in to find the silver sword gleaming among the folds of knotted rope. Elkaiu was amazed, not only because he had found an object for which he had no name, but because the sword bore no mark of rust or tarnish even though it had drifted for untold years along the currents of the salty sea. Elkaiu had brought the sword to his Lady, who had sensed a great power in it. She sensed, too, that it had been cast into the sea to be cleansed, and so she had ordered it kept beneath the lake to continue its purification. The Lady had eventually grown old and died, but she had passed on the knowledge of the sword to her successor. And so it had gone, generation after generation for many hundreds of years, the secret of the sword known only to the various Ladies of the Lake, who preserved it. Over the centuries, Lady Nimaiu said, there arose a legend that one day the sword's true owner would come to take it away.

"Is that you, Sar Valashu?" she asked as she pointed at my sheathed kalama whose hilt was also carved with swans and stars. Then she looked at the bright blade in my hands. "Have you come to claim this *sword,* as you call it, as your own?"

Yes, I thought as I stared at the shimmering wonder of it, I have. *I must.*

"The silver gelstei," Master Juwain said, breathing deeply. "This must be the one of which the Sea People told."

He went on to say that on all Ea, throughout all the ages, he knew of no greater work of silver gelstei than this sword. "*If* this truly is the Sword of Light."

"The Sword of Fate," Atara said softly, "it was also called."

For a moment, everyone fell silent as they looked at this long blade gleaming in the bright sunlight. Kane, who loved good weaponry almost more than life, seemed to gaze at it the longest and most deeply. "Alkaladur—so, Alkaladur."

Here Alphanderry, standing by his side, rested his hand on his shoulder as he sang out:

> Alkaladur! Alkaladur!
> The Sword of Flame, the Sword of Light,
> Which men have named Awakener
> From ages dark and dream-dark night.

"What words are these?" Maram asked.

"So, they're from a much longer song telling of how Kalkamesh forged the Bright Sword," Kane said. "This was in the time after the First Quest when Morjin had nearly killed Kalkamesh and taken the Lightstone for himself."

"Do you know the whole song?" Maram asked Alphanderry. "Will you sing it?"

Alphanderry nodded his head, but then looked at Lady Nimaiu, whose attendants were combing out her tangled hair. It would have been rude for him to sing words that Liljana could have no hope of translating quickly and faithfully enough to be appreciated. But Lady Nimaiu, when apprised of this difficulty, asked Alphanderry to continue. She said that the spirit of the song would come through in his voice, and that was all that mattered. And so she stood smiling encouragingly at Alphanderry as all the Maii turned toward him and he began to sing. When he came to the verses that told of Kalkamesh's forging of the sword, I listened raptly:

> When last the Dragon ruled the land,
> The ancient warrior came to Mesh.
> He sought for vengeance with his hand,
> And vengeance bitter burned his flesh.
>
> And yet a finer flame he held,
> The sacred spark, aglow, unseen,
> In hand and heart it brightly dwelled:
> The fire of the Galadin.

He brought this flame into the realm
Of swans and stars and moonlit knolls
Where rivers ran through oak and elm
And diamond warriors called swords souls.

To Godhra thus the warrior came
Beside the ancient silver lake.
By might of mind, by forge and flame,
A sacred sword he vowed to make.

Alkaladur! Alkaladur!
The Sword of Flame, the Sword of Light,
Which men have named Awakener
From ages dark and dream-dark night.

No noble metal, gem, or stone—
Its blade of finer substance wrought;
Of essence rare and form unknown,
The secret crystal ever sought.

Silustria, like silver steel,
Like silk, like diamond-frozen light,
Which angel fire has set its seal
And breath of angels polished bright.

Ten years it took to forge, ten years
To shape the crystal, make it whole;
The blade he quenched in blood and tears,
And in its length he left his soul.

A diamond for its pommel stone
Its swan-carved hilt was blackest jade
And set with seven gems that shone:
White diamonds in which starlight played.

My hand pressed against the sword's diamond pommel as for a long time I disappeared into the past. And Alphanderry recounted how Aramesh, at the Sarburn, had used Alkaladur's silustria to seek out Morjin on the battlefield and the golden cup that he had stolen. Aramesh, of course, at last had thrown down Morjin and imprisoned him—and then taken the Lightstone into his keeping. In great bitterness, Kalkamesh had then cast his great work of silustria into the sea. But the prophecies told that one day Alkaladur would come forth again. The final verses that Alphanderry sang to us burned themselves into my mind:

> *And there it dwelled beneath the waves,*
> *Through ages new and ages old.*
> *But so it's told in ancient caves:*
> *The silver gelstei seeks the gold.*
>
> *Alkaladur! Alkaladur!*
> *The ageless blade, immortal sword*
> *Which men have named Deliverer—*
> *To pure of heart will be restored.*

Alphanderry fell silent as he stared at the sword; I stared at it, too, as did everyone else gathered around the lake.

Maram slowly nodded his head. Then he looked at Kane. "If Kalkamesh did cast the sword into the sea in his anger at King Aramesh's sparing of Morjin, then it seems a rare chance that the sea carried it a thousand miles to this island only to be caught in this man Elkaiu's net."

"Ha, chance," Kane called out. "There's much more at work here than mere chance."

Now Alphanderry asked Liljana to tell the sword's story in the Maiian language, which she did. When she had finished, Lady Nimaiu gazed at the sword. "Now I understand why it lay so long beneath the lake—and in the sea perhaps longer. Upon this sword, there must have been much blood."

Perhaps once there had been, I thought. But now, as I held it up to the sun, the blade's silver surface reflected its light so perfectly that it seemed nothing could ever stain it or mar its beauty.

Master Juwain, whose mind turned over thoughts more times than the wind tossing about a leaf, nodded his bald head toward the sword and said, "This must be the Awakener told of in the song. But we must be sure that it is before Val claims it as his own."

"But, sir, how can we be any more sure than we are?" Maram asked.

"Well, there is the test to be made," Master Juwain said. "If it is truly of silustria and not some lesser gelstei, it will pass this test."

"What test?" I asked him sharply.

"The silver gelstei is said to be very hard—harder than any stone save the Lightstone itself."

He motioned for me to hold the sword with its blade flat to the earth so that he could get a better look at it. "The sea carried it a thousand miles across its rocks and sands. Did they make many scratches? Do you see any mark upon it?"

I turned the sword over and over, trying to detect on its gleaming blade the faintest featherstroke of a line or scratch. But it was as unmarked as the surface of a still mountain lake.

"Hard is silustria—harder than adamant," Master Juwain said as he looked at the two sparkling stones of my knight's ring. "Why don't you use these diamonds to try to scratch this blade?"

Again I looked at the sword's wondrous finish. I no more wanted to scratch it than I did the lens of my eye.

"It must be tested, Val. It must be known."

Yes, I thought, it must be. And so, making a fist, I touched my ring's diamonds to the blade and drew them in a small arc across it near the hilt. The silver remained untouched. Now I singled out one of the stones and positioned it precisely; I found a point where three of its facets came together and pressed it as hard as I could against the silver, all the while trying to dig and drag the diamond down the entire length of the sword. But it slid off like light from a mirror and left not the slightest mark.

"Alkaladur," Master Juwain breathed out. "It is the Bright Sword."

Now many of the Maii tried to get a better glimpse of this miraculous thing that had lain in their lake for so long unknown to them. Although they craned their necks to see it, none tried to touch it, nor would I have let them if they had.

"There are lines from the song I would like to understand better," Maram said as he came up by my side. "What does it mean that the silver gelstei seeks the gold?"

"Hmmph, that should be clear," Atara told him. "Weren't you listening to what Alphanderry said?" Her eyes fixed on the sword as she sang out:

The silver sword, from starlight formed,
Sought that which formed the stellar light,
And in its presence flared and warmed
Until it blazed a brilliant white.

"Yes, I see," Master Juwain said, rubbing his shiny pate. "The lines tell truly. Some believe that the Lightstone, far from merely coming from the stars, is source of their light. It is known that the silver gelstei was first sought in an attempt to forge the gold. And so it has a deep resonance with it. It's said to love the Lightstone as a mirror does the sun. But whether it flares in its presence as the song has it, I do not know."

"It must flare!" Lady Nimaiu called out to us.

My companions and I, and all the Maii, looked at her.

"In the hands of its true keeper, the sword must flare," she went on. "The Old Ones have told of this."

My hands tightened around the sword's black jade hilt. I felt certain that the sword must be mine.

"You cannot claim this sword, Valashu Elahad, merely with words and wishes," Lady Nimaiu told us. "Even as your Master Juwain has said, it must be tested. It must be known."

The sadness in her voice hinted of some dark thing, as of iron buried in the earth. And I said to her, "Tested . . . how?"

She looked at me for what seemed a long time as the sadness seemed to build into dread. And then she told me, "You have said that you are willing to die for your dream of finding the Great Gelstei. The sword must flare, in the hands of the one who would point the way to this stone. It must flare, or he cannot be the sword's keeper, do you understand? And if he is not, he must die."

Upon these ominous words, I noticed half a hundred of the largest Maiian men making their way through the crowd toward us like a closing net. Then Kane's hand moved toward his sword, while Atara quickly fit an arrow to her bow. I gripped Alkaladur's hilt even more tightly.

"What do you mean, he must die?" Maram shouted, reaching for his sword, too.

"The Old Ones," Lady Nimaiu said, looking me, "have told that Valashu will leave this island in glory or death. They are waiting to see which it will be."

I peered through the crowd at the Maiian men moving in, now more than a hundred strong and now ten feet closer. Then I glanced up at the smoking mountain above the lake. And I said, "Then you would give me to Ea's mouth of fire, yes? But why?"

"The Old Ones have told of this, too," Lady Nimaiu informed me. "They say that you, the seventh son, will show the way toward the light—either that, or bring the shaida dark. That is your fate."

"My fate," I whispered, looking at the bright sword I held in my hands. "The Old Ones said that I would find my fate upon this island."

At this, Alphanderry repeated one of the refrains from his song:

> Alkaladur! Alkaladur!
> The Sword of Sight, the Sword of Fate,
> Which men have named the Harbinger
> Of death to those who rule by hate.

I wondered, then, if this sword was to be my death. I knew that I could not just cast it back into the lake or give it to Lady Nimaiu to return it there. The prophecy told that the seven brothers and sisters with the seven gelstei would set forth into the darkness and the Lightstone be found. This sword, I was sure, must be my gelstei. And the darkness lay all around me, waiting for me to find my way through it if only I could shine a bright enough light.

"No one," Kane growled out, looking from the crowd of Maiians then back to Lady Nimaiu, "is going to throw anyone into that damn mountain so long as I am alive!"

Could the gentle, unarmed Maii, I wondered, stop us from cutting our way back to the beach? Perhaps—considering that they were, by blood, in their hearts, true Valari. But could anyone stop Kane from laying about with his sword and slaughtering the men around us with all the fury of an enraged tiger?

Only one, I thought. As there is only one way to save these people—and Ea, as well.

"The sword will flare," I finally said to Lady Nimaiu. "Alkaladur must be the Sword of Sight—and I must find the way to point it toward the Lightstone."

At my acceptance of the trial that had been put upon me,

many hundreds of Maiians sighed in relief, though they did not relax their intense concentration upon me.

Then Kane muttered to me: "Who are these people to test you?"

"Who is anyone?" I asked him, resting my hand on his sword arm. "But there is no choice."

Kane thought about this as he stared down the Maiian men closest to us. Then he snapped out, "All right. But if you're to get any light out of this sword, you must first find it in yourself."

Master Juwain nodded his head at this. "Why don't you try holding the image of the Lightstone inside yourself while you point the sword?"

"But point the sword where?" Liljana asked. "Surely the Sea People told truly: there is a great gelstei on this island. But not the Lightstone, it seems."

I, too, believed what the great whales had said—and Lady Nimaiu. But I turned to look at the temple even so.

"Why don't you point the sword toward it?" Atara said to me.

I did as she suggested, extending the sword's point directly toward the temple's pillars behind us to the south. But the silver blade, while marvelously full of light, seemed not to brighten even slightly.

"It's not there," Maram muttered. "I don't think it's there."

We all fell silent as we stared at Lady Nimaiu and the waiting Maiians. And then Master Juwain said to me, "It might help if you meditated, Val. This, too, is said of the silustria:

> To use the silver stone,
> The soul must dwell alone;
> The mind must be clear,
> Unclouded by fear.

As I stood there gazing at the reflection of my dark eyes in the sword's polished contours, I remembered what Master Juwain had once taught me about the silver gelstei: that it was the stone of the soul and therefore of the mind which arose out of it. At the moment, with thousands of people staring at me and this fateful blade catching the bright morning sunlight, my mind was anything but clear.

"Why don't you try the seventh light meditation?" Master Juwain suggested.

And so I did. With Kane gripping his sword and staring at the Maiians in their bright-colored kirtles, I closed my eyes and envisioned a perfect diamond floating in the air. This diamond was just myself. Nothing could mar its incredibly hard substance—not even my fear of failing to gain the Lightstone. And certainly not my dread of death. The diamond was cut with thousands of facets, each one of which let in the sun's rays with perfect clarity, there to gather in its starlike heart with a brilliant fire that grew brighter and brighter and . . .

"Well, it seems there's nothing," Master Juwain said, his voice coming as from far away. "Nothing at all."

I opened my eyes to find the blade unchanged.

"It seems the Lightstone really isn't on this island," Maram said. And then he fell despondent and muttered, "Ah, perhaps it's nowhere—perhaps your brothers were right that it's been destroyed."

"No, it can't have been," I said.

"Then perhaps . . ."

His voice died into the deathly silence of the thousands of Maiians surrounding us. He could not bring himself to say that I might not be the sword's rightful keeper, and therefore not the one fated to find the Lightstone.

I tried to reassure him, and myself, saying, "I can almost feel it, Maram. I know it exists, somewhere on Ea."

And with that, I held the image of the diamond inside myself again even as I held the sword out toward the Garden of Life to the west. But still its blade grew no brighter.

"Again, Val," Kane encouraged me. "Try a different direction."

I slowly nodded my head. And then I lifted the sword toward the smoking mountain to the north, with as little result.

"Again, Val, again."

I lightened my grip around the swan-carved hilt so that the seven diamonds set into the jade there wouldn't cut my hands so painfully. Then I pointed this sword that men had named Awakener toward that part of the world where the Morning Star arises in the east.

"*Sa natu,*" I heard one of the Maiian men standing nearby

say with a terrible finality. I did not need Liljana to translate the meaning of his words: There is nothing.

"Valashu," Kane said to me, "what is in your heart?"

Darkness was in my heart; the icy cold of nothingness gripped me there, too. My death would be Kane's death, I thought, and that of Atara and my other friends along with them. The pain of this unbearable thought pierced me like one of Atara's arrows in my deepest part. There I felt gathering something hot and bright, for love, too, dwelled inside me. The Old Ones had said my fate would be darkness or light, but could I choose which one? When I opened my heart to my friends, it was as if I touched them with the valarda: this blazing fire of the stars.

"It flares!" Kane called out suddenly. "Do you see how it flares?"

As I opened my entire being to Alkaladur, the fire there suddenly blazed hotter, both purifying and reforging the secret sword that I had carried inside myself since my birth. I felt the two swords, the inner and outer, resonate like perfectly tuned crystals chiming out harmonies older than time. It was as if they quickened each other's essence, aligning with each other, a fiery light passing back and forth, down the length of the sword, up and down the length of my spine and then out through my heart along the line of my arms held pointed out away from me and into Alkaladur.

"It flares!" Kane shouted. "It flares!"

I opened my eyes to see the silver sword glowing as from a light within. When my arms trembled and the sword's point wavered from slightly south of due east, so did its light.

"It does flare!" Lady Nimaiu said, with Liljana translating for her. I saw tears filling up Lady Nimaiu's eyes as with the waters of the lake. "And so it is proven: you are the sword's true keeper, Valashu Elahad. We will hope that it will lead you to this Lightstone you seek."

Her words set off a rumbling thunder of happy cries and conversations among her people. The Maiians, who had witnessed glories of the earth before but never one like this, gathered around gazing at my sword in wonder. Everyone seemed to be relieved that we would be taking this ancient sword—and all our other weapons—from their island.

"Then the Lightstone must lie somewhere east of us," Kane said, looking at my luminous sword. "But it seems it's still far away."

To the east of us, I thought, lay the Dragon Channel, Surrapam, and the great Crescent Mountains. And farther: Eanna, Yarkona, and the library at Khaisham. And beyond that, the even greater White Mountains of Sakai and the plains of the Wendrush. And finally, the Morning Mountains of Mesh.

"You have a long journey still ahead of you, don't you?" Lady Nimaiu said to me.

"Yes, we do," I told her, though I did not know how long or how far we must travel.

"We should celebrate your triumph—and your life! Will you share a meal with us before you leave?"

My friends, even Kane, seemed to bear the Maiians no ill will for putting me to such a deadly test. I saw Maram gazing at Lalaiu as if it was already arranged that he would share with her that night much more than a meal. I thought of the *Snowy Owl,* which would be sailing the next day on the morning tide.

"Yes," I said, "we'd be honored to dine with you."

As the Maii began walking off toward the temple and the feast to be held there, Lady Nimaiu embraced me. Then she touched her wounded finger to Alkaladur's blade and looked at me deeply.

Atara moved closer to me then, along with Liljana, Maram, and Master Juwain. Alphanderry gazed at my sword as if wanting to compose a song that would tell of what had happened here. Flick spun fiery spirals around it. Kane alone of my friends dared to lay his hand on Alkaladur's blade; I sensed that somehow he was testing it and wondering if it really would lead us to the Lightstone.

"So, Val, so," he said to me.

And Maram, clasping my hand, added, "Then it seems the Quest really will go on."

For a while we stood there by the shimmering lake, as seven brothers and sisters whose destinies and very lives were as one.

Then it came time for me put away my new sword. But first I had to draw forth my old one. This I did, and I stared at the pieces of it with a great sadness in my heart. But there was a great joy there, too: a warm surging of my blood that seemed to swell out from the center of my being like a star's radiance. With Lady Nimaiu's permission, I flung the shards of my broken kalama far out into the lake. They sank into its dark blue depths without a trace. Then I slid Alkaladur into the sheath. It fit perfectly. Every piece and part of the world and all my dreams seemed suddenly to fit into a great plan. The Quest, I was sure, would go on until the very end, wherever that might be. My friends and I would venture into the darkness, and in its deeps we would find the Lightstone, for that must be our fate. And so tomorrow, I thought, as I rested my hand on my sword's swan-carved hilt, we would take to the road once more and journey on eastward, toward the great rising sun.

APPENDICES

APPENDICES

HERALDRY

The Nine Kingdoms

The shield and surcoat arms of the warriors of the Nine Kingdoms differ from those of the other lands in two respects. First, they tend to be simpler, with a single, bold charge emblazoned on a field of a single color. Second, every fighting man, from the simple warrior up through the ranks of knight, master, and lord to the king himself, is entitled to bear the arms of his line.

There is no mark or insignia of service to any lord save the king. Loyalty to one's ruling king is displayed on shield borders as a field that matches the color of the king's field and that displays a repeating motif of the king's charge. Thus, for instance, every fighting man of Ishka, from warrior to lord, will display a red shield border with white bears surrounding whatever arms have been passed down to him. With the exception of the lords of Anjo, only the kings and the royal families of the Nine Kingdoms bear unbordered shields and surcoats.

In Anjo, although a king in name still rules in Jathay, the lords of the other regions have broken away from his rule to assert their own sovereignty. Thus, for instance, Baron Yashur of Vishal bears a shield of simple green emblazoned with a white crescent moon without bordure, as if he were already a king or aspiring to be one.

Once there was a time when all Valari kings bore the seven stars of the Swan constellation on their shields as a reminder of the Elijin and Galadin to whom they owed allegiance. But by the time of the Second Lightstone Quest, only the House of Elahad has as part of its emblem the seven silver stars.

In the heraldry of the Nine Kingdoms, white and silver are used interchangeably, as are silver and gold. Marks of cadence—those smaller charges that distinguish individual members of a line, house, or family—are usually placed at the point of the shield.

Mesh

HOUSE OF ELAHAD—black field; a silver-white swan with spread wings gazes upon the seven silver-white stars of the Swan constellation

LORD HARSHA—blue field; gold lion rampant filling nearly all of it

LORD TOMAVAR—white field; black tower

LORD TANU—white field; black, double-headed eagle

LORD RAASHARU—gold field; blue rose

LORD NAVARU—blue field; gold sunburst

LORD JULUVAL—gold field; three red roses

LORD DURRIVAR—red field; white bull

LORD ARSHAN—white field; three blue stars

Ishka

KING HADARU ARADAR—red field; great white bear

LORD MESTIVAN—gold field; black dragon

LORD NADHRU—green field; three white swords, points touching upward

LORD SOLHTAR—red field; gold sunburst

Athar

KING MOHAN—gold field; blue horse

Lagash

KING KURSHAN—blue field; white Tree of Life

Waas

KING SANDARKAN—black field; two crossed silver swords

Taron

KING WARAY—red field; white winged horse

Kaash

KING TALANU SOLARU—blue field; white snow tiger

Anjo

KING DANASHU—blue field; gold dragon
DUKE GORADOR SHURVAR OF DAKSH—white field; red heart
DUKE REZU OF RAJAK—white field; green falcon
DUKE BARWAN OF ADAR—blue field; white candle
BARON YASHUR OF VISHAL—green field; white crescent moon
COUNT RODRU NARVU OF YARVANU—white field; two green lions rampant
COUNT ATANU TUVAL OF ONKAR—white field; red maple leaf
BARON YUVAL OF NATESH—black field; golden flute

Free Kingdoms

As in the Nine Kingdoms, the bordure pattern is that of the field and charge of the ruling king. But in the Free Kingdoms, only nobles and knights are permitted to display arms on their shields and surcoats. Common soldiers wear two badges: the first, usually on their right arm, displaying the emblems of their kings, and the second, worn on their left arm, displaying those of the baron, duke, or knight to whom they have sworn allegiance.

In the houses of Free Kingdoms, excepting the ancient Five Families of Tria, from whom Alonia has drawn most of her kings, the heraldry tends toward more complicated and geometric patterns than in the Nine Kingdoms.

Alonia

HOUSE OF NARMADA—blue field; gold caduceus
HOUSE OF ERIADES—field divided per bend; blue upper, white lower; white star on blue, blue star on white
HOUSE OF KIRRILAND—white field; black raven
HOUSE OF HASTAR—black field; two gold lions rampant

HOUSE OF MARSHAN—white field; red star inside black circle

BARON NARCAVAGE OF ARNGIN—white field; red bend; black oak lower; black eagle upper

BARON MARUTH OF AQUANTIR—green field; gold cross; two gold arrows on each quadrant

DUKE ASHVAR OF RAANAN—gold field; repeating pattern of black swords

BARON MONTEER OF IVIENDENHALL—white and black checkered shield

BARON MUAR OF IVIUNN—black field; white cross of Ashtoreth

DUKE MALATAM OF TARLAN—white field; black saltire; repeating red roses on white quadrants

Eanna

KING HANNIBAN DUJAR—gold field; red cross; blue lions rampant on each gold quadrant

Surrapaœ

KING KAIMAN—red field; white saltire; blue star at center

Thalu

KING ARYAMAN—black and white gyronny; white swords on four black sectors

Delu

KING SANTOVAL MARSHAYK—green field; two gold lions rampant facing each other

The Elyssu

KING THEODOR JARDAN—blue field; repeating breaching silver dolphins

Nedu

KING TAL—blue field; gold cross; gold eagle volant on each blue quadrant

The Dragon Kingdoms

With one exception, in these lands, only Morjin himself bears his own arms: a great red dragon on a gold field. Kings who have sworn fealty to him—King Orunjan, King Arsu—have been forced to surrender their ancient arms and display a somewhat smaller red dragon on their shields and surcoats. Kallimun priests who have been appointed to kingship or who have conquered realms in Morjin's name—King Mansul, King Yarkul, Count Ulanu—also display this emblem but are proud to do so.

Nobles serving these kings bear slightly smaller dragons, and the knights serving them bear yet smaller ones. Common soldiers wear a yellow livery displaying a repeating pattern of very small red dragons.

King Angand of Sunguru, as an ally of Morjin, bears his family's arms as does any free king.

The kings of Hesperu and Uskudar have been allowed to retain their family crests as a mark of their kingship, though they have surrendered their arms.

Sunguru

KING ANGAND—blue field; white heart with wings

Uskudar

KING ORUNJAN—gold field; ¾ red dragon

Karabuk

KING MANSUL—gold field; ¾ red dragon

Hesperu

KING ARSU—gold field; ¾ red dragon

Galda

KING YARKUL—gold field; ¾ red dragon

Yarkona

COUNT ULANU—gold field; ½ red dragon

THE GELSTEI

The Gold

The history of the gold gelstei, called the Lightstone, is shrouded in mystery. Most people believe the legend of Elahad: that this Valari king of the Star People made the Lightstone and brought it to earth. Some schools of the Brotherhood, however, teach that the Elijin or the Galadin made the Lightstone. Some teach that the mythical Ieldra, who are like gods, made the Lightstone millions of years earlier. A few hold that the Lightstone may be a transcendental, increate object from before the beginning of time, and that as such, much as the One or the universe itself, it has always existed and always will. Also, there are people who believe that this golden cup, the greatest of the gelstei, was made in Ea during the great Age of Law.

The Lightstone is the image of solar light, the sun, and hence of divine intelligence. It is made into the shape of a plain golden cup because it holds the whole universe inside. Upon being activated by a powerful enough being, the gold begins to turn clear like a crystal and to radiate light like the sun. As it connects with the infinite power of the universe, the One, it radiates light like that of ten thousand suns. Ultimately, its light is pure, clear, and infinite—the light of pure consciousness. The light inside light, the light inside all things that *is* all things. The Lightstone quickens consciousness in itself, the power of consciousness to enfold itself and form up as matter and thus evolve into infinite possibilities. It enables certain human beings to channel and magnify this power. Its power is infinitely greater than that of the red gelstei, the firestones. Indeed, the Lightstone gives power over the other gelstei, the green, purple, blue, and white, the black and perhaps the silver—and potentially over all matter, energy, space, and time. The final secret of the Lightstone is that, as the very consciousness and substance of the universe itself, it is found within each human being, interwoven and interfused with each separate soul. To quote from the *Saganom Elu*, it is "the perfect jewel within the lotus found inside the human heart."

The Lightstone has many specific powers, and each person finds in it a reflection of himself. Those seeking healing are healed. In some, it recalls their true nature and origins as Star People; others, in their lust for immortality, find only the hell of endless life. Some—such as Morjin or Angra Mainyu—it blinds with its terrible and beautiful light. Its potential to be misused by such maddened beings is vast: ultimately it has the power to blow up the sun and destroy the stars, perhaps the whole universe itself.

Used properly, the Lightstone can quicken the evolution of all beings. In its light, Star People may transcend to their higher angelic natures while angels evolve into archangels. And the Galadin themselves, in the act of creation only, may use the Lightstone to create whole new universes.

The Lightstone is activated at once by individual consciousness, the collective unconscious, and the energies of the stars. It also becomes somewhat active at certain key times, such as when the Seven Sisters are rising in the sky. Its most transcendental powers manifest when it is in the presence of an enlightened being or when the earth enters the Golden Band.

It is not known if there are many Lightstones throughout the universe or only one that somehow appears at the same time in different places. One of the greatest mysteries of the Lightstone is that on Ea, only a human man, woman, or child can use it for its best and highest purpose: to bring the sacred light to others and awaken each being to his angelic nature. Neither the Elijin nor the Galadin, the archangels, possess this special resonance. And only a very few of the Star People do.

These rare beings are the Maitreyas who come forth every few millennia or so to share their enlightenment with the world. They have cast off all illusion and apprehend the One in all things and all things as manifestations of the One. Thus they are the deadly enemies of Morjin and the Dark Angel, and other Lords of the Lie.

THE GREATER
GELSTEI

The SILVER

The silver gelstei is made of a marvelous substance called silustria. The crystal resembles pure silver but is brighter, reflecting even more light. Depending on how forged, the silver gelstei can be much harder than diamond.

The silver gelstei is the stone of reflection and thus of the soul, for the soul is that part of man that reflects the light of the universe. The silver reflects and magnifies the powers of the soul, including, in its lower emanations, those of mind: logic, deduction, calculation, awareness, ordinary memory, judgment, and insight. It can confer upon those who wield it holistic vision: the ability to see whole patterns and reach astonishing conclusions from only a few details or clues. Its higher emanations allow one to see how the individual soul must align itself with the universal soul to achieve the unfolding of fate.

In its reflective qualities, the silver gelstei may be used as a shield against various energies: vital, mental, or physical. In other ages, it has been shaped into arms and armor, such as swords, mail shirts, and actual shields. Although not giving power *over* another, in body or in mind, the silver can be used to quicken the working of another's mind and is thus a great pedagogical tool leading to knowledge and laying bare truth. A sword made of silver gelstei can cut through all things physical as the mind cuts through ignorance and darkness.

In its fundamental composition, the silver is very much like the gold gelstei and is one of the two noble stones.

The WHITE

These stones are called the white, but in appearance they are usually clear like diamonds. During the Age of Law, many of them were cast into the form of crystal balls to be used by scryers and are thus often called scryers' spheres.

These are the stones of far-seeing: of perceiving events distant in either space or time. They are sometimes used by remembrancers to uncover the secrets of the past. The kristei, as they are called, have helped the master healers of the Brotherhood read the auras of the sick that they might be brought back to strength and health.

The Blue

The blue gelstei, or blestei, have been fabricated on Ea at least as far back as the Age of the Mother. The crystals range in color from a deep cobalt to a bright lapis blue. They have been cast into many forms: amulets, cups, figurines, rings, and others.

The blue gelstei quicken and deepen all kinds of knowing and communication. They are an aid to mindspeakers and truthsayers and confer a greater sensitivity to music, poetry, painting, languages, and dreams.

The Green

Other than the Lightstone itself, these are the oldest of the gelstei. Many books of the *Saganom Elu* tell of how the Star People brought twelve of the green stones with them to Ea. The varistei look like beautiful emeralds; they are usually cast—or grown—in the shape of baguettes or astragals and range in size from that of a pin or bead to great jewels nearly a foot in length.

The green gelstei resonate with the vital fires of plants and animals and of the earth. They are the stones of healing and can be used to quicken and strengthen life and lengthen its span. As the purple gelstei can be used to mold crystals and other inanimate substances into new shapes, the green gelstei have powers over the forms of living things. In the Lost Ages, it was said that masters of the varistei used them to create new races of man (and sometimes monsters), but this art is thought to be long since lost.

These crystals confer great vitality on those who use them in harmony with nature; they can open the body's chakras and awaken the kundalini fire so the whole body and soul vibrate at a higher level of being.

The Red

The red gelstei—also called tuaoi stones or firestones—are blood-red crystals like rubies in appearance and color. They are often cast into baguettes at least a foot in length, though during the Age of Law much larger ones were made. The greatest ever fabricated was the hundred-foot Eluli's Spire, mounted on top of the Tower of the Sun. It was said to cast its fiery light up into the heavens as a beacon calling out to the Star People to return to earth.

The firestones quicken, channel, and control the physical energies. They draw upon the sun's rays, as well as the earth's magnetic and telluric currents, to generate beams of light, lightning, heat, or fire. They are thought to be the most dangerous of the gelstei; it is said that a great pyramid of red gelstei unleashed a terrible lightning that split asunder the world of Iviunn and destroyed its star.

The Black

The black gelstei, or baalstei, are black crystals like obsidian. Many are cast into the shape of eyes, either flattened or rounded like large marbles. They devour light and are the stones of negation.

Many believe them to be evil stones, but they were created for a good purpose: to control the awesome lightning of the firestones. Theirs is the power to damp the fires of material things, both living and living crystals such as the gelstei. Used properly, they can negate the working of all the other kinds of gelstei except the silver and the gold, over which they have no power.

Their power over living things *is* most often put to evil purpose. The Kallimun priests and other servants of Morjin such as the Grays have wielded them as weapons to attack people physically, mentally, and spiritually, literally sucking away their vital energies and will. Thus the black stones can be used to cause disease, degeneration, and death.

It is believed that the baalstei might be potentially more dangerous than even the firestones. For in the *Beginnings* is told of an utterly black place that is at once the negation of all things and paradoxically also their source. Out of this place may come the fire and light of the universe itself. It is said that the Baaloch, Angra Mainyu, before he was imprisoned on the world of Damoom, used a great black gelstei to destroy whole suns in his war of rebellion against the Galadin and the rule of the Ieldra.

The Purple

The lilastei are the stones of shaping and making. They are a bright violet in hue and are cast into crystals of variety of shapes and sizes. Their power is unlocking the light locked up in matter so that matter might be changed, molded, and transformed. Thus the lilastei are sometimes called the alchemists' stones, according to the alchemists' age-old dream of transmuting baser matter into true gold and casting true gold into a new Lightstone.

The purple gelstei's greatest effects are on crystals of all sorts, but mostly those in metal and rocks. It can unlock the crystals in these substances so that they might be more easily worked. Or they can be used to grow crystals of great size and beauty; they are the stone shapers and stone growers spoken of in legend. It is said that Kalkamesh used a lilastei in forging the silustria of the Bright Sword, Alkaladur.

Some believe the potential power of the purple gelstei to be very great and perhaps very perilous. Lilastei have been known to freeze water into an alternate crystal called shatar, which is clear and as hard as quartz. Some fear that these gelstei might be used thus to crystallize the water in the sea and so destroy all life on earth. The stone masters of old, who probed the mysteries of the lilastei too deeply, are said to have accidentally turned themselves *into* stone, but most believe this to be only a cautionary tale out of legend.

The Seven Openers

If man's purpose is seen as in progressing to the orders of the Star People, Elijin, and Galadin, then the seven stones known as the openers might fairly be called greater gelstei. Indeed, there are those of the Great White Brotherhood and the Green Brotherhood who revere them in this way. For, with much study and work, the openers each activate one of the body's chakras: the energy centers known as wheels of light. As the chakras are opened, from the base of the spine to the crown of the head, so is opened a pathway for the fires of life to reconnect to the heavens in a great burst of lightning called the angel's fire. Only then can a man or a woman undertake the advanced work necessary for advancement to the higher orders.

The openers are each small, clear stones the color of their respective chakras. They are easily mistaken for gemstones.

The First (also called bloodstones)

These are a clear, deep red in color, like rubies. The first stones open the chakra of the physical body and activate the vital energies.

The Second (also called passion stones or old gold)

These gelstei are gold-orange in color and are sometimes mistaken for amber. The second stones open the chakra of the emotional body and activate the currents of sensation and feeling.

The Third (also called sun stones)

The third stones are clear and bright yellow, like citrine; they open the third chakra of the mental body and activate the mind.

The Fourth (also called dream stones or heart stones)

These beautiful stones—clear and pure green in color like emeralds—open the heart chakra. Thus they open one's second feeling, a truer and deeper sense than the emotions of the second chakra. The fourth stones work upon the astral body and activate the dreamer.

The Fifth (also called soul stones)

Bright blue in color like sapphires, the fifth stones open the chakra of the etheric body and activate the intuitive knower, or the soul.

The Sixth (also called angel eyes)

The sixth stones are bright purple like amethyst. They open the chakra of the celestial body located just above and between the eyes. Thus their more common name: theirs is the power of activating one's second sight. Indeed, these gelstei activate the seer in the realm of light and open one to the powers of scrying, visualization, and deep insight.

The Seventh (also called clear crowns or true diamonds)

One of the rarest of the gelstei, the seventh stones are clear and bright as diamonds. Indeed, some say they are nothing more than perfect diamonds, without flaw or taint of color. These stones open the chakra of the ketheric body and free the spirit for reunion with the One.

The Lesser Gelstei

During the Age of Law, hundreds of kinds of gelstei were made for purposes ranging from the commonplace to the sublime. Few of these have survived the passage of the centuries. Some of those that have are:

Glowstones

Also called glowglobes, these stones are cast into solid, round shapes resembling opals of various sizes—some quite huge. They give a soft and beautiful light. Those of lesser quality must be frequently refired beneath the sun, while those of the highest quality drink in even the faintest candlelight, hold it, and give it back in a steady illumination.

Sleep Stones

A gelstei of many shifting and swirling colors, the sleep stones have a calming effect on the human nervous system. They look something like agates.

Warders

Usually blood-red in color and opaque, like carnelians, these stones deflect or ward off psychic energies directed at a person. This includes thoughts, emotions, curses—and even the debilitating energy drain of the black gelstei. One who wears a warder can be rendered invisible to scryers and opaque to mindspeakers.

Love Stones

Often called true amber and sometimes mistaken for the second stones of the openers, these gelstei partake of some of their properties. They are specific to arousing feelings of infatuation and love; sometimes love stones are ground into a powder and made into potions to achieve the same end. They are soft stones and look much like amber.

Wish Stones

These little stones—they look something like white pearls—help the wearer remember his dreams and visions of the future; they activate the will to manifest these visualizations.

Dragon Bones

The color of old, translucent ivory, the dragon bones strengthen the life fires and quicken one's courage—and all too often one's wrath.

Hot Slate

A dark gray, opaque stone of considerable size—hot slate is usually cast into yard-long bricks—this gelstei is related in powers and purpose, if not form, to the glowstones. It absorbs heat directly from the air and radiates it back over a period of hours or days.

Music Marbles

Often called song stones, these gelstei of variegated, swirling hues record and play music, whether performed by a human voice or an instrument. They are very rare.

Touch Stones

These are related to the song stones and have a similar appearance. However, they record and play emotions and tactile sensations instead of music. A man or a woman, upon touching one of these gelstei, will leave a trace of emotions that a sensitive can read from contact with the stone.

Thought Stones

Almost indistinguishable from song stones and touch stones, thought stones absorb and hold one's thoughts as a cotton garment might retain the smell of perfume or sweat. The ability to read back these thoughts from touching this gelstei is not nearly so rare as that of mindspeaking.

Turn the page and read a preview of

David Zindell's

THE
▓ SILVER SWORD ▓

(0-7653-1674-9)

Available now in hardcover

THE ANGELS, IT is written, at the beginning of time sang into creation the stars. With the aid of the Lightstone, their golden voices brought forth out of the black void Solaru, Aras, Varshara, and a million other bright bursts of fire. I have heard the stars sing back. All men and women can apprehend the heavens' music as well as the angels, but who can hold inside such blazing, infinite songs? Only one, I believe, who finds the golden Cup of Heaven in which to contain their light, in whatever place on earth this greatest of all gelstei has been lost.

At the western edge of the world, the stars shine the same as those of the Morning Mountains of my home. Having called my six companions and me across the length of Ea on a great quest, these bright points of light put a song in each of our hearts and led us back east. Bright hopes we held, and bright gelstei, too: a ruby firestone, a bit of black jade, a scryer's clear sphere that gave visions of the future. Other ancient crystals we had gained on our long journey; into my hands had come the legendary silver sword, Alkaladur. Must I, I wondered, use this Sword of Fate to fight the Red Dragon named Morjin as we had for so many months and miles—perhaps even to the death? Or would my blade's shining silustria point the way toward the Lightstone as told in the ancient songs?

In the warmest days of Marud in the year 2812, as we sailed across the Dragon Channel from the Island of the Swans to Surrapam on a stout bilander called the *Snowy Owl*, these questions burned through my mind. Through my blood still burned the kirax that one of Morjin's assassins had struck into me with a poisoned arrow. The pain of this foul substance would always torment me, even as in some mysterious way it connected me to the foulness of Morjin's mind and heart. Miraculously, though, whenever I gripped my newly acquired sword and pointed it toward the stars, the fire of the kirax seemed to go away.

"So, that sword seems almost to have been made for you." Kane, the fiercest of my friends, spoke these words to me on the last night of our voyage. We stood on the deck of the *Snowy Owl*, looking for warships on the glistening black waters to the east. "And even as it now belongs to you, you belong to it."

It was a strange thing for him to say, but then Kane was a strange man. He was tall, like the Valari people from which I came, and he had the same bright, black eyes as did my brothers and my father, King Shavashar Elahad. But his hair had turned white, and he wore it cropped short instead of long and black and tied with brightly colored battle ribbons. And where the bold faces of my people most often recalled those of hawks or eagles, Kane's grim visage brought to mind the wildness and fury of a tiger. He moved, too, with all the power of such a beast. At times, though, as when we stood together looking up at the stars, he came alive with a terrible beauty, and then he seemed the most graceful and glorious of men.

"Well, I am a Valari warrior, aren't I?" I told him. "And isn't it said that a warrior's sword is his soul?"

I looked down the length of Alkaladur's blade, double-edged and sharp enough to cut steel. Its silustria, hardest of all substances except the gold gelstei of the Lightstone, caught the starlight and cast it back with a silvery sheen. The sword's maker had set seven diamonds into its black jade hilt, carved with swans like unto those of my family's emblem. A great round diamond formed the sword's pommel stone. When I pointed the sword to the east, the silustria filled with a bright white radiance as it flared in resonance with the lost Lightstone.

"It is said," Kane told me, "that this sword has many powers, and you have called upon one of them. But *you* have many powers, too, eh? Soon enough, I think, this sword will call upon all that dwells most deeply within you, Valashu Elahad."

I thought about this as I listened to the ship's timbers creaking and the wind whipping at the sails. I looked out across the deck. There, near the bow, stretched out beneath their traveling cloaks, lay four of our other friends: Master Juwain of the Great White Brotherhood; the minstrel Alphanderry; Lady Liljana Ashvaran of Tria; and Atara Ars Narmada, daughter of Ea's greatest king, warrior of the Manslayer Society—and the woman I loved. Already, it seemed, whenever Alkaladur's deepest light pierced my heart, I felt myself opening to passions almost too beautiful to bear.

"What are you looking at, my friend?" a low, rumbling voice called out to me.

Just then, Prince Maram Marshayk, the seventh member of our company, came staggering out of the darkness with a bottle of brandy clenched in his huge hand. A great, dense beard bloomed from his heavy face; he stood nearly as tall as Kane, and was even thicker in his body and limbs, though less from hard sinew than jiggling fat. He wore a stained cloak over his rather ostentatious scarlet woolens, while on each of his fingers he sported a jeweled ring. Of all my friends, he had suffered the worst from the rigors of our quest—or, at least, had complained the most about them.

"Why aren't you sleeping, Maram?" I asked in a low voice.

"Ah, why must you answer a question with a question?" He belched loudly as he looked through the darkness at me—and my sword. "I am not sleeping because one of Captain Kharald's fine sailors offered to share this fine brandy with me. And because it's too lovely of a night to sleep. *And*, most of all, because whenever I close my eyes, I can still smell the perfume of Lalaiu's hair upon my face, and that keeps me awake."

He spoke of the Maiian woman that he had left behind on the Island of the Swans. Listening to the wistfulness that came into his heavy voice, I could almost believe that he loved her.

"The question," he said to me, glancing at Atara, "is why *you* aren't making the most of this splendid night and taking few moments of joy with *your* beloved while you still can?"

I felt my cheeks burning with the heat of my blood. I looked at Atara, whose beautiful blue eyes had finally closed in sleep. Her long blond hair half-covered the most beautiful face I had ever seen. At that moment, I thought, she looked much more like a gentle maiden than a skilled warrior who had vowed to slay a hundred of her enemies before marrying. And I remembered well enough my promise to her father, King Kiritan of Alonia: that before taking her hand in mine, I would find the Lightstone and bring it into the City of Light. This, surely, was not vainglory on my part (or not just), but only good sense.

With all of Ea about to go up in flames, who would want to marry anyone and bring children into the world—unless the Lightstone *was* found and war ended forever?

"You know why," I said quietly to Maram.

As Maram's brown eyes softened with his regard for me, I thought that he *did* know the real reason that I could not take Atara to me, the deepest and most painful reason that I tried to keep a secret, even from myself. And I loved him for that.

"Someday," he promised me, "I'll stand with you in Tria when you wed Atara. *If* we make it across this water without the damn Hesperuk warships attacking us. And across Surrapam without running into the damn Hesperuk army. And then through the mountains without . . ."

For a while, as we stood with the salty sea wind blowing at our faces, Maram recited a litany of all the dangers he supposed might lie ahead of us. Then his attention fell upon my sword, and he said, "There might have been much blood upon this blade, once, but surely the ages have washed it clean. I have to tell you that I'm not ready to see you bloody it again."

"Nor am I," I told him. "It might be that we can reach our journey's end in peace."

"It *might* be," Maram sighed out. "But already, Morjin has sent an assassin to murder you. And a great bear he made into a ghul. And the damn Grays with their stone eyes that nearly sucked out our souls. And in Tria, more assassins, with that damn Kallimun priest, and of course that monster Meliadus in the Vardaloon—not to mention whole plagues of mosquitoes, leeches, and ticks. Ah, am I forgetting anything?"

If he *had* forgotten any of Morjin's assaults, I would not remind him, for he needed no extra fuel to stoke the fires of his vivid imagination.

"And what if Morjin finds you with his damn illusions again?"

"Then I will fight them off, as I have before," I reassured him.

"We can only hope so," he said with a belch of brandy. "But now we propose to cross Surrapam in secret—what if someone gives us away? What if Morjin somehow *sees* you carrying that bright sword of yours? Even with twenty Alkaladurs, you couldn't fight off the whole damn Hesperuk army!"

His words seemed to hang in the air as the ship pitched and rolled beneath us and sent up a salty spray. Then Captain Kharald, pacing the deck midships, walked over to us. His heavy boots thumped across worn wood. He was a heavyset man dressed in a thick wool shirt, pantaloons, and a black belt from which hung a spyglass and a cutlass. The dark of full night bled away the colors of his bright red hair and his green eyes, but I could easily make out the careworn lines of his blunt face. As captain of a ship running the Dragon Channel with a hold full of grain for his starving people, he had many cares and concerns.

"That is a great sword you gained on the island," he said to me. "I've never seen its like."

I stood pointing Alkaladur down toward the deck of the ship. It wouldn't do for Captain Kharald—or anyone—to see it light up like a star.

"A great sword indeed," he went on, stroking his beard. "And it's said that you Valari are the greatest warriors in the world."

His rough, wrinkled face, in the light of the waning moon, tightened with calculation. But he said no more to me that night. He bade Kane, Maram, and me to lie back down with our friends to take some rest. Then he walked over to the *Snowy Owl*'s mainmast to check on the lookout in the crow's nest high above us.

As we rejoined our other friends and tried to sleep, I had to fight back a gnawing sickness in my belly. I felt too poignantly Captain Kharald's dread of the Hesperuks who had invaded Surrapam. What would it be like, I wondered, to see my land ravaged by one of Morjin's murderous and crucifying armies?

With a strong wind blowing at our backs, we fairly flew across the glittering waters of the Dragon Channel. It took us only a day and night, altogether, of fast sailing to complete our passage. Fortune favored us, for the lookout gave no cry of alarm as to Hesperuk warships, but only called out near dawn that he had sighted Surrapam. There, in the morning, at Artram, the last of Surrapam's free ports and therefore crowded with ships coming and going through its bustling harbor, we made landfall. Immediately we set to work bringing our horses up from below deck and down the gangplank onto the dock.

I led forth, keeping a firm hold on the reins of Altaru, my

fierce black stallion, so that he wouldn't rear up and strike out at any of Captain Kharald's crew with his great hooves. Atara, walking beside her roan mare, Fire, came next. She had a gift for gentling horses—perhaps inherited from her grandfather's people. Like most of the fierce Sarni who roam the grasslands of the Wendrush, she stood tall and straight, with a great strength that seemed to well up from her lithely muscled body. The Surrapamers crowding the dock stared at her in wonder. Although Atara had the same blond hair and brilliant blue eyes as the many Thalunes common in Surrapam, she carried herself with a barbaric grace. She certainly had the look of a barbarian, with her black leather armor studded with steel and the leather trousers beneath her traveling cloak. Her bare, brown arms showed circlets of gold, and a torque of lapis and gold shone from her neck. And no Thalune woman would wear a sword at her side or bear a bow and arrows as if ready to put a shaft through any man who insulted her.

It did not take long for the rest of our companions—Kane, Maram, Master Juwain, Liljana, and Alphanderry—to join us on the dock. As we stood checking our horses' loads, Captain Kharald came down the gangplank to speak with us.

"I have just had news," he told us, standing in close. "All the countryside north of the Maron River is lost. King Kaiman has rallied our army and is making a stand near Azam only forty miles from here. It seems our wheat is needed very badly."

I watched the lean, hungry-looking Surrapam dockmen who had already gone to work unloading the bags of wheat from the *Snowy Owl*'s holds. From nearby smithies down Artram's busy streets came the sounds of hammered steel and the clamor of preparations for war.

Captain Kharald looked from Atara to Maram, and then at Kane and me. And he said, "Your swords are needed badly, too. Would you be willing to raise them against the enemy that you say you oppose?"

I remembered Thaman, his countryman, who had requested help from the Valari in Duke Rezu's castle; in the months since then, I thought, it had gone very badly for his people.

"We do indeed oppose him," Liljana said in her calm, controlled voice. "But there are other ways of fighting the Red Dragon than with *this*."

She set her hand on the hilt of the cutlass that she had reluctantly strapped to her side in Tria, upon her vow to make the quest. Despite this weapon, few would mistake her for a warrior. She was middling old, with iron-gray hair bound tight and coiled like a matron's and a rather stout body that seemed all softness and curves. Her round, almost jolly face readily broke into warm smiles. With her wide hips and great breasts, one could easily imagine her as a mother of many children—and a grandmother of many more. It always surprised people, I thought, to discover that beneath her comely exterior, she possessed a will of steel.

"I think," Captain Kharald said to her, nodding toward her sword, "that you might do very well fighting the Red Dragon with *that*. But you still might help. Cooking for our soldiers. Or caring for the wounded."

Liljana remained quiet while she studied Captain Kharald with her wise hazel eyes. I sensed that she did want to tend to Surrapam's wounded warriors and make them well—as she did almost everyone in the world.

"And you, Master Juwain," Captain Kharald said, turning slightly, "are a healer, are you not?"

Master Juwain, short and compact and tough as old tree roots, slowly nodded his bald head. His rather ugly face shone with the keenest of intelligence as he considered Captain Kharald's words. I saw torment working at his luminous gray eyes. I noticed him pressing his hand against the pocket of his woolens where he kept his varistei: the green healing crystal that he had been given far away in a magical wood.

"I am a master healer," he said to Captain Kharald without pride. "But even such as I can do little when the dogs of war are loosed upon the world."

"What little you can do would be greatly appreciated. Even one life saved is one more soldier who might recover to fight the Dragon. And one less grieving mother."

At this, Master Juwain bowed his head in thought, and stared down at the ground.

"And you, minstrel," Captain Kharald said, looking at Alphanderry, "such a voice you have! Such a gift with music! You could sing to the soldiers before battle and put the fire of the angels into their hearts."

Alphanderry's soft, sad eyes brightened at this. He was a slender man, handsome of face and form, and at once lively and dreamy in his manner. His black, curly hair seemed to catch the sun's rays in a crown of light. Upon his back he bore a six-stringed mandolet, from which he could summon the most beautiful of melodies. Everything about him—his fine, tapering fingers, his sensual lips, the poise of his head, his innate curiosity and imagination—bespoke his deep love for beauty.

"I would gladly play for the soldiers," Alphanderry told Captain Kharald. "But then it seems that I must gladly die, for the Hesperuks will surely prevail."

He spoke these words simply and almost happily, as if fate was only fate and should be celebrated as with everything in life—and later sung about with passion and reverence.

But his carefree way seemed only to irritate Maram, who huffed out, "Well, *I* am not so ready to die, gladly or otherwise. And I don't think you are either."

At this, Alphanderry just shrugged his shoulders as he smiled at Maram.

"Val," Maram said to me, "would you talk some sense into our foolish friend?"

In answer, I could only let my hand rest upon Alkaladur's hilt as I looked from Alphanderry and then at Captain Kharald.

"Val," Maram said again, this time in alarm, "please don't tell me that you're thinking of offering King Kaiman your sword!"

Now all the rest of my friends looked at me, too. I thought it strange that although I was the youngest of our company, at only a score of years, it had fallen upon me to be their leader.

"Captain Kharald and his people," I said to Maram, "have given us their aid."

"For which we paid them good gold!"

I considered this as I turned toward Atara. And she told me, "Whatever we do, Surrapam will fall."

I wondered what visions she might have seen in her scryer's crystal, and I asked her, "Have you *seen* this, then?"

Her bright blue eyes fixed on mine. "Any soldier in King Kaiman's army could see that. A child could, Val."

A clacking sound on the wharf drew my attention. There, two boys in front of a sailmaker's shop played with wooden swords. And I said to Atara, "Yes, the *children*."

Atara looked at them, too, and said with some certainty: "If we stay, we *will* die. Surely, though, knowing this cannot be the basis for determining the rightness or wrongness of such a course."

"It can for *me*!" Maram said.

At that moment, a whirl of little crimson and silver lights broke out of the still air above us. Flick, the strange being that had attached himself to us in the Lokilani's wood, spun about like a constellation of stars. He remained invisible to Captain Kharald and others who had not partaken of the wood's magic. But to me, he seemed to speak in bright bursts of radiance that I could almost understand.

Then Kane caught my attention, and shot me a look that struck deep into my soul. I could almost feel his heart surging savagely in time with my own. His purpose dwelled with *my* purpose, and that was both a bright and a terrible thing. I recalled that my father, in the course of his kingship, had from evil necessity had to make many hard decisions.

Finally I turned to Captain Kharald and said, "It is one thing to risk one's life in a noble cause, and another to throw it away. Even a hundred regiments arrayed against the Red Dragon wouldn't be enough to bring him down. But the finding of the Lightstone might be."

Captain Kharald's face reddened with anger and disappointment. "Then you intend to continue your quest?"

"Yes, we must. It is our calling."